Harvest of Gold

**Center Point
Large Print**

Also by Tessa Afshar and available from Center Point Large Print:

Harvest of Rubies

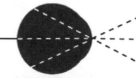

This Large Print Book carries the Seal of Approval of N.A.V.H.

Harvest of Gold

TESSA AFSHAR

CENTER POINT LARGE PRINT
THORNDIKE, MAINE

This Center Point Large Print edition ꝯ
is published in the year 2014 by arrangement with
Moody Publishers.

Scripture references are from Psalm 16:10–11; Psalm
139:13; Psalm 127:1; Psalm 23:6; Judges 6:15; Nehemiah
6:2–3; 6:6–7; Deuteronomy 6:4–5; 14–15; 7:7–10; 30: 6.
Some Scripture quotations are taken from the *Holy Bible,
New International Version®*, NIV®. Copyright ©1973,
1978, 1984, 2011 by Biblica, Inc.™
Used by permission of Zondervan. All rights reserved
worldwide. www.zondervan.com
Some Scripture quotations are taken from the *Holy Bible,
New Living Translation*, copyright © 1996, 2004. Used by
permission of Tyndale House Publishers, Inc., Wheaton,
Illinois 60189, U.S.A. All rights reserved.

The text of this Large Print edition is unabridged.
In other aspects, this book may vary
from the original edition.
Printed in the United States of America
on permanent paper.
Set in 16-point Times New Roman type.

ISBN: 978-1-61173-983-1

Library of Congress Cataloging-in-Publication Data

Afshar, Tessa.
Harvest of gold / Tessa Afshar. — Center Point Large Print edition.
pages ; cm.
ISBN 978-1-61173-983-1 (library binding : alk. paper)
1. Marriage—Fiction. 2. Jewish families—Fiction. 3. Large type
books. I. Title.
PS3601.F47H37 2014
813′.6—dc23

2013033465

For my brother:
Thank you for your loyalty, generosity,
and unwavering belief in me.

587–586 BC   Judah is captured by Babylon, and the Temple is destroyed.

559–530 BC   Cyrus the Great establishes the largest empire the world has ever known and founds the Achaemenid dynasty. In 538 Cyrus sets Israel free from its Babylonian captivity as foretold by Isaiah (44:24–45:5). He donates money from his own treasury toward the rebuilding of the Temple in Jerusalem.

530–522 BC   Cambyses, Cyrus's eldest son, conquers Egypt. His reign is briefly followed by his younger brother, Bardia, who dies shortly thereafter under strange circumstances.

521–486 BC   Darius the Great expands the Persian Empire so that at its height it encompasses approximately eight million miles of territory. Next to Cyrus, he is the most admired Achaemenid king. He is probably not the king referred to in the book of Daniel 6:1–28, since Daniel would be quite old at this time.

486–465 BC   Xerxes takes over his father's great dynasty. He is best known for his notorious attack on Greece and for choosing a simple Jewish girl named Esther as his queen. The date of this event is not known. For details, see the book of Esther.

465–424 BC   Artaxerxes is known as a benevolent king who replaces several harsh laws with more humane rulings. He sends his cupbearer, Nehemiah, back to Jerusalem in 445 in order to rebuild its ruined walls.

334 BC   Alexander the Great conquers Persia.

Approx. 33 AD   Jesus of Nazareth is crucified.

CHARACTERS
in order of appearance or mention

Sarah—former scribe to the queen; wife of Darius
Darius Pasargadae–Persian aristocrat; Sarah's husband
Pari—handmaiden to Sarah
Damaspia—queen of Persia
Artaxerxes—king of Persia
Nehemiah—cupbearer to the king; relative of Sarah
Arta and Meres—members of Darius's personal guard
Niq, Nassir—Babylonian brothers
Megabyzus—Persian general
Mardonius—member of the Immortals
Lysander—friend of Darius
Hanani—brother of Nehemiah
Pyrus—nephew of Megabyzus and a provincial governor
Zikir—high-ranking official from Damascus
Roxanna—daughter of a Persian aristocrat and woman of many talents
Sanballat the Horonite—leader of Samaria who opposes Nehemiah
Tobiah—Ammonite leader who opposes Nehemiah
Zenobia—daughter of Zikir

Part 1
The Assault

Chapter 1

THE TWENTIETH YEAR
OF KING ARTAXERXES' REIGN (446 BC)
WINTER, PERSEPOLIS

Sarah's head snapped up as the door to her chamber burst open with uncharacteristic force. Her friend and handmaiden, Pari, rushed in, tunic askew, strands of usually pristine brown hair hanging around her face in a haphazard tangle.

"The baby's here!" she said, her voice high as she waved a long arm for emphasis.

Sarah jumped to her feet. "And Apama? How is she?" Apama, the wife of the second assistant gardener, had gone into labor with her first baby three days ago. The baby had proven reluctant to come. By the end of the second day everyone had started to fear the worst.

Pari's lips flattened into a straight line. "Bardia says she is too weak. They allowed me a glimpse of her before I came over. She's whiter than a bowl of yogurt, and lies shaking in spite of the fire burning in the brazier next to her pallet."

A shiver ran through Sarah. Bardia, the head gardener and practically a member of Darius's family, was not in the habit of careless pronouncements. "That doesn't sound encouraging. Perhaps we can do something to help."

She strode to the bank of shelves built into a niche in one corner of her bedchamber. Neat piles of soft sheets, wool blankets, and cotton-filled quilts stacked on top of each other. Sarah chose an exquisite linen quilt made of various shades of blue and green fabric, embroidered with silver thread. "This should help keep her warm."

Pari's eyebrows climbed toward her hairline. "Didn't the queen give you that coverlet?"

"She has stunning taste, hasn't she?"

"Indeed, my lady. More to the point, won't she mind your giving away the gift she chose for *you* with her own stunning taste?"

"Not if she doesn't find out," Sarah said, unable to keep the smile from her voice. "Besides, having suffered through a difficult birth herself, she is likely to approve. We should send a few things for the baby as well. Is it a boy or a girl?"

Pari slapped a hand over her mouth. "In all the excitement, I forgot to ask. I only know it is healthy."

Sarah tucked a loose curl behind her ear. "That's the important thing. I saw some linens in the storehouse that should suit a new baby. Let's fetch them." She and Pari paid a brief visit to the storehouse and retrieved a few appropriate articles for the newborn.

"His lordship has already sent over a lamb," Pari

said as they walked back to Sarah's apartments. "He had instructed Bardia to bring it over as soon as Apama gave birth."

Sarah was not surprised by Darius's thoughtfulness. Children were highly cherished by the Persians. The whole household rejoiced at the birth of a baby, even one belonging to a lesser servant.

She frowned at the thought of Darius. It had been five long days since he had sent for her. His lack of interest ate at her with a sharpness that robbed her of sleep at night and of rest during the day. Was he losing interest in her already? The thought made her want to weep.

She had not always been desperate for his company. When her marriage had first been arranged by the queen, it had felt like a blight that ruined her life. She had chosen neither her husband nor the state of matrimony.

Everyone assumed that a simple Jewish girl should be overjoyed at the prospect of marrying the king's cousin. But at the time Sarah had wanted nothing more than to continue serving as the queen's senior scribe, the only woman in the empire to have ever been honored with such a post. The first four months of her marriage had been a nightmare of mutual resentment. But in time, she and Darius had learned to accept each other and settled into a happy companionship. She gave a wry twist of her mouth as she sat on a purple linen couch. Her feelings for Darius were far more complex than companionship.

The problem was that she loved him.

She *loved* him.

Much good it did her, for he did not return her feelings. She knew he cared for her. He had set his concubines free, and settled them in their own independent establishments, and made Sarah the only woman in his life. By his own admission, he enjoyed her company and admired her. But he never confessed love for her.

Her puppy, Anousya, tired of being ignored, interrupted her reverie by jumping up and putting his head on her lap, gazing at her with adoring eyes. At six months, he was already large, and beginning to develop the massive structure that had marked his cousin Caspian, Darius's favorite dog. Sarah still missed Caspian, who had been the most astounding dog she had ever met.

She leaned over and caressed Anousya behind his ears, drawing comfort from the warmth of his solid body. He gave her a puppy smile full of pleasure.

He had been a present from Darius. Her mouth softened as she remembered the night she had named him. Her first suggestion that they call him Silk—because he was so soft—had met with undisguised disapproval.

"Silk!" Darius had exclaimed, sounding offended. "He's not a little girl's toy dog. He is from a noble bloodline, worthy of kings and princes."

Sarah had smoothed the lines of her flowing skirt over her thigh. "How about *Honey?* He is so sweet; that would be a perfect name."

Darius's dark brows lowered with displeasure.

"You don't like *Honey* either?" She pretended to pout. "You said I could name him anything I liked."

"Ah. I did say that. I beg your pardon. *Honey* . . . *Honey,* it is." He spoke the name as if he was chewing on a mouthful of salted sour cherries.

"Thank you, my lord! How perfect. I can imagine it vividly. Having a house full of your mighty friends, and you calling out in front of them: *Here, Honey. Fetch, Honey.* They will be delighted by such a spectacle."

"Wench." The grooves in his cheeks deepened. "I'd be looking at you the whole time I said it. *Here, Honey,*" he said, patting his lap.

She burst into laughter and threw herself into his arms.

"I have a better idea. What if we call him *Anousya?*" She suggested the name, knowing that her husband would approve of the allusion to the king's elite royal guard, better known as the Immortals.

"Now that's a fitting name," he said. "He shall be a warrior dog."

She poked him in the side where she knew him

17

to be ticklish. "He shall be a *companion* dog," she said, reminding him of the original meaning of the Persian word.

Sarah sighed. She could not understand her husband. Sometimes, it seemed to her, he battled his own heart, wanting her with half and rejecting her with the other. Then again, he had never gone five whole days without sending for her, not since they had committed to living as true husband and wife.

"Apama and her husband will be thrilled with your gifts, my lady," Pari said, interrupting Sarah's thoughts. She lifted her arms, now piled with the linens they had fetched from the storehouse sitting precariously on top of the queen's coverlet. "Would you like to come with me as I deliver them?"

"I think not. They always seem flustered when I visit, though I do my best to put them at ease. What they need is peace and quiet. You take those with my compliments. And I will pray for Apama."

Pari wasn't absent for long. She returned, carrying a tray loaded with food. "Shushan has sent you thick herb soup with wheat noodles and hot bread from the ovens," she said as she set the table.

"She read my mind!" Sarah exclaimed as the fragrance of mint and fried onions filled her room. "I've been craving one of her hearty soups all day." Sarah bent over the bowl and inhaled the

18

complex aroma of herbs and spices with pleasure. Darius's one-eyed, skinny cook could transform simple vegetables and meat into an unforgettable feast for the senses.

"Bardia says Apama shows improvement. She smiled when I covered her with your quilt. She is too weak to speak, but her eyes filled with tears when I told her the coverlet had once belonged to the queen. Her husband more than made up for her silence. He bid me to thank you and his lordship so many times that I had to escape while he was midsentence. He'll probably fall at your feet or something equally embarrassing when next he sees you." She lifted the tray on which she had carried the food and turned as if to leave before coming to a sudden halt. "I almost forgot. A messenger just arrived from Susa. He has a missive from Her Majesty for you."

Damaspia, the queen of Persia, was kind enough to consider Sarah a friend—a privilege that sometimes exacted a terrible price, as Sarah well knew. The queen had entered into the habit of writing Sarah, sharing the latest news since she and Darius had moved to his lavish estate near Persepolis six months ago, while the rest of the court resided in Susa for the winter months.

Sarah looked from the steaming bowl to the roll of papyrus in Pari's hand. In a low voice, she spoke a prayer of thanksgiving over her food. As soon as she finished, she held out one hand for the missive while grasping a spoon to start eating. She was too hungry to wait on the soup and too curious to wait on the letter. Pari gave her a disapproving look, but surrendered the missive. Sarah knew she did not have the most graceful table manners even when she was focused on the task. Reading and eating at the same time spelled disaster for either the upholstery or her delicate clothing. Or, most likely, both. She offered Pari her best conciliatory expression before tearing into Damaspia's seal.

She had the skills of a fast and accurate reader, but she read the letter twice to ensure she had understood the queen's command. She looked at the date of its composition with a frown. It had been written two months ago. With a swift motion that almost upended her soup bowl, she rose from the couch.

"Artaxerxes and Damaspia have asked us to visit them at Susa. But they want us to be there in eighteen days!"

"Under three weeks? You would have to fly to arrive in time," Pari said with a gasp.

"I know. Would you please fetch the courier who brought this letter? At once."

A few moments later a young man, still in riding gear, stood at her door next to Pari. Sarah thanked him for his prompt presence. "Can you tell me when this missive was first given to the royal courier service?"

He searched through his leather satchel and retrieved a papyrus scroll. After a few moments of study, he nodded. "Here it is. It was part of a larger batch from the queen's offices. The whole packet was given to us three weeks ago."

Sarah dismissed him with her thanks. His answer confirmed what she had suspected. Damaspia's scribe must have missed the fact that this letter was time sensitive and delayed sending it until a larger packet became ready for dispatch. Deferments of mail were common practice, which saved money and resources. But the scribe was supposed to know when a letter should not be delayed. Sarah quashed an uncomplimentary thought about the inattention of Damaspia's new senior scribe.

"Is his lordship at home?" she asked Pari.

"Yes, my lady."

"Then take this letter to him. Tell him it's from the queen, and that it's urgent."

Sarah wondered if Darius would come to her in response to the queen's letter, or if he would make arrangements without consulting her. It had become his habit to speak to her about most of his affairs of business in the past few months. Given his recent distance, however, he might choose to attend the matter without involving her.

Darius returned from the palace at Persepolis nursing the start of a pesky headache. Hours of dealing with one of Artaxerxes' foreign officials had proven exceptionally dreary. Halfway through the meeting he'd thought of Sarah. An intense longing for her company overcame him, tempting him to cut the meeting short.

He controlled the urge, not out of concern that the official might take offense, but because this disconcerting yearning for Sarah was exactly what he had been trying to battle against for weeks. He felt as if he was losing control and did not enjoy that feeling. Staying away from her seemed the safest course.

But keeping his distance failed to curb his hunger for his wife. He had spent the whole hour since his return from Persepolis staring at new maps from the cartographer while thinking of the outline of Sarah's curves.

The last time she had visited his apartments, she had accidentally left a sheer scarf behind. Instead of returning it to her, he had held on to it, draping the turquoise silk over the back of a sofa. He leaned against the folds of fabric now, and pulled one corner against his lips. The faint smell of roses still clung to the delicate shawl. He inhaled the scent before shoving the fabric away.

She had sent him into convulsions of laughter the night she left the scarf behind, pulling it low over her forehead and scrunching her lips, mimicking with astonishing accuracy the voice of Artaxerxes' dreaded mother, Amestris. "Eat your spinach or it will be the dungeons for you, my boy. I'll chop off your nose, don't think I won't. Your handsome features don't impress *me*."

"You keep that up and you'll be the one in the dungeons. Amestris has spies everywhere. For all you know, I'm one of them."

Sarah gave a nonchalant shrug of one shoulder. "Or I might be one of her spies, setting a trap for *you*."

"Hasn't worked."

"You haven't eaten your spinach, have you? Shows a distinct lack of obedience. Even the vague likeness of the queen mother should motivate you into submission."

Darius laughed. "Submission and I don't get along. You should have learned that by now."

She leaned over. For a breathless moment he thought she would kiss him. Instead, she stretched a hand and pulled a tiny piece of lint from his hair. She blew on the fragile thread and watched it fly into the air. "One can always hope."

He felt the tug of challenge in her voice. Something ancient and intensely male rose up in him, filled with excitement at the thought of that challenge.

And that was the trouble with the woman. She managed to hold his interest in a thousand ways. Peace as well as entertainment seemed to follow in her wake, though she offered both without conscious effort.

Her intelligence impressed him, and that was not an easy accomplishment with a man who spent his days around the most brilliant minds of the world. And yet, instead of giving herself airs, she got on her hands and knees and scrubbed the head gardener's floor when his cottage became infested from the damp.

When Pari came to tell him that an urgent summons had arrived from the queen, he leapt to his feet with the alacrity of a hungry lion. He no longer had to fight against his own urges. He had no choice, after all. It was his duty to go to his wife. As he made his way to Sarah's apartments, he realized with sheepish relief that his headache had disappeared.

A brief knock on Sarah's door heralded a visitor. The knock proved a polite formality, as her husband let himself in before she could respond. Darius appeared every inch the courtier today, dressed in a tunic of soft, midnight blue wool that clung to his tall figure, emphasizing long, toned muscles. As if he needed sartorial enhancement to improve his looks. Darius turned heads even when wearing old hunting gear. Deep green eyes narrowed as Sarah bowed before him.

"How formal," he said, when she rose.

"It seemed appropriate." She gestured toward his elegant outfit. Earlier that morning she had been for a walk with Anousya and had found, discarded, a few alluring tail feathers from the priceless peacocks that roamed the grounds. She picked the most colorful one and tucked it into his belt. "Here. I think you must have dropped this earlier."

He pulled out the feather, intending to stroke Sarah's cheek with its soft plume. She sidestepped the caress. Darius frowned. "Such audacity," he said with mock rage. "Are you implying I am a peacock? I've been closeted with one of the king's officials most of the morning. Had to dress the part, that's all."

He waved the queen's letter. "What's this about, do you know? Why the great rush? We have to be on the road in two days and ride the back roads light and fast to arrive in time."

"I don't know why Damaspia and the king have requested our presence in Susa. It might be a routine visit."

Darius arched a dark brow, speaking volumes without needing to use words. Artaxerxes and his queen rarely wasted time with routine anything. The fact that they had summoned Darius and Sarah meant they had a purpose to the visit.

Sarah raised her chin. "I'm afraid I have no idea what is behind this royal invitation. But I can explain the inconvenient timing. That would be the fault of Damaspia's new senior scribe. If you look at the date, you will find that she dictated this message two months ago, in good time for us to make arrangements and arrive at Susa with utmost convenience. So whatever her reason for summoning us, it could not have been an emergency. Unfortunately, her new scribe must have overlooked the date the queen has mentioned. I checked with the courier. The letter was not sent until three weeks ago, which places us in an awkward position."

"I see." Darius took a few steps toward Sarah. "I cannot complain then, since it was my fault she lost her brilliant scribe and now has to bear with inferior service."

He stood so close that she could feel his breath on her face. But he refrained from touching her.

Longing, confusion, frustration, and hurt roiled inside Sarah until she felt like a tangled skein of wool. What ailed the man? Why did he have to blow so hot and cold? She backed away from him. "I could write Damaspia a letter to explain. She would understand if we arrived late, under the circumstances."

"No. I think it best that we try to arrive at the requested date. The king might have need of us. The fact that Damaspia's servant is incompetent does not alter the original reason for this request. Neither Damaspia nor Artaxerxes makes requests lightly."

Sarah nodded. "Shall Pari and I begin to pack? If you wish to be on the road in two days, there is much to do."

Darius took another step forward, which brought him too close again. This time he reached a hand to play with a fat curl on her shoulder. Pari had spent a whole hour yesterday turning Sarah's straight hair into a profusion of curls. Darius seemed fascinated by the change.

"Pari will have to come later with the baggage train. They can travel on the royal highway, which will be more comfortable for her. She would never keep up with us on the mountain passes. It won't be a pleasant ride for you either. I doubt we'll even take time to set up tents in the evenings if we are to make the trip faster than a royal courier. But you have become very competent on a horse. One would never know you didn't spent your childhood on the back of one." He pulled on the curl to draw her nearer, but there was something reluctant about the way he touched her, as if he drew her to him against his own will.

A bubble of resentment rose to the surface of Sarah's mind. First he avoided her, and now he came to her half willing. Offended, she pulled her hair out of his fingers and walked to the other side of the room. The wall stopped her retreat and she leaned against it. "I will make the arrangements," she said, her face stony.

Darius spied a flagon of pressed apple juice on a side table and poured himself a cup. He took a deep swallow, his movements lazy. Why was he lingering here? Annoyed with his perplexing moods, Sarah wished he would take himself back to his private world now that he had given his orders.

Looking thoughtful, Darius swirled the juice in its silver cup before placing it back on the table. He sauntered toward her, silent as a cat. Her eyes widened when he raised one hand and placed it on the wall so close to her waist that she felt the heat of it through her wool dress and linen shift. Sarah swiveled to the other side, intent on slithering away. With a sudden move, he placed his other hand close to her head, trapping her against the wall.

"Why are you running from me?" he asked, bringing his fingers to rest on her back, drawing her close to him.

She stiffened in his arms. "Why are you?"

He half laughed, half groaned. "I can't seem to get my fill of you." Then he kissed her, and whatever part of him had been trying so hard to resist her, to reject her even, gave way. She felt his defenses crashing as he drew her tighter still. Her own resistance melted as she sensed that for a while, at least, he would be hers.

Chapter 2

S arah looked from the heap of clothes that had begun to gather on her bed to the pile of scrolls and clay tablets that were mounting on her cedar desk and sighed. Ignoring both, she decided to write a letter to her cousin Nehemiah, informing him of her imminent arrival. As cupbearer to the king, her Jewish relative held a position of high authority. In spite of his being a Jew, Artaxerxes had bestowed on him considerable influence, which allowed him regular proximity to the person of the king.

If secret trouble were brewing, Nehemiah would see to it that Darius and she were armed with the right information before entering the king's presence. Artaxerxes was a kind and generous king, as Sarah had reason to know. But he was also dedicated to his empire with a single-minded passion that could at times make extreme demands. A little preparation for Artaxerxes never went amiss.

"You'll be riding on horseback the whole way with only two or three pack horses," Pari said, interrupting her train of thought. "I hope Lord Darius has plenty of clothes in his storehouses in Susa, for I cannot fit but two outfits in the space he has allotted me. *It's all about speed, Pari,* he says to me. But once my lord arrives, I wager he won't care a snap for speed. He'll want you as elegant as a princess; he wouldn't want you to feel embarrassed before the court again."

Sarah rested her head in her hands for a moment. She had not slept well the night before, remaining awake and fretting about the mountain of tasks she had to accomplish before leaving for Susa. Sleeplessness had not helped her accomplish a single chore, of course. But she had not been able to make herself rest by logical arguments. After over an hour of anxiety-ridden thoughts, she had finally remembered to pray. In her worry, even her prayers had kept turning into a list of things she had to accomplish, for she had focused more on her burdens than on God. She had fallen asleep close to dawn and had awakened bleary-eyed.

"Do your best," she mumbled through her fingers. "I only need to fend for myself the first two weeks, and then you will arrive with the baggage train." Thanks to Pari's gentle instructions, she had learned how to navigate the rigid formalities of court life as the wife of an aristocrat. She would never walk into another royal feast looking like a demon from the outer darkness, the way she had on her wedding day.

She finished the letter for Nehemiah and had it delivered to the royal courier who was leaving that day for Susa. Abandoning the packing to Pari, Sarah focused on the estate accounts. For many hours, she lost herself in the work. Darius's new steward in Persepolis, Vidarna, had turned out to be a gem. He had the sense of humor of a goose, and still blanched every time he had to give an accounting to Sarah. He could not grow accustomed to the fact that he had to report to a woman, and an aristocratic one at that, even if only by marriage. But he had proven honest and competent, two qualities that no shortcoming could diminish.

Late that evening, having arrived at a semblance of order, Sarah surrendered the accounts to Vidarna. "I've left some gaps, I'm afraid. But I know you'll manage, Vidarna. Your work is always exemplary."

The scribe's bald head bent low in a respectful bow. "I am certain you've taken the most difficult matters upon yourself, my lady. As always."

Exhaustion mingled with relief as she handed the accounts over. She liked knowing that she left the estate in good order before departing for what might turn out to be a lengthy trip. One could never guess how long a royal audience might last, especially with the New Year only four weeks away.

Sarah then sent for Bardia, who arrived bearing a scarlet pomegranate. "The last of the autumn fruit, to put a smile on your face on these final days of winter," he said, his wide smile revealing five solitary teeth.

"How thoughtful, Bardia. It looks perfect. Tell me, how is Apama?"

"She has turned a corner, my lady. I believe she will recover completely. And that daughter of hers never stops eating. She will no doubt grow strong and plump before the month is out."

"I am relieved to hear it. Now you must go to bed, my friend. You've been working too hard this week."

Bardia nodded. At the door, he turned back to her. "It shall be your turn soon, my lady. You'll see."

Coming from anyone else, such a comment would have been intrusive. But Bardia had a unique gift of saying intimate things without appearing impertinent. Sarah gazed into space for a moment, a hand resting against her flat belly. The truth was that the incessant talk about childbearing over the past few days had made her more conscious than ever of how desperate she was to have a babe of her own. After over eleven months of marriage, she showed no signs of fecundity. Of course the first five months of her marriage did not count on that score. She gave Bardia a sad smile and turned away.

Pari held up two outfits for her inspection. "Which one for the great feast: the blue or the red?"

Sarah nibbled on her lower lip. "Do you think Darius will like the red?"

"He'd have to be blind not to. My advice is not to breathe deeply while you are wearing it. The latest fashions are very tight on top."

Sarah groaned. "Pack the blue, then. I didn't realize you had made the red so formfitting. No wonder you didn't let me try it on when you were finished."

"I've already packed the red," Pari said, her soft mouth pulled into a stubborn line. "I wish I could see Lord Darius's expression when he sees you in it."

Well. If wearing tight, scarlet garments was going to grab her husband's attention, perhaps she should stop arguing and allow Pari to choose her wardrobe. "You will land me in a heap of trouble one of these days," she said.

"You don't need *me* for that." Pari sat down on a couch and picked up Sarah's winter riding tunic, which needed minor mending. "Why are the New Year celebrations in Susa? I thought they were always held in Persepolis."

"This year, the king decided to change the venue and remain in the old palace. I think he wished to avoid the aggravation of travel."

Foreign officials from around the empire had been notified of the change; in a matter of weeks they would be descending into Susa's ancient halls, bringing gifts for Artaxerxes as a sign of their continued fealty to the empire. There would be special ceremonies and endless feasts.

"You will attend at least ten separate events in the first week of the year alone, regardless of the location," Pari said, her head bent to her task. "A separate outfit for each occasion, with matching jewels. This is your first New Year as a lady of rank. There will be many demands on your time."

Sarah groaned at the thought of the ceaseless gatherings and the constant social activity. "I abhor the fuss. Give me the company of close friends over a large, formal affair any day."

Having grown up as the daughter of a Jewish scribe, she still found the requirements of life for an aristocratic woman trying. It was easy to forget Darius's privileged background when they were alone together. He offered amenable company and never pointed out her ignorance. But in public, the differences became uncomfortably obvious. His speech, manner, and every gesture marked him as a highborn lord, while she struggled to fit into a world that always felt foreign.

If only she weren't so tired. She forced herself to her feet. Pari continued to apply her ivory needle into the padded, moss-green garment of her winter riding tunic with careful expertise. Although they were at the tail end of the season, it would be cold through the mountainous trails. Sarah made a face. She wasn't looking forward to freezing on horseback for twelve days straight.

"Would you please organize a bath for me?" Sarah asked. A hot soak might ease her muscles, cramped from hours of sitting and squinting over detailed documents.

"Of course, my lady." Pari set aside her needle and left to arrange Sarah's late-night wash.

Hot steam and the scent of roses filled the bathhouse when Sarah arrived. Pari handed her a pumice stone and a perfumed scrub, and, sensing Sarah's need for quiet, retreated to a far corner of the bathhouse. Sarah stepped into the small sunken pool, sighing with pleasure as the hot water lapped about her. Slowly, the knots of tension began to melt. It would be many days before she could enjoy this luxury again. Traveling on the back roads, far from the royal stage houses, meant hurried washing with freezing water drawn from rivers and streams—*if* a river was available.

Even in the summer months when bathing in a stream might prove a delightful distraction from the heat, tradition forbade it. Persians believed washing dirty linen or even the human body in a river brought pollution into creation. One was permitted to draw water for the purpose of ablution, but the Persians considered outdoor bathing an act of irreverence. Sarah closed her eyes and sank deeper, determined to derive as much enjoyment out of *this* bath as she could.

She finished rinsing her hair, and for a few moments allowed herself to float in the water, enjoying the sensation of doing nothing. A hand began to wash her back with a cloth. "That feels so good, Pari. Thank you." The touch became soft. Sensual. Sarah's eyes snapped open and she twisted her head to find her husband squatting on one knee on the tiles surrounding the sunken pool, a wicked grin making his eyes sparkle.

Sputtering, Sarah pulled away into the middle of the bath, keeping her back to him, her arms wrapped securely about her body. "What are you doing?" She sounded like one of his peacocks sporting a head cold. In all her months of marriage, he had never visited the bathhouse while she occupied it. She felt ridiculously shy about his presence. There was something vulnerable about sitting in a bath while Darius crouched above her, fully clothed, not a wave of his long hair out of place.

He shrugged as he twirled the wet washcloth. "I needed to speak with you."

Sarah tried to regain her composure, and said with as much aplomb as she could muster, "Would you please wait until I return to my chamber?"

"It's late already. I would prefer to speak now. Besides, this is more fun. I've never visited you here. An oversight on my part."

Sarah gaped. "Where is Pari? I saw her a few moments ago."

"I dismissed her. That poor girl appeared beyond fatigued; she was half asleep on the wet tiles."

Caught between guilt for not noticing Pari's need for slumber and pique at her husband's high-handed manner, she said, "How thoughtful."

Darius nodded, his smile widening. "Would you like to come out?"

"Yes." Her towel, folded neatly, lay on a marble bench out of her reach. Sarah pointed to it. "May I have my towel?"

He seemed to think for a moment. "Certainly." He made no move to fetch it. Instead, he lifted a courteous hand. "Please. Help yourself."

Sarah lowered her lashes. He wished to play games, did he? An abrupt determination to beat her husband at his own antics brought new vigor to her sluggish mind. She knew that if Darius had noted the steely glint of resolve in the cast of her face, he would have been more prepared for a challenge. As it was, he perched behind her on the tiled floor, as innocent as an infant, thinking himself in complete control. Which suited her well.

"Upon reflection, perhaps *you* should come *in?*" Over her shoulder, she gave him an inviting smile. It was impossible to miss the sudden blaze in the forest green eyes. She lifted her own arm in a parody of his movements from a moment before. With her back to him, the gesture lost some of its blithe hilarity. But it would have to do. "Please. Help yourself." She motioned to the water.

Darius shot up and began to take off one leather shoe, then the other, hopping in his haste.

"I think your men will appreciate the scent of roses on your hair tomorrow as we set out for Susa," Sarah said sweetly, hiding behind her hair.

Darius went still mid-hop, one foot in the grasp of his hands. With slow movements, he straightened. Then he burst into laughter. "I concede the victory to you, my lady. I do not wish to smell like roses." He fetched the linen towels that Pari had left behind and offered them to her.

"What did you want to discuss?" Sarah asked as she toweled her hair dry.

"Vidarna came to see me. He said you had worn yourself out working on the estate records since yesterday before dawn, and you looked exhausted. I'm sorry about that. When I asked you to help me with the management of my estates, I didn't mean that you should work like a slave."

Sarah experienced a pang of fond appreciation for Vidarna. She found it hard to believe that the taciturn scribe had looked at her long enough to notice how tired she was. "Please don't concern yourself, my lord. I wanted to finish before leaving. I made my own decision."

"Nonetheless, I can see you are weary. I came to tell you that I have delayed our departure by one day. Tomorrow, I wish you to rest."

"There is no need! We cannot afford the extra day, Darius. It could make us late."

"That's not as important as you." He reached out and grasped her hand. With a slow, deliberate pull, he drew her into his arms and cradled her. His touch was comforting, void of demand. He didn't even seem to mind that her damp towel was leaving a wet smudge over the front of his tunic. "Not nearly as important as you," he said again, his lips close to her ear.

His words, spoken with solemn sincerity, melted her heart. She felt protected in the folds of his embrace. Her body relaxed and she felt enveloped by a sense of peace. It occurred to her that in spite of his inward struggles, in spite of the fact that he did not fully trust her, in spite of his divided heart, her husband cherished her. He wanted to keep her safe. He wanted her happy. Because of his neglect over the past several days, she had allowed herself to sink into insecurity, and then into resentment. She had focused on his shortcomings and forgotten that he was a true gift to her.

She turned with a slight motion and kissed his neck. He went still. Sarah kissed him again, more boldly. He tangled his hand in her wet hair and turned her face toward his so that he could see her more clearly.

"You aren't too tired?"

She shook her head and, standing on tiptoe, kissed him on the mouth, her lips shy. "I love you," she said. It was the first time she had said the words without his prompting. The fact that he never made a similar declaration made her want to keep her own feelings hidden inside. But Darius coaxed and cajoled them out of her. Tonight, she offered up the words as a free gift. Her pride could not compare with his joy.

He drew a sharp breath at her words. "Say it again."

"I love you."

With an inarticulate sound, he dragged her tighter against him. For the span of a moment he studied her, his dark lashes lowered, his expression unreadable. Then he kissed her with an explosive tenderness that dissolved the last of her reserve.

Chapter 3

Darius snapped into full consciousness, aware that an unfamiliar noise had dragged him out of sleep. Years of military training had honed his instincts for danger so that he was already taking inventory of the surroundings before his eyes adjusted to the starlight. With relief he noted that Sarah slept undisturbed next to him, her body squeezed tight against his side in an unconscious effort to ward off the night chill.

He shifted his head to look for Arta, who had been assigned guard duty. In the firelight, he could see the man sprawled on the ground, his head slumped forward at an awkward angle. Darius's heart pumped with an unpleasant rush as he noticed the dark liquid clinging to the side of Arta's slack face.

Besides Arta, he had three men riding with him. One was gagged and tied. He caught the attention of the second man, Meres, who remained alert and unbound, faking sleep. Meres pointed behind him with a subtle rising of his brow.

Following his signal, Darius noted that there were four intruders busy with gagging and tying the remaining member of his company. *Five,* he amended, taking in the massive shoulders of a leather-bound man skulking toward him, holding a wide short sword. Darius grasped his knife, the only weapon he had kept strapped against his thigh when he had fallen into his pallet last night after an exhausting journey through treacherous slopes.

The wide-shouldered man stood over him now. Filled with the peculiar calm that often came to him in the heat of battle, Darius realized that the man held his sword at a curious angle, like a club. He wasn't intent on killing him so much as subduing him, then.

With a lightning-quick movement, Darius swept his leg, catching his attacker in the ankles. Surprised, the man lost his balance for a moment. Darius rolled to his feet, and, taking advantage of his opponent's unsteadiness, kicked him hard in the groin. The man dropped his sword and doubled over, in too much agony to cry out.

Darius grabbed the discarded sword and hit the man on the back of the head with the dense, bronze handle. With a grunt he fell over, unconscious.

"Consider it a favor," Darius said, knowing from old experience that his attacker wouldn't want to be awake through *that* pain.

"Darius?" Sarah was kneeling on her pallet, her eyes wide with shock. Darius swallowed hard. When he had consented to having her join him on their trip, he had not expected anything more dangerous than their daily rides, which, upon occasion, brought them to high mountain passes. The thought of what might happen to her in the midst of a melee made his gut twist into a tight knot.

He forced his voice to sound calm. "Hide behind that rock. Don't move unless I call!"

She didn't stir. *"Hurry,"* he whispered, a sharp bite underlying the command. To his relief, she obeyed.

The rest of their unknown attackers were now aware that he was not asleep and could no longer be taken by surprise. He saw Meres engaging two men while the other two headed in his direction. Darius frowned, perplexed by the fact that they seemed unarmed except for a long, skinny stick which one of them held casually in one hand. He used the moments he had before they reached him to try to cut one of his men, Sama, loose from his bonds. He had time to cut the ties about Sama's wrists and grab a shield before his two opponents were almost upon him.

Darius turned, taking note of small details that might give him an advantage in the unequal fight. In a corner of his mind he became aware that the grass felt cool and damp beneath his bare feet and the air crisp in his chest. To his astonishment, he saw that only one man approached him, his gait slow. The pale light of the fire could not hide the fact that even though he was of slim build— shorter and thinner than Darius—his compact body displayed an impressive array of hard muscles. The man's companion held back, in no haste to come to his aid. They certainly did not seem to expect much trouble from their prey, Darius thought.

Unsure of how the man intended to use such a thin reed of a staff in a fight, Darius flexed his sharp knife in one hand, considering. He stepped forward into a well-practiced stance, and put his weight behind the knife as he lunged at the man. To his surprise the man did not veer either to left or right, but in the last moment, stretched out an arm, and with what felt like a soft touch, pushed against Darius's wrist in an arc. Darius found his knife hand travelling wide off the mark, his own strength being used against him.

He regained his balance and turned to face his opponent again. The white staff suddenly whirled in the air, sounding more like a whip than a wooden stick. Darius pulled his shield in front of his face just in time to catch its downward strike. Amazingly, the wood did not splinter as it came into contact with Darius's thick wicker-and-leather shield. Instead, it bent and found its way around the shield, whipping the side of Darius's face with a painful strike. He put a hand to his stinging face; it came away bloody. He had never experienced anything like it in battle before.

Darius gripped his knife harder. The man had taken a strange pose, his knees bent, one arm forward, his palm flat, the other fisted around the staff and pulled back. Darius rushed at him, intending to use the weight of his core body to wrestle the man to the ground. Before he had the opportunity, however, his opponent uncoiled with tremendous speed and brought down the edge of his hand diagonally against the side of Darius's neck. The blow bore down on Darius with the force of metal instead of mere flesh and blood. He knew he would have lost consciousness if his neck muscles were not so strong. Darius resisted the dizziness that enveloped him, swallowing hard to overcome the urge to vomit.

With a growl, he threw aside the shield and rushed at his attacker, hoping to surprise him with an unexpected counterattack. The man grabbed Darius just above the elbow and pressed. It was as if a string had been pulled from his elbow all the way down into his fingers; Darius lost his grasp on the knife, his fingers nerveless.

He managed to break contact and took up a defensive stance, but realized that he was losing control of the fight. It was clear that his opponent was proficient in a form of combat hitherto unknown to Darius. With sudden speed, the man rushed toward him and flew high in the air as if he had grown a set of wings, landing a forceful kick straight into Darius's solar plexus. It felt like being hit by a tree trunk. Darius collapsed, unable to breathe.

Time slowed. As the world came to a standstill, he remained aware that everything was happening much faster than it seemed. From the side of his eye he saw his opponent's companion standing to the side, his arms crossed, a relaxed grin on his face as he watched, secure in the knowledge of his opponent's extraordinary ability in battle. Without warning, the man's grin wavered and his eyes rolled back before he slid to the ground with a noisy crash. Sama stood behind him, holding a fat rock in his hand.

Darius's opponent grew distracted for a moment by the noise of his companion dropping to the ground. It was the opening Darius needed. The thought of what this man could do to his wife should he lose gave Darius the strength to get back on his feet, ignoring the fire in his ribs. Taking advantage of his opponent's slack-jawed surprise, he landed his elbow into the man's belly and knocked him in the side of the head with a double-handed punch. The man staggered to one side. Darius swept a kick against his knees in the opposite direction and his opponent toppled. On the ground, he could not use the staff. Sama joined the melee, and between the two of them they finally subdued the adversary. He lay unconscious, a trickle of blood falling from his fast swelling lip.

They rushed to help Meres; Darius experienced a rush of relief when he realized that although the others in the gang of attackers were skilled fighters, they were nowhere near as extraordinary as the man whom he had faced. Within minutes, Meres's two challengers were quashed and tied with severe knots that held them helpless against one another. The other three men in the gang, now in various stages of unconsciousness, were restrained in similar fashion.

He had barely finished tying up the last man when Sarah ran to his side. "Are you all right?" She couldn't manage to hide a small quiver in her voice.

"You were supposed to wait until I called you." He tried to sound stern, but heard relief drown out every other emotion in his words.

"Pardon, my lord. In all the excitement, I forgot."

Barefoot as she was now, the top of her head came to his chest. Her hair, wild from sleep and her haphazard run, tangled about her face. The full mouth, trembling with fear only moments ago, now grew flat into a stubborn line as she tried to regain her composure. If not for the carefully averted gaze of his men and the deep bruise at his side, he would have clasped her to him and kissed her—to reassure her or himself, he could not be certain.

"You took a few hard hits," she said, trying to sound casual. "Anything broken?"

It occurred to him that for a woman unused to battle and bloodshed, she was acting with admirable self-possession. No tears. No hysterics.

No embarrassing scene before his men. He knew that self-control came at a high cost, and appreciated it all the more. "I may have a few cracked ribs," he said, keeping his voice light.

"And your cheek is bleeding. It will probably scar. Too bad. You won't be as good looking as Meres anymore."

Darius swallowed a smile, enchanted by her indomitable humor. "Saucy wench. You'd better attend me, then. Or will you faint at the sight of a little blood?"

He would have laughed at her offended expression if the moan of one of the captives hadn't forced him back to the present situation.

"Search them," Darius said through gritted teeth as Sarah bound his ribs with bandage. "Strip them naked if you have to. I want to know who they are and why they attacked us."

Arta, who had regained consciousness and sat nursing a prodigious headache, growled. "Thieves and rascals—that's who they are. Looking for our silver, no doubt."

Darius made a noncommittal sound in his throat. The five men did not strike him as ordinary robbers. They fought like professionals, not bandits. Their high-quality horses were well cared for. He could still picture the unusual moves of the slim man he had fought; if not for Sama's help, he would have lost that clash. Those were not the moves of a common thief.

He deliberated for a moment on whether to take the time and solve the puzzle of this mysterious attack, or bundle the culprits on their horses and deliver them to the magistrate in Susa and let him untangle this enigma. After all, the king, who had summoned him and Sarah for a special audience, expected their speedy presence.

Yet, something about these men continued to nag at him. He felt uneasy at the thought of leaving the investigation to someone else. A baffling mystery was at work here, and he grew convinced that he needed to solve it, even if it meant a delay in meeting with the king.

The sun had risen high by the time his men had made a small mound of their attackers' belongings in the middle of the campground. Darius picked up the white staff and examined it. It was made of a kind of wood he had never seen. He flexed it in opposite directions several times. It gave with incredible ease, bending in ways that would have broken any other wooden stick. He wondered how the staff had been fashioned in order to have at once the solidity of wood and the flexibility of leather. He discarded it and began to go through the pile of sacks and parcels in front of him.

At the top of the pile rested a flawless box, carved from ivory. Inside, Darius found a dagger decorated with exquisite jewels on one side of the handle and plain gold on the other. The delicate construction allowed the dagger to rest comfortably in one's hand. He hefted it in his palm and tested the edge; although it had been designed as a ceremonial piece, it proved more than battle worthy. The blade was well balanced, honed, and sturdy.

This was no ordinary dagger. The consummate craftsmanship and the rare jewels used in its creation marked it a worthy offering for a nobleman of high rank. Darius examined it a moment longer, looking for identifying marks or clues to its ownership. Finding none, he replaced it in the box and set it aside.

Unlike the dagger, everything else in the pile appeared commonplace and well-used. Extra clothes, coins, a couple of jars of oil for the treatment of leather and metal, camping gear. Wine. Dried date cakes. Nothing incriminating. At the bottom of the pile, a sealed leather pouch caught his eye. He did not recognize the seal; the palm tree and stylized lion motif weren't Persian. He showed it to Sarah. "Do you recognize this seal?"

She studied it before responding. "It's unfamiliar to me."

"Can you break the wax, but retain the integrity of the design? I need to figure out its source once we arrive in Susa."

"I think so. It depends on the quality of the wax." She pulled out her knife and drew a careful line into the seal. With a delicate snap, she broke it into two undamaged sections.

"What do you think you're doing?" The voice was deep and calm. Darius turned and found the broad-shouldered man who had attacked him regarding him through intelligent brown eyes.

"Ah. Awake at last. Did you have a pleasant nap?"

"You better leave that package alone."

Darius crossed his arms. "You aren't in a position to make demands, are you? Who is it for?"

The man said nothing. Darius unrolled the leather and found a short letter inside. "Not very illuminating," he said after he read it.

"What does it say?" the man asked, shifting against his tight bonds.

"You don't know?"

"I just carry them. I don't read them."

"How noble." He held out the letter to Sarah. "What do you think?"

She studied it in silence for a time. "Interesting."

"Really? I found it disappointing. *Carry out the instructions I send you. You now have everything you need for the New Year ceremonies. May you walk in safety.* How is that of any help? What are the instructions? That's what I need to find out."

"Your problem is that you don't know your grammar. You see the way the author of the letter has used the verb *send?*"

Darius gave a desultory kick against a round pebble, sending it spinning into the air. "Are you trying to put me to sleep?"

Sarah tapped the rolled letter against her thigh. "Listen, your lordship, and you might learn something of benefit. The way the author has used this verb indicates that the instructions are not coming later. Nor have they been sent ahead. Whoever wrote this letter is saying that the instructions should be delivered at the same time as the missive, which strongly indicates that these gentlemen have them hidden somewhere. Possibly on their persons."

Darius whistled softly at that bit of news. He executed a showy, court-worthy bow before Sarah. She pushed against his shoulder with an exasperated hand. The hand, soft and mildly ink-stained from her furious work on the estate records before their departure, was speckled with dirt—no doubt a result of her dive behind the outcropping of rocks.

"That is an excellent grammar lesson." He turned to the intruder. "Impressive, isn't she? Too bad for you. Would you like to tell me where these blessed instructions are?" He sighed as the man stared back, turning mute. "I didn't think so."

He bade his men to search the intruders again while he went through the pile of their possessions once more. There were no other items of interest in the remaining pouches—nothing that pointed to the missing instructions. With sudden insight, Darius began to search through the piles again. This time, he wasn't trying to *find* something, but to ensure that a certain crucial article was missing.

"Where are your travel visas—your *viyataka*?" he asked.

The man's head snapped up. "What?"

"Your permits. You can't be travelling on the king's roads without the required documents. Yours seem to be missing."

"Must have lost them."

Darius patted the pile in front of him. "I don't think so. I think that's what you were after when you attacked us. There happen to be five men in our party and five in yours. It must have proven too convenient a coincidence for you to overlook. You are travelling the back roads, so your chances of running into the king's soldiers are diminished. But to enter a large city like Susa, where this road leads, you will need the official *viyataka*. Much easier to enter the city with the appropriate documents than to try to sneak in without them, which must have been your original plan."

"You forget—you also have a woman, which we don't. So you see, your travel documents would be of no use to me."

Darius knelt in front of his captive and poked him in the chest with his index finger. "You underestimate yourself. It would be easy enough to pay a woman at the gates of Susa to pretend to be a member of your party."

The man turned his face away from Darius's penetrating gaze. "So what?"

"So, this proves that you aren't simple thieves looking for money. You are on a mission of some kind—a mission secret enough to prevent you from applying for travel documents. Would you care to share what that mission is?"

He snorted. "Would you care to share yours?"

Darius sighed. "You insist on making this difficult."

By now, his men had searched the intruders and their horses down to the skin, but had found nothing. The whole troop had regained consciousness and sat brooding in their ropes, but made no move to resist the thorough examination.

With a sudden move, Sarah sprang to her feet and walked over to the owner of the staff. "That's an unusually short haircut," she said.

Darius frowned. It wasn't like his wife to be fashion conscious, or to make public statements about someone's lack of style. He edged closer to her, not liking her proximity to the exceptional fighter in spite of his being bound.

"You must have cut it within the past month," Sarah continued, refusing to budge from the subject. "Shaved it even, I would guess, from the way it has grown back."

Darius gave his wife a sidelong glance before bending to examine the man's scalp. The sun had risen while they were interrogating the thieves, its light winter bright. Under its luminous reflection the man's skin shone white beneath the covering

54

of hair. Then with bewilderment Darius noticed black marks on parts of the scalp. "Tattoos. You have tattoos on your scalp."

The man turned to Darius and gave him a pleasant smile. "First your woman, now you. Are you people obsessed with scalps?"

Darius restrained the urge to give him a good kick and signaled Meres to shave the man's head.

"Leave my head alone!" the man yelled, but was helpless, trussed up as he was, to prevent Meres from completing his task.

His head was shaved in a matter of moments. Meres wiped the blood that flowed from several shallow cuts, a consequence of the man's futile struggles. A short message written in Aramaic became legible on the white scalp, tattooed in black ink.

Sarah gasped as she read it in silence. "That's about the king!"

Chapter 4

W hat?" The man whose skull was the focus of intense attention twisted his head to address Darius. "What's it say?"

"As if you don't know."

"Can't read my own head, can I? What does it say? Tell me."

Darius, who had grown rigid after perusing the strange missive, emptied his voice of inflection and began to read the tattoo aloud. "Poison the jeweled side of the dagger only. Present it with a roasted pigeon as our gift. Cut the bird in half. Make certain he consumes the poisoned side."

Darius's men looked at one another, puzzled. Arta scratched his wounded head. "What does that mean, besides the fact that some poor sod is going to get murdered?"

"The message is about the king," Sarah explained.

"What?" Several masculine voices, including their attackers, spoke at the same time.

"How can you tell?" Arta asked.

"His Majesty receives gifts from ambassadors around the empire on the first day of spring. You remember the mention of New Year in the letter we found among their gear? This is what the author meant.

"Often the gifts presented to the king are symbolic: water from a river, to indicate that the whole river belongs to Artaxerxes; earth, to signify that the land itself is offered to the king. A bird would be a pretty way of claiming that the sky is also the dominion of the Persian monarch. A cooked bird would be tasted by the king as a sign of his approval, which, one assumes, is why they have included the knife."

"That's why the knife is so exquisite," Darius said. "It's meant as a gift for His Majesty on the feast of the New Year."

Sarah nodded. "Although the king would eat of the proffered fowl, he would take the precaution of sharing it with the one who has brought it in order to ensure that it is not poisoned. However, the person behind this plot has concocted a clever ploy to bypass that difficulty. Both will eat from the same bird, but the king's portion will be deadly, while the assassin's remains free of venom. There would be no proving such a plot; you could not tie the death of the king to the killer, for many would have witnessed that both ate of the same food and only one sickened and died."

"The king!" Arta almost exploded as he pronounced the word. "Are you certain? I thought the New Year offerings were made in Persepolis."

Darius pressed his forefinger and thumb to the bridge of his nose. "Usually, they are. This year the king changed the venue to Susa as he did not wish to travel. The heads of state from around the empire—governors, satraps, and important officials—are at this moment descending on Susa to bring their offerings to His Majesty. Except that one of them has been planning to use this occasion as a means of assassinating the king. Only an official of high rank would have access to the king on New Year's Day, so this plot has its origins in a person of consequence someplace in the empire."

There was a moment of stunned silence. Then everyone began to speak at once, the loudest voices belonging to the intruders, swearing ignorance of the plot.

Aggravated by the noise and confusion, Darius bellowed, "Silence!"

An uncomfortable quiet settled over the camp.

Darius took a deep breath; the movement strained his bruised side, and he shifted to ease the pain. Facing the intruders he said, "How can you have the gall to profess innocence? The only thing we lack in evidence against you is the dead body of the king himself."

The man who had forbidden Darius from opening the sealed letter now addressed the gathering. Darius guessed that he was the leader of their party and set his attention on him.

The man nodded his dark head. "My lords, my lady, my name is Nassir, from Babylon. These are my four brothers: Nur, Naram, Nutesh. And that one," he said, pointing with his chin to the man with the tattoo, "is our youngest brother, Niqquulamuusu. Everyone calls him Niq."

"That's a relief," Darius said.

"First, please accept our humble apologies for the manner of our introduction."

Darius noticed Sarah's mouth twitching at the use of the word *introduction*. This fellow was entertaining for a cur and a murderer, he had to admit.

Nassir continued. "We intended you no harm. You must have noticed that we went to great lengths to ensure no one was truly hurt. We don't kill people."

"That tattoo bears witness against your claim."

"This is a terrible misunderstanding, my lord. Allow me to explain."

Darius, who now had the task of interrogating the Babylonian brothers, motioned for him to continue, curious as to the story he would concoct.

"My brothers and I are couriers, in a manner of speaking."

"Couriers work for the empire. I doubt the royal administration hired you or"—Darius waved his hand vaguely toward the group of tied-up men—"your siblings."

"That is true, sire. Perhaps *courier* is stretching the word a little. We transport things. As you noted, travel in Persia is guarded by strict regulations. Even mail, if sent without royal approval, is read and destroyed upon discovery. But there are those who, for personal reasons, can neither apply for a travel permit nor entrust their mail to official couriers. Most people have secrets they would rather not share with the king's bureaucrats, who could sell a juicy morsel for extra money on the side. In my experience, these secrets are often harmless to the empire. They concern matters of a personal nature—inheritance, love, family squabbles. Our rule is that we never look inside the packages and letters entrusted to us. People's private sorrows and pain are not our concern."

"How convenient. And you don't think that such rules attract murderers and villains of every kind?"

"No, my lord. Folks who have murder in mind wouldn't entrust a stranger with their secrets, generally speaking. We are honest men of business. We have no interest in murder. We merely transport documents and goods from one part of the empire to another for a reasonable fee."

"Honest men, you call it?" Arta gaped. "My head is still aching from your honesty."

"That was business, sir. It's not as if we were going to rob you of your gold or silver. As his lordship so wisely deduced, we needed to borrow your travel documents."

At his side, Sarah tried to stifle a snort; she did not succeed. Darius decided to redirect the conversation. "Explain the tattoo."

"Ah, that. Believe me, my lord, I had no idea what the content of that vile message was or I would never have placed my brother's scalp at the disposal of such roguery. Here is what happened. A man contacted me and offered a great deal of money for my brothers and me to carry that dagger and a couple of missives into Susa."

"What man?" Now they were getting somewhere, Darius thought.

"There's the rub, my lord. He met me at night, wearing a hooded cloak. I hardly saw his face. His only introduction was a bag of gold. He sounded like an aristocrat. But I never found out his name."

"Where was this?"

"In Babylon. But the man was not Babylonian; I could tell from his accent. I don't know where he came from. I found it hard to place him, as though he had distorted his speech. He paid extra because he wanted to tattoo his letter on the messenger's scalp. He said it was the only way he could be certain that it would not be discovered by royal spies."

"But for my wife's sharp eyes he might have proven right. How came he to tattoo your head without your knowing what the message said?" he asked Niq.

Niq shrugged. "They kept me hidden in a room for a month. Except for the man who shaved and tattooed me, I saw no one, not even my brothers.

My room had no window, so I couldn't send or receive any messages. I had no idea what they had written on my head. They locked me in until my hair had grown out and covered the message beneath. At the time I thought it a mere inconvenience: the pay had been so enormous that I figured it was worth a month of my life. It never occurred to me that they had tattooed treason on my head. When I find the rascal who marred me with dishonor, I'll flatten him."

"Why did you not ask your brother to try to decipher the message?"

"By then my hair had grown in, and we could read nothing. I couldn't shave my head. The purpose of waiting for a month was to have the hair grow in so that we could travel with the message hidden."

"Was the man who tattooed you the same person who spoke to Nassir, do you think?"

Niq shook his head. "No. He had no lordly ways about him. He must be a simple servant, judging by his manner. His master must've held him in deep confidence, though, if he entrusted him with such a job."

Darius chewed on his lower lip. The origin of the plot was proving a dead end if the brothers were to be believed. Although he had foiled the plan by discovering it, he knew it was essential that he find the traitor. No doubt whoever intended to assassinate Artaxerxes would try again. "To whom were you supposed to deliver the dagger and the missives in Susa?"

"I have no name," Nassir said.

"Of course not."

"But I have a place and time of meeting."

Darius smiled slowly.

Sarah had finally stopped shaking by the time they began to mount their horses. She had known—of course she had known—that she had married a warrior. She had given her heart to a man of military rank and function, who spent much of his time on secret or open missions for the king, quashing rebellions and conquering new territories. It was one thing to have intellectual awareness of such a reality, however, and another to witness it. To see the kicks land in her husband's ribs and the blood flow from his flesh. And this was a mere skirmish. She began to tremble again at the thought of the full onslaught of a large-scale war.

She had only known Darius in the role of courtier and landowner. In the months since their marriage had become a reality, Darius had remained mostly by her side, serving Artaxerxes as a diplomat on occasion, and tending to his lands. His properties had needed his attention after the tangle his dishonest steward, Teispes, had left behind.

The sudden attack of the Babylonians now forced the reality of the full scope of Darius's profession into the forefront of Sarah's mind. He would not thank her for becoming an over-protective wife, nagging him to avoid every uncertain venture. In Persia, men were expected to serve the empire. She had to learn to accept the danger in which he walked. She would have to learn to swallow her fears and let him go with a smile when the time came for him to ride into battle.

She jumped in her saddle when Darius interrupted her reverie. "You seem deep in thought."

She had not heard him draw near, which was a good indication of her appalling preoccupation, given the size of his horse, Samson. "Yes, my lord."

He grabbed her hand, bringing his giant of a horse near enough that their thighs touched. It had been many days since he had drawn so close to her. The rigors of outdoor travel and the constant presence of others had kept them apart since they had left Persepolis. He seemed uncaring of curious eyes now.

"Some elaboration might be in order," he said, bending his face close to hers so that she could feel his warm breath tickling her ear.

Sarah leaned forward to caress her horse's neck, hiding her face from Darius's scrutiny. "I was thinking of how well you fought."

"You were thinking how close I came to being killed."

"That too."

"I'm sorry you saw that, Sarah."

She felt the heat of tears pricking the back of her eyes. Turning her head so that Darius's sharp gaze would not notice her distress, she focused her attention on the Babylonians. The brothers were trussed up like roasted lamb, and could only manage a plodding gait on their horses.

She asked in an undertone only Darius could hear, "Do you believe their story?"

He leaned back in the saddle. "It's a wild tale. And yet it rings true. I've heard of private couriers. There aren't many of them. Understandable, since the empire frowns on their trade."

"I believe them too, in spite of their shady occupation."

When Niq had attacked Darius, she had been desperate to rush out of her hiding place to lend a hand, terrified lest Darius be hurt. Beyond that mind-numbing fear, however, she had been shocked at the instinctive rage and violence that overcame her. She would have torn Niq apart if she could. Only a dread of her husband's wrath had kept her obedient to his demand that she stay hidden. Now that the danger was past, the flood of her violent emotions had ebbed. She had no desire for revenge. The sight of the brothers, bound up and helpless, roused her pity.

"What will happen to them, do you think? If they can prove that they are innocent in the plot against the king, I mean." If they were guilty, they would die under horrible conditions. The punishment for dabbling in murder through the use of poison was severe in Persia. The punishment for attempting to kill a king, worse.

"Even if they are not assassins, they are still lawbreakers. They aren't going to walk away free men."

"It's a pity. They aren't ordinary thieves, you have to concede."

Darius laid his hand against his side and stretched in the saddle. "Apart from being more charming than most criminals, what recommends them to you?"

"They seem to have a certain code of honor. You said yourself they went to some lengths to avoid seriously injuring any member of our party. Niq, you said, would have defeated you in the first pass if he weren't being careful of your life. I don't believe they are truly evil."

"Perhaps it would be a waste to stuff them in a mouse-infested prison somewhere. I admit, Niq shows interesting potential. His unique fighting skills might benefit the empire."

"Or think of the many contacts Nassir must have made during years of working on the underside of the law. Such connections are bound to prove useful."

Darius swatted away at a family of gnats congregating near his face. "*Such connections* are called treason in some circles. In any case, at the moment I need them in order to solve this plot. If they are telling the truth, only Niq and Nassir have ever seen any of the men connected to the conspiracy. Without them, I have no way of breaking through this case and securing Artaxerxes' life. Whether I trust them or not, I have to work with them for the time being."

A shiver went through Sarah as she realized the danger Darius was courting. Someone brazen enough to plan to kill the king would not balk at killing his cousin to maintain anonymity. "Cold?" he asked.

"No, my lord."

He reached over their horses to hold her hand. "You need not worry, Sarah. I have survived graver dangers than this."

She wondered if *he* worried for his own safety. Did he ever struggle with fear or self-doubt? He was not in the habit of sharing his deepest feelings. She sensed that he would spurn such questions. Sometimes she hungered to touch the recesses of his heart—those places he guarded and hid with long-practiced ease. She desired to know the man, stripped bare of his defenses. But he never invited that depth of intimacy.

She forced herself to give a smile. "So, how are you going to catch this assassin?"

"I'll begin by setting up a trap for his agent in Susa. We know the time and place for the rendezvous. That's a fortunate development. We will capture him and make him spill what he knows."

"Sounds simple enough."

He rubbed the back of his neck with the flat of his hand. "It does."

Somehow she was even less reassured by his agreement. "At least you'll be able to put Artaxerxes on his guard. That should protect him from harm."

Chapter 5

Darius met with Artaxerxes within hours of arriving in Susa. Thanks to his personal connection to the monarch, he secured an immediate private audience, a privilege that could take weeks to arrange for most officials. The king paled as he heard Darius's news. Artaxerxes was no stranger to assassination plots. His own father, King Xerxes, had been killed by the treachery of Artabanus, the commander of the royal bodyguard.

If it were not for the intervention of the great general Megabyzus, Artaxerxes would have fallen prey to the same plot and be occupying a royal grave instead of a golden throne. On any given day the king of Persia lived one betrayal away from death, one ambitious man away from mutiny.

Artaxerxes subjected Darius to an intense but silent scrutiny. Darius knew that his loyalty was being weighed. How much could the king trust him? With an important mission? With the discovery of a complex secret? With his very life? The fact that they were related was of no consequence. Plenty of dangerous plots were hatched by blood relatives far closer than a second cousin. What mattered to the king was Darius's heart. Darius hoped he had proven himself trustworthy through the years. But he was also honest enough to recognize that he could not guarantee the safety of the king. He might fail to fulfill this mission, not due to duplicity or incompetence, but simply by virtue of unforeseen circumstances. Even the most well prepared plan could go awry. The responsibility of the king's life weighed heavy on him.

Artaxerxes finally broke the long silence. "So. My fate rests in the hands of two dishonest Babylonian brothers and an anonymous assassin for hire. They alone can point us to the origin of this conspiracy."

"We also have the seal, Your Majesty." Darius leaned back against the sumptuous cushion of his couch. His cracked ribs were in agony after the long ride to Susa, and he could not find a comfortable position. "I doubt it will lead us to the man's door," he continued. "I believe he is too careful to give himself away by such obvious means. A murderer who goes to the trouble of tattooing his letter on a messenger's scalp is more careful than the average man. But he has still left us the clue of that seal. Sarah is delving into its origins now."

The king's mouth softened at the mention of Sarah. "I always said I should have made her a spy. Discovering that tattoo and its significance was nothing short of genius. I must give her a worthy gift."

Darius bent his head in gratitude. "Your Majesty, Nassir and his brother are scheduled to meet with the assassin in a public tavern tomorrow. I don't have enough men in Susa at my disposal to guard the perimeter effectively."

"I will inform the captain of the guard. You can take your pick of the Immortals."

The Immortals, the king's special bodyguard, were famed to be faster, keener, and better trained than any fighting men the world had ever seen. Darius himself had served a stint with them in his younger days.

"My thanks, Your Majesty. I almost forgot. What was the original reason Your Royal Majesties summoned us to Susa?"

Artaxerxes gave a narrow smile. "I felt you and Sarah would both be useful in court. You've been away from us long enough. The queen and I merely felt it time you returned to us. And yet, if not for that casual summons, I might have been dead on New Year's Day."

Darius knew that the success of his mission lay in the element of surprise. If the assassin grew suspicious, he might bolt before the appointed meeting. He needed men who could lose themselves in a crowd, men who would have no problem looking like the average commoner loitering in a tavern.

Most of the Immortals shouted professional

soldier by their very bearing—by their muscle-bound frames and military posture. You could dress them as peasants, smear their fingernails with dirt, and ruin the perfect order of their curled hair and beards. But any man trained for combat would be able to detect twelve such men trying to melt into their surroundings.

When the captain of the guard paraded one accomplished Immortal after another before Darius, he rejected them all. He wasn't looking for the best Immortal. He was looking for men wily as foxes. From the corner of his eye, he saw a young man practicing archery. His clothes, wrinkled and far from clean, hung about him in loose, neglected folds. He had tied his uncombed hair back with a grey piece of rag. Darius suspected that the man had not bathed for a good many days. His appearance, from the perspective of the captain of the guard, was nothing short of disgraceful, Darius knew. Because of their close association with the monarch, the Immortals were expected to look as elegant as courtiers.

Darius grew absorbed in his study of the young man. He handled his bow with an uncanny precision. The ease with which he loosed his arrows and landed them dead center within their target belied the difficulty of the task. Archery was one of the most admired arts of the Persian arsenal, but few men managed it with the accuracy and distinction of this young soldier.

"Who is that?" Darius asked the captain.

"*Mardonius?* Not worthy of your notice, my lord."

"He is adept with the bow and arrow."

The captain crossed his arms. "His skill wins him a place among us. But his manners are deplorable. A commoner, as many among the ranks of the Immortals are. He refuses to learn the ways of the court, however. Just look at him!"

"I *am* looking at him, Captain. Can he follow orders?"

The captain shrugged. "Depends. Orders dealing with battle, always."

"Then I'll take him. And any other men like him that you have."

In the end, Darius left the practice field of the Immortals with eleven men. None of them would have won the prize for top-ranking officer. They had shown formidable talent in various areas of combat, yet had managed to displease the establishment with their idiosyncrasies. As such, they had never been given the opportunity to rise into positions of higher rank or perform the kind of sensitive and crucial service Darius had in mind.

To be chosen as part of an important mission was a new experience for these men. Darius knew being handpicked by him—being considered worthy by a respected leader—was already leaving a mark in them. He would bet a month of his military wages that they were bursting to prove his trust justified. After years of rejection, a superior had *seen* them. Had wanted them. Darius understood that he had won them heart and soul. He needed that commitment. There was too much at stake to settle for less than wholehearted service.

He took the men to his own mansion, built on the outskirts of Susa. For an hour, he debriefed them on the details of their assignment. Then he introduced them to Niq and Nassir, who were also his houseguests, though house arrest was a more apt description of their confinement.

The other three Babylonian brothers were guests of the king at the royal palace—a means of ensuring Niq and Nassir's cooperation. The brothers swore fealty to the king and promised to do everything in their power to uncover the identity of the man behind this plot, but Darius preferred caution to regret. While he believed them, he recognized the possibility that he might be wrong about the brothers' innocence.

Darius had spent the better part of an hour debriefing Niq in private as they rode toward Susa. He frowned thoughtfully as he recalled that conversation.

"Where did you learn to fight like that?"

Niq's narrow face lit up. "You liked it?"

"Not at the time. I've never seen anything like it. It's not Babylonian training."

"You noticed."

Darius ignored the sarcasm. "Where then?"

"Not so much where as who."

Darius loosened his feet from the confinement of their stirrups in order to stretch his legs. "Who?"

"When I was a young lad—nine, maybe, or ten—my father brought home a strange man. Near death, he remained unconscious for days. He had been set upon by a large band of robbers while travelling, and the brigands had left him for dead. My mother said he had more broken bones and bruises than a chicken has feathers. By some miracle, he survived his grave injuries.

"He seemed odd-looking to me, with exotic narrow eyes and a wiry build that appeared deceptively small. He said he came from a faraway land called China. His country had suffered a great war and he had been banished, I think. He never did tell us his full story."

"He taught you to fight?" Darius guessed.

"That's right. His people knew a whole new manner of combat. My brothers were too old, he said, to become adroit in these new methods. But he declared that I had tolerable talent and was young enough to mold."

"How long did it take him to train you?"

"Years! It isn't merely the body that needs to be trained." He tapped his bound hands against his forehead. "You start here." He tapped his chest. "Then your heart. Your body follows."

With subtle pressure from his thigh, Darius nudged his horse closer. "Where is this man now?"

Niq gave a wry twist of his lips. "Your guess is as good as mine. One day he was there. The next he vanished like smoke." He made his fingers wriggle and float upward, an impressive feat given the tightness of the bonds around his wrists. "He left me his staff though. That was a special gift, I'll own. You experienced its bite earlier." He pointed his chin at Darius's wounded face and smiled.

Darius touched his bruised cheek gingerly and wondered how the cocky young Babylonian riding next to him had survived as long as he had considering his annoying tongue. Then again, not many people could beat him in a fight.

"I might be able to arrange a suspension of your punishment if you agree to teach some of our men your combat techniques."

"What's the pay?"

"Your life. Interested?"

Niq and Nassir answered the questions of the new recruits, adding as many helpful details to Darius's debriefing as they could. After stressing the need for secrecy, Darius left upon one final errand in preparation for their upcoming confrontation.

He found his friend Lysander in his usual haunt in Susa—a disreputable tavern with a secret stash of decent wine. Darius lingered in the shadows of the doorway and studied his friend.

Lysander was a Spartan by birth, bred for war from early childhood, and thickly muscled from years of intense training. His long blond hair spread about him in a disorganized tangle. Before him sat a half-finished cup of wine, not his first of the day, judging by the relaxed posture of the wide shoulders as they leaned against the rough wall. Scarred fingers were engaged in carving a delicate statue from a block of light-colored wood. Darius could not make out the image, but he knew from old experience that when his friend completed the carving, it would be a trinket worthy of a royal household.

"Well? Are you going to stand there forever, Darius Pasargadae, and gawk? Or are you going to show some manners and come out of hiding to greet me?"

Darius smiled. "You always had the eyesight of a jackal. How did you know it was me?"

Lysander sniffed. "You stink of courtly spices. And I could see the glint of your gold finery a *parsang* away. Besides, the sun shone on you for a moment and I saw your face."

Darius sat across from his friend on a rickety wooden stool. Placing his foot on the edge of the table, he pushed the two front legs of the stool off the floor, tilting himself backward. "I was with the king earlier. I have a royal commission for you."

"Agh. The last time I had a royal commission, I broke my nose." He touched the offended organ with a forefinger, tracing the slight kink that marred an otherwise perfect feature.

"Do you want to know what the commission is, or moon over your pretty face?"

Lysander took a deep swallow of his wine. "By all means. Entertain me."

When Darius finished doing just that, Lysander shoved his cup away and set down his forgotten carving. "You swim in dangerous waters, Darius."

"Will you join me or not?"

"Keep your beard on, Persian. Of course I will join you. I was merely making an observation."

The tavern—Pardis—had been named after the lush Persian gardens that reminded visitors of paradise. There were a couple of pots of droopy yellow violets outside the tavern's peeling walls, but beyond that, Darius could not find any similarities to the formal gardens.

He had already looked over the place and directed each of his men to their assigned location. The men blended well with the crowd that had gathered in the dark corners of Pardis, drinking cheap wine and making noisy conversation. There was one entrance and one back door. Reconnaissance should prove simple.

They were more than an hour early. Darius, aware that their target might have taken the same precaution, studied the place, looking for signs of danger. Niq and Nassir came in together and sat on torn cushions arranged against a wall. Darius placed himself in a dark corner facing the brothers. They put a filthy sack before them on the dirt floor. He had given them the sack as a hiding place for the ivory box, which contained the dagger. In a place such as Pardis, a priceless box would draw as much attention as the bejeweled dagger lying snug within.

Near their meeting time, a slender man approached the brothers. Without invitation, he sat down, his movements fluid. Darius could feel his team of men growing tense as a strung bow. He withheld the signal for attack, however, wanting to make certain there was no mistake. If they captured the wrong man, the right one, were he present, would fly without detection.

The noise in the tavern had risen to a crescendo, preventing him from hearing the conversation between the man and the brothers. Darius studied him minutely, looking for clues to his identity. He could be a soldier; he had the bearing of one— the ease of movement, the athletic build. Slowly, the man reached a hand inside his outer garment to extract something. Darius straightened, ready to spring. But the man merely withdrew a couple of coins and gestured to a pin that rested on Nassir's shoulder. Nassir shook his head. With a subtle movement of eyes and neck, he shifted the direction of his gaze so that it encompassed Darius. Then he shook his head again.

Loud enough so that Darius could hear, he bellowed, "I said my father gave it to me, and I don't want to sell it. Now put your money away and leave us in peace. My brother and I don't want company."

The man responded with a rude gesture and rose. Darius nodded to two of his men, indicating that they should keep an eye on him. The possibility existed that Nassir and Niq had betrayed him—that this *was,* after all, the assassin, and the brothers had just tipped him off. The man left the tavern shortly, followed by Darius's guard. Now he was two men short.

Darius resumed his watch. Lysander, his bright hair darkened with oil and slicked back, sat to the right of the brothers, keeping an eye on the entrance as well as on Niq and Nassir. He had an interesting trick of folding his massive body into a twisted stoop that made it seem shrunken and unimpressive. In spite of his arresting looks, he could make himself seem invisible in any crowd.

With a casual motion, Lysander lifted up the back of his hand and wiped it across his nose. Darius tensed. This had been the agreed-upon signal between them of a possible development.

A new man approached the Babylonians. He was tall and carried himself with a regal air. His clothes, though plain, were made of fine cloth. No sweat stains. No repairs. He made a furtive examination of the room. He had intelligent eyes, Darius thought. For a moment those eyes rested on him. Darius buried his head in his cup, letting his hair fall across his face. When next he lifted his head, the man was taking a seat with the brothers.

A shiver tickled the back of Darius's neck. The conviction that he was looking at his prey filled him. *Wait. Wait,* he cautioned himself.

The man pointed to Niq's head and said something. Niq ran a hand through his short hair and shrugged. The man then pointed at the sack. Nassir leaned forward and whispered in the man's ear. In the ebb and flow of noise in the tavern, several moments of quiet settled over the room. In the relative silence, Darius could hear the man's voice, accented with a guttural undertone that he could not recognize.

"You brought me the package?" he asked, and gestured toward the sack again. Nassir hesitated and then pushed the sack toward him. The man pulled the sack open. Without extracting the ivory box into common view, he opened the lid and examined the dagger.

Darius gave the signal to his crew, and they descended on him in a purposeful circle of menace. The man saw his betrayal instantly. He cursed, jumping away from the brothers, the sack still in his hand. Darius picked up speed, hurtling his body toward the man, but someone slammed into him drunkenly, slowing his progress by a fraction of a moment. He shoved the drunk aside, once again gaining speed as well as a free view. Then he saw the flash of the dagger.

Their prey had no chance of fighting his way out, no matter how skilled he might be, Darius reasoned. The odds were simply against him. But he could not silence a nagging premonition. He observed Niq taking a battle stance, stepping cautiously forward.

And then the unthinkable happened. The man did not fight. He turned the dagger and, in a flash, before any of them could reach him or have hope of disarming him, drew its sharp edge against his own neck. Niq was upon him, and then Darius and Lysander. Darius pulled the dagger away from his still-clutching fingers and laid him on the ground.

They had arrived too late. With knowledgeable precision, their prey had severed an artery. Copious waves of blood gushed out of the self-inflicted wound and pooled in the hollow of his neck, overflowing onto the dirt floor.

"Who?" Darius screamed in impotent rage. "Who sent you? A name. Give me a name and I will take care of your family."

Gathering the last of his strength, the man moved his lips. It wasn't to speak. He spat into Darius's face and then went still.

Chapter 6

The crowd began to gather like flies around stinking carrion. "Get rid of them," Darius told one of his men. His lips barely moved. Shock gripped him. He forced himself to focus past the dead man, trying to salvage what he could of the wreck of their mission.

"Carry him outside and put him in the cart. You three, stay here and search this area. Perhaps before killing himself he discarded something that might reveal his identity. Look under the cushions where they sat. Examine every unlikely hiding place."

Outside the tavern, he turned on Niq. "How could you let him do it? You were much closer to him than I. Why didn't you stop him?"

Niq flushed. He drew a hand down his face, his expression drawn. "I ask pardon, my lord. I thought he was preparing to fight. I took my time, calculating how to bring him down without harming him. I never thought he would turn the dagger on himself." His mouth opened and closed like a fish. "I am mortally sorry, my lord."

If he weren't so horrified by the events of the past few minutes, Darius would have enjoyed Niq's first foray into humility. Instead, he tried to determine if the young Babylonian was putting on an act. In truth, Niq's reading of the situation had been identical to his own. Suicide had not entered his mind. In Niq's expression and words Darius saw a reflection of his own feelings. Shame. Failure. Shock.

In spite of his conviction that the boy was innocent of wrongdoing, he turned to two of his men and bid them to search Niq and Nassir to ensure they were not hiding a secret message from the assassin. The brothers said nothing, but he could tell that they were offended by this order, which brought their integrity into question.

"It's for your own good," Darius said. "This way no one can accuse you of offense later." His words seemed to calm them.

He dispatched the remaining four Immortals. "Go back inside and interview the landlord. See if our man arrived on foot or on horseback. Take charge of his horse if he has one. Find out if he has been here before."

He threw a handful of gold coins at Mardonius. "Find out if anyone in there knew him. Perhaps someone might have at least noticed which direction he came from today."

Motioning to Lysander, Darius went to the cart where they had laid the dead man. He was young—not yet past his twenties. Glazed black eyes stared unseeing into the overcast sky. Darius did not close them. "Did you notice the hatred in his face when I said that I would care for his family if he supplied me with a name? He spent the last of his meager strength spitting in my face. That's not the act of a detached professional."

"I thought the same. It might be that he hated Persian officials in general. There are plenty of men who bear a grudge against your empire."

Darius leaned further into the cart until the assassin's dead face was only a hand's breadth away. The man's beard had been carefully trimmed and curled. The scent of sandalwood still lingered in his hair, now mingling with the odor of blood. Everything from his expensive leather shoes to his clean skin indicated that he had been a man of some wealth. "True. But unless he has no family, it takes a lot of hate to refuse protection for those you love when you know you won't be there to provide it yourself."

He lifted the man's hand and examined the well-groomed fingernails more closely. "He's not the typical assassin, you must admit. We'd best search him and see if we can unearth any secrets from his corpse. He certainly refused to divulge anything whilst living."

As Darius expected, the man carried nothing on his person that hinted at his identity. He had a dagger with a serviceable bronze blade and a plain wooden handle tucked into his belt. Good enough to carve an enemy's belly. Too nondescript to be useful for their purposes. A thousand men might own a similar weapon. His clothes, new and immaculate, hid nothing, not even a coin that might reveal a location by virtue of where it had been minted. He wore no jewels and did not carry a seal. The man was like a blank clay tablet.

They stripped him, layer by layer, until he was naked. Suddenly, Darius went still. "He had strange taste in tattoos for someone who hated the empire." He pointed at the man's arm. The stylized image of a hawk with open wings, the sun shining above him, had been tattooed in black ink into the flesh of his bicep. It was one of the official symbols that Cyrus the Great had adopted to represent his rule over Persia. Cyrus's heirs had continued to use the spread-winged hawk through the generations. Artaxerxes still used it on some of his flags.

Lysander frowned. "A royal mark, symbolizing Achaemenes, the ancestor of King Cyrus, and your own ancestor, if I am correct. Why would he bear a Persian royal symbol but spit upon a Persian official?"

"There are deep secrets at work here. The more I know, the less I understand."

They covered the body, placing the clothes and the dagger in a separate bag, intending to study them further once they returned home. The Immortals who had been sent to search for hidden clues came back empty-handed. Darius was past disappointment. Then Mardonius ran out.

"I have a lead, my lord. One of the customers walked here from his house. He said he saw our man partway down the road, walking toward the tavern."

"In which direction?"

"To the south, my lord."

"Good work." Darius said, trying to sound calm. "Can you lead us to where he was first seen?"

Darius and Lysander followed Mardonius, leaving behind the rest of the men to guard the body and the Babylonian brothers. Mardonius marched down a narrow road with high walls on either side. He took several turns, arriving at an even narrower road jammed with small houses, which were joined together by virtue of shared walls on either side.

"Here is where our witness lives," Mardonius indicated a small house with a brown curtain for a door. "When he came out of his house a couple of hours ago, he saw our man striding further ahead down the road. He remembers him because although his clothes were plain, they appeared new and of good quality. He said he displayed a regal bearing."

"Did he go straight to Pardis? He stopped nowhere on the way?"

"Nowhere, my lord."

Darius looked around. "So, in order to get from his lodgings to Pardis, he had to walk down this road. Mardonius, fetch four of your comrades and search this area. Go house to house and ask if anyone has lodged our man or seen him over the past few weeks. It is possible that he rented a room or house somewhere nearby from one of the locals. The landlord probably has no idea that he has been harboring a criminal. But if we find his lodgings, we might discover some evidence amongst his possessions. Lysander and I will question the people down this road. You and the others check out the roads and alleys to the east and west."

Mardonius sprinted away. Lysander scratched his square jaw. "I thought of something. In two days, the representatives of the provinces will bring their tributes to the king for the New Year. There must be an official list. If this misbegotten son of a donkey was supposed to offer a gift from a certain province, we'll know where he is from by virtue of his absence."

"Good thinking. We'd best begin our search, though. Every bit of information will help."

Darius lost count of the number of residents they questioned. Several of them remembered seeing the man over the past month, but could not recall the location of his lodgings. Nor had they seen him communicating with anyone in particular. It was a girl—young enough to be unmarried and old enough to have discovered the thrill of speaking to the opposite sex—who finally provided them with a solid lead. Darius did not reveal that the object of their search now lay dead at the bottom of a cart.

Instead, he hinted that he wished to find him in order to give him some beneficial news.

"I know the one you mean," she said, managing to swish her hair, play with her long earrings, and giggle at the same time. "Always clean, that one, and smelling of exotic perfumes. Very pleasant to speak to."

"You've spoken to him?" Darius tried to hide his impatience and smiled at her with inviting warmth he did not feel.

"Certainly. He compliments me every time he sees me."

Lysander leaned forward, enveloping the girl in a blue gaze so fervent she blushed. The poor child, Darius thought, his conscience a little stung. She stood no chance against two men who could wrap a roomful of aristocratic women around their fingers.

"And why shouldn't he compliment you?" Lysander said. "Such a pretty girl. Look at the size of those eyes. A man could drown in them."

More giggles. Darius rolled his eyes. "Did he tell you his name?"

"Achaemenes."

Darius's spine stiffened. "Are you certain?"

"Of course. It's not a name I would forget, being so royal sounding and all. He's an important man, I'm sure of it, although he never brags."

"Does he have friends? Anyone in particular he speaks to or spends time with?"

"Not that one. He likes to keep to himself."

"Do you know where he lives?"

"What do you mean? I would never visit the home of an unmarried man."

"I meant no offence. Only, seeing as you are friends, I thought perhaps he has let you know." Darius knew that Achaemenes—if that were his real name—would never reveal the location of his lodgings to an indiscriminate young woman with a loose tongue. Their man might have a taste for flirtation, but that did not render him careless. However, Darius did not put it past the girl to follow him puppy-eyed, determined to find out for herself.

He was not disappointed. Ten minutes later, he and Lysander were inside the modest house the man had rented while in Susa. They lit a lamp and began a thorough search, sparing nothing in their zeal to unearth the man's secrets.

As he shoved his hand through one pillow, then another, Darius vented his questions. "Achaemenes? A Persian name to be sure, and very royal. One of the rulers of the Pasargadae tribe. I believe Xerxes named one of his sons after him as well. But our man did not come from Persia; he spoke with a foreign accent. He had arrived here with the express purpose of killing the king. How could he be called Achaemenes? He must have made it up."

"Then again, there is that tattoo." Lysander rummaged through a sparsely-filled chest. "A foreigner who is Persian and yet hates Persia. An admirer of the Achaemenid dynasty who plans to kill the king. What a riddle."

"It gives me a headache. Artaxerxes is going to have a conniption when he finds the man is dead, and I have no viable lead to follow." Frustration boiled over. With uncharacteristic violence, Darius shoved a fist into the wall above where Achaemenes had laid out his pallet. The wall was made of thin, cheap boards. It rang hollow. Darius sucked his bruised knuckles thoughtfully before tapping another long plank with a probing knock.

"Whoever put up these boards performed a shoddy job and left a space between them and the outer wall. If I were going to hide something, I'd pick the other side of one of these panels." He continued to walk around the room, knocking against the boards, with Lysander doing the same in the opposite direction.

Darius jumped back as a long wooden plank swung up and almost hit him in the chin. Then his eyes lit up. "Finally!"

He fished out a leather pouch and a diminutive flask from inside the hidden cavity behind the board. Lifting the lid of the amphora, he sniffed. "Poison," he said, his voice grim. "This is what he intended to use on the dagger."

With a quick motion, he undid the leather strap around the pouch and upended the contents into his palm. Gold coins. Darius blew out a deep breath and smiled. Here at last, was the clue he had sought. Those coins could lead him to the location where the plot had originated.

The Persian Empire allowed the nations under their standard to rule themselves by their own laws, mint their own coins, speak their own languages, and practice their own religions. So long as each province paid its annual tribute in a timely fashion, good will abounded to everyone. The Persians had proven themselves magnanimous in their mastery. Different provinces in the empire enjoyed a great deal of freedom, retaining their unique traditions and customs.

The coins in the Persian Empire were, therefore, not uniform. Depending on where they were minted, they portrayed a variety of images. Thus the coins Darius had found brought them one step closer to the mastermind behind the plot. The man who had planned to kill the king had likely paid his assassin with local coins.

"Phoenician?" Lysander guessed.

"I'm not sure. Sarah will know."

"Your wife?"

"Yes. She was the queen's senior scribe before she married me and is a fount of astounding information."

"Ah. I look forward to meeting this paragon. You have kept her hidden far too long. Let us finish our search, collect our corpse, and head to your house. Is there any food to be found in that great mansion of yours? Dead bodies make me hungry."

Chapter 7

SPRING, SUSA

T he satrapy of Beyond the River," Sarah declared as she examined the coins. "If I had to guess, I would say these were coined in Damascus, the principal city of Syria." They had gathered in the dining room and settled themselves on comfortable cushions around a low, silver and gold table. Tantalizing wafts of herbs and spices filled the room. Sarah, preoccupied with her exploration, forgot to offer to serve the men.

When she lifted her head, she found Pari, always more aware of social necessities than her mistress, filling the gap by heaping mouthwatering food on golden plates for Darius and his friend. She smiled at her handmaiden before returning her focus to her husband and Lysander.

They had come in directly from their grueling day, sparing no time to change. Both wore ragged, ill-fitting clothing that must have once belonged to other men. The ripe smell clinging to the folds of threadbare fabric suggested that the original owners of the robes had not been too particular about cleanliness. Sarah tried to ignore the bloodstains on Darius's knees and chest, knowing they belonged to the dead assassin.

In spite of their gruesome costumes, the sweat that clung to their dirt-covered faces, and the general air of disrepute with which they had arrayed themselves, the two men still presented a striking picture. Darius's olive-skinned, masculine beauty contrasted with Lysander's blond comeliness. Where Darius was tall and rippled with narrow muscles, Lysander was of average height and massive. Beneath the trappings of their disguise, and the deeper physical power that rags could not cover, Sarah noticed that they were bone weary.

"So you now have a name and a location. That's a good start," she said.

"He may have given a false name," Darius said. "We need more specific clues than that if we are to find the identity of one man. How about the seal? Did you find anything promising connected with it?"

Sarah looked down. "It's been a disappointment, I fear. The whole purpose of a seal is to reveal the identity of the sender, thereby establishing the authenticity of the message being sent. In this case, you would think they had created a seal to *cover* their identity. It is entirely anonymous as far as I can make out."

"Meant to be recognized by only a few, no doubt. A secret group who would know the sender by his secret seal." Darius set down his cup.

"Precisely. I found a tiny fragment of lapis lazuli in the cavity of the wax, suggesting that is what the seal is made of. Not a rare enough material to point us to a particular location. But they do use lapis seals in Damascus, which supports the location. The style of the palm trees is also a good match. I think we should begin our search there."

"You had better return the seal to me if you are finished with it. The king can send agents to Damascus to try and unearth the artist who designed it."

Lysander reached for another piece of roasted venison. "We know this plot has its origin in high places. The fact that our assassin would be bearing gifts to the king on New Year's Day suggests that the plan to kill the king might have originated with a governor or even someone as high as a satrap. Who is the satrap of Trans-Euphrates these days?"

"Megabyzus," Darius said.

"Megabyzus, as in the king's brother-in-law? That old goat? He must be nearly eighty years old by now. He goes as far back as the king's father, Xerxes."

Sarah leaned forward as she remembered an old piece of palace gossip. "Wasn't there a scandal involving Megabyzus and his sons several years ago? As I recall, they rose in revolt against Artaxerxes."

"Yes, they did," Darius said. "Then the king negotiated an unconditional pardon for him. Artaxerxes loves that old man. Not only did Megabyzus save his life decades ago, he also secured Artaxerxes' throne after his father was murdered. Artaxerxes is not a man to forget such service."

Sarah cleared her throat. "Perhaps Megabyzus has decided to throw the king's pardon back in his face. Perhaps whatever caused the uprising in the first place has not been resolved." Accusing the king's favorite general and brother-in-law of treason, even in the privacy of her home, was no light matter. But if the king's life were to be secured, every angle needed to be examined with care.

Darius lowered his brows. "It's a good theory. It fits enough of the facts of our case to merit a careful follow-up. Still, something nags at me. Megabyzus is not a man who would resort to poison. It would be more like him to rise up again in open revolt."

"Perhaps he's grown too old for revolts but remains spry enough to bear a grudge," Sarah said. "Poison might be the weapon of choice when you can no longer wield a sword."

Darius placed a palm against his side, wincing. Sarah remembered his cracked ribs, and realized that the day's physical activities must have placed an additional strain on his injured body. She wished she could make him rest, but knew that he would resist the suggestion. His upcoming interview with the king weighed heavily on his mind. Sarah suspected that he felt he had failed his monarch by allowing their man to die.

When he had first arrived home she had tried to comfort him. Instead of opening up to her, she had sensed him recede behind a wall, hiding his emotions. She felt shut out and unwelcome. He had sought her out because he trusted her knowledge. But his feelings were locked away from her.

"There is too much mystery. I fear for the safety of the king," he said, pushing away his full plate.

"Let's look at things from a different angle," she said. "Let's examine the trail that has led us thus far.

"If the king and queen had not decided to invite us to Susa when they did, and if the queen's letter had not tarried due to a mistake, you and I would not have been on that road at exactly the moment when the Babylonian brothers were travelling. Furthermore, if you had not chosen to ride with fewer men than usual—five, including you—Nassir would never have attacked us. And if the sun had not shone at just the right angle, I probably would have missed the tattoos on Niq's head. Think of how many details had to fall into place in order for us to intercept the assassination plot."

With a shy movement, Sarah reached across the table and placed her hand on his. "Do you not feel that we were meant to discover this plot? If that is the case, then perhaps we are meant to solve it as well."

Darius's lashes swept down to hide his expression. With a gentle motion he disentangled his hand from Sarah's hold. "I do not believe in your Lord, Sarah. These things were mere coincidences, not God's intervention. If I want to protect the king, I need to rely on hard work and clever planning. I cannot depend on the help of your God."

Darius spent a poor night, tossing and turning with physical pain and mental stress. With some discomfort, he remembered his harsh words to Sarah. She had only been trying to help. In a way, he wished he could have her faith. It would bring him a measure of peace. He had spent so many years running from his mother's God, however, that it had become second nature. Darius knew that the fastest way to displeasing his father was to chase after this Jewish God. He had made his decision to walk away from that part of his heritage long ago. When his mother had been near death, and had spent hours enchanting him with tales of her God's faithfulness and love, he had known that he would have to choose between her world and the one in which he had grown up.

And he had made his choice. His father's world over his mother's. And now his wife's. He would not go back on that decision.

Early in the morning, he made his way to Artaxerxes' palace for the interview he dreaded. The king's mellow response came as a surprise. Darius had expected coldness. Open displeasure. Even a royal tantrum. Instead, Artaxerxes, paler than usual, listened with gravity and asked the piercing, intelligent questions that Darius had come to expect from him.

"Megabyzus?" he asked, when Darius made the connection. "I don't believe it. The man saved my life and my throne when I was but a lad. Why do you suspect him?"

"He has already risen in revolt against you once, Your Majesty."

"Those days are over. He was angry with my mother for meddling in his business, and with me for not stopping her. That revolt was an anomaly in the life of a man who has spent his days serving the empire and her kings. Serving *me*." He plucked a fat purple grape from its stem and played with it before replacing it on the plate. "What other evidence do you hold against him?"

"As the satrap of the Trans-Euphrates, he lives in Damascus and uses Syrian coin."

"He has not lived in Damascus for some years. Though he remains satrap in name, others do the work. He has no need to tip his hand by using Syrian coin."

Darius blinked in surprise. "I had not realized."

"It is not publicized. I do not wish to embarrass him, but the daily work of running a region as large as Trans-Euphrates is too much for him now."

"There is another concern which seems to point to Megabyzus. The assassin's name and tattoo both had royal Persian connections. Megabyzus is part of the royal family by virtue of having married your older sister, Your Majesty. Therefore he loves the royal family and is faithful to the Achaemenid line. But perhaps he has not forgotten his grudge against you. Perhaps he loves the dynasty, just not you."

Artaxerxes stretched his feet on an ornate footstool. "We deal with a paradox here, I grant you. I shall send an agent to Damascus to look into the matter."

Darius's head snapped up. "I thought I . . ."

The king waved his hand. "No. I want you here for now. We must still weather the coming weeks and the endless rounds of visitations by foreign dignitaries. I will be more vulnerable to plots during this time. I could use you here.

"In the meantime, I will have my agents keep an eye on Megabyzus. But if you are mistaken about him, we need to continue our search to find the true culprit. Once he finds out that his plot has been foiled, he might try again."

The New Year dawned blue and hot, an annoyance for the hundreds of officials who had to don layers of formal court attire, cover their heads with appropriate hats, caps, and crowns, wear long sleeves and trousers under their voluminous robes, and apply fake beards and hairpieces in order to look presentable for the most punctilious day of the year. The royal presentation of gifts lasted for hours, sometimes days. Darius did not know how Artaxerxes could bear the ceremonial weight with such apparent good grace. He supposed that replenishing the national coffers with fresh wealth gave him extra forbearance. Feeding large armies and navies, crushing rebellions, aiding allies, and conquering new territories required a generous treasury. If Artaxerxes had to entertain half the world in order to have it, he would make the necessary sacrifice and smile through what must have been only one step better than torture.

Wives and daughters of officials celebrated the Great Feast in the women's quarters as Queen Damaspia's guests. They were invited to attend the king's banquet for part of the royal presentation of gifts, however. Darius searched for Sarah as the women gathered in a corner gallery especially prepared for them. Having spent most of his time away from home, several days had passed since he had been in her company.

He found her listening with polite interest to a lady dressed in Phoenician garb. As if sensing his scrutiny, she turned her face toward him. Eyes the color of mahogany brightened as soon as she detected him. The tilt of her mouth tinged with secret warmth aimed solely at him. Darius felt a jolt of satisfaction at the private welcome in her smile. An official with a tall hat who had obscured his view moved. Darius's heart picked up speed.

She had donned a new dress the color of rubies. His mouth ran dry as he saw her generous curves hugged in the outrageously tight outfit, cinched at the waist with a belt of golden rosettes and flaring into a long skirt made of hundreds of tiny pleats.

He narrowed his eyes and dug in his heels as a violent urge to stride across the hall and cover her with something large—and very bulky—over-whelmed him. If he had caught a man looking at her at that particular moment, he did not think he could have controlled his impulse to flatten him with a well-placed blow. In the back of his mind he registered that other women were dressed in a similar fashion, and that Sarah was following the dictates of the latest court styles. The knowledge did nothing to cool the fiery kick of possessive-ness that had overcome him. He closed his eyes for a moment, trying to rein in the unaccustomed emotions.

It took every bit of his inner resolve to focus his

attention back on the king. He lingered near the monarch for the length of the ceremonies, not taking his eyes off him for one moment. As the end of the evening approached, Darius bid Lysander to take charge of the special guard over the king for several hours. Knowing Sarah would have made her way home already, Darius rode to his estate not bothering to change from his court finery, driving Samson so hard the horse arrived covered in sweat.

He found Sarah sitting on a stool before a mirror, still adorned in her ruby dress. A servant girl whose name escaped him had taken down the elaborate braids and tucks of Sarah's hair and was busy combing through the thick mass. Dispensing with formalities, Darius snapped his head to the side, signaling for the girl to leave. Sensing his dark mood, she scurried out. He prowled over to his wife. He had to kneel to be at eye level with her. Words stuck in his throat. Instead, he kissed her, his touch rough from feelings he had not been able to fully master. She gasped and he pulled away.

"Don't ever . . . *ever* . . . wear that dress again. Ever."

Her eyes widened. "You didn't like it?"

He kissed her again. He could not seem to help himself. "No." His mouth slid to her neck. "Yes." His kiss grew soft. "You can wear it. But only for me."

She giggled. He could feel the rise and fall of her chest under his lips. "I love you, Darius."

He tangled his fingers into the folds of the silken skirt and pulled so that she slithered forward on the stool.

"Darius, do you—?"

With a quick movement, he covered her mouth with a hard hand. "Don't," he commanded. He knew what she was about to ask. Softening his voice, he said again, "Don't ask that. I won't lie to you, Sarah. I don't want to hurt you. But I won't say what I don't feel."

She lowered her lashes to cover the sheen of hot tears from him. He drew her closer, spending long hours trying to make her forget what he could not give her, cradling her in his arms until she fell into an exhausted sleep.

Far into the night he lay awake, thinking of the question he had not allowed her to ask. He remembered how he had once longed to be married for love. Like most men of his station, he had had to settle for an arranged marriage, however. He had thought that dream buried because of the circumstances. Now he began to ask himself a more difficult question. Was he *capable* of love? Had his heart so hardened that in spite of longing for the idea of love, he could not enter the reality of it? He punched his pillow and turned over.

Unlike previous years when Artaxerxes stayed to sup with his guests during the magnificent feasts of the New Year, he now took his meals in private with the queen. Darius was relieved by this precaution. Nehemiah the cupbearer, privy to the danger that threatened the king, remained near him even after he finished his meals in case Artaxerxes became thirsty or had to taste wine during the ceremonies. Darius felt grateful for Nehemiah's vigilance. For once, he set aside his discomfort around his wife's cousin and rested in the knowledge that, whether he liked the man or not, he could trust him with the king's life.

Darius had acquired the official list of visitors, and had checked each one in person before they were allowed to approach the king. By the third day, every single official visitor had shown up with an appropriate gift. Not one was missing. The officials representing the provinces within the Trans-Euphrates satrapy had been scrutinized with extra care. Each ambassador had proven genuine. Achaemenes must have planned to replace one of them at the last moment.

Darius set up private interviews with the delegates from the Trans-Euphrates provinces. Not one of them had heard of a man named Achaemenes.

As the thirteenth day of the New Year with its closing picnic celebrations finally dawned, Darius grew no closer to solving the riddle of the assassination plot than he had when he first discovered it on Niq's shaven scalp. At least the king remained alive.

According to royal spies, old Megabyzus had been behaving himself. Darius hoped Megabyzus did not have them duped. Even if he were innocent of this crime, it was small comfort to Darius, who fretted about the possibility of an unknown enemy while continuing to suspect the old general.

Darius understood the gravity of the threat. More than Artaxerxes' life was at stake. The king's sons were young—some would consider them too young to rule. Were he to die now, the empire would slide into a bloodbath of ambitious men, each trying to wrest power from the other. Persia could not afford to lose its king yet. And it was up to Darius to ensure his safety. The days glided by until spring was no longer new. Darius, who by the king's permission had retained his special band of twelve warriors in addition to the two Babylonian brothers, discovered no break-throughs.

Unaccustomed to failure, he chafed under its weight. In the hidden darkness of his soul, the knowledge of that failure ate at him with slow persistence.

Part 2
The Unraveling

Chapter 8

Jerusalem! Jerusalem!

Nehemiah's chest tightened at the thought of the city he had never visited. In less than an hour his brother Hanani would arrive, bringing with him reports of the city of their fathers. Hanani, who along with a group of friends had returned from Judah only the night before, would know the latest news of the land.

Although his apartment in the palace was spacious, Nehemiah felt as if the walls were collapsing in, and strode into the marble-floored hallway, his steps impatient. He paced, first in one direction and then in the opposite.

Autumn had settled on the land, and the air in Susa had grown crisp with the change of season. The trees were already naked, having shed their foliage weeks before. A few golden leaves had escaped the attentions of the army of gardeners, and brightened the palace grounds with their colorful death. Nehemiah gazed outside a latticed window, craning his neck. Too soon to see any sign of his guests. He sighed and resumed his clipped gait.

Hearing a sound, he rushed to the window again and saw a group of men walking toward the gate that would lead them to his section of the palace. He grinned and turned to wait for them, his fingers drumming an absent rhythm against each other. At the end of the corridor, he could see the men approaching and he frowned. They were strangers to him.

His shoulders drooped as he walked back down the long hallway. Not having seen his younger brother for over a year, he was eager for the sight of him. But he was even more eager for news of Jerusalem. He could not explain the longing for his ancestral home that had filled his soul in recent months. Nehemiah had been born in Persia. His job as cupbearer to the king placed him in constant proximity to the most powerful man in the world, giving him authority and influence few Jewish men in his generation enjoyed. Yet it was Jerusalem that had filled his thoughts for months.

He stared through the window again. It was growing late. He wondered why Hanani tarried. To his astonishment, he felt a strong urge to bite the corner of a nail, a habit he had outgrown in boyhood. With an impatient gesture, he crushed the impulse. In the distance he saw another group of men approaching the gate. With relief, he recognized Hanani at the head of them.

He lifted a light-hearted arm in greeting as he strode toward the group in the wide palace hallway. "Welcome! Welcome back! Peace be upon you," he said, his voice carrying in the enclosed space.

No one answered him, not even with a wave. He examined the faces of his guests. What he saw caused a chill to go through him. Shadowed eyes, downturned lips, sweaty brows, fisted hands. He told himself that his guests were weary from their travels. They had been on the road for months, and he knew from experience how exhausting such arduous journeys could prove. But he had an inkling that something serious had gone amiss.

As they came abreast of each other, Hanani introduced him to several of his friends whom Nehemiah had never met. He extended a warm welcome to each and led them to his quarters where he settled them around the table his servant had prepared. He had ensured that the fringed linen pillows strewn on the floor had been cleaned and aired for the occasion. Silk carpets tickled their bare feet, already washed and perfumed by his servant.

The food, which Nehemiah had ordered with special care to their religious dietary restrictions, was served and they were left alone. The scent of fried onions and garlic filled the air. Nehemiah gave a heartfelt thanks to the Lord, his deep voice rolling out the Hebrew syllables with care.

Unable to contain his questions another moment, he unleashed them on his quiet companions. "Tell me about Jerusalem. And our fellow countrymen who have returned from exile to live in the province of Judah. How are they faring these days?"

Hanani dropped his neck as if an ox yoke weighed it down. "Our people are in great disgrace, Nehemiah."

"What has happened?" the cupbearer took a deep breath to keep his voice from rising. "Hold nothing back. Tell me everything."

"Last year, I embarked for Judah with so much hope, Nehemiah. I thought I would find our people settled and Jerusalem in good order. I thought I would find a glimpse of our former glory after over a generation of resettlement."

Nehemiah nodded. "Of course. Is it not so?"

It had been over ninety years since Cyrus the Great freed the people of Israel from their captivity to Babylon. With his support, more than forty thousand of their most talented men and women had returned to Judah during that initial relocation alone. While Nehemiah had been aware of a number of discouraging setbacks throughout the decades, he had expected that with the return of Ezra the priest almost a decade ago, Jerusalem would be on its way back to prosperity.

Hanani leaned over, his hands over his belly as though he ached. "The whole region has become a shambles."

Nehemiah's mouth turned dry. He leaned back against the wall. "And the Temple?"

"The new Temple is complete, but it does not compare to its original glory. The structure could hardly be called magnificent, and in spite of King Cyrus's generosity, its furnishings are sparse. The Holy of Holies remains empty. And the sacrifices offered are a tiny fraction of what you hear about from the days of Solomon.

"Still, that half-empty building is the best thing in Jerusalem right now. The work of revitalizing the City of David and restoring Judah has ground to a halt."

Nehemiah's shoulders slumped. "I don't understand. How can this be?"

"Several years ago, just after the latest group of settlers had arrived from Babylon intending to rebuild Jerusalem, the enemies of Judah sent a letter to King Artaxerxes, accusing the Jews of rebellion. They told the king we were troublemakers. Once Jerusalem was strengthened, they said, we would refuse to pay our tribute to the empire."

Nehemiah felt suddenly cold and drew his robe closer around him. "I had not heard."

"At the time, the restoration of Jerusalem was within reach. We had laid the foundations of the

113

city again, and its walls could have been finished within a year or two. But it was not to be. Our foes prevailed."

"What?"

"The king believed the accusations of our enemies and ordered the work in Jerusalem to be stopped."

"Artaxerxes?" By virtue of his job, Nehemiah spent many hours with the monarch. The king often treated him as a trusted advisor as much as a servant, and shared his concerns on many matters. But he did not know all of Artaxerxes' policies. It was impossible to keep up with the constant demands on the king's life. This was one decision about which the royal cupbearer had known nothing.

Hanani nodded his head. "The results have been devastating. The walls of Jerusalem have been torn down. They are in ruin, Nehemiah. The gates—the beautiful gates of the city—have been destroyed by fire."

Nehemiah could not utter a single word. The setback described by his brother tore at his heart. After a long silence, he managed to say, "I had no idea things were so bad in Judah."

"This is not all."

His brother's warning made the hair on Nehemiah's arms stand on end. He untangled his legs and rose, his movements as hesitant as an old man's. "There is more?"

"Without the walls, Jerusalem is no longer safe. They have suffered a recent famine so there is little food. The rich take advantage of the poor. Most of the residents have left the city to eke out a living from the lands beyond. There are barely a thousand people left in Jerusalem. Our enemies laugh at our disgrace, for we are hardly better than a ruin. I think God has abandoned us, after all."

When he heard those words, Nehemiah sank to the floor. Unmindful of the men before him, some of whom he had met for the first time that evening, he began to weep. He wept like a child who had lost his mother.

For days Nehemiah mourned. He fasted. And he prayed.

He performed his duties on an empty stomach and with a broken heart. To honor royal protocol, he pasted a smile on his face and hid the misery that ate at his soul. But whenever he had a private hour, he gave it to the Lord. His prayers rent the heavens with their passion.

He asked God for favor, because he knew that he had to approach the king. Artaxerxes had interrupted the work in Jerusalem, and only Artaxerxes could start it again. Nehemiah could not change the heart of a king. But he believed that the Lord could.

For four and a half months he prayed. He sought the Lord. He asked for strength. He begged for direction. His friends joined him in the fervor of their own requests.

No doors opened. Nothing changed. The king offered no opportunity for the cupbearer to present the plight of his land.

Nehemiah prayed harder. God remained silent.

Slowly, a new voice began to seep into his thoughts. *Give up,* it goaded. *Give up!* If God had wished to move, He would have done so by now. What was the point of hours of supplication? *Forsake your prayers! Give up! Who are you to think you can make a difference?*

Nehemiah dug in his heels and increased his vigilance. He did not understand why God delayed. He could not explain why his prayers were ignored, when surely the Lord Himself must desire the welfare of Jerusalem. All Nehemiah could do was persevere. So he ignored the words of discouragement in his head and persisted, even when his strength ebbed.

Hanani came to visit him late one evening. Nehemiah's servant had just finished curling his beard and perfuming his hair.

"Mercy, brother, but you smell better than the king's gardens," Hanani said. "With your hair as red as Esau's, you could pass for a flower."

Nehemiah gave Hanani a quelling look. "It's part of the requirements of my position. I cannot come before the king and his esteemed guests smelling like a camel."

In truth, the discrepancy between his circumstances and those experienced by the people in Judah had begun to grate on his conscience. Day after day he prepared himself for his duties as usual. He bathed and covered his body with silks and linen, knowing his countrymen were poor and naked. He inhabited some of the most luxurious edifices the world had ever seen, aware that his fellow Jews lived with inadequate shelter, exposed to the cruel elements. As his leather-shod feet touched marble walkways and silken carpets, he was mindful that his people only had dirt to rest their feet on.

Hanani held up a hand. "I meant no disrespect. Any breakthroughs with the king?"

"None. I try to remember that walking in the will of God might mean waiting as much as it might mean moving forward."

Hanani sighed and found a large cushion to sit on. "I've always admired your faith, brother. For myself, I find this delay senseless and frustrating."

Nehemiah smoothed his wide sleeves until no ripple remained in the rich fabric. "One thing *has* changed."

"I could use some good news."

Nehemiah's smile was tight. "I'm not certain you will consider this good news. The months of prayer, though seeming to reap no reward, have produced an unexpected shift in my own heart.

"When I'd first begun to pray, I had merely

intended to ask Artaxerxes to reverse his decision. I believed my role was that of intercessor on behalf of the people of Jerusalem. I thought, like Esther, the Lord had planted me close to the king for this hour. I was supposed to intervene for Jerusalem and plead their cause to the king."

Hanani shifted on his cushion to find a more comfortable spot. "That's what we have been praying for."

"My heart has changed, Hanani. The longer I've carried on with my supplications, the more I've become convinced that Judah needs a strong leader. If the enemies of Jerusalem have already succeeded in interrupting its restoration once, what would prevent them from doing so again? Life at court has taught me that only a faithful commander could see such a demanding task through to its completion. Jerusalem needs more than a building project; it requires a leader who knows how to overcome powerful enemies and draw our people back to the Lord."

"What are you saying?"

"I want to be that leader."

"Lord have mercy, Nehemiah!" his brother said, his voice a squeak. "Have you lost your mind? Do you know the trouble you are asking for? This is no job for a pampered courtier, if you'll pardon my frankness. The foes of our nation are hungry wolves who will swallow you whole. Besides, what will the king say? Would he release you from a job you perform well in order to allow you to traipse into a far-flung corner of his empire?"

"Do you think I haven't asked myself these questions a hundred times over? I know I have no power to secure what I want. I'm helpless to change anything. Neither my talent nor my experience will prevail. God alone has the strength to provide for Jerusalem."

Nehemiah picked up an exquisite silver goblet, a gift from the king on his last birthday. Absently, he turned it this way and that, blind to its beauty. "You must remember that the descendants of Abraham are supposed to change the world. We are supposed to bless the nations. Instead, we are practically homeless. The provision of God is faithful, Hanani. He hasn't forgotten that promise. But He asks us to act as His hands and feet on this earth. Should I refuse the Lord's call because the world might set itself against me? Because the cost is too high?"

Hanani stuck a finger under his high woolen collar and tugged hard. "We were talking about the king of Persia, not God."

Nehemiah rubbed his hands together. "That is your mistake. This whole endeavor is about the Lord. And *His* path is never smooth, brother. That does not mean I can veer from it. No. I tell you, I *refuse* to give up."

Chapter 9

ONE MONTH AFTER THE DISCOVERY
OF THE PLOT TO KILL THE KING
THE TWENTIETH YEAR
OF KING ARTAXERXES' REIGN (445 BC)
THE MONTH OF NISAN
(BETWEEN APRIL AND MAY)

Nehemiah carried the king's golden chalice with three graceful fingers, folding the last two into his palm according to royal etiquette. When he reached the king's side, he placed the chalice on a carved ebony table. The base of the cup made not the slightest whisper of a sound as it connected with the table. No ripple disturbed the surface of the dark liquid. Using a bejeweled ladle, Nehemiah drew a small amount of wine from the cup and drank from it.

A servant rushed to his side carrying a folded linen napkin and a bowl of water perfumed with jasmine blossoms. With practiced movements, the cupbearer dipped his hand for a thorough washing before drying it. He had performed this duty too many times to consider the danger; he was testing for poison, after all. He waited the required moments. There was no sudden, excruciating pain, no rush of nausea, no telltale signs of venom at work in his body. He offered the chalice to Artaxerxes. The queen, who was supping with her royal husband that evening, had her own cupbearer perform the same duty for her.

She tasted the wine. A deep sigh of appreciation escaped her lips. "This is from Darius's vineyard in Persepolis if I'm not mistaken."

"Your Majesty's palate is discriminating as always," Nehemiah said. "My lord Darius's baggage train arrived last week after an unforeseeable delay. Lady Sarah sent the wine over as soon as it had settled."

Artaxerxes gave a good-natured smile. "She is a thoughtful girl."

Nehemiah didn't have it in him to return the king's smile. He was weary with a burden of sorrow that refused to be lifted no matter how he prayed. Thoughts of his shattered native land had haunted him for four and a half months. Jerusalem's ruined walls kept him awake at night and tormented his thoughts in the daylight hours.

"Yes, Your Majesty."

Turning aside, he busied himself with the practical details of his duty. In the back of his mind Nehemiah could hear Artaxerxes speaking. It must have been an amusing comment as it made Damaspia laugh. Unexpectedly, the king said, "What do you think, Nehemiah?"

Nehemiah reddened. He had been so steeped in

his thoughts that he had no idea what the king had said. He looked down; without warning he felt overwhelmed by such a wave of sorrow that he could barely prevent himself from bursting into tears, an unforgivable offence during a royal audience.

The king gazed at Damaspia for a moment before returning his attention to the cupbearer. "Why are you so sad? What grieves you, Nehemiah?"

Nehemiah tried to speak. Words failed him.

Again Artaxerxes spoke. "You don't appear sick. It must be your thoughts that trouble you."

Cold sweat broke out over Nehemiah's forehead. He clasped his hands together in order to hide their trembling. Intense fear made his heart race. This was the moment he had prayed for. The king had given him the opening he needed in order to make his request. Nehemiah knew that the king might be offended by what he was about to ask. After all, Artaxerxes' own life was in danger from an unknown assassin; why should he care about a cupbearer's troubles? Nehemiah might lose the favor of the monarch forever without gaining an advantage for Jerusalem.

"Long live the king!" he said, through dry lips, and plunged ahead. "You are right to say that I am sad, Your Majesty. How could I be anything else when the city of my ancestors lies in ruins?"

Artaxerxes leaned forward on his couch. "I see.

Is it about Jerusalem that you speak? What do you want me to do, cupbearer?"

Nehemiah took a moment to send a lightning prayer to the Lord of heaven. After the months of wearing himself out with his supplications, he still felt unprepared for this conversation. "If it please the king, and if I have found favor with Your Majesty, please send me to Judah so that I can rebuild the city where my fathers are buried."

The queen raised a delicate eyebrow. "You wish to leave us, Nehemiah?"

"Leave you? No, my lady. I only want to go for a short while to help rebuild Jerusalem."

Artaxerxes heaved a sigh. "How long will you be gone? When do you plan to return to us?"

"As soon as the walls are completed and a semblance of order and safety is restored to the city, I shall return. I hope it will not take me overlong."

Artaxerxes seemed to consider Nehemiah's words. With a sharp movement, he leaned back. "Jerusalem is in the satrapy of Beyond the River, isn't it? How far is that from Damascus?"

"The whole province of Judah is located Beyond the River, sire, or as your scholars call it, the Trans-Euphrates. I am not certain of the distance from Damascus. But it cannot be far."

"Perhaps there is wisdom in sending you to the land of your forefathers. I do not wish for any part of my kingdom to crumble from neglect. What do you need for this journey?"

Nehemiah took a deep breath. An exuberant sense of hope filled him as he realized that the king had not only granted him permission to go to Jerusalem, but was also open to helping him.

"If it please the king, may I have letters addressed to the governors from Beyond the River? Our convoy will have to travel through their provinces to get to Judah, and a word from you would make our journey safe."

Artaxerxes signaled for his personal scribe; the man, a reedy-looking eunuch, rushed forward and began to work on the letters immediately.

"You must need some provisions, surely," Damaspia said.

Nehemiah turned to her, bestowing a grateful smile in her direction. "Indeed, Your Majesty. A work of construction of this magnitude will need extra lumber. If it please the king, may I have a letter to Asaph, the manager of the royal forests, instructing him to give me timber? We need beams for the gates of the Temple fortress, for the city walls, and for a house where I can reside."

Artaxerxes did not demur. With a royal nod, he set his eunuch to write a letter to Asaph. Overwhelmed by the king's generous consent to every request, Nehemiah felt relief flood through his limbs. *The gracious hand of God is on me,* he thought. *He has opened this door.* A new strength filled him as soon as his mind grasped hold of this realization. No matter how hard the journey ahead might prove, he knew now that it was the will of God. The Lord had called Nehemiah, and He would provide for him.

"You cannot go as a cupbearer, Nehemiah. You would have no authority for governance."

"Your Majesty?"

"You need a new title. I am making you governor of Judah until you return."

Nehemiah bowed, overwhelmed. "The king's generosity knows no bounds."

"Don't be foolish. It's a demotion. To go from being my cupbearer—a position that gives you daily access to me and nestles you in the kind of affluence few ever see—to go from *that* to being the governor of a forsaken region with barely enough food to keep you alive is a questionable move. It is not the act of an ambitious man. You are moving backwards, in order to serve the land of your fathers."

"Yes, Your Majesty. Thank you, Your Majesty."

Artaxerxes and Damaspia laughed. "The man asks for a demotion and thanks me for giving it to him. Either he has lost his wits or he has interesting values." Artaxerxes took a sip from his cup.

"There is also the matter of an escort. It is a long way to Beyond the River. Without proper escort, your convoy may find itself under attack by highwaymen. You need military accompaniment. And I have just the man to lead it."

"Jerusalem!" Darius stood before Artaxerxes, his hands clasped like a knot behind his back. "I am to become the wet nurse to the cupbearer, roaming around the backwaters of the world in order to make certain he doesn't get himself robbed? Your Majesty, there are more urgent matters for us to consider."

Artaxerxes' expression became blank. "I thought you would be pleased, Darius. Between your mother and your wife you are bound to find some interesting relations hanging about Jerusalem. Think of it as a family reunion, with the empire footing the bill."

Darius made sure that his face was as blank as the king's. "Thank you, sire. But my Persian relations are quite enough for me to deal with at the moment," he said, looking straight into the dark eyes of his second cousin. "I don't need a new passel of them."

"Point well taken," the king said mildly. Darius flushed. Nothing could make a man squirm like Artaxerxes' gentle responses.

"I am concerned about the ongoing investigation of this failed assassination plot, Your Majesty. A journey to Jerusalem and back will take months."

Artaxerxes rested his jaw into the palm of his hand and leaned forward. "Of course, Judah *is* located in the satrapy of Beyond the River. And since you are convinced the plot originated there, it might give you an opportunity to conduct a discreet investigation. You will have a perfect cover as Nehemiah's military escort; no one is likely to suspect you of being my spy when you already have a job."

Darius broke into a grin. "You had me worried, sire. Now I see your mind remains as subtle as ever. May I take my men?"

"*My* men, you mean, since their wages come out of my pocket. By all means, take them with you."

"Have you heard from your agent in Syria yet, sire? I would like to pay him a visit when we arrive at Beyond the River. Perhaps we can help each other." For reasons of his own, which he did not deign to share with Darius, Artaxerxes had kept the identity of his spy in Damascus a secret. It was obvious that the man had made as few inroads in his investigations in Syria as Darius had in Susa, for he had nothing of use to report. But Darius thought that together they might be able to accomplish more.

"If it becomes necessary for my agent to meet with you, I will ensure that the meeting will take place. In the meantime, for safety if nothing else, it's best that you remain strangers to each other."

"As Your Majesty wishes."

Artaxerxes' reticence puzzled Darius. The king's network of spies, notorious in its ability to uncover furtive information, had become one of his strongest weapons in the maintenance of his sprawling dominion. Artaxerxes did what he could to protect them from discovery, but Darius had not known him to keep his operatives secret from one another.

He shifted his weight from one foot to the other. "When does the cupbearer plan to leave?"

"Nehemiah? I wouldn't be surprised if his trunks are already packed. He is in a tearing hurry to get himself to the province of Judah. You better bring fast horses if you want to keep up with him."

"No doubt he will be encumbered by an enormous baggage train." The thought made Darius's shoulders droop. Nothing was more boring than escorting a lumbering baggage train for months. He had done his share of such work in his younger years. Under normal circumstances, an experienced military commander like Darius would never have been assigned to such a menial task. But Artaxerxes was right. It was the perfect cover.

The king shifted on his throne. "And what of your wife?"

"My wife?"

"I believe her name is Sarah? Does that jog your memory? Do you plan to take her with you?"

"I doubt it. It presents too great a danger. When we were attacked on our way to Susa, I thought my hair would turn white when I considered what might have befallen her. She would be a distraction."

Artaxerxes shrugged. "On the other hand, she might prove helpful. Think of how she has aided us already. Besides, Nehemiah could use her help. He is going into a hotbed of jealousy and discord. Their neighbors are none too fond of the Jews. You should see some of the letters the court has received from them through the years. They'll be kicking up a fuss before Nehemiah has laid the foundation of that wall, you mark my words.

"Sarah's skills as an experienced royal scribe would be a formidable asset to the new governor. In any case, I don't imagine she will relish the thought of being parted from you for such a lengthy period."

"Sire, are you ordering me to take my wife?"

Artaxerxes smiled. "Merely a suggestion."

"In that case, the cupbearer can scrounge another scribe for himself. I don't wish to risk Sarah's neck on a long journey to the pit of the empire, especially when I will be busy trying to uncover a clever assassin."

"You must do as you think best."

Darius was disconcerted to find the king gazing at him with a mixture of amusement and pity.

"One more thing before you leave." Artaxerxes nodded to his steward who rushed forward bearing a plain ebony box, shiny from careful polishing. Artaxerxes snapped the box open and showed the contents to Darius. "For Sarah, as I promised. With my thanks."

A delicate gold necklace set in terra cotta–colored carnelian sparkled in its black nest. Darius bowed. "Your Majesty's generosity is beyond compare."

Artaxerxes waved a hand, his expression sour. "Away with you, if you are going to spout flattery at me." He stretched his feet before him with a sigh. "Besides, you'll need every minute to get ready for this mission. I doubt if it will prove easy."

Chapter 10

Sarah set aside the letter from Nehemiah, her eyes shining. Jerusalem! She tried to picture Nehemiah in their native land acting as governor, rebuilding the city, and organizing the city's officials. She did not know whether to pity them or envy them.

Since the previous year when she had given up striving against God and had surrendered her life to His care, a desire to see the new Temple had so burned in her heart that she used to pray fervently about it. With a frown, she acknowledged that it had been some time since she had done so. Her prayer life was no longer as passionate as it once had been, if she were honest. Settling into her new home with her husband had taken much of her focus and her time. She bit her lip. The joys of being a wife to Darius and helping to run his estates had not replaced her need for the Lord. She needed to return to the discipline of coming before Him more often.

And yet, in spite of her unintentional distance, He had answered her old prayers about seeing the Temple. It seemed as if God in His mercy had gathered the desires of her heart and saved them for the right time. Even her faithlessness had not cancelled His goodness. For here was Nehemiah, asking her to accompany him to Judah as his scribe. The best part of the invitation was that Darius would lead the military contingent attached to the convoy. In fact, the reason Nehemiah had extended the invitation to Sarah could only be because he knew that Darius would bring her along.

Since the king himself had given the assignment to Darius, he could not decline to go. Sarah was painfully aware that her husband had no interest in going to Jerusalem. On several occasions, she had asked him to take her for a visit to the city of her fathers. He had refused, proclaiming it a pointless journey to a shattered land.

Sarah almost laughed. The Lord had His own plans and used His own means. Darius might resist his wife's requests, but he was no match against the God of heaven and earth. And now she would see Jerusalem with Darius. Perhaps he would even come to believe in the Lord.

Her grin turned into a grimace as a wave of nausea overwhelmed her with sudden force. She had learned to keep a basin under her bed, for the nausea had proven unpredictable. She managed to make it to the basin just in time. For the past two weeks she had found herself teetering between glowing health and debilitating bouts of inexplicable nausea. At first, she had assumed she had eaten something that disagreed with her body.

Then she realized that she had missed her monthly cycle and hope had bloomed in her heart.

She thought of the tender evening spent with Darius in the bathhouse, and began to believe that she had conceived a baby as a result, although it was early days yet and hard to be certain. Shyness and something like fear had prevented her from sharing her suspicions with her husband. What if she was wrong? What if she built up a hope in him, only to find out that she had been mistaken? So she had kept her secret, hugging it close, not ready to share it with anyone.

Pari suspected, but kept her thoughts to herself, too wise to press Sarah before she felt ready to share her suspicions. She cleaned up the befouled basins without comment, and left plain bread by Sarah's bedside to calm her heaving stomach in the mornings before she rose.

Sarah considered Nehemiah's invitation in the light of this new development. For the first time it occurred to her that Darius might not allow her to go, not if she were pregnant. Running deep through his character was a protective streak as hard as iron. He would not risk her safety on such a grueling journey. From Nehemiah's letter, Sarah had received the impression that Judah stood on the verge of ruin, poor and endangered by ruthless enemies. This was no pleasure holiday. It would be an arduous task, taxing her strength as well as her heart.

Would she place her baby in danger by participating in this journey? Sarah considered not going. It would mean that she would be apart from Darius for many months. The baby would flourish within her in his absence. He would miss the first quickening, miss the increase in the size of her belly as their son or daughter grew within her. They would not be able to celebrate the small joys of her pregnancy together. Alone, she would have to walk through the pregnancy day after day, without her husband to comfort and encourage her.

He might not even be back for the birth. Sarah did not know the length of this assignment. Yet it seemed reasonable to assume that including the months of travel, it could last a year. She did not want to be parted from him for so long!

She wanted to see Jerusalem with every fiber of her being. She wanted Darius to be by her side when she visited the Temple, because she hoped that the seeds planted by his devout Jewish mother might bear fruit once he experienced the presence of God. But none of these desires were grave enough to endanger the health of her child.

Sarah considered the choices before her. The real question was whether this journey would indeed place her baby's life at risk. She remembered several of the king's concubines who had travelled with the court while expecting. Journeying on royal highways in a baggage train was not nearly as rough as the way Darius preferred to travel. Nehemiah would have a large baggage train, and must therefore journey more slowly. If the king's concubines were considered safe on such roads, surely Sarah posed no danger to her child by travelling in the same manner?

She felt better the longer she considered it. But she knew that Darius would never agree. He would not listen to reason. He would force her to stay at home, where she would be safe, surrounded by friends and court physicians. No amount of cajoling, convincing, crying, or wheedling would move him.

Sarah began to pace around her apartment. Her puppy, Anousya, kept pace with her. He skipped by her side backward and forward, occasionally making plaintive sounds, as though wondering what ailed his mistress. Absently she bent down to pet him before resuming her agitated walk.

She needed a physician, first to confirm that she was indeed expecting a baby, and second to ascertain if travel to Judah would be safe for her and the child. Where could she find a competent physician who would not betray her secret to her husband? For if she were to go to Jerusalem, her only option would be to keep her pregnancy a secret from Darius until they were too far from Susa for him to send her back.

She had given him her word to be forthright and honest, to keep nothing hidden from him. Was it wise to risk their relationship by withholding this secret?

The alternative would be to part from him for endless months. She would not be lying. She would just be delaying telling her husband the truth.

The thought brought on another wave of nausea. Sarah tried to breathe deeply, calming herself. Darius would interpret her actions as a betrayal. He would be furious. He had once told her that he could not abide lies. The mere suspicion that she had lied to him at the start of their marriage had kept him apart from her for months. She could not risk her marriage by hiding her pregnancy from him. But neither could she face the prospect of living without him for a year and bringing their baby into the world in his absence.

With a frantic motion she doubled over into the basin and retched, even though there was nothing left in her stomach to bring up. She curled up on her bed, exhausted and sick. And still no solution presented itself.

"From the king, for you," Darius said as he dropped a black box on the bed next to her. Sarah picked the box up in surprise.

"For me?"

"In appreciation for your part in discovering the murder plot."

Sarah, whose stomach had thankfully settled down for the past few hours, felt well enough to enjoy the gift. She pulled out the carnelian necklace and examined it with care. "It's breathtaking." She held it against her throat for a moment before dropping it back in its box. "I will write the king a letter of thanks. And I will not mention the fact that the queen's gift is exceedingly more to my taste than His Majesty's."

Darius sat on the bed next to her, stretching his legs to the floor. "Am I expected to feel flattered at being considered more worthy than a bauble?"

Sarah had been rewarded with an aristocratic marriage to Darius after solving a potentially damaging plot against Damaspia. She blew a kiss to her husband and nodded. "Baubles are very appealing, my lord. They often appreciate in value and come in handy during times of economic distress. Besides, they are never moody or unreasonable."

"Unlike husbands, you mean?" With a sudden shifting of long limbs, Darius pushed Sarah back into the pillows for a deep kiss that melted her insides. "But can they do this?" he asked.

"I told you I preferred the queen's gift."

He turned a half revolution from her so that he lay on his side next to her. "Pari tells me you've been sick all day. It's not the first time you have felt unwell in the past week or two. It should have passed by now if it were a simple stomach sickness." His hand felt cool against Sarah's heated cheek. "You feel warm."

She shook her head and shifted on the bed, looking for a more comfortable position. "I'm not feverish." Until today, she had managed to downplay her sickness and exhaustion around Darius. It was impossible to do so anymore, given the increased frequency and violence of how wretched she felt.

He stroked her hair with a gentle hand. "Perhaps not. But I am sending for a physician nonetheless. I don't like this lingering malaise."

Guilt churned Sarah's insides. She still had not decided on a course of action. He would be elated to know that he was about to become a father. Her heart melted as she imagined his face when she told him the news. She almost blurted it out then. She stifled the desire, because she knew that telling him was the same as engineering their separation. With difficulty she forced herself to keep her secret for a while longer.

"So what did the king want to see you about? Any news?"

Darius leaned back, resting his elbow on the covers. "He wants to send me to Jerusalem with your cousin Nehemiah."

From his hesitant manner, Sarah deduced that he expected her to be shocked by his news. "So Nehemiah tells me."

"You have spoken to the cupbearer?" Darius's frown was thunderous.

"He sent me a letter, describing his upcoming journey. He said you would be leading his military escort and asked if I would be willing to help. Competent scribes are not easy to come by in Jerusalem, it seems."

Darius swiveled to sit up. "He reaches above himself! He assumes he has the authority to command you to travel to Jerusalem?"

Sarah's eyes widened. "Command me? Of course not. He believed you would be taking me with you. You know I have always wanted to visit Jerusalem. Besides, you would be gone for a year. You wouldn't leave me behind for that length of time. His letter intended no disrespect. He said that since I was already coming on the journey, I could be of tremendous help as a scribe."

Two spots of bright color burned on Darius's cheeks. He shifted on the bed as if he could not find a comfortable position.

Sarah's mouth fell open. "I *am* coming, aren't I? You don't intend to leave me behind?"

"It's too dangerous, Sarah." Darius avoided looking at her. "Going as Nehemiah's escort is a mere cover. My real mission is to get to the root of this plot while we are in the Trans-Euphrates. If the assassin begins to suspect me as the king's agent, you would be in danger. They could take you hostage to get to me.

"In any case, according to reports from area officials, your beloved Jerusalem has become a cauldron of unrest. Hostile nations surround the city. They will be none too pleased by Judah's sudden favor with the king. Who knows what they might do. It's too risky to take you along."

Sarah sat up straight. He planned to leave her behind! Was it so easy for him to abandon her for a whole year? Here she had been agonizing over how not to be parted from him, and he had already decided that he would leave her at home. All considerations of telling him about the baby vanished. "You seem eager to be parted from me." Her lips felt stiff as she spoke.

Darius shot up and stood over her like a tall column of fury. "Don't be dim-witted, Sarah. I hate the thought of leaving you. But I won't endanger your life for the sake of my own selfish desires. As I've already told the king, your presence would prove a dangerous distraction."

"The king? Artaxerxes told you to take me with you?"

An elegant hand waved in the air. "He made a mere suggestion."

"So even the king agrees with me."

"The king is interested in your usefulness. He knows your talents would serve him well on this trip. He is looking out for the interests of the empire. I am looking out for you."

"Darius, you can't protect me from every

danger. The last time my life was threatened, I was safely ensconced in your mansion. And it wasn't some bloodthirsty enemy of the empire that stabbed me in the woods of Ecbatana. Your own servant did that." Sarah forced herself to be calm. Her voice grew soft and pleading. "I am safest when I am with you. Please take me."

Darius raked his fingers through his long hair. "I will think on it."

Chapter 11

The physician Darius summoned to Sarah's bedside proved too competent. A lanky Egyptian with a smoothly shaven face that betrayed little emotion, he wasted no time and examined Sarah with thorough expertise. As he washed his hands in a basin of warm water, he said, "No malady ails you, my lady. I believe you are with child, although it's early days. Two months, perhaps. You must have guessed?"

Sarah flushed. "I suspected it."

"Judging by what your husband said, he is unaware of your condition. He fears you are ill."

"I haven't told him yet. I wanted to be certain."

"You can be certain. A baby grows in your womb."

A rush of joy swept over Sarah so that she could not speak for some time. In that short moment, the physician's pronouncement made the baby real to her—real enough to love. To protect. She closed her eyes. She was carrying Darius's child. Her eyes grew moist as an avalanche of tangled feelings gathered force in her heart. *She was going to be a mother!*

Her mind was finally able to think beyond the emotions of the moment. "Can I travel? Will it endanger the baby?"

"Not if you take care. No galloping on horseback, mind. If you go at a gentle pace and take plenty of rest, you should both be fine."

He then gave her a list of foods to eat and to avoid. Sarah took the list and studied it with care, memorizing it on the spot.

"I have a favor to ask of you, master physician. Don't inform my husband of my pregnancy yet."

The smooth mask of the Egyptian's face remained impassive. "I don't mean to be disobliging, my lady, but to withhold such information from the man who hired me would be wrong. I would not betray his lordship's trust, nor would I invite his justified affront."

"I had no right to ask. Forgive me."

"Why do you wish to withhold such happy news from your husband? It is clear that you are delighted with the child. Your husband will be equally thrilled, I assure you."

Sarah plucked at the soft sheets. "He will be leaving on a long assignment shortly. As it is, he does not want to take me along due to the possible dangers we might encounter. Once he knows I am with child, he will tie me up to a wooden post rather than risk taking me with him."

"I see. When I inform him of your condition, I will try to reassure him that travel poses no threat to the health of your baby."

"My thanks," Sarah said. "Not that it will make any difference."

• • •

Darius was beginning to understand why Artaxerxes had given him such a pitying look on their last meeting. The king had once allowed his own wife and queen to accompany him on a military campaign. Darius began to suspect that bringing Damaspia along on that occasion had not been Artaxerxes' original intention. Damaspia must have forced his hand. He could just see her, the dazzling cerulean blue eyes flooding with fat tears, begging her husband to allow her to go. He realized he was no more immune to Sarah's soft plea than Artaxerxes had been to Damaspia. *I am safest when I am with you.* Those words had wormed their way into his heart. He could not deny the impact they had on him. The woman knew how to get under his skin.

He had spent the afternoon away from home, overseeing details of his trip to Beyond the River. Impressed by how much the cupbearer had already accomplished in a short time, Darius had to admit that his wife's cousin had a genius for administration.

The knowledge did not soften his heart toward Nehemiah. Since his wedding day he had harbored a dislike for his wife's cousin. The reason for his initial animosity no longer existed, for he felt happy with Sarah. His suspicion that Nehemiah had engineered the wedding as a means of elevating himself in the court had turned out to be false. And yet Darius could not shake his antagonism toward the cupbearer. It made no sense, even to him. Nehemiah had been a close friend of his parents; moreover, he was kin to his wife. She loved and respected him with a devotion that grated on Darius's nerves. He wondered if he might be jealous and dismissed the thought. He? Jealous of his wife's affections toward another man? A ludicrous thought.

He pushed the matter aside, preferring to forget about the cupbearer as long as possible, and sent a servant to fetch Vidarna. "Has the physician examined Lady Sarah?"

"Yes my lord. He waited for over an hour to give you his report. He could not linger as another patient was expecting him."

"Ah. I am sorry to have missed him. I wished to know what he made of Sarah's condition."

"He said he would be back this week to discuss it with you, my lord. He did not seem overly concerned. I am sure it's nothing serious."

Darius never met with the physician. To his astonishment, Nehemiah managed to procure the myriad of provisions necessary for the trip to Jerusalem before the week's end. Darius had never known such a complex undertaking to be organized so quickly. Yet the cupbearer's preparations remained meticulous in every detail. Darius could find no fault in his arrangements. In order to be ready to leave with Nehemiah, Darius found himself busy from morning till dusk, missing the physician on several occasions.

Sarah assured him that the physician seemed satisfied that she suffered from no serious malady. She appeared better to him, her skin less pale, the bouts of nausea decreasing with each day, though in spite of her reassurances, he suspected that they had not altogether abated.

To his surprise, his wife did not bring up the topic of Jerusalem again. He had half expected her to badger him from one hour to the next. Her silence caused him more discomfort than if she had nagged him. He could have dismissed the carping of a pestering wife; he found it harder to dismiss the sweet silence of a sad wife.

The idea of leaving her for a whole year left a bad taste in his mouth. If he were honest, he missed her after three days of absence. Her conversation, her humor, her tenderness had enriched his life so much that when he was without them, he felt bereft. No one stood up to him the way this little woman did. She had never shown him the slightest fear. She seemed unimpressed by his rank or riches or looks. Could he really bear to be separated from her for twelve long months?

How dangerous was this journey? Because they would travel along the royal highways, with a large convoy, and accompanied by a military escort, he felt that the months on the road would offer relative safety. Even a strong gang of thieves would think better than to attempt attacking such a cavalcade. Once in Jerusalem, she would remain under his watchful care as well as Nehemiah's. He could assign one of his men to protect her day and night. If he did not take her to Syria with him, she would not be thrown into the path of unnecessary danger.

The more he thought on it, the more convinced he became that bringing her was not the act of an irresponsible husband. He knew how desperately she desired to see the city of her fathers and to worship in their Temple. She would glow as brightly as one of Persepolis's famed lamps if he told her that he planned to take her with him. Besides, she would be amenable to his every whim for months. He chuckled. Well, days, anyway.

Nehemiah had set the date of their departure three days hence. If he wanted to include Sarah he had better tell her right away; she had little time to prepare for such a long absence from home.

"I have thought upon your request, and have decided to take you with me to Jerusalem."

Sarah froze, the piece of rag in her hand, which she had been holding just beyond reach of Anousya forgotten. The puppy barked. With an absent air, she surrendered the rag and sprang from the couch. "I can come?"

"Yes."

It was one of the few times Darius had seen her lost for words. He felt a tremor of satisfaction go through him.

An odd emotion crossed her face. It wasn't happiness. More like an inner struggle, he would have guessed. Before he could examine the source of that inexplicable reaction, her expression changed. Delight lit up her eyes as she ran to him and threw her arms about him.

"Thank you! Thank you!"

"You will be assigned a guard at all times. I don't want you venturing anywhere without him. Do you promise?"

"I'll take two guards if you wish. I'll even take Mardonius, though he never bathes and smells like the rump of a dead bear."

Darius laughed. "When he was a boy, his father died of a fierce chill after a bath. His childish brain connected the two events and he has since avoided bathing as much as possible."

Sarah took his hand and drew him down to sit next to her on the couch. "When do we leave?"

"In three days."

She squeaked. "You jest! Even Nehemiah couldn't pull that off."

"He has. Having second thoughts?"

To his surprise she reddened and looked away. "Darius, I . . ."

"What is it?" Again he caught that odd expression on her face, as if she felt conscience-stricken. "Sarah?"

She waved a hand before her. "Don't mind me. I can be ready. May I bring Pari? I thought the two of us would travel in one of the carts. I would rather avoid the back of a horse on such a long journey, if it's all right."

"That's a wise decision."

An hour later, Darius left his wife with a nagging feeling in the back of his mind. He sensed there was something wrong—that she held something back. He chided himself for his ridiculous misgivings. But the nagging feeling would not leave.

Pari clapped when she heard the news of their upcoming travel.

Sarah gave a wan smile. "Are you certain that you wish to come? We are not travelling to palaces and mansions, but to a broken-down city. The food will be simple and the conditions primitive. I would understand if you chose to stay."

"And be parted from you for a whole year, especially now when you need me most? I think not. Besides, you've been reading King David's poetry to me for months, and now I will have an opportunity to visit his city."

"There might not be much worth seeing. Jerusalem has suffered war and neglect."

"No matter. I am going."

Sarah was relieved to hear of Pari's determination to accompany her. The imminence of their departure had loosed a terrible anxiety in her. Had she lost her mind? In spite of the physician's assurance, she worried that she might jeopardize her baby's health. She knew nothing about pregnancy. Not having grown up amongst women, she had not gleaned the wisdom common to most women her age. Having a friend like Pari as her companion would prove an enormous comfort.

She had almost blurted the news out to Darius after he had asked her to come. Guilt had overwhelmed her. He deserved to know that he was about to become a father. He deserved to have a part in making the decision about this journey. Her silence robbed him of that crucial choice. She recognized that she was wrong. She told herself that she had three days to reveal her secret. Perhaps if she told him just before leaving, he would be so pressed for time that he would be forced to take her.

She wondered if there were midwives in Jerusalem. Surely the women there didn't give birth without help. But here in Susa she would have access to the best. Damaspia would no doubt send her personal midwife to see to her needs. Not in Judah.

She had no information about the timing of this assignment. For all she knew, Darius and she might have to turn around and return home within weeks of having arrived. By then she would be growing large with child. Could she stand four months of bumping along royal highways with her belly sticking out over her feet?

Then again, Darius would never stand for it. He would find somewhere safe for her to stay until her time came. If the king needed him, however, he would have to leave her side. What an irony that would be if, after traipsing behind him through half the length of the empire, she still ended up having the baby alone.

She would tell him, she decided. She would tell him as soon as he returned home. But by the time Darius came to her that evening, she had lost her nerve.

The day of their departure dawned hazy with dry heat. It was the middle of spring, but felt more like high summer. They gathered outside the west gate of the city. Sarah counted one hundred and three people including Darius's military escort. Most were men. She recognized several of Nehemiah's relatives and Jewish officials from Susa. Many others were hired servants. Horses, donkeys, and asses loaded up with men or gear made a noisy cavalcade. A large number of sturdy carts filled with food, tents, and other necessities lined up along the road, waiting to start. Most were covered and pulled by donkeys. Some smaller carts, fashioned from wood planks, only had high sides, covered on top with canvas and ropes.

Sarah searched frantically for Darius and spotted him near the head of the column, speaking to a man she did not recognize. There was no more time to vacillate. She had already left it too late. She needed to tell him now.

"My lord, may I speak to you?"

He turned to her, his manner distracted. "Not now, Sarah. Go to your cart with Pari."

"But my lord . . ."

"Sarah, this is poor timing. I shall speak with you later."

Half relieved and half panicking, Sarah walked down the column of travellers until she found the wide cart Darius had prepared for her and Pari. A large portion of the floor had been fitted with thick mattresses to shield them from the uneven road, and a removable stretch of canvas over the cart gave them respite from the elements. He had even installed thick curtains for privacy.

She climbed in with Pari's help and sat with her knees up against her chest. If she told him after they started on the road, he would be furious. He would feel manipulated, and with good reason. Thanks to her many delays, however, she had run out of options. It was unreasonable to expect that he would be free to have an intimate conversation with her just before the start of the journey.

Nehemiah silenced the group and led them in

prayer, asking God to take care of them, and to give them safe passage. And then with a ponderous gait as dignified as a royal barge embarking on a long quest, their convoy began its journey.

Sarah put her head on her knees and moaned. This did not bode well. Again, she determined that she would tell him as soon as he came to her that day. She would begin by asking his pardon and would even volunteer to go back, if he wished it.

The heat and the monotonous bump of the cart hour after hour added an extra layer of exhaustion to her ever-present, pregnancy-induced weariness. Since the spring sunlight had lingered late into the afternoon, the caravan had pushed past the first royal staging house. No doubt they would have to spend the night camped on the roadside, for they would be unable to make it to the next staging house before nightfall. Sarah stretched on the mattress, exhausted. Sleep overcame her with a heavy hand by early evening.

Through a veil she heard Darius's voice inquiring after her. She must rise, she told herself. There was something crucial he had to know. But the pull of sleep had too strong a hold on her body. As if in a dream, she felt a soft touch on her cheek and the indistinct murmur of Darius's voice in her ear. Then she fell asleep again and lost her chance to make things right.

She rose early the next day, feeling refreshed. The carts had stopped after she had fallen asleep, and the cessation of movement had helped her body to recover from the day's travel. Dressing with Pari's help, she covered her hair with a cinnamon-colored scarf and disembarked to look for her husband. She could not bear to delay her confession for another moment. Better to face the fire of his anger than to hide her news from him.

As she searched the column, she noticed a royal messenger riding toward them at such a swift speed that the dust of the road almost hid him from sight. He galloped past where Sarah stood toward the head of their cavalcade. Sarah shielded her eyes with a hand. The courier signaled to Darius and both men dismounted. Sarah wound her way toward them. By the time she reached her husband's side, he had read the missive. She noticed with astonishment that his eyes brimmed with unshed tears.

Chapter 12

Gasping, Sarah clutched Darius's arm. "What's wrong?"

He bent his head toward her, but his expression remained dazed, as if he had not comprehended her words.

"What has happened?" she prompted again.

"It's . . ." His voice caught. The silence stretched while Sarah writhed with worry. Darius cleared his throat. "It's my father. His servants have brought him home with a terrible fever. The king bids me come to Susa immediately. There is no time to waste."

"Oh, Darius. I'm so sorry." She squeezed his hand. It felt cold and clammy in her hold. "What will you do?"

"Leave at once. Lysander can lead the military escort in my absence. The train is moving so slowly that I should be able to catch up with you even if I am gone for a week or more."

"Shall I come with you?" she asked, forgetting that she was not supposed to ride.

"You won't be able to keep up with me, Sarah. I need to get there as soon as possible. There may not be much time."

She nodded. Without considering their curious

audience, she wrapped her arms around him. "May the Lord go with you, my love."

Darius pulled her into a hard embrace and buried his face in the fork of her neck. "Look after yourself." He vaulted onto his horse and, after a short conversation with Lysander, thundered back on the road toward Susa. With the loose sleeves of his light tunic floating behind him, he looked like he was flying.

Back in her cart, Sarah shared the news with Pari and spent an hour praying for Lord Vivan. Perhaps the Lord would spare his life for Darius's sake. Having lost his mother when he was only seventeen, he had a particularly deep attachment to his father.

She had not told Darius about their babe after all. The news of his father's grave illness had driven it from her mind. She regretted her omission. He had gone to his sick father without the one piece of news that would have bolstered Lord Vivan's heart.

Ten days after their departure, Nehemiah came to visit Sarah when the caravan had stopped for the night.

"Any news from Darius?" he asked as he stood at the foot of her cart.

Sarah shifted to the edge of the mattress until her legs were dangling over the edge of the cart. "None, my lord."

Nehemiah looked away. In the firelight his face appeared drawn. "You and Lord Vivan were good friends, weren't you?" Sarah said, her voice softening.

"We still are, although due to his frequent travels, we no longer have the luxury of much time spent together."

"He has forgiven you for the debacle I made of my wedding, then? For recommending me as a suitable bride for his son?"

Nehemiah gave a tight smile of remembrance. "Once he understood the circumstances, he overcame his reservations. He can see that Darius is happy, which is what he cares about. For a short time our friendship grew strained, when he thought that I had led him wrong."

"I ask your pardon, cousin Nehemiah."

"And I give it. Long forgotten, now." He took a deep breath. "I pray the Lord will restore Lord Vivan. He is a good man."

Sarah rested her elbows on her knees. "Did you know Darius's mother too?"

"I knew her since we were children. No one was surprised when Lord Vivan fell in love with her. She was extraordinary. But we were all amazed that she accepted him. She loved the Lord, you see. To marry him, she sacrificed a great deal."

"She never gave up her faith?"

"No. She worshiped the Lord as best she could in a Persian household. Of course, she could not raise her only son as a Jew. She shed many tears over that loss. No child ever received such depth of prayer."

"Does Darius know anything about the Lord?"

"More than you might imagine. Toward the end of her life, when Darius was sixteen or seventeen, they spoke about her faith often. She knew she was dying, and she wanted him to understand her better. She did not break her word to Lord Vivan by suggesting that Darius should pursue the Lord, however. Nor did she burden Darius with guilt for choosing to live as his father expected of him. She only told him of her faith and what it meant to her."

"I've not heard him speak of the Lord. He avoids all reference to my faith if he can help it."

"It cannot be easy for him. A Persian prince, bound by love and tradition to his way of life, and yet having a whole other world laying claim on his heart. If he feels any pull toward the Lord, he must feel compelled to fight it with his whole strength."

Sarah rubbed the corner of her nose. "I understand Lady Rachel's struggles better than anyone. My life seems to have become a repetition of hers. It isn't easy to have to swallow my thoughts and feelings around my own husband. Like a wall, his hostile unbelief divides us. And then there is the way he keeps his emotions hidden behind a dam I cannot touch. Such a pair we are! I stuff anything to do with my faith away from his hearing and he hides his heart away from me. It makes for a lonely life, sometimes."

"You do sound like Rachel."

Lysander had taken to riding behind Sarah's cart for several hours each day. He had also assigned two of Darius's personal guard—Arta and Meres—to stand watch over Sarah while he was absent. Both men were familiar to her, and comfortable to be around. Lysander was altogether different.

Sarah had caught him carving a hand-sized wooden figure on the first day that he had ridden near her. Like Darius, he was so at home on his horse that he guided the animal by the pressure of his legs, leaving both his hands free.

Curious, Sarah had asked to see the figure. He had used light-colored wood, which had been bleached to an ivory color. She gasped as she held the figure in her hand. It was a miniature bust—an unmistakable likeness of Darius. He had managed to capture the symmetry, the sheer force of beauty in his face. What made the small bust remarkable, however, was the subtlety of expression. Strength, kindness, and a slight air of cynical humor made the features come alive. Fascinated, Sarah studied the bust. It made her miss her husband with renewed intensity.

She handed the sculpture to Pari, who had been

studying it over her shoulder. "That is fine work," she said. "One of the best I have seen. You could be a professional sculptor."

"Hmm. It's for you. To help with Darius's absence."

Within days, Sarah realized that the abrupt communication, as well as the thoughtful consideration, were typical of the Spartan. Though he seldom shared his thoughts, when he did choose to give a glimpse of his mind or heart, one felt like the recipient of a grand privilege. He rarely smiled, but when he did, his countenance became suffused with an intelligent light that made his handsome face more welcoming. Sarah and Pari did what they could to make him laugh, but they never succeeded. His infrequent smiles, they decided, were more than compensation for the lack.

Sarah wondered why a man so talented with his hands would risk his life at soldiering. She would have to ask Darius for Lysander's story; she sensed hidden depths in him that hinted at an interesting past.

On the next day of their journey, one of Nehemiah's servants fell asleep on his donkey and toppled onto the road, hitting his head on a stone, causing a nasty gash. Sarah could see the commotion from her cart. Someone fetched Lysander, and to her surprise, he ministered to the servant with sure, knowledgeable hands. He even had a chest of medicinal herbs and prepared bandages, which he used to treat the servant.

Sarah knew that Persian military officers were given the rudiments of medical training in case of injury on the battlefield. Perhaps Lysander had been given similar training in Sparta. Yet Darius did not carry around a well-stocked chest of medicine as Lysander did, which looked more like something a physician would use. The Spartan's interest in medicine clearly went further than that of the average officer.

In the evening, Nehemiah came to her for a short visit. Sarah remained sitting in her cart, while Nehemiah stood outside for the sake of propriety.

"How is your servant, my lord? He took quite a tumble today."

"He will recover. Lysander is more experienced than most physicians."

"How is that? I thought he had trained as a soldier."

Nehemiah waved a hand. Sarah was amused to note his nails were as clean and well-manicured as ever, his clothing free from the dust of the road. Her cousin managed to keep himself groomed and dignified even after hours of travel on dry roads.

"The man is a mystery. He has many skills, among them how to keep his mouth shut. Darius knows more about him than anyone else does. Which reminds me, any news?"

"Not as yet."

"I wished I could go myself. I have a great respect, not to mention affection, for your father-in-law. But my place is here."

"Of course. It's better that Darius have this time alone with his father, in any case."

Nehemiah nodded, his red hair glinting in the firelight. "Send for me if you need anything. I shall not require your help until we arrive at the king's forest in Lebanon. After that, there will be many opportunities for you to lend a hand."

For a moment Sarah considered telling Nehemiah her news and asking for his prayers and guidance regarding Darius. Then she realized that she could not share her secret with her cousin before letting her own husband know. How hurt Darius would be upon finding out.

When they had been on the road for twelve days, Darius returned with the setting sun. He came to see Sarah before reporting to Nehemiah or his men. She had had no chance to ask him a single question when he took her into his arms and held her, his hands encircling her waist.

She noted the dark circles under his eyes and the pallor of his skin when she stepped away from him. But he was not wearing mourning attire, and his expression, though weary, was devoid of grief.

"He is well?" Her voice sounded like the squeak of an excited child.

Darius broke into a smile. "He is past danger and expected to make a full recovery. When I arrived, he had been in a deep sleep for three days and nights. The physicians who tended him said he would die within hours." Darius rubbed his forehead as if the memory pained him. "He refused to die. He has never been fond of physicians, and I'm certain he did not wish to oblige them."

Sarah chuckled. "He was asleep when you arrived, then?"

"Yes. At first I sat by his side in silence." He said nothing for a few moments. Sarah wondered how hard it must have been for him, listening to the labored breathing of his father, thinking whether each breath might be his last. Wondering if he would never hear the sound of his father's voice again.

Darius closed his eyes for a moment as if the memory pained him. "In desperation, I began to speak to him, though I believed he could not hear me. There were so many things I wished to tell him."

Sarah longed to ask him what he had said to his father. She knew better than to ask, and held him instead, physical touch her only means of increasing their intimacy. He would reveal what he wished, and she had to be content with that.

"After a few hours of tiring both of us with my chatter, I told him that I did not want him to die."

Sarah leaned into Darius and tightened her hold on him for a moment. He rested there as though her arms were the sanctuary he had sought and missed for long days.

"What happened then?" she prompted.

"Then I fell off the bed."

"You did not!"

"I assure you I did. For with a loud and firm voice my father replied, 'I have no plans for dying, my son.'"

A bubble of laughter escaped Sarah's lips. "That's extraordinary! I would have fallen off the bed, also."

Darius grinned. "He woke up with a vengeance after that, demanding food and fresh clothes and a report from his post. It was no easy task convincing him to rest."

Sarah sighed with relief. "I was so worried."

"The physicians said his recovery was no less than a miracle. I stayed with him until I felt assured that the danger had passed."

"Have you had any sleep?

"Not much. I rode through most of the night to catch up with you."

"You must have ridden faster than a hurricane since you left Susa."

He stretched. "I am weary. But I must receive reports from my men and your cousin first."

"I have something to tell you, Darius."

"Tell me tomorrow. I don't think I could take anything in tonight. My mind is numb with exhaustion. I am for bed as soon as I have finished my rounds."

Sarah nodded and gave him another embrace. She would rather have him fresh and in good humor when she told him her news.

The persistent throbbing in her back awakened Sarah from a sound sleep. Once again, the convoy had managed to ride past the staging house and stopped for the night by the side of the road, which meant that she had slept in her cart rather than in a comfortable inn with a tolerable bed. The sun would not rise for some time yet, and the camp rested in silence. She turned to the right and then to the left, trying to find relief. The ache followed no matter how she positioned her body. Pari had told her that lower back pain was a common complaint during later pregnancy; she must have started earlier than usual. She felt the bite of nausea, sharper than usual, and reached for the stale bread Pari left by her bedside every night. While she no longer grew sick with the same violence of her early pregnancy, she had never entirely outgrown the discomfort of a bilious stomach.

The ache lingered, and after over an hour of tossing and turning, Sarah decided to stretch her legs and walk a little, hoping to find relief. By the time she left the cart, a greyish dawn had begun to cast soft shadows over the landscape. She leaned against the cart's wooden side, letting her body adjust to being upright before beginning a slow walk.

Without warning, a severe cramp slashed through her belly with such force that Sarah doubled over. Her breathing became ragged from the force of it. Fear mingled with pain. This did not feel normal. She placed a protective hand over her belly, trying to calm the alarm that raced through her mind.

After a few moments, the cramp loosened its grip and Sarah was able to straighten. She walked back to her cart and whispered Pari's name. A light sleeper, her friend was by her side in a moment.

"What's wrong, my lady?"

Sarah gripped Pari's hand. "It's past now, so hopefully it is nothing. But I had a heavy cramp seize me a few moments ago. And my back has been aching for several hours."

Pari jumped down to stand by her side. "Let's take you back inside where you can lie down."

"No. The walls close in on me. Let me stay here."

Pari continued to hold her hand. The sun was rising in the east, its pace lazy. In the pale light Sarah could see Pari's face pinched with worry.

She gave her a reassuring smile. The smile widened as she saw Darius striding toward them. Pari, also noting his approach, said she would go to fetch water, though Sarah knew she wished to give them privacy.

"I thought I would have to wake you," he said. "You're up early."

"You are visiting early."

He tangled his hands into her hair and drew her close. "I missed you."

"And I . . ." The words she intended to speak were forgotten as another knife-sharp cramp invaded her belly. She closed her mouth on the groan that rose up from her depths. Her breath came out in short puffs of air. Grasping Darius's arm for support she bent over, doubling in on herself.

O Lord, have mercy on me. Have mercy on my baby.

"Sarah? Sarah, where do you hurt?" Peripherally, she noted that Darius's voice exuded calm.

She could not think of anything to say. She had yet to inform him of her pregnancy; was she now to tell him that she feared she was losing the babe he did not know she had conceived? She shook her head and clutched at him harder as the pain made her forget everything else.

He picked her up and carried her into the cart and laid her down on her mattress. The interior of the cart remained enveloped in shadows; he turned to light a lamp. The pain ceased as suddenly as it had begun, and Sarah forced herself to sit up.

"I'm all right now." She sounded weak and shaky to her own ears.

Darius turned back to face her, holding the lamp in one hand. He looked frozen. "I am going to fetch Lysander," he said.

"I don't think it's necessary. The pain is gone."

"It's necessary." He held out his hand. It was scarlet. "You are bleeding."

Sarah sucked in her breath. For the first time she became aware of the sticky feeling between her legs. She looked down and saw that her shoes were stained with blood. Denial was no longer an option. It dawned on her that her baby was dying. She squeezed her eyes shut and buried her face in the pillow, hoping to drown the wail that was rising, rising from the depth of her being. Darius lifted her into his arms and cradled her. "I must fetch Lysander, sweetheart. I'll return quickly."

Pari came to her side moments later.

"My baby," Sarah said, her voice broken. "My baby."

Pari's eyes filled with tears. "I'm so sorry." She sponged the blood from her skin and changed her into fresh garments. With soothing movements, she began to rub Sarah's back. Another wave of contractions overtook her, not as intense as before, but painful enough to make her retch.

Lysander and Darius appeared at the foot of the cart. "May I come in, my lady?" Lysander asked.

She nodded, beyond words. Darius tried to follow, but Lysander held up a hand. "Give me a few moments alone with your wife, Darius. Her maid can remain."

"I want to be by her side."

"I understand. And you will be. But first, I need to examine her in private."

Darius gave a curt nod. "Don't take long."

Lysander's examination was thorough. Sarah's misery overrode her embarrassment.

"You are losing a babe," he said, not trying to cushion the news.

"Can you save him?"

He shook his head. "He was not meant to be. Nothing would have saved him. Now we must make certain that you do not hemorrhage and your flesh does not fester. If you take good care, there is no reason you should not conceive again and give birth to a healthy baby. Many women have miscarriages and recover fully to have a brood of children."

Tears soaked Sarah's cheeks. "He is the one I want. I love him so much."

"My lady, am I right in assuming that your husband does not know?"

"Yes. I ought to have told him before coming. I tried several times since. We were always interrupted. I intended to tell him today. Now, it's too late."

"It will be hard on him. I'll call him in now. Shall I tell him the news, or do you want to do it yourself?"

"Since I never told him that we had conceived a child, I should at least be the one to inform him that his child has died."

Darius leapt into the cart as soon as Lysander opened the heavy curtains. He rushed to Sarah's side and sat near her, careful not to cause her discomfort. "What is wrong with her?" he asked Lysander without taking his gaze off Sarah. With heartrending tenderness, he stroked the damp hair off her face. "You'll be well."

"Darius." Sarah bit her lip, unsure how to go on. "My lord, forgive me. I have lost our baby."

An impassive mask dropped over the perfect features. She knew that trick. Whenever his emotions erupted, he hid them with the dexterity of a magician with his staff. "You were with child?"

"Yes, my lord."

"Is she going to be all right?" He turned to Lysander. "There was a lot of blood." In the dispassionate voice, Sarah thought she detected a thread of fear. She reached for his hand, desperate for his comfort. Desperate to give him comfort.

Lysander said, "With good care, she will recover quickly. I am confident she will conceive again, Darius."

"Was it the travel?"

"I doubt it. I have known women engaged in more vigorous activity during pregnancy who carried their babies to term without difficulty, as well as women who avoided all strenuous exertion and miscarried, nonetheless."

"But you don't know for certain?"

Lysander pushed his hand through his flaxen hair. "No. Not for certain. No one really knows why these things happen. I think the body recognizes the existence of a problem, and expels the baby."

Darius said nothing. His eyes, heavy-lidded and red, betrayed a weight of sorrow he could not hide entirely. He lingered by Sarah's side, his hand in hers, keeping quiet vigil until she fell asleep.

She did not slumber for long. Darius was still there when she woke up. "How do you feel?"

Still groggy from sleep, Sarah tried to gauge his mood and failed. "Better."

He leaned away from her. "I need to ask you a question, Sarah. Will you tell me the truth?"

"Yes." She knew what he was about to ask. She knew that telling him the truth would drive him away from her. But she also knew that she could not lie. It was bad enough that she had hidden the truth from him. She would not make matters worse by trying to cover her offense with more lies.

His voice sounded brittle and hoarse. "Did

you know you were pregnant when we embarked on this journey?"

Sarah's mouth turned dry. "Yes, my lord. I knew."

Darius rose to his feet, his movements awkward, as if he could not access the innate physical grace that marked his usual bearing. Without a word, he left.

Chapter 13

Lysander remained with Sarah until the bleeding and cramping subsided. According to him, these were favorable signs, indicating that she would recover from her miscarriage without any lasting effects. As long as she passed the afterbirth in its entirety, he remained confident of her full recovery.

The convoy had begun to move again. Sarah hardly felt the uneven terrain of the road. A heavy curtain of grief descended over her mind. Her thinking became cloudy. She felt only anguish. Her baby was gone. Her husband was gone. And she had brought Darius's abandonment on herself.

In the afternoon, Darius came. He stood over her, his green eyes accusing. But he could not hide the sorrow that mingled with the bitterness. She remembered how he had once told her of his longing to have children. The loss of this baby had wounded his heart as much as hers.

He laid a hand on her forehead, his touch impersonal. "Is she still bleeding?" he asked Pari, ignoring Sarah.

"Not copiously, my lord. And she has shown no sign of chills or fever. She is recovering well."

Darius nodded and turned to leave.

"Forgive me, my lord!" Sarah cried.

He stopped, his broad back rigid. "It's too late."

"Please! I love you!"

"I don't care," he said, and vaulted out of the cart while it was still moving.

Sarah turned into her pillow and wept.

"He will come round," Pari said, patting her shoulder.

"No. He won't."

Darius sat on his pallet, ready to bed down for the night. Not that he would get much sleep. Since Sarah's miscarriage, his nights had consisted of long hours of torturous thought, interspersed with short spurts of restless slumber and nightmarish dreams. In the shadows he saw the wide-shouldered outline of Lysander walking toward him.

"I need to speak with you."

"So speak."

Lysander hunched down next to Darius. "Not here. What I have to say is for your ears alone."

With a sudden rush, he felt the blood drain from his face. "Sarah?"

"Come."

Darius almost throttled Lysander in his haste to make the man disgorge his secret. Was she sick? Was her life in danger? His friend refused to say another word, however, until they were out of earshot of the camp.

"Your wife is not in immediate danger, but I am worried for her. It has been three days since the miscarriage, and she still can't eat. She is nauseous all the time and too weak to leave her bed."

"Has her womb begun to fester?"

"I don't believe so. She has no fever. The bleeding and the cramping have ceased. But she is not returning to health as she should. Women's maladies are not my specialty. I know of nothing else to do. She won't mind me when I tell her to eat. You have to do something, Darius."

Darius had visited Sarah every day for the past three days. His visits were always the same—silent, brooding affairs that left her shaking with nerves. He checked on her physical well-being, yet refused to speak to her. It was as if he came against his own will, she thought. As if part of him hated her and wished to be as far away from her as the sun from the moon. And yet part of him could not resist being near her—resist ensuring that she was recovering her health. In spite of his great anger, he could not entirely sever his heart from her. Sometimes, she found a wisp of hope in that connection. More often, she felt swallowed up by a despair that seemed unending.

She wanted to share her husband's sorrow, for who understood better than she what it felt to have a beloved child ripped out of her life? But he had raised such a wall between them that she could not reach him. His bitterness breathed like a living thing, separating them. Every day she had begged for his forgiveness. Every day he had ignored her and left without a word.

She had trouble eating. Her body rejected food. The very sight of it made her ill.

On the fourth evening, just after the convoy had stopped for the day, Darius came in bearing a bowl of soup.

"You are going to eat this," he said.

"I cannot."

He placed the bowl on the floor of the cart next to her. Bending, he put a long arm behind her back and lifted her up. He piled a few cushions behind her to support her back before straightening up. His touch made the blood rush to her face.

"You are going to eat."

"I don't wish to be contrary, my lord. The smell of it alone is making me nauseous."

"Nonetheless, you must eat. You have gone too many days without food, and Lysander says that if you go on like this, you could bring on a long sickness."

He sat next to her on the mattress and reached for the bowl. He held a spoonful of the soup to her mouth. "Eat." His voice brooked no disobedience.

If he had shown a glimmer of tenderness or even compassion, she might have believed that he still cared for her. But his manner was brusque. He would have done as much for a sick dog or a horse.

Not wishing to anger him more than she already had, she forced herself to gulp down the spoonful of soup. For a moment, her belly roiled with discontent. She closed her eyes and breathed deep.

"Good. Now another," he said, unrelenting.

By the time he was done, a sheen of sweat covered her skin, and she shook with the effort not to purge the contents of her stomach.

He wet a towel and wiped her face and neck. "It will pass soon."

To her surprise and relief, he proved right. The nausea passed and her stomach settled. For the first time since losing the baby, she felt almost well.

"You look better. Your cheeks have a tinge of color."

"I feel better. Thank you."

She expected him to leave now that he had accomplished his purpose in visiting her, but he lingered.

"Why, Sarah? Why did you keep the child from me?" He sounded more anguished than angry.

Sarah closed her eyes for a moment. "I feared you would not let me come."

"You wanted to see Jerusalem that badly? Visiting Judah seemed more important to you than the health of our baby? Than my feelings?"

"*No!* Never. I kept the news from you because I did not wish to be parted from you for a whole year. Or to have our baby alone. I asked the physician you sent me if travel would be dangerous to the child. I would never have risked his life, Darius. Not even for the sake of being with you. He assured me that if I took care, the babe would be in no particular danger. Even the king brought his pregnant concubines on the road with him."

He leaned back on the stool. "You had no right to keep this child from me. I was his father! I deserved to know, Sarah."

"I know you did. I wronged you, Darius. I couldn't believe you did not find out after the physician's visit. He told me he would inform you."

"No doubt against your wishes. You blush. I have made the right assumption, I see." He crossed his arms in a tense movement. "You cannot blame this on him, though the poor man tried to visit me many times. This was your responsibility as my wife! You were the one to share it with me. You were the one to tell me that we had made a child together. Do you think I wished to hear such news from the mouth of a physician?"

"Oh Darius. Forgive me. I kept thinking that I would tell you soon. But then I knew you would leave me behind, and the fear of that parting made me mute.

"At first I thought I would have weeks. I had

not bargained on Nehemiah's speed, which hastened our departure beyond my expectations. I tried to tell you on the morning before we left. Do you recall?"

"You really imagined that I would have time to sit and chat with you moments before the convoy took off? That is an excuse. You wished to tell me when I could do nothing about it."

Sarah could not refute his accusation. The silence in the cart grew heavy with the rupture between them. It felt to her as if talking had pulled the bitterness into the open, but nothing had been resolved. She realized now that speech could not heal what ailed them. Unreasonable mercy was the only solution to their plight. Mercy and forgiveness.

Her husband was a man who gave his trust frugally. And she had already breached that trust when she first came to him as wife. It had taken a disaster to soften his heart. It wasn't until she had been stabbed and lay severely ill that he made peace with her. From Darius's perspective, this new betrayal must seem incomprehensible.

"I should have entrusted myself to your decision," she said.

He shrugged and rose, his movements heavy. "You should have entrusted yourself to my *care*. But you robbed me of the opportunity. Because of you, I had to mourn my child before I ever had the chance to celebrate him.

"You might have lost this babe even if you had stayed in Susa. But at least we would have both known that we had done our best for him. Now we will always have to struggle with that question."

Nehemiah visited her in the evening. Pari leapt from the stool and offered the only seat in the cart to him. He gave a gracious nod, arranged himself neatly on the stool next to Sarah, and leaned over. "I'm so sorry, my girl."

The gentle sympathy in his voice caused her to melt into tears. She had cried more in four days than she remembered doing since childhood.

"Why did God take my baby?"

"That's too great a mystery for me, child. It was the same for your mother, you know. She lost a babe before she conceived you."

Sarah's eyes widened. "No one told me."

"At the time she was as heartbroken as you are now. But then great joy returned to her when you came along. She didn't seem to stop smiling for months after you were born."

"She never spoke to me about it."

"Perhaps she felt you were too young to understand."

"I wish she were here now. She would know how I feel. I would be so comforted if I could snuggle in her arms like I used to do when I was a child."

"Dear girl. I am so sorry that the one loss

highlights the other. But the Lord can be as loving as a mother to you."

"I feel that He has left me too. I feel abandoned by the Lord."

"Sometimes the heart goes through such a deep valley that the Lord is overshadowed by its darkness. The trick is, when you feel God has let go of you, you don't let go of God. Cling to Him anyway. And you will find that He never abandoned you—He remained near all along.

"I am convinced that He knows your pain and desires to give you rest in the midst of it, for does He not seek to comfort all who mourn, and provide for those who grieve in Zion?"

Sarah struggled to sit up. Pari rushed forward to help her. She felt her meager strength abandon her after expending so small an effort. Even speaking was depleting her. "Cousin Nehemiah, I don't feel that this wound will heal. This loss is too much for me to bear. I have wanted this baby so much. Why would God give him to me only to take him away?"

"All I can say is that your child was precious to Him. Planned by Him. For how could you have conceived him unless the hand of the Lord rested on you? No life can form in the womb without God's breath. Didn't King David say, *You knit me together in my mother's womb?* So you see, the little one that you had for such a brief time, grew inside you by the will of the Lord. God's awesome power knit him together within you. And this sweet life was treasured by Him."

"What good is it to know that God sorrows with me? It will not change my loss."

If Nehemiah noticed the bitterness in Sarah's outburst, he did not mention it. No reproach marred his voice as he answered. "King David said:

You will not leave my soul among the dead
or allow your holy one to rot in the grave.
You will show me the way of life,
Granting me the joy of your presence
And the pleasures of living with you forever.

"Not all the leaders of our people agree with me on this, but when I meditate on the words of our prophets, I grow convinced that your child will have the pleasures of living with God forever. Though you'll not have him in this lifetime, you can have the comfort of knowing that the grave will not have the last word. He'll be granted the joy of God's presence. And who knows but that in the world to come, you will be reunited?"

Sarah went still. Until that moment, she had been so drowned in her own grief and Darius's loss that she had thought of little else. Death had always seemed so final to her. For the first time she began to realize that God's sorrow might surpass her own. And that God's power might somehow surpass death.

She could not comprehend such mystery. But the God who had parted the sea in order to save her people surely had enough glory to rule over the destiny of an unborn baby.

The comfort Sarah had longed for, but could not grasp began to work its way against the great sadness that had enveloped her. "Will you pray for me?"

"Indeed, that is the reason I came."

Sarah put her face in her hands. She could feel her fingers shaking. "I have driven Darius away, Cousin Nehemiah. I did not tell him about the baby for fear that he would leave me behind in Susa. Now, he cannot forgive me. I think he blames me for the loss of the child."

A sigh trickled out of Nehemiah. If he felt any criticism or disappointment at Sarah's behavior, he kept it to himself. "We must leave these troubles in the Lord's hands. He is great enough to carry your burdens." Nehemiah began their prayers with a time of repentance on behalf of himself and Sarah, as well as on behalf of their forefathers before them. And then he prayed for the precious baby whose loss was like a sword piercing Sarah's heart.

"O Lord, God of heaven, we thank You for the gift of this child, though he was with us for such a brief time. We thank You for the blessing of the life that grew in Sarah's womb. We praise You that You hold that life in Your tender hands, and underneath are Your everlasting arms.

"Lord, cleanse Sarah's flesh and soul from the spirit of death that has touched her. Restore her with the breath of Your life.

"We return this babe to You, knowing that Your faithful love for him endures forever. Into Your hands we commit his spirit. Keep him safe under the shadow of Your wings.

"God, our Provider, heal the grief that has overwhelmed his mother and father. Bring Darius to forgive his wife. Draw him to You. Protect this marriage, and let it grow into a godly union. And Lord, bless this man and woman with more children."

As Nehemiah prayed, Sarah's tears flowed. It was as if her soul was being washed. It felt to her that the Lord Himself had drawn near, had caressed her with the tender love of a mother.

Her breath caught in her throat. She had blocked the sweet companionship of God's presence for a long time—blocked it by refusing to trust Him. She had grown so obsessed with arranging her own life that, unknowingly, she had withdrawn from Him bit by bit. And yet, here He was, the Lord of Eternity, offering her His peace. She became aware that God understood her loneliness and weakness. In the shadow of that discovery, she realized that although her sorrow had not departed, it no longer suffocated her with its weight.

Chapter 14

S arah straightened after trying to battle another attack of weakness and nausea. Pari handed her a damp towel. "It's as if you never lost the babe. You have the same symptoms as when you were pregnant."

"I know." Sarah sighed, leaning back against the pillows to give her belly a chance to settle. "I have retained the adverse effects of pregnancy without the joy of carrying a healthy baby in my womb."

"I suppose your body needs time to adjust."

"After more than eight weeks, you'd think it would have received the message that my womb is empty. I still haven't had my monthly cycle. And although I eat no more than before, I seem to be growing larger by the week."

"You will return to normal soon." Pari began to dust the walls of the cart. It had not rained once since they had started their journey ten weeks ago. The roads were rendered so dusty that the movement of their caravan created a whirlwind of interminably swirling dirt. The particles of fine dust found their way into their cart even when they kept their curtains shut. When the heat became too much to bear, they would open the curtains and roll back the canvas covering over their heads, braving the swirling muck for the sake of a bit of air.

Either way, their cart would become filthy. Pari and Sarah wiped every surface down two or three times a day. Within hours, however, a film of dirt covered everything—the sheets, the boards, the floors, their skin. There were times when the only thing Sarah could taste was dust.

Occasionally, Darius allowed their caravan to stop at a royal staging house for the evening. The women would linger in wooden baths, scrubbing themselves so that for a few lovely hours they felt clean. It did not last. As soon as they were on the road the next day, the sand wound its way into their clothes and their hair again.

Pari shook a pillow with fastidious vigor. "At least you have your appetite back. I tell you, my lady, you scared me half to death that first week. But now you are almost restored to your former strength."

"A good thing considering the pace my husband has set for us. We are no more than a few days' journey from Tadmore."

Pari plunked her slim body on a stool. "I thought I would cry when he wouldn't even allow us to stop for a few hours at the bazaars of Babylonia. It was sunset by the time we arrived and the sun had barely risen when we left. My first journey to Babylonia and the only thing I saw was the barest hint of the temple of Marduk from a great distance. I couldn't even purchase a handkerchief as a keepsake."

Sarah gave a wan smile. "Perhaps on our way back we shall have time to dawdle and shop."

"I doubt it."

Sarah felt a jolt at the sound of Darius's voice. He leapt from the back of his giant horse into the moving cart, his movements as lithe as a young wolf's.

"My lord." Sarah stood, holding on to a corner post before giving her husband a formal bow. Darius had fallen into the habit of stopping by every day for a short visit. He even deigned to speak to her, although his manner remained painfully distant. Gone was any display of tenderness. Gone were the playful remarks that brought quick laughter between them. Gone was any form of intimate warmth. Sarah did not understand why he bothered to visit her given the fact that he clearly did not enjoy her company.

He remained near the entrance of the cart, his posture stiff. "We are nearing Tadmore. We should be there in less than a week."

"So I have heard. It's an amazing feat, how far you and Nehemiah have managed to bring us in such a short time."

"Artaxerxes' letters to the governors of the region helped. Once we were west of the Euphrates River, many a ruler would have delayed us upon discovering our destination. No one dares to displease the king, however."

"Or his soldiers. I think the leader of every region we travelled through made up his mind not to make trouble for us before he saw Nehemiah's letters from the king. One look at you and your men and they became as friendly as a shepherd's dog."

Darius brushed at a piece of lint on his tunic. "I will part company with you in Tadmore."

Sarah's stomach gave a somersault. "With *me?*"

Darius's cheeks turned ruddy. "With the whole convoy, I mean. I go to Damascus, but the rest of you will proceed west to Lebanon to meet with Asaph, the keeper of the king's forests. We have already sent him a message so that he will have the timber Nehemiah needs ready for collection. From there, you will proceed to Jerusalem via secondary roads."

"I see. You will not come with us to Lebanon?"

"I must deal with this plot against the king. Nehemiah has more than adequate protection in the men I leave with him. Lysander shall be in charge of the military escort; he can deal with any trouble that might arise.

"I am certain that a number of the rulers we met in the Trans-Euphrates have already sent messages to their allies near Judah, warning them of Nehemiah's arrival. There will be no end of trouble."

"Does Nehemiah know?"

"Of course. The politics of this region are more familiar to him than to me. But foreknowledge is not enough to protect you. The situation remains volatile and dangerous. I have given Lysander instructions regarding your protection, Sarah. You will continue to have a detail of guards on the road, as well as later when you arrive in Jerusalem. I don't relish having to deal with a hostage situation. Do you understand me?"

"Yes, my lord. I will go nowhere without my guards."

"Good." He nodded once and hesitated, as if there was more he wished to say. Slowly, he reached out a hand toward her. Sarah held her breath. But the hand dropped with an awkward motion before it reached her. Without wasting time on common pleasantries or leave-taking, he jumped out of the cart with the same ease that he had hurtled into it.

Pari stared out into the bright day for a moment before putting a gentle arm around Sarah's waist. "He won't stay angry forever."

Sarah splayed her palms on her belly. She felt its emptiness like an unspoken indictment. "You underestimate my husband."

Sarah's life changed when they arrived in Tadmore. In the morning she waited for Darius to come and bid her goodbye. She did not expect a display of tenderness or kind words. She did, however, expect the formality of a leave-taking. He did not come. Knowing he was riding into danger, knowing that he might never see her again, he did not come.

Hurriedly, Sarah put on a loose garment and covered her hair with a cinnamon-colored scarf and ran to the road, worried she might miss him altogether. She felt too shy to force her company on him. Hiding behind Lysander's wide shoulders, she listened as Darius gave his final orders. His words flowed over her like a shower of meaningless sound. She could not make sense of them. She could make sense of nothing save that he was leaving.

He noticed her as he came forward to place a hand on Lysander's arm. Their eyes locked. In the early morning light, the black pupils of his eyes had contracted to tiny pinpoints so that the irises looked like green jewels—shiny, brittle, and ice-cold. Then he looked away and mounted his horse without a word. He did not look back—not once. Sarah lingered, gazing at his retreating back until he disappeared over the horizon, the sand whipping around his horse's hooves, Niq, Nassir, Arta, and Meres barely keeping up with him.

The convoy remained in Tadmore for three extra days, replenishing supplies and resting the animals. On the evening of the third day, Sarah was outside helping Nehemiah with some light record-keeping when a wave of weakness over-came her. Lysander happened to be standing near her; for a moment Sarah's knees buckled so that she half crashed into him. He whipped his face toward her. With the ease of athletic reflexes, he held her up.

She pulled away. "I beg your pardon. It's the heat. Sometimes it overcomes me."

"I doubt it. Lady Sarah, I need to examine you."

"A cool glass of water and I shall be restored. You need not worry."

"I don't believe water will cure what ails you. Come. Is your maid in your room at the inn?"

"Yes. But I don't see why this is necessary."

"Oh, it's necessary. Believe me."

Lysander leaned back after covering Sarah with the sheet again. He looked pale. For the first time Sarah began to feel an inkling of fear.

"What's wrong with me?"

"Nothing. You are in perfect health." There was a slight tremor in his voice. He shoved his hand through his flaxen hair and shook his head. "You see . . . well. I have some news."

Pari sank next to Sarah. "What is it? Will you spit it out, man?"

"My lady, you are pregnant."

"What?" Pari's voice mingled with her own as they stared wide-eyed at Lysander.

Sarah swallowed. "Were you mistaken when you said I had miscarried?"

"No. I was right about that."

"I can assure you I could not have conceived since."

"I believe you were pregnant with twins. It's the only explanation. You lost one of the babes. But the other has been flourishing in your womb. You must be about five months along. When you collapsed against me earlier, the idea seized me with sudden conviction. Your continued struggle with nausea, your lingering tiredness, the interruption of your cycle—they all pointed to one conclusion: that you must still be pregnant."

Sarah turned to her friend and saw a reflection of her own shock in Pari's face. They were too overcome to say anything for long moments.

"Are you certain?" Sarah croaked. "I mean—could you be mistaken? Perhaps I'm simply fat. That's what I thought."

Lysander shook his head. "There's no mistake. I am confident you are with child. The babe may be small. You don't show as much as other women at this stage. He will make his presence unmistakable in the next few weeks, no doubt."

Slowly, Lysander's incredible news began to sink its way into Sarah's benumbed heart. A flood of emotions overcame her. Joy. Astonishment. Doubt. Longing. Hope. Fear. Regret. There was such a tangle of feelings that she could not make sense of them. A babe grew within her. She was still pregnant. In four months, she would hold her child, wailing and squirming, in her arms. She had lost one child. Then against all expectation, against all reason, she had gained another.

God be praised . . . God be praised . . . God be praised . . . God be praised . . .

She began to laugh, overcome. Tears mingled with the laughter. Pari enfolded her in her long arms and the sound of their joy and weeping filled the room. When she had spent the last of her strength, Sarah looked up. Lysander stood near the door, pulling on his ear with an awkward repeated motion. Sarah wanted to run and grasp him in a sisterly embrace of jubilation, but she doubted he would welcome it. As it was, he appeared desperate to leave the room and escape the bubbling over of feminine sentimentality.

She realized that the person she truly wished to embrace in that moment was her husband. To share with him this unexpected joy and celebrate the miracle of the child they had made together. The desire was so strong that she would have jumped on the back of a horse and chased after him if she were not concerned for the well-being of her child.

"If only Darius knew," she said, springing up from the bed. "I did not tell him the first time. I wish I could tell him this very instant that he is going to be a father. I could write him a letter, couldn't I?"

The Greek shrugged. "It would be too dangerous to put that kind of news in a written message. If it fell into the wrong hands, your safety would be compromised. We assume that Darius's mission remains secret from the king's enemy, but we cannot be certain. If he has uncovered Darius's true intentions, the knowledge that his pregnant wife is within easy reach could prove too tempting, leading into a thorny hostage situation. Best you wait until he returns." He turned to leave.

"Lysander!" Sarah cried.

"Yes, my lady?"

"You are sure? Positive? I am truly with child?"

The pale blue eyes crinkled in the corners. "I would stake my life on it. You need have no worry on that score."

God be praised . . . God be praised . . . God be praised . . . God be praised . . . And yet, while her joy grew explosively, Sarah also felt a deeper ache for the baby she had lost. To have the one did not wipe away the grief of the other.

By the time they arrived in Lebanon, Sarah's battle with nausea faded, restoring her to a vitality she had not enjoyed for four months. They intended to collect an enormous shipment of timber from Asaph, the keeper of the king's

194

forests. Nehemiah came to visit Sarah on the afternoon they were to meet with Asaph.

"I need a competent scribe, Sarah. Someone has to keep accurate records of that timber. Are you well enough to accompany me and help?"

"I am feeling in excellent health, Cousin Nehemiah. Thank you." Sarah found herself at a quandary. She wanted Darius to be the first to find out about her pregnancy. But given the rapid expansion of her stomach and his prolonged absence, she could not hide this secret for long. In addition, she could not receive a commission from Nehemiah without letting him know of the added complexity and risks that were involved with her condition. If he wished her to work for him, he deserved to know. She prayed that Darius would find no offence in her decision. That he would not feel left out once again.

"I do have a surprise that I must share with you, my lord. You will find out for yourself soon enough; there will be no hiding this. I am with child."

The brown eyes widened; the dark red eyebrows raised so high they almost touched his hairline. Sarah could barely keep herself from laughing out loud at his utter astonishment.

"You are with child *again?*"

"I am with child *still*. Lysander thinks I was carrying twins. I lost one, but the other is healthy. I'm about five months along."

"I . . . I did not notice."

"Neither did I, if that is any comfort to you. I just thought I was growing fat."

Nehemiah pulled on his beard and made a noncommittal noise. "The Lord is merciful!"

"Words cannot capture my thankfulness. He has blessed me with His goodness."

"Does your husband know?"

"No. I found out after he left."

"We best let you rest then. He would never forgive me if I put you to work now."

"I can do light record-keeping. It will be good for me to occupy my mind with beneficial things. I worry about Darius when I have nothing to do."

Nehemiah finally gave in and assigned several tasks to Sarah. With the knowledge of her pregnancy buoying her spirits, and work she enjoyed, she began to feel she could face life again. Not a day went by that she did not miss Darius. His absence ate at her like a bleeding wound. If they had not parted in such grave disharmony, she would have borne their separation better. As it was, she wondered if even knowing that she carried his child would soften his heart toward her. Once, she had hoped that he would come to love her. Now she wondered if he would stop hating her.

She spent long hours in prayer, like in the days she had first come to the Lord. He grew more real to her than Jerusalem itself.

Joy and grief settled in her soul like uneasy housemates. Guilt ate at her when she felt happy, for it seemed obscene that she should experience so much joy when she had lost a child, and when her husband seemed to have abandoned her.

Chapter 15

Darius concealed Niq and Nassir just outside Damascus in a small inn, leaving Meres to keep an eye on them. They had strict instructions to keep out of the way until he sent for them. The last thing he needed was for the assassin to spot the Babylonian brothers. Darius knew his best weapon against the king's enemy was the element of surprise. If the assassin found out that they had followed his scent to Damascus, he would burrow so far underground that no one would ever discover him.

The palace in Damascus resembled a miniature paradise. Luxury ruled the court. Silk hangings and carpets, the effulgence of hundreds of lamps burning late into the night, endless wine served in gold and silver chalices, priceless perfumes. Darius thought that old general Megabyzus would roar with disapproval if he saw the waste. But he lived safely tucked away in Persia, spending his waning years in comfort. Artaxerxes wished to spare him from the pressures of rule. He remained satrap in name only, receiving the honor and financial reward without having direct command.

Darius presented himself to Pyrus, the man appointed by Artaxerxes to govern the province of Beyond the River in Megabyzus's permanent absence. The appointment was another nod in the old general's direction since Pyrus was Megabyzus's nephew. No doubt a few strings had been pulled to make the appointment possible. Nepotism had grown rampant amongst the new generations of Persian royalty.

"Lord Darius, welcome!" Pyrus pronounced with loud enthusiasm when Darius introduced himself. Darius, who had never set eyes on him until that day, had to endure a wine-soaked kiss and an intimate embrace from the acting governor.

He gave a stiff bow. "His Majesty sends me with his compliments."

"How thoughtful of him! I hope our tribute pleased him? I would have come myself, except that I had a terrible bout of toothache." The smile he flashed was grim enough to indicate he continued to harbor a decaying tooth.

"The king expressed immense satisfaction with your offering."

"And what brings you to our court?" The lax face sharpened. It occurred to Darius that the man might not be as frivolous as he might seem. He seemed keen enough to know he was being measured, at any rate.

"I travel with the new governor to the province of Judah. The king wished me to stop in Damascus and inquire after your well-being as well as to inform you of the new developments in

Judah. The new governor, Nehemiah, intends to rebuild the walls of Jerusalem. The king wishes you to know in case trouble arises in the region."

"His Majesty is famed for his generous consideration."

Was that a touch of irony Darius detected? Or merely too much wine? The acting satrap was young—no older than thirty. Garbed in embroidered silk from head to foot, his jewelry could probably stock the treasury of the whole empire for a good many days. Darius was no longer surprised at the extent of extravagance in the court. Indeed, he wondered at it not being worse.

After a long dinner with more courses than one of Damaspia's formal affairs, a new high official arrived who was introduced to Darius as Zikir. Dressed in mourning, Zikir met Darius with a stiff bow and few words.

"Lost his grandson to some unfortunate accident recently, poor sod," Pyrus mumbled in Darius's ear. "He was never a cheerful man. But now! May the divine Ahura Mazda help us. He is like a mobile funeral. It's as if he sucks all cheer when he walks into a room."

"I am sorry to hear of his loss. How did his grandson die?"

"No one's bothered to tell me about it. He used to work around here. I liked him. He had gratifying taste in clothes and the kind of style one does not expect to find Beyond the River in Damascus. Much better company than his grandfather."

Darius racked his memory for more information on Zikir, but could not recall anything. He observed the man give orders with dignity. He seemed to have a lot of influence in the court of Damascus. Other officials treated him with a grave respect, which they lacked when they addressed Pyrus.

As Darius studied the faces around the hall, a young man caught his attention. He seemed familiar. He had dark blond hair, curled in the Persian fashion, and his beard and mustache were dark for such light skin. His loose tunic hid a slim build. Lounging behind a table as he was made it hard to assess his height. Darius guessed it to be just above average. No matter how hard he tried, Darius could not remember where he had seen him before.

He leaned toward Pyrus. The overpowering scent of sandalwood assailed his nose and he pulled back. "Who is that young man?" he asked, pointing with a subtle move of his chin. "The one in the green robe, sitting toward the end of the hall?"

"That one? He is a pretty boy, isn't he? A mere merchant, sadly. Belongs to the king. He's been here for some weeks in order to commission something or other. Because we are located conveniently between Egypt and Babylonia, we are a haven for merchants. Many such men visit us."

"His name?"

Pyrus straightened the wide sleeve of his tunic. "Cyrus, I believe. Not terribly original."

Darius could not recall having met a merchant named Cyrus. Yet something about the man nagged at him. He felt certain they had met before.

With a sudden move, his host swiveled with enthusiasm, spitting a piece of half-eaten date on the table in his haste. "I forgot to mention it earlier, my lord! You have arrived on an auspicious day. We have arranged for a horse race tomorrow. It will be as exciting as anything you would have experienced in Persepolis, I assure you. Would you like to enter the race?"

"I appreciate your invitation. Given the fact that I have been on horseback without interruption for three months, I must resist the temptation. I shall enjoy attending, of course."

"Excellent. Would you like to place a wager? I can give you a few insightful tips."

Darius wiped a round froth of Pyrus's spittle from his chest. "Thank you. I believe I will enjoy the races better if I am merely observing."

"Ah. That's too bad. One of the favored odds is on that fellow Cyrus you inquired about. You should see him on the back of a horse."

"Indeed? How interesting, considering he is a merchant."

"Yes. But he rides like a cavalry officer."

• • •

The races were held early in the morning. Pyrus arrived late, holding up the ceremonies by his delay, looking puffy-eyed and pale. He found his way to Darius.

"Abominable hour. But it's the only time of day when the sun does not make physical exertion unbearable. It's no easy task standing around and watching a race this time of year."

Darius gave an amused sidelong glance at his host. "It's not very easy for those running the race either."

"Oh, them." Pyrus waved a pristine white handkerchief in the air. "They are accustomed to it."

Darius, who had run his share of races, didn't bother to correct him. Instead, he began to examine the riders. He found Cyrus the merchant sitting astride a magnificent horse, lingering toward the back of the line. Again, something about him niggled at Darius's mind. The way he sat his horse, the way he held the reins, the way he tapped the animal's neck with an affectionate hand—it all seemed familiar. Where had Darius seen him? He was no merchant—of that, he was certain.

The race began, and before long Cyrus the merchant had settled himself comfortably in the middle of the pack. It was a long race, and he appeared wise enough to pace himself. Darius admired the young man's seat, his mastery over the horse, and the ease with which he navigated the crowded racetrack. With unconscious grace, Cyrus leaned forward and signaled his horse to break out. The horse flew.

Darius stiffened. He had seen that exact move one year before. A different horse, but the same rider. He tightened his mouth in an unconscious gesture of displeasure. Cyrus, indeed.

Cyrus won the race. He deserved it; Darius had to give him that. No one on the track matched his technique or sheer grace. When the crowd of admirers surrounding him thinned, Darius drew near.

"Hello, Roxanna," he whispered in her ear. "That beard does not become you."

She did not blink. "It's as itchy as a thousand mosquito bites. But one must put up with these inconveniences for the greater good."

Darius wrapped a peremptory hand around her arm. "Let's go somewhere we can talk without interruption, shall we?"

To his utter amazement, she threw him a nonchalant smile. "I am at your service, my lord."

He had to admire her nerve. Any other high-born woman caught in the guise of a man and misrepresenting herself as an agent of the king would be trembling with fear. Roxanna seemed to be enjoying herself.

Not far from the racetrack, Darius spotted a verdant garden and began to guide Roxanna that way. After scanning the area to make certain they were alone, he turned on her. "What do you think you are doing? Last year was bad enough. But this is insanity."

Roxanna was the daughter of an aristocrat—a lady of high rank. She also happened to be one of the best riders in Persia. The year before, she had donned male disguise and entered a race in Ecbatana. Although royal women were taught to ride and allowed to participate in hunts with men, their freedom did not extend to public races. No woman with aristocratic blood dared enter such a spectacle.

Except Roxanna. As any witless fool could have predicted, her ruse ended in disgrace.

Roxanna had not only broken the rules, but she had also shown the poor judgment to win the race. Unfortunately for the girl, several people had recognized her, since she had been surrounded by family and friends in Ecbatana. The court was scandalized. Last he had heard, her betrothed had broken their engagement, saying he could not join his life to a woman who would no doubt continue to embarrass him in public.

Come to think of it, Darius owed her something of a debt. The scandal of her race had overshadowed the wagging tongues about the debacle of his wedding. At the time, he had been hiding in Ecbatana, trying to forget his disaster of a bride.

The thought of his wife made him harsher than he intended to be. "What would your father say if he saw you now?"

"No doubt he would say he was glad he had disowned me."

Darius swallowed the string of words he was about to unleash. "He *disowned* you?"

Roxanna shrugged. "Sad, isn't it?"

"Never mind that. Do you know what the king would do to you if he found out you were impersonating one of his merchants? Have you lost your wits?"

"Artaxerxes is a forgiving man, unlike my father. I don't think *he* would disown me."

Darius's eyes widened. "Great holy fires! *You* are the king's agent. You are his spy in Damascus."

Roxanna clapped him on the back. "Excellent powers of deduction. Artaxerxes must adore you."

"I don't understand. How did you end up working for him?"

"After my father disowned me, he arranged to send me to a distant village near Ionia where he owns extensive property. He expected me to spend the rest of my life in lonely exile there. Artaxerxes heard of the arrangement and disapproved. He sent a few of his men to kidnap me while on my way to Ionia."

"He forced you to work for him?"

"Heavens, no. He had no need of that. He gave me a choice. Ionia or his service. Of course I jumped at the chance of becoming one of his spies. He put me to train under one of his masterminds before setting me loose on the world. It'd make your hair stand on end, the things I can do now."

"Does your father know?"

"Of course not. He was told I was kidnapped. By whom or why, he has no idea."

Darius began to pace. "This is the height of irresponsibility, Roxanna. I don't know what Artaxerxes was thinking. You have no idea how much danger you are in. This is no job for a highborn girl."

"That's for me and the king to decide." The honey-colored eyes grew narrow and cool.

"So you're going to spend the rest of your life donning men's clothing and wearing a false beard, pretending to be something you're not?"

"Don't be an idiot. There are plenty of situations where a woman has more use as a spy than a man. This case presents an exception. Artaxerxes didn't feel I would be effective around Pyrus as a woman. Now, do you want my report?"

"Confound it. Yes, I want your report."

"Good decision. I have followed the trail of the seal the king sent me and found the designer. As you surmised, it was commissioned here in Damascus."

"Oh, good work, Roxanna," Darius cried, forgetting his disapproval of moments before. "Who commissioned it?"

"Alas, I could not find that out. The designer never knew. He discovered a pouch on his workbench when he arrived at his shop some months ago. A letter inside gave him directions for the design of the seal."

"Where did he drop it off? Who paid him?"

"The payment was included with the commission letter. He was directed to leave the pouch with the seal at the base of a particular tree in the woods. He obeyed his absent employer's instructions and never heard about it again."

"Another dead end. This man begins to exasperate me. At least we now know for certain that our assassin is in Damascus. That rules out general Megabyzus himself. How about Pyrus? He is Megabyzus's nephew, after all. Could he be working for his uncle behind the scenes?"

"I would be surprised if Pyrus is involved in anything more drastic than accepting a few juicy bribes. He loves his position and title, not to mention the luxury they afford him. He would not jeopardize them. I cannot see him masterminding an assassination plot, or even acting as a lackey on behalf of his uncle. I've never even known him to be fully sober."

"Who is Zikir? He seems to wield considerable power."

"Astute observation. He carries a lot of weight in this court. Before Artaxerxes named Pyrus acting satrap, everyone expected Zikir to ascend to power. He hails from Damascus and has considerable connections both with the old guard Beyond the River, and with the Persian government. His authority has not waned although the king has withheld the title from him. Pyrus might be the official leader here, but Zikir rules by force of old influences."

"Perhaps he holds a grudge against the king for overlooking him."

Roxanna slashed her hand in a dismissive gesture. "He's famed for being a faithful vassal to the Persian Empire. Why would he risk everything by trying to murder the king for the sake of a promotion? He still holds most of the practical power in Trans-Euphrates."

"Well *someone* tried to kill the king."

"Don't look at me with that accusing expression. I didn't do it."

"Wished that you had. Then I would wring your little neck and be done."

"Sorry to disappoint you. Look, I've just run an exhausting race. Now, I am going to collect my prize, eat a hearty lunch, bathe, and take a nap. Meanwhile, I shall leave you to discover who lies behind this twisted plot."

Darius kicked a loose rock and sent it hurtling into the air. "Marvelous. I have to save the Persian Empire and who do I have to help me? A girl in a fake beard who likes to take naps and two brothers who think the law is a mild suggestion."

Chapter 16

The heat wave broke the afternoon the convoy arrived in Jerusalem. A gentle drizzle started as they entered Judah's boundaries, and it continued until they reached their destination. After weeks of scorching heat, the cool rain felt like balm on a throbbing burn.

Tears mingled with rain on Sarah's skin as they entered the city. She wasn't the only one weeping; every man and woman belonging to the lineage of Abraham cried as they came within sight of Jerusalem. They were tears of joy for returning to their ancestral home. They were also tears of horror as they saw the state of the city.

City was a euphemism. Except for a few extensive buildings and its large territory, Jerusalem had been reduced to a village—and a dilapidated one at that. The walls had sustained considerable damage; in some places they had been razed to the ground. Debris was scattered around in chaotic disorder. As far as the eye could see, the evidence of fire seared the land. The convoy rode through what must have once been a gate. A few pieces of scorched timber were all that remained of the frame. They must have been magnificent in their day, judging by their width and height. Now they were a withered reminder of lost dreams.

"*This* is the City of David?" Pari asked, her voice high with shock.

"What remains of it."

"Lord Nehemiah will need a miracle to restore this place, my lady," Pari whispered so that no one could overhear them.

There were few on the convoy from Persia who were privy to Nehemiah's plans to restore Jerusalem. Those who knew had been instructed by Nehemiah to keep his intentions secret, particularly in Judah, until such time as he was ready to unveil his purpose. The only thing that the city officials knew was that the king had appointed Nehemiah as the new governor of the region.

"I fear you're right, my friend. Even Nehemiah cannot manage to turn this rubble into a city. Not without God's intervention."

"Why don't the people who live here clean up the debris? It's such a mess."

"It's as if the inhabitants have descended so far into despair that they no longer care about the state of their home."

Until such time as Nehemiah could build his own house, he and his retinue took residence in an old building belonging to one of Jerusalem's noble families. The house had remained uninhabited for a decade, and the city's desolation had not helped its state. Sarah and Pari were given a small room with peeling clay walls. Flies competed with spiders for residency. Sarah would have preferred to remain in their cart and sleep outdoors. But Nehemiah and Lysander both deemed it unsafe and packed her into her unpleasant room.

For Sarah, the first three days in Judah passed in a haze. Whenever possible she followed Nehemiah, writing letters, taking down information, and gathering old records while her cousin met with the leaders of Jerusalem. He hid his intentions during those meetings, choosing instead to listen to each official's report. Mostly, the men griped about how difficult their situation was. None of them took responsibility for the state of the city. They blamed everyone but themselves. Sarah noticed with amusement that her cousin would turn bright red during such discourses. He did manage to control his tongue however—an impressive feat considering the provocation.

Late on the evening of the third day, Sarah heard hushed voices outside her door. Startled by an intrusion so late at night, she cracked her door open and caught the tail of Nehemiah's robes swishing down the stairs, accompanied by his brother.

"What is it, my lady?" Pari said, her tones too soft to be overheard.

"The new governor is up to something. He's

sneaking about in the night. Shall we discover his intentions?"

Pari shook her head. "It's precisely this attitude that gets you into trouble, you do realize?"

"Does it? I had not noticed," Sarah said, as she covered her head in a modest linen scarf.

In the courtyard, her cousin was surrounded by a handful of men, his brother Hanani and Lysander among them. One small torch lit their way. There were no pack animals; obviously, Nehemiah was more interested in secrecy than in comfort, and the noise of the animals would have alerted half the city to their late-night activities. Nehemiah rode a biddable donkey; the rest were on foot.

Sarah cleared her throat. Seven heads swiveled in her direction.

"Good grief, girl! What are you about, sneaking around this time of night?" her cousin said.

"Funny you should mention, sir. I wanted to ask you the same thing."

"A few of us are going to inspect the city secretly, if you must know. And before you ask— no! You cannot come. It is too dangerous for a pregnant woman. Go back to bed, where you belong."

"I have no intention of coming. However, I would appreciate a report after your return. For the records, of course."

"Of course."

• • •

Once they left the densely populated area of the city, Nehemiah directed several torches to be lit. They proceeded through the Valley Gate, located southwest of the city where there were few settlements, past the Jackal's Well. Then they trudged over to the Dung Gate at the southern end of the eastern wall.

Just beyond the gate lay the Hinnom Valley, where the people of Jerusalem discarded their garbage. The smell of rotting rubbish was so overwhelming that it almost made Nehemiah gag. He wrapped his face in a kerchief and noticed that even Lysander was doing the same.

From the back of his donkey Nehemiah could observe the devastation of the walls with grim clarity. No part of the once impenetrable structure stood whole. The foundation remained solid in parts; in other places, the wall was halfway up. Most sections, however, had suffered utter destruction. In the white light of the moon, brightened by the fire of their torches, the desolation of Jerusalem cried out like the howling of mourning women. Defeat sat at their door like a living presence.

The men of his party had to walk with care, for their path was strewn with broken masonry and rubble. While this became an inconvenience, it also proved promising. Some of the stones scattered about on the ground were whole enough to be used again. Many large pieces had survived the devastation. Already cut, and having sustained minimum damage, they were ready for building again.

Without uttering a word, the group walked all the way to the Fountain Gate and from there to the King's Pool. The debris became so bad at one point that Nehemiah's donkey could no longer get through. He changed their course, heading for the Kidron Valley instead to inspect the state of the wall there.

No improvement could be found in this section of the wall; it seemed as ruined as everything else they had seen thus far. They ended their expedition here and backtracked, returning to Jerusalem through the Valley Gate. Their inspection had only covered the southern part of the city. Nehemiah reckoned it was more than enough to give him the information he needed.

Sarah awoke early the next morning and found Judah's governor already busy.

"Ah, good. I can use your help," he said when he saw her. "I've sent for the Jewish leaders. They are about to find that their lives are going to change." He pointed to a diminutive alcove set behind the farthest edge of the hall. "Sit in that corner, behind the half wall. Don't say a word, mind. Not one chirp. I doubt the men of Judah will take kindly to a female scribe. A *pregnant* female scribe."

Sarah patted the growing bulge of her belly and grinned.

"I've kept my own notes and memoirs concerning this journey since we were in Susa. But having your records will add details that I might not have time to include. Have you brought your writing implements? Good."

Soon, the priests, the nobles, the officials, and other important administrative staff of Judah began to trickle in.

Judah's new governor began the meeting with a description of his findings the night before. Sarah wrote down his words as fast as she was able.

"But I tell you nothing that you don't already know," he said when he finished recounting what he had seen. "You see the trouble we are in. People of Judah, the city of our fathers lies in ruins. There is not one gate that remains standing."

Nehemiah pulled an elegant hand through his dark red hair. The rustling of his silk garments sounded stark in the heavy silence. "The state of our nation disgraces us. Our enemies gloat over our diminished circumstances. The Lord's people suffer because of it. A vibrant life cannot be established in this city unless it enjoys the protection of well-made walls. As it stands, the city of Jerusalem is not large enough to sustain farming; it's not busy enough for commerce; and it is not safe enough for crowds. We cannot build our homes in Jerusalem unless it can be defended against raiders.

"Let us end this shame, brothers. Let us rebuild the wall of Jerusalem. The Lord has opened a way for us. The king himself, who stopped this project when he believed our enemies' lies, has given me leave to commence it once more."

A quiet murmur rose in the room. Men's voices gathered strength as they questioned the new governor's news. Nehemiah held up his arms, silencing the chatter.

"Don't think I have accomplished this because I am a friend of the king's or because I am a good politician. The gracious hand of my God was upon me when I was in Artaxerxes' presence. That's the reason I gained his favor. Because of it, the king has given me authority to inaugurate this mission.

"We've even been given timber from the royal forests. But the tallest trees of Persia and all the gold from its treasury cannot fulfill this task unless you give the Lord your wholehearted cooperation. I cannot manage this work alone. It requires every leader, every man and woman of Jerusalem, to band together. Come then: Let us commit to the task; let us face the battle; let us put our backs to the toil—each to our part, each to our position; there is not a week, nor a day, nor a moment to lose."

Sarah's heart rose like thunder, motivated to do anything that her cousin demanded. Nehemiah could persuade the dead. She was not the only one affected by his speech. He spurred such a passion in the leadership of Judah that they forgot their fears and complaints and began to shout their agreement. They would begin the good work. They would rebuild the walls. And nothing would stop them.

Nehemiah gave a modest smile and held up his hands. "We need to organize our people if we are to progress. I have made some plans."

When the leaders left, Sarah rose from her cramped hiding place. Her body was changing rapidly so that what might have been comfortable one day before, grew challenging hours later. She stretched and bit her lip as pain shot through her hip. A small movement in the core of her belly brought her up short. Her baby was quickening.

"What's wrong, dear girl?" Nehemiah's worried voice interrupted the incredible moment of discovery.

"I felt the babe move in my womb for the first time."

"Ah. He must have liked my speech."

Sarah laughed. For an old bachelor, her cousin handled her pregnancy with great aplomb. "My child has auspicious timing." She patted the rise of her stomach. "That went well. I had expected resistance from them. Instead, you had them agreeing to your every suggestion."

Nehemiah returned to his table, which boasted

a pile of parchments he had been studying earlier. "Don't be fooled. There will be trouble. From within and from without. We shall have many hard battles ahead of us."

"Cousin Nehemiah? What makes you so determined? If you know the work is going to be hard and mired in discouragement, why do you persist?"

Nehemiah rolled up a parchment and tapped its end against his palm. "Because I believe I was called to this. What do you think destiny is? A smooth path that never jostles you? No. When you walk in your destiny, you will crash and fall more times than you can count. But the secret is to hold on to God's vision for your life—and for the lives of those He puts under your charge. No matter how many times you fall, crash, and fail, you get up. You get up and face your obstacles."

As he began to coordinate the enormous project before him, Nehemiah directed Sarah to keep an exact record of the individuals constructing the wall. He wanted her to archive their names as well as the location of their work.

"Don't go chasing after each one around Jerusalem. Stay away from the walls, Sarah. I will charge Lysander's men to bring you reports twice a day."

Searching through her writing box for fresh ink on the first afternoon that the work began, Sarah noticed a short roll of parchment. With an unpleasant chill, she recognized the ivory-colored sheepskin: the note that had been given to Nassir by the mastermind of the plot to kill the king. It had been some months since she had studied it. Unrolling the parchment, she began to read.

Carry out the instructions I send you. You now have everything you need for the New Year ceremonies.

It had never been delivered to the intended assassin, of course. Sarah read the words again, this time with more intensity. The distance of months must have swept aside the cobwebs of her mind. For the first time she noticed a vital clue, which she had missed during the first round of her inspections.

This note was not addressed to a stranger.

As fast as her growing stomach allowed, she sprang to her feet and went in search of Lysander. She found him in the courtyard, parceling out fresh orders to his men. He gave her a sidelong glance and dismissed his men.

"I need to speak to you. It's urgent."

Lysander wasted no time on questions, following her inside the dilapidated residence. She put the parchment in his hand. "I've found out something important. This note is not addressed to a stranger."

"Start from the beginning. What note?"

"The one we found on the Babylonians."

Lysander unrolled the parchment and, after a

brief glance, gave it back to Sarah. "I can't read Aramaic. What does it say?"

Curbing her impatience, Sarah read it to him. "What I realized as I reread it is that it is addressed to someone familiar. This is not a letter to some unknown assassin. It's a missive addressed to a person whom the author knew. *May you walk in safety.* That's almost sentimental. They knew each other. They might even have been fond of each other."

"I see. I will send a messenger to your husband. It's a subtle distinction, but perhaps he will find it of use."

Sarah nodded and turned to leave. Without warning, a sharp pain, like a small arrow, pierced her abdomen. Unlike the muscular twinges that plagued her when she stayed in one spot for too long, this pain came low and deep, as if from the center of her womb. Her eyes widened with shock. The discomfort passed quickly, but fear settled over her like a boulder. The memory of her miscarriage remained too fresh for her to ignore such a peculiar sensation.

"My lady? Are you unwell?"

"A passing pain. Do you think . . . ?"

Lysander frowned. "Let's not arrive at premature conclusions. I must examine you."

Lysander's expression remained bland as he dried his hands on a clean towel. "I cannot be certain.

This is not a branch of medicine with which I have sufficient familiarity. You have bled a small amount. I believe this happens to some women. The sharp pain you describe may also be normal for this stage of your travail. But given your recent miscarriage, I am unprepared to take undue chances. You need a physician who specializes in women and birthing, and there is none to be found in this dilapidated province. All I have unearthed so far is midwives who know less than I."

Sarah glanced over at Pari; reflected in her friend's face she saw the same grim fear that had hold of her own mind. Lacing her fingers together, she squeezed them to hide their wild trembling. The thought of losing another baby was too much for her. "What do you suggest?"

"I know of a physician in Damascus who is famed for his expertise in this area. I myself met him years ago when I was stationed there, and I have great respect for his ability. But he has a terror of travelling and would never come to us. We would have to take you to him." He looped his hands as they hung between his knees.

"Bringing you to Damascus would be risky in the midst of this plot business. Your husband will no doubt have my hide for exposing you to danger before I have the opportunity to explain. I see no other way, however. I cannot leave you here and just wait for nature to take its course. If we travel very slowly to ensure your well-being, we should arrive in a few days. And then you can have the best of care."

Sarah nodded, grasping at this ray of hope. "Darius will understand once you explain. He only wants my safety. I know that now. If being in Damascus provides that, he will come to approve of your decision, and even applaud your initiative."

Lysander raised a skeptical eyebrow. "Applaud it or no, he will have to live with it. I cannot make any other choice under the circumstances." He stood up. "I'll send him a message to prepare him for our arrival. We'll leave at first light."

"Thank you, Lysander. I will let the governor know of our departure." Nehemiah would miss both of them, she thought.

"Try not to worry, my lady. The baby rests soundly within you. This journey to Damascus is a mere precaution."

Chapter 17

Disbelief gripped Darius as he studied the message from Lysander. With narrowed eyes he read the words again. Lysander had kept it brief, no doubt in deference to the possibility that the letter might fall into the wrong hands. He only said that due to an urgent development he was personally escorting Sarah to Damascus.

Darius crumbled the bit of papyrus in his fist. Had the Spartan lost his mind? What could have possessed him, dragging his wife into the middle of danger when he knew this was the one situation that Darius had been determined to avoid?

He pushed his hand through his hair. Tomorrow, he would see Sarah. Not an hour had gone by since he had left her that he had not thought of her. Sometimes longing for her filled him like a tidal wave. More often, the thought of his lost baby cooled his ardor. Grief and resentment made powerful defenses against tenderness. He still could not stomach her betrayal. How could a woman who seemed so loving act with such manipulative self-interest?

And how could a soldier as experienced as Lysander justify conveying his superior officer's wife to Damascus while Darius was neck deep in a delicate investigation? He considered landing a powerful punch on the man's square jaw upon his arrival in advance of conducting a reasonable investigation. The thought brought a grim smile to his face.

Before he lost all focus, he scripted a quick note, ordering Lysander to bring Sarah to the inn where he had already concealed the Babylonians, hoping the obscure location might protect her. He handed the letter to the messenger with orders for an expeditious delivery, making certain the man knew where to find the party on the road.

Alone, Darius poured himself a goblet of wine and inclined against a cushion, trying to make sense of the day's events. The sound of footsteps forced him out of his reverie. He looked up with shock at the sight of Roxanna, who paraded in and threw herself on the iron bed.

"You look like you just tasted water from a camel's trough," she said. "Bad news?"

"Who let you in here?" He was outraged by her audacity, traipsing into his private chamber as if she were not an unmarried woman from the flower of Persian society. The beard did ruin the effect somewhat. But that was not the point. Had the world lost its collective wits? Was he the only sane person left on earth?

"I let myself in. Your guard found himself pre-occupied, I'm afraid. I could not spy for Artaxerxes if I asked permission every time I tried to enter a room."

"Next time, knock. You're not spying on me."

"Says who? The king is very interested in the activities of his most faithful servants. Just in case."

Darius threw a pillow at her with the precision of a spear. It landed on her face before she could dodge, and knocked her beard askew. She sat up, her face red with rage. "Very comical."

At any other time, he would have laughed at her odd, lopsided appearance. He could not muster the will for humor just then, however. "You had better repair that. No one would believe you're a man if they saw you now."

Roxanna settled herself on a stool with her back to him and peered into a silver mirror. "Blast. It took me an hour to get that right."

"While you see to your frippery, allow me to fill you in on important new information I just received." He described Lysander's letter.

"A conjugal visit in the midst of secret investigations. How nice for you. I heard your wife was a handful. The details of your wedding feast entertained the women in my father's household for weeks. I've been dying to meet her ever since. She's the only woman besides the queen who sounds remotely entertaining."

"You aren't coming anywhere near her, Roxanna. The two of you together will probably bring about the end of the empire as we know it."

Roxanna turned to face Darius, once again looking convincingly male. "Don't be such a tyrant, Darius. I'm certain she would enjoy my company."

A loud knock brought their discourse to an abrupt end. Darius threw Roxanna a tense glance and placed a silencing finger to his lips. Without warning, he whipped the door open. Roxanna's servant waited on the other side. He did not seem startled by the violence of his welcome. After bowing with admirable calm, he offered his mistress a long package.

"This came for you directly from the king's secretary, my lord. According to his letter, I was to bring it to you without delay."

Roxanna took the package. "What is it?"

"A gift for the satrap of Egypt. The royal secretary bids that you deliver it when you are finished with your work in Damascus."

"Thank you. I'll see to it." She dismissed the man with a nod.

Darius leaned against a crooked wall. "Does your servant know who you are? He called you *my lord*."

"He knows. He's too discreet to slip his guard when we are in public. Like all the king's men, he knows his craft well."

"Why couldn't he wait until you returned to your chambers to give you the satrap's gift?"

"Because," Roxanna said as she began to unwrap

the folds of fabric, "there is a message from the king hidden in here somewhere."

Inside the fabric packaging they found a thick linen robe, decorated with gold thread and jewels of a size that were more vulgar than elegant.

Darius stroked the fabric. "Revolting, but expensive."

"Not everyone has your superior taste, my lord." Roxanna removed a thin knife from an inside pocket in her loose robe. She began feeling around the Egyptian satrap's gift. To Darius's surprise she slashed open a section in the hem of the robe.

"I hope you are good at mending."

"Can't sew a stitch. Thankfully, the king's servant is handy with a needle." She searched through the torn area until a small roll of parchment dropped out of the hem onto the ground.

She took a moment to read it and swore. "The king has been attacked again."

"Is he injured?"

"Not seriously. They were hunting in the royal enclosure when someone shot an arrow at him. It grazed him in the arm. His armor deflected most of the damage, but it was a close call."

Darius sank to the edge of his bed. "Did they catch the culprit?"

"I'm afraid not. By the time they found his perch, he was long gone. The king grows impatient with the delay in our investigations."

"I can imagine how grating this must be from

his point of view. He sits on his throne, helpless, knowing that every time he eats or sleeps or rides, it is an opportunity for a clever assassin to put an end to his life. We cannot afford to dawdle with cautious investigations, anymore. Our assassin is growing bolder. We must take a more aggressive stance in our inquiry."

Darius rode to the inn, his stomach turning somersaults with tension. In a few moments, he would see Sarah. He had spent half the night trying to figure out what could motivate Lysander to bring her to Damascus. The more he had pondered the strange circumstance, the heavier his anxiety had grown. He knew Lysander would not have made such a decision lightly.

Nothing could have prepared him for what awaited him in the diminutive, private bedchamber. He noticed inconsequential details as he walked in: the whitewashed walls; Pari's downcast face; Sarah's hair, lying loose down her back like a waterfall of silk; the green embroidery on her blue linen dress; the way her eyes softened when she saw him. And then, with speech-robbing, mind-numbing shock, the rise of her belly, which pressed against the fabric of her loose gown. His wife, who had bled the life of their baby into his arms only weeks ago, was clearly with child.

Darius had spent a significant part of his childhood learning to control his emotions. Learning to conceal the expression of them. His long-practiced defenses failed him. He had to remind himself to close his mouth. He whipped his head to the corner of the room where Lysander waited.

"Did you . . . did you misdiagnose her condition?"

"No. She must have been carrying twins. She lost one that morning. The other . . ." He made a vague gesture toward Sarah. "As you see."

Darius felt torn between the desire to pull his wife into his arms, to feel the new curves of her body pressed against him, their child cradled between them, and the equally strong need to keep his distance. He leaned against the wall, crossing his legs at the ankles to give the impression that he hadn't a care in the world. He would rather have fought against Niq and his staff for a week straight than admit he needed the wall for support.

"I see. You brought her all the way to Damascus in order to show me this?"

"Of course not. I brought her because there's a complication."

Darius straightened. He forced himself to look at Sarah. "You'd better sit down."

She obeyed him, her movements awkward. For the first time he noted her pallor and the dark circles under her wide eyes. She was tired. As Lysander spelled out the risk to the pregnancy, Darius studied her from the corner of his eye. She was on the verge of tears. The thought of losing this child weighed heavy on her.

"Is Sarah's life in peril?" he asked Lysander, careful to keep his voice neutral.

"I don't think so. I don't even know if the baby is at risk. But I could not take a chance, given what happened before."

Darius gave a slow nod. "You made the right decision. Thank you for bringing her."

Lysander gave a tight smile. "I'm relieved you think so. I feared you'd strike me first and ask questions later."

"I considered it." He lifted his chin toward Sarah. "The sight of her made me forget my intentions."

"I was counting on that. Now, I'd better go fetch the physician."

"Take Pari with you."

Alone with Sarah, Darius found himself at a loss for words. "Are you hungry?" he asked, trying to sound solicitous. He felt stupid. Here she was, carrying his baby, the child he had wanted with such desperation, and all he could ask was whether she wanted food?

"No, thank you." Her voice was soft. Uncertain. "Are you . . . are you happy about the baby?"

His heart contracted at the hesitance in her voice. "Of course. I'm very happy." *Astounded. Dumbfounded. But happy.*

"It would have been lovely to have had twins."

Darius sank into a stool. "One is good too."

She looked up. Her large brown eyes were swimming and vulnerable. He felt his breath catch. "Would you like to feel him? You never had the chance before."

He went down to kneel beside her. She had sat down on the edge of the bed. The mattress, stuffed with straw, must have been old, for lumps poked out in various places. She bent forward and caught his hand in hers. Gently, she laid his palm flat against the bulge of her stomach. She was large enough to be unmistakably pregnant, but not so large as a woman near her term. Her flesh under the soft fabric of her garments felt taut. He allowed his hand to linger there in an aching caress.

"Sometimes I can feel him flutter within me. I doubt you'll be able to tell; he's very small yet."

"He?"

"Or she. Do you have a preference?"

He shrugged and removed his hand. "As long as the child is healthy, I care not. She is welcome either way."

"I know this baby cannot magically undo the wrong I've done you, Darius. I don't expect you to forgive me just because I am carrying your child."

He rose up and turned his back. To his surprise, he felt something like relief wash over him. At least she did not expect him to act as if everything was well between them.

He heard her stir on the bed to come and stand near him. "Do you know, with the drama of the baby, I believe Lysander forgot to send you a message about my new discovery."

He turned around, grateful for a new topic, knowing she had changed the course of their conversation on purpose in order to allay his discomfort. These uncanny intuitions had always made her an irresistible companion. Which made her betrayal even harder to bear. He forced his thoughts away from that gaping wound. "What new discovery?"

"While I was searching for parchment in my trunks, I happened to come upon the note the assassin gave the Babylonian brothers. When I studied it again, I had an interesting insight. That note was not written to a stranger. It wasn't for a hired man at all. The man who wrote it knew its recipient. Knew him well, even. Perhaps intimately."

Darius went still. "Well enough to be in mourning at the news of his death?"

"I imagine so. Do you know such a man?"

"A high official named Zikir. He is in mourning for the death of his grandson, and fits every criteria we know about. He is from Damascus and occupies a high place in the court. He is in mourning. And he has reason to hold a grudge against Artaxerxes."

They were interrupted by a knock at the door.

"Your physician," Darius said, as he pulled the door open.

A rotund man with balding head and a bushy salt and pepper beard came in. His forehead shone with perspiration. Darius imagined Lysander had treated the man to a taste of friendly pressure and was grateful for his friend's interention. His stomach turned into a sour mass at the thought of Sarah growing weak. Bleeding. Dying. If it came to a choice between his wife and his baby, he knew what his decision would be. The realization confounded him.

"Would you like to wait outside, my lord, while I examine your wife?" The tone of his voice suggested that was exactly what he expected Darius to do.

"No, I would not."

The physician cleared his throat. "As you wish."

The exam took a long time. He saw that it hurt Sarah, and could barely keep himself from grabbing the physician by the nape of his fat neck and pulling his probing fingers off her. He reached for her hand at one point and held it, trying to give her his own strength. He was touched by the way she gripped him, driven by fear and pain. Without meaning to, he caressed the hair away from her perspiring face.

"Shhh. It will be over soon."

After finishing his thorough exam, the physician asked Sarah many questions about her pregnancy, as well as the initial miscarriage. He had small, clever eyes that didn't seem to miss any details. Darius felt his tense muscles begin to relax.

Finally, the physician stood up and stretched. "Well. Your friend Lysander is not as unskilled in matters of childbirth as he surmises. He's right that your wife was pregnant with twins originally. One she lost. Why, I could not tell you. No one understands these things. The child might not have formed right from the start. In any case, *this* baby," he gestured toward Sarah on the bed, "is healthy and growing. There's nothing wrong with him or with your wife. She should carry him to term without complications. The slight bleeding and birth pangs she experienced are not out of the ordinary. Many women have them. I see nothing to concern you. Nothing at all. Enjoy your good fortune, and worry no more."

Darius heard a choked sound from the bed and turned to see Sarah bury her face in a pillow, her shoulders shaking. Without planning to, he reached out and caressed her back, rubbing the nape of her neck. As if he could not resist the touch, his hand lingered there for a moment, absorbing the shivers that were going through her. Wordlessly he remained by her side until he felt her body settle into calm.

He felt as if the weight of a mountain had lifted from his own shoulders. The physician departed with a considerably fatter purse; Darius had never been so happy to part with his gold. When he returned, he found that Sarah had wiped her face and was already sitting up, looking sheepish.

"What a fuss I made over nothing. I feel very foolish."

"You did right to come to Damascus. If I'd been there myself, I would have wanted you to see the physician too."

She gave a watery smile. "I'm so relieved the baby is well."

Darius nodded. "Why don't you rest for a while?"

The noise of a muffled altercation outside made them both go rigid with alarm. Darius pulled out his dagger and whipped into attack stance as the door burst open.

"I beg pardon, my lord. She would not abide," Meres cried through clenched teeth, trying to hold on to the silky skirts of a tall woman who danced into the chamber with admirable aplomb, as if she had not broken twenty-three rules of social decorum by her brazen behavior.

"Slippery thing," Meres said, as the woman's scarf came off in his hands and she continued to advance into the room.

It had been a while since Darius had seen her in woman's garb. He had forgotten how exotically attractive she was. Her mouth was too wide; her nose too short, the nostrils flared in a curious curl to each side; her eyes too narrow. And yet the overall effect left the viewer a little breathless. More trouble for him. He closed his eyes. "Roxanna."

Chapter 18

Sarah's jaw almost hit the floor as the ravishing woman made her way inside, her wide smile devoid of any embarrassment at having interrupted husband and wife. Darius nodded at Meres who left the chamber, closing the door behind him, creating a measure of privacy again. The woman named Roxanna sauntered further into the chamber, her steps wide and leisurely. She flopped on the dilapidated stool Darius had vacated earlier, and spreading her legs, placed her elbows on her knees.

Darius blew out an impatient breath and nudged her leg with the tip of his shoe. "You aren't wearing trousers anymore. Try to at least give the impression that you are a woman or you'll be recognized."

Roxanna grinned and pulled her long limbs into a semblance of demure femininity. "Aren't you going to introduce me to your wife?"

Sarah gathered her mouth into a tight line. Clearly this woman knew her husband well. "Yes, my lord. Won't you introduce us?"

If Darius felt uncomfortable with this unusual visit, it did not show on his face. "Sarah, this is the king's secret agent in Damascus. Obviously, that is not information you can repeat to anyone else. Her name is Roxanna. Everyone in the court of Damascus knows her as Cyrus, however."

The king's secret agent! Sarah felt momentary relief at that bit of information, until she realized that the woman's vocation meant she must have spent considerable time with *her* husband over the past few weeks. Then it sank into her benumbed mind that Darius had given her a man's name. She came to her feet, her movements slow. "How curious."

"Not as curious as you might think, given the fact that she has been sporting a false beard and men's disguise until today. She is pretending to be one of Artaxerxes' merchants while helping to solve his attempted murder."

Sarah sent Roxanna a calculating glance. She was tall and athletic, with dark blond curls and eyes the color of spring honey. She was also entrancingly beautiful. Hard to swallow that such a creature could convincingly switch genders at will. "And you have managed to make everyone believe you are a man all this time? How clever."

Roxanna shrugged. "One must do what one can for the empire."

Her accent was crisp and aristocratic. Sarah felt a stab of jealousy. This was precisely the kind of woman Darius would have wanted for his wife if the choice had been left up to him. Stunning, supple, with the inherent brand of self-confidence that seemed bred into their class. She felt short and dumpy in comparison.

"How close are you to solving the plot?" Sarah asked. "Any breakthroughs?"

For a moment, the young woman seemed flustered. "Not yet. But we draw close."

Darius rubbed the back of his neck. "Sarah has brought news that might give us a new insight."

To Sarah's surprise, Roxanna gave her a genuine smile when Darius explained her discovery. "I'd heard you had a brilliant mind. Glad to have your help."

It occurred to Sarah that living the life of an agent could not be easy for a woman. No matter how adventurous, Roxanna must struggle with loneliness. She would always be an outsider, never belonging to anyone. Sarah wondered if the girl's crude intrusion was more than a bid to satisfy her curiosity. Perhaps she had wanted to meet another woman who in some small way promised a meaningful connection. Because she had once served as the queen's senior scribe, Sarah might be the closest Roxanna had come to another woman who broke the normal rules that governed women's lives.

The hard, defensive wall around Sarah's heart cracked. She felt ashamed of her own spiteful attitude toward Roxanna. Jealousy was not an emotion with which Sarah battled often. She was shocked at the depth of her own envy. Could the woman help being lovely? Did she have to pay the price of Sarah's lack of confidence?

Sarah could not retain Darius's attachment by showing her claws to every attractive woman who came near him. Pulling other women down with waspish words was no way to keep her husband. She would have a much better chance at holding on to him if she proved loving and trustworthy herself. Raising herself up in his esteem was the one sure way to secure his affections.

There was a respectful knock at the door. Their little room had turned into the Throne Hall of Persepolis, it seemed. Everyone was lining up to enter. Darius pulled the door open with impatience and barked, "What?" at Meres, who stood on the other side.

"My lord. If you are available, may I have a word?"

Darius raised a brow. "The Babylonian brothers giving you trouble?"

"No. We uncovered something enlightening earlier this morning. I would have ridden to tell you, except that I didn't want to leave our guests to their own devices. I don't think they would get into trouble intentionally, but they have been cooped up for some days and grow restless. In their desire to clear their name, they're liable to cause havoc. Since you are here already, perhaps you and my lady might wish to hear this news."

Darius looked over his shoulder at Sarah, his

eyebrows raised in question. Another man would not have considered exposing his wife to a bunch of wild men. From the start, Sarah had found her husband unusually tolerant in such matters, however. As long as he judged her to be out of harm's way, he allowed her contact with many of his friends and associates, esteeming her opinion in various situations. He wasn't lax enough to put up with her going off on her own. But he permitted her a wider access to the world than was normal in his circles.

"I would love to come," she said, unable to hide the eagerness in her voice.

"Are you not tired after your journey?"

"I would never raise a murmur of complaint against Lysander, but I must confess that in deference to my condition, he drove our cart so slowly from Jerusalem that at one point I saw a small lizard slither past us. Any more rest, and I might lose my mind. I'd much rather come with you."

"And you're not leaving me behind," Roxanna said, bouncing to her feet. "If there is news, I need to hear it."

On the way out, they ran into the proprietress of the inn. She bowed to Darius and murmured, "My lord," and then bowed to Sarah as she came out, though not quite as low as she had to Darius. Then she froze as she saw Roxanna bringing up the rear.

"Here now! I don't know what you're all doing in there. This is a respectable establishment."

Roxanna shrugged a shoulder. Sarah had to put a hand over her mouth to strangle her laughter when Roxanna said, "Don't worry. No one is perfect."

Niq and Nassir stood to attention as Sarah and the rest of Darius's entourage walked into the room. Darius had left Lysander outside as guard; everyone else crowded into the tight chamber, trying to find a spot big enough that did not squish them against someone else.

Nassir was holding a block of wood he had been carving in one hand, and a thin blade in the other. His hands were dusted with fine wood shavings from the deepening hole in the middle of the block. On the table in one corner sat four identical wooden chalices. Sarah was impressed. Another week, and he would have a complete set.

Niq was covered in perspiration, his hair lank. Sarah guessed that he had been engaged in intense physical exercise. Keeping up with his odd combat training, no doubt. After a short greeting, Darius motioned for everyone to sit, and settled himself on a skinny cushion after finding a sturdy stool for Sarah.

Roxanna leaned against the closed door. "These are the Babylonian brothers, I presume?"

Sarah bit down a smile at the way Niq marched

forward, pushing out his chest, sucking in a deep breath to flatten an already muscled belly. "I'm Niq, my lady. And this is my brother Nassir."

"Never mind that!" Darius said. "Tell me your news. Meres says you have something of import to tell me."

Niq scratched his head and sent a doubtful look first in Sarah's direction, and then in Roxanna's.

"You can speak in front of my wife."

"Yes, sir. It's just that the story is a bit colorful."

"How colorful?"

"It involves a baby. Out of wedlock, so to speak."

"My wife is an old expert at babies. And Roxanna knows more swear words than you do. Go on. You won't corrupt them with your tale." Sarah pretended a deep interest in the fringe of her scarf.

"Yes, my lord. We discovered an interesting piece of information from an old woman who works here. She's been kind to us. She has no sons of her own, and likes to spoil us now and then."

Meres rolled his eyes. "She likes to spoil *him*. That boy can charm the grey out of a storm cloud."

Niq shrugged. "I was born with natural talent."

"Am I to understand you found out something worthwhile?" Darius crossed his arms.

"Yes, my lord. This old woman told me an interesting story. It's from years past, but I think it may prove significant to your search. You see, at one time she worked in the household of a Syrian official named Zikir. He lives in Damascus now."

That name again, Sarah thought. She noticed that Darius sat up straighter. "Go on," he said.

"Our story concerns something that happened twenty-five years ago. And it involves no less a dignitary than our king's own father. Xerxes ruled in Persia at the time. He was on a tour through the empire when he chose to stop in Damascus for a royal visit. He stayed at the palace, of course.

"According to the woman who works here, one night, he was sleepless and he went for a stroll in the palace gardens. To his delight, he found a young maiden bathing in a pool in the starlight."

How convenient for the old king, Sarah thought. She shifted on the stool to make herself more comfortable.

Niq scratched through his thick beard. "That maiden was Zenobia, the daughter of Zikir. He had brought his family to the palace for the royal visit so that they might enjoy the glamor of the royal entourage. Zenobia was his only child and he doted on her. The old woman says that she was a little wild. Spoiled, probably. Not many virgins go frolicking in the palace pool after dusk. But on that fateful night, Zenobia would not be dissuaded. She dragged her servant with her into the garden for that forbidden midnight swim.

And when the king happened upon her, he was smitten. Apparently Zikir's daughter was famed for her beauty. Anyhow, according to the old woman, she received the king's advances with open arms."

"If she'd been my daughter, I would have—" Nassir made a garroting gesture against his throat. "No daughter of mine would be allowed to throw herself into the arms of a strange man, be he royalty or not."

Sarah arched an eyebrow and gave silent thanks to the Lord that she had not been born into Nassir's family.

Meres flicked a well-fed fly that had sat on his sleeve. "Fortunately for the girl, her father did not have your stringent standards, Nassir. The point is that Zenobia became pregnant."

"With Xerxes' child?" Darius asked.

"According to the old woman, yes."

"Why did the king not take her as concubine?"

Niq flipped a hand in the air. "Do I understand the way of kings? By the time they found she was pregnant, he was long gone. Before leaving, he gave this Zikir a hefty gift of land and cattle, and entrusted him with high office. Apparently, Zikir was from a noble Syrian family, but they were impoverished. There would have been no advantage in the king taking the woman into his household. He probably thought he had more than paid his debt for a girl who came to him willingly enough, and without asking for a lifelong bond."

"What was the name of Zikir's grandson, do you know?"

Roxanna twirled the tip of her scarf in the air. "Xerxes. Like the king's father."

"That seems to support the old woman's story." Darius leaned forward. "Why else would a Syrian name his grandson after a Persian king?"

"Of course Zenobia did marry," Roxanna said, twirling her scarf in the opposite direction. "This son we are bestowing upon King Xerxes in fact has a legal father."

"Who?"

"The daughter married some minor Syrian official. A forgettable man who was far beneath her, by all accounts. The one thing he seemed to have done right was to drop dead after they had been married a couple of years. What is interesting, however, is that their son, Xerxes, was born six months into the marriage. And he was a strapping, fat, healthy child. Nothing like a babe brought forth so prematurely."

Sarah abandoned her uncomfortable stool. "So, Zenobia's midnight indiscretion got her pregnant by Xerxes. Her father, desperate to alleviate scandal, found her a husband who was too grateful for the association with a now-wealthy family to be offended by her lack of purity."

Roxanna nodded. "That would be my guess. A bride who is carrying another man's child is not such a bad deal if she comes with a fat dowry and excellent connections."

"This explains how the child came to be born three months early," Darius said. "Now we need to connect that old story to the new plot. Was the assassin who cut his own throat in Susa none other than Zikir's grandson? That man claimed to be called Achaemenes. A Persian name to be sure. But not Xerxes."

Darius used the tip of his dagger to smooth out a sliver of wood sticking out of the floor. "This is what we have so far: Zikir's grandson has the blood of kings. So at the outset, Zikir loves the Persian line; he's famed for his service to the empire. At the same time, those kings have withheld every royal right from his grandson. He has never been officially acknowledged as the son of Xerxes. Zikir has lived with that shame. Borne it. Then, Artaxerxes unknowingly delivered an unforgivable insult by not giving Zikir the position of satrap in Trans-Euphrates. A position that was almost royal. A position that he had long deserved both by virtue of his service and abilities.

"Instead, Artaxerxes honored a bumbling man who was drunk more often than sober. Why? Because Pyrus was the acknowledged scion of an aristocratic Persian family. This must have proven too much for Zikir. Finally, his hatred must have overtaken his love of the royal line."

Nassir dug his blade deep into the block of wood he held in his hand. "Revenge is a common motive for murder."

"This is still conjecture. We don't have proof," Darius said. "There are a few key pieces of evidence we are missing. Roxanna, since you have conveniently turned yourself into a woman again, pay a visit to Zenobia and get what you can out of her. I've heard she's a recluse who does not visit the palace. Find her. Use your charm. Lie. Pretend you are the undertaker. I don't care what you do. Just get her to talk to you. We need to unearth the truth about how Xerxes died. No one at court seems to know the details, except that he was not in Syria at the time of his death. We must establish whether he is the man who killed himself in that tavern in Susa or not. If he is the assassin, then it stands to reason that his grandfather would have been the mastermind."

Sarah was beginning to feel heavy and uncomfortable. She decided to try sitting on her stool again. "Don't you have one more advantage that the murderer doesn't know about?"

"Niq and Nassir. Yes. They can identify him and his servant. I've kept them out of the way so far, not having a good suspect at hand that would be worth exposing them for. But we now have enough information to risk coming out into the open. I'm going to take you men out of hiding and bring you into the palace today. What I need from you is to identify Zikir. Once I have your testimony, the case is closed.

"I'll try to sneak you into Damascus without being noticed. At the palace, I'll set up some kind of trap for Zikir so that you can see him without being seen. Roxanna, bring your report to me as soon as you have seen Zenobia. Sarah, you and Pari will remain here with Lysander until this business is wrapped up."

Sarah, who was beginning to feel herself wilt with pregnancy fatigue, said, "Yes, my lord."

Darius turned to her. She thought his lips softened for a moment. "So biddable, my lady."

"I try, my lord."

He wrapped his fingers around her arm. "You mean you are too exhausted to argue. Come. I'll take you to your chamber. I want to see you eat and rest before I leave."

Chapter 19

The first men who volunteered to work on the walls of Jerusalem were priests. Nehemiah had expected farmers or laborers—men accustomed to manual exertion—to step forward before others. The priests, however, jumped first at the chance to restore Jerusalem.

It came to Nehemiah that they knew better than most the spiritual significance behind the shattered walls of the city. They were a reminder of their people's sin, which had caused God to remove His hand of protection from them. If the Lord was opening the doors for the restoration of Jerusalem as Nehemiah promised, then He must have forgiven His covenant people. To rebuild the walls meant that they were cooperating not with the governor, but with God Himself. And they set the example for the rest of the people.

Before the high priest Eliashib picked up a single stone, he and his priests dedicated the Sheep Gate to the Lord. They blessed the people who would one day bring their sheep through these gates again, on their way to be sacrificed at the Temple.

Afterward Nehemiah watched Eliashib tuck his long robe into his belt and begin to sweat under the hot sun of northern Jerusalem, his dignified priests looking like a bunch of laborers as they toiled alongside him. This portion of the wall was large and of particular importance, for this part of the city stood undefended by steep hills.

Under their hands, the blistering work of laying stone upon stone became an act of worship. They were honoring God. They sought to show Him their obedience. They started at the Sheep Gate and toiled their way westward for uninterrupted hours as if God Himself empowered every small accomplishment.

Nehemiah sent a carpenter to oversee their efforts when they began to set the framework of the door. Even the religious enthusiasm of a priest could not compensate for a lack of construction experience.

"We don't want the doors to fall upon our heads the first time we open them," Nehemiah told his brother. "I don't care how much they pray as they are building. You need a bit of human expertise as well."

Sanballat the Horonite delivered a fierce kick to the stool next to his oak table. The stool crashed against a wall, shattering one of its delicately carved legs. He cursed under his breath. Carved stools were not cheap.

He picked up the letter from Tobiah and handed it to his son. "Selemyah, what do you make of this?

Tobiah says that Judah has a new governor. And what do you think he is doing? Rebuilding the walls of that pockmarked Jerusalem, that's what!"

Selemyah grasped the delicate papyrus in careful fingers. "Let that backwater city do what they will. You are the leader of troops from Samaria. What harm can a little stretch of wall do to you?"

"Don't be shortsighted! Why are these Israelites roaring to rebuild their dear Jerusalem, do you think? They chase after power and profit. And if they get their way, will not the governor of Judah curry more favor and authority than the rest of us in the region? I plan to become governor of Samaria one day. As such, I don't intend to tolerate a new power rising up next door, breathing down my neck."

Selemyah perched on the edge of the oak table. "What do you aim to do?"

"First, we must establish if this building project has the Persian stamp of approval. Not many years ago, the king stopped the very same project. I suspect these people are probably in outright rebellion. In which case, we threaten them with exposure and that should bring their precious wall to an end.

"Let us send for Tobiah. Come to think of it, I will call in the aid of Geshem the Qedarite as well. He is another powerful man in our region and is bound to be equally displeased with the developments in Judah."

• • •

Nehemiah read the letter that bore the seals of Sanballat, Tobiah, and Geshem. It was short. But in the few lines, Nehemiah could detect scathing contempt. He read it aloud for the grim-faced Jewish leaders who surrounded him, his voice devoid of expression.

People of Judah,

What do you think you are doing? Hasn't the king already forbidden the rebuilding of Jerusalem once? Are you now rebelling against the king?

Nehemiah gazed at the young man who had delivered the missive. "Did your master, Sanballat, have an additional message for us?"

"He was laughing too hard to say much."

"Tell your master that not only do we have the king's permission, but we also have the help of the God of heaven. He is the One who will make us prosper. We, His servants, will rise up and rebuild this city.

"But you, Sanballat, Tobiah, and Geshem, you will have no share in or claim to our Jerusalem." He handed the letter back to the messenger. "Will you remember my words or shall I write them down?"

"No. I . . . I . . . er . . . will remember."

"Excellent. Don't let us keep you."

Before the young man was out of earshot, Nehemiah addressed his leaders. "Nothing but the buzzing of a fly. Let them mock away. We'll see who is laughing when we accomplish the task God has placed before us. Let's return to work. Everyone to his post."

Nehemiah knew that every day of building was crucial. There was no time to waste. The faster they could accomplish their task, the less chance they would have of being derailed by unforeseeable forces. For the sake of efficiency, he had divided the building project into forty-two sectors, with various leaders overseeing the work in each section.

It was a daunting project. In places, the original wall had been as wide as the length of five tall men lying down end-to-end. The enormous width had been necessary in order to support the wall's considerable height. Nehemiah had directed the laborers to build directly on top of the old foundations where possible, changing the location of the wall only when absolutely necessary. Some of the ancient foundations had been laid at the time of King David. Others, like the Broad Wall, were from the time of King Hezekiah, a reminder of a time in Judah's history when its enemies had breathed down its neck, requiring extraordinary defenses. But in the end, those defenses had failed. What use was a wall without the hand of God behind it to hold it up? There were times when the builders wept as they worked, remembering what they had lost.

Nehemiah recognized that the structure they were building would lack the splendor of the City of David. But he did not concern himself with grandeur now. What Jerusalem needed was practical protection. In order to grow and prosper into a true city, they needed to surround it with an effective shield.

He fell into the habit of visiting several sites each day. On the fifteenth day of building he began with Eliashib's section of the wall. He noted that the high priest was not as fast on his feet as he had been at the beginning of his labors.

The governor recalled that Sanballat's daughter was married to one of Eliashib's grandsons. It was one thing to toil for the glory of God, but quite another to get tangled up with disgruntled family members. In addition, if what he heard was true, Tobiah was a personal friend of the high priest. Nehemiah pursed his lower lip for a moment. He had not counted on having enemies who were related to his friends.

Immediately to the west of Eliashib and his priests, a group from Jericho labored on the wall. They were simple men. Nehemiah doubted if they could read and write. And yet they stood next to the high priest of the land, shoulder to shoulder, strengthening their city. There was something sacred about the way the wall was bringing people of such diverse backgrounds together. They were united by their commitment to serve God with one heart. Differences were set aside for the sake of their goal.

Beyond them, Zaccur the son of Imri worked with his family and servants. The sound of jovial chatter was interspersed with occasional grunts and strained groaning. Masonry was heavy. The builders had to pick through the stones left over from the old walls and dust and clean them before setting them in place. Some pieces were small enough for one man to lift. Many were so heavy that it required several men to shove one boulder onto a lever and fulcrum so that they could lift the stone to the appropriate height.

Nehemiah bent down to run a hand across the first round of stones that had been set over the foundation. "Your work progresses well."

Zaccur wiped a hand across his sweat-soaked brow, leaving a streak. "Thank you, my lord."

Nehemiah clasped him on the shoulder. "You have done a fine job." Their portion was small compared to the priests', but they worked with gratifying zeal.

The governor walked westward to the Fish Gate, where the residents of the city once sold fish from the Sea of Galilee. *One day again, God willing, crowds of fishermen will walk through these gates!* The sons of Hassenaah—four young men with shoulders as broad as a Persian beam—worked hard on the Gate.

"How goes it?" Nehemiah called out.

"Come see for yourself, my lord," said a brother with curly hair and brown eyes that sparkled. Nehemiah could not remember his name, and if he was honest, could not even tell the brothers apart. They all had curly hair and sparkling brown eyes, as well as thick muscles.

They were working on the doors. Lebanon's rich timber had already been cut into planks and laid on a large table hefted from somewhere to accommodate their task. Nehemiah stroked the surface of one plank. As smooth as an ancient stone, the young men had sanded it until the grain of the wood stood out with the beauty of an artist's pattern.

"This shall be a gate worthy of the city to which it belongs."

Four broad smiles enveloped him with appreciation.

Meremoth was busy repairing the section of the wall that stood next to the Fish Gate. He came from an important family; both his father and grandfather were known as men of rank in Judah. Yet he exchanged good-natured jests with the four simple brothers as if they had been boyhood friends. As if a world of wealth, education, and lineage did not stand between them.

Meremoth's hands were covered in mud, which he was using as mortar between the stones. His face, his hair, his work clothes, even his brows were speckled with it. He looked a mess. But the echo of his loud laughter rang through the valley beyond. He sounded like a man who had discovered what he loved best in the world.

Judah's governor shook his head and continued his systematic inspection westward, then southward, encouraging and strengthening the builders as he walked by each section. He exchanged pleasantries with Meshullam followed by Zadok. The people of Tekoa were next.

The men of Tekoa were dressed in homespun, no shoes on their feet, their clothing—what they had of it—threadbare. Their women had come along to help, cleaning the pale limestone, helping to heft and position some of the smaller pieces. It was backbreaking work, with an occasional surprise when they moved the rocks. Scorpions. Sometimes, to escape the incessant summer heat, little creatures hid under the fallen stones. Nehemiah had seen scorpions scuttle out from under the weight of a shifting boulder, running with blind fear toward the people who had disturbed their rest. How no one had been stung so far had been due more to God's mercy than human ingenuity.

The small band of peasants from Tekoa occupied a special place in Nehemiah's heart. It had taken monumental courage for them to come and help in the building effort. Tekoa was a city in the highlands to the south of Jerusalem. The prophet Amos had once been a shepherd of Tekoa, called by God to preach to Israel.

Geshem the Qedarite ruled a vast area near there. Which might explain the visit Nehemiah had received from the nobles of Tekoa several days before.

The delegation of eight men had looked more suited to a royal visit in Persepolis than the back-waters of Judah. They were garbed in Egyptian linen, dyed in fine colors of the sea and the air. A bigger bunch of peacocks would have been hard to find throughout Judah.

"How may I help you?" Nehemiah had asked in polite inquiry.

"You may stop building this atrocity you call a wall." The speaker, the shortest man in the group, took a long step forward as if he owned the ground he walked on. Nehemiah had seen him before when he had called the leaders of Judah for their initial meeting. When everyone had cheered with enthusiasm after he revealed his intentions, this Tekoan lord had sat sour-faced and stared through thick lashes that curled like a girl's.

"Why would I do that? Jerusalem will fall into complete ruin if we don't provide an appropriate defensive structure around her."

"You know nothing about it. You come from Persia, wet behind the ears, without a single clue as to how we survive here. You think you know what you are doing. Instead, you are offending every good friend Jerusalem has."

"Good friends like Geshem, I assume?"

"Yes, and Sanballat and Tobiah, too. They are related to half the nobility of Judah. How dare you offend them?"

"You forget. I am the new governor." Nehemiah spoke the reminder in a mild tone.

A fat hand slashed through the air. "What's a governor worth if no one will follow him? We certainly won't. Not one of us from Tekoa will take part in building your pathetic wall."

Another of the men nodded. "As if we would ever stoop to working with your construction supervisors. *Supervisors,* you call them! We are nobility and you expect us to report to a bunch of rough peasants?"

Nehemiah felt himself turning color. "They are masons and carpenters who know how to build a safe wall. You may have cleaner fingernails, but I doubt you know a plane from a chisel."

"And you haven't the faintest idea how to run Judah. You shall not receive aid from the men of Tekoa in fulfilling your disaster of a scheme."

Except that the Peacock Delegation had been proven wrong. Against the express commands of their leaders, this group of peasants had walked to the City of David in order to lend a hand in its restoration. Yes, Nehemiah was fond of the men of Tekoa. He greeted each one by name, his voice colored by warmth he seldom showed men with ten times the influence.

He was about to walk toward the Jeshanah Gate

when his brother Hanani found him. "We have trouble," he said without preamble.

"We always have trouble."

Hanani pumped his long chin up and down. "Too many friends. That's your problem."

Nehemiah smoothed the wide sleeve of his robe. "What now?"

"Sanballat has been making public pronouncements in front of his highborn friends, not to mention the whole army of Samaria. He makes a mockery of us with his words. Of course, the content of his speech has made its way into Judah as he intended. By tonight everyone will have heard of it. He's trying to spread hopelessness and discouragement, and brother, he's good at what he does."

"I didn't expect he would become my faithful supporter."

Hanani's smile was bitter. "That, he is not. He's incensed by the fact that you have persisted in this project. You've certainly managed to rile him."

Nehemiah lifted a shoulder. "He'll have to take that up with the Lord. What has he been saying?"

Hanani was quiet for a moment. Nehemiah had the impression that he was working up to something unpleasant. "He calls our people feeble and ineffectual, and says that we don't know what we are doing. He implies that these walls will never be finished, and that we'll be unable to offer sacrifices in the Temple again. *Will they finish in a day? Can they bring the stones back to life from those heaps of rubble—burned as they are?"* Hanani made his voice high and tonal, adopting Sanballat's Samarian accents.

"Ah. And the people? How are they responding?"

"From what I can tell, discouragement is already spreading among the ranks. Nehemiah, this is an enormous project. It's unreasonable to think we can finish it. It took kings and armies with substantial resources to build these walls once. We are just a ragged and poor people, working with burned limestone. We don't have what it takes to succeed. These men may be our enemies. But their objections are reasonable. I think Tobiah the Ammonite is right."

Nehemiah felt his throat grow dry. Even his own brother was falling under the pressure of Sanballat's intimidation. "The problem with discouragement is that it always sounds like the truth. Tell me what Tobiah said."

Hanani hung his head. "He said that even if something as slight as a fox climbed upon our wall, it would crumble under its feet. Because what we have built is so pathetic."

Nehemiah lowered himself on one of the pieces of charred stone that his enemies had scoffed. "Don't you know, Hanani, that your adversary always wants you to believe that even an insignificant obstacle will defeat you? Don't you know that your enemy will belittle your efforts so that you will give up before you have started? He wants to breed insecurity and self-doubt in your heart."

"Well, he's succeeding. Nehemiah, these men are right. We must have lost our minds to think we could complete a project this huge."

"It's easy to believe these lies. I know. It's easy to believe in your own weakness. Right now, even the smallest interference feels overwhelming. But if you give in to these lies, you will give up on your destiny. You will overestimate the power of every obstacle that comes against you, and underestimate the power of God to rescue you.

"Are we weak? I won't deny it. Are we facing a challenge that is greater than us? Of course! But, brother, you and our people must learn that you are more than equal to any fox when the Lord stands by your side."

Chapter 20

Dressed in the distinctive outfit of Persian cavalry, the Babylonian brothers rode into Damascus under the cover of night. Darius had made them curl their hair and beards, and they looked like different men. No one would recognize them for the highway robbers who had set upon him on the road to Susa. As he brought them into his chambers, he hoped the disguise would fool Zikir and any spies he might have in the palace.

Once in his room, he showed the two men the curtained alcove to one side of the chamber where they would have to hide. The nook had been designed for the storage of goods and offered little space. The brothers tried hiding there in order to make sure they would fit when the time came; they were too wide in the shoulders to be comfortable standing and had no room for sitting. The side of Darius's mouth tipped up as the two men jostled to find a viable position that did not crunch one part of someone's body.

He sent Arta with an invitation for Zikir to come to his chambers in the morning. "Tell him it will prove to his advantage." He knew that appealing to a man's greed was often a strong motivator. At the same time, leaving the message vague meant that an honest man would still be intrigued.

"Tomorrow, I want you to come out as soon as you recognize his voice," he told Nassir. "I doubt he'll bring his servant with him, so initially, Nassir, you must be our witness. After you confirm that he is our man, I will search for the servant who tattooed Niq's head and we shall arrest him also."

It was almost midnight when Roxanna returned. She had taken the time to get back into her male disguise.

"Did you find Zenobia?"

"I did, poor creature. She's overcome by the death of her only child. Can you imagine losing your twenty-five-year-old son?"

Darius did not want to think about the woman's sorrow. Having so recently lost an unborn child, his heart was too quick to pity. He could not afford to go down emotional alleys with this case. "Did you uncover anything of interest?"

"For one thing, Xerxes' full name was Xerxes Achaemenes. He was commonly known by his first name; few people knew his middle name. It had been a whim of his mother's. She could not claim his heritage in public. The names were her secret way of acknowledging her son's true parentage."

Darius sat down, his movements slow. "Finally, we have irrefutable proof. He was our man in Susa."

"I fear so."

"Who sent him there?"

"His mother did not know. She remains unaware of his part in the plot, or even that there was a plot against the king. I doubt she would believe it. But here is an important detail: Zikir is the one who told her of his death. He said it was an accident, and that his body could not be recovered. He did give her the accurate date of his death, however."

"How could he have known the time of his death unless he knew everything else? We leaked nothing. Zikir must have had his own sources of information. And they had to be in Susa to know."

Darius came to his feet. "We have more than enough information to convict him of plotting to kill the king. Tomorrow, we shall wrap up the case against him and send him to Susa for trial."

"I pity Zenobia. To lose a son and father in a matter of months for the sake of a dried-up old grudge is a bitter fate."

To Darius's surprise, Zikir took his time coming in the morning. He arrived alone, as Darius had suspected. Garbed in mourning as he was, his face chalk-white and drawn, Darius felt an ambiguous tug of compassion for him. Not enough to loosen his razor-sharp focus on trapping him, however. Killing kings was not something you could sweep under a rug, no matter how good your motive.

He invited the old man to lounge at a wooden table that sat in the center of the room. Although the cushions were plump, Zikir had a hard time bending his knees to sit on the floor. His joints suffered from the stiffness and pain that afflicted some old people. Darius had to quash another wave of sympathy. He offered wine, which Zikir refused with polite dignity, explaining that his belly could not tolerate the drink.

"I have asked you here because I want to speak to you about Pyrus. What do you think of him?"

Zikir's wrinkled face grew shuttered. "His Majesty chose him. That's what I think of him."

Darius gave a reassuring smile. "Yes. But His Majesty is open to changing his mind. It occurs to me that Pyrus might not be the man the king thought him. It would be helpful to me if you would give me your true opinion of the man. He seems to drink too much, for one thing."

Zikir looked down. "That was not always the case."

"No?"

"He has had his troubles like the rest of us."

Darius nodded. Only half his mind was on Zikir's answers. With the other half he was fretting over Nassir's delay. Surely he had heard enough of Zikir's voice to be able to recognize him? He could see the man's face through the thin opening in the curtains. Why did he not come out?

"As you say, we all have troubles. That is no excuse for doing your job poorly." Darius cleared his throat, hoping that Nassir would catch the hint and move.

Zikir gave a tight smile. "Far be it from me to sit in defense of the acting satrap. I don't mean to imply that I approve of his actions."

"Good. Good."

To his shock, Zikir began to rise. It took him long moments to arrange his legs and his hips until he could put the weight of his body on them. "Forgive me, my lord. I must leave."

Darius sprang to his feet. "But we have not discussed Pyrus's situation!"

"Nor shall we. If you want to form an opinion of the acting satrap, it's best you look elsewhere. I have too many personal grievances against the man to be trusted with an accurate summation. If he must go down, it won't be by my hand."

Darius found himself lost for words. It was not often that a man gave up the opportunity to crush an enemy. Zikir's scrupulous attitude confused him. *This* was the murderer he wanted to trap?

He looked around the room with vague desperation. Where was that benighted Babylonian, Nassir? Why did he not come out to identify Zikir as the one who had hired him?

He forced himself to pick up the thread of conversation, hoping to make Zikir open up. "I understand that Pyrus took the job that rightly belonged to you. You must, of course, bear resentment to him for that injustice."

The old man walked stiffly to the door. "You understand nothing, my lord." Pulling the door open, he walked out before Meres, who was standing guard, had a chance to come to attention.

Darius stood for a silent moment and gazed at the empty hallway, the sound of Zikir's fading steps echoing around him. Controlling the urge to kick the door, he closed it with a soft movement. The Babylonian brothers had come out of their hiding and were standing at attention when he turned around.

"Why did you not come out to confront Zikir?" he asked Nassir, his voice soft. He had learned that trick from his father. The deeper his anger, the harder his control.

Nassir's face grew a shade whiter. "Because he was not the man who commissioned me."

Darius's eyes narrowed. For the first time he began to genuinely doubt Nassir's honesty. "You lie. You lie in order to protect your employer."

"I swear to you, my lord, I speak the truth. This is not the man who hired me. His voice is different."

"He put on an accent and a false voice when he engaged you!"

"The tone of his voice is too old. He could not have made himself sound younger, could he? He is too short. I tell you, you have the wrong man, my lord. It cannot be him just because you want it to be so."

Darius took a deep breath. "As it so happens, I do not want it to be so. But everything points to him. Everything except your finger!"

Nassir wiped his sweating brow with a hand that trembled. "Nonetheless, I cannot point my finger at an innocent man."

"How scrupulous you grow of a sudden. I warn you, Babylonian, you better begin to speak the truth, or I will put your head on top of a pike taller than Zikir's."

The man squirmed under Darius's scrutiny. "I speak the truth, my lord. It was not him who engaged me. Perhaps he sent a servant to employ me. But this was not the man who hired me. That is all I know."

Darius ignored the niggling doubt that churned in the pit of his stomach like a sickness. The evidence of logic had piled high enough to convince the most stringent judge. "I do not understand this discrepancy. We arrest him, anyway. I don't need your testimony to carry my case against him. There is enough external evidence to convict him."

The problem, however, was not that he needed Nassir's testimony. It was that Nassir's testimony pointed away from Zikir. Rather than indicting him, Nassir was testifying to his innocence.

Darius ground his teeth and summoned Meres. Roxanna came in dressed as Cyrus just as they were getting ready to leave. "Are we going to arrest Zikir?"

He rolled his eyes. "I suppose you wish to participate in the festivities?"

Her wide mouth opened to show a row of very even, white teeth. "I believe you're beginning to know me."

"Lucky me. We have a complication. Nassir claims that Zikir isn't the man who hired him."

"Oh. If you arrest the wrong man, the real culprit might take advantage of the confusion to get away."

Darius pulled a hand through his hair. "Do you think I haven't considered that possibility? Yet how could he be the wrong man? Everything else fits. If we don't move now, he is sure to attempt on the king's life again."

They departed, en masse, for Zikir's offices in the palace. Darius decided that he would rather have the Babylonian brothers near him than leave them alone in his room, coming up with ways to create new mischief.

Zikir's arrest proved an anticlimax. The old man did not seem surprised by their appearance or by the charges that Darius laid against him. He came to his feet with the slow movements Darius had come to recognize. "You are making a mistake."

Something in the tone of Zikir's voice struck Darius. He sounded resigned. He sounded innocent. Annoyed at his lingering doubts in the face of a mountain of evidence, Darius said nothing, waiting for the old man to move. He gave him his dignity, leaving him free from fetters as they walked down the long passageway in the palace.

A man walked toward them from the opposite direction, his head bent. He seemed lost in thought. With an incoherent shout, Niq sprinted after him, yelling, "It's him! It's him!"

Before Darius could make a single reasonable inquiry, Niq had the man sprawled on the floor, and was sitting on him, bending his arm behind his back until the man began to moan and mumble for mercy.

Darius made his way over to the ignoble heap on the floor. He bent to see if he recognized Niq's prey. The man's face was squished into the marble tiles until his nose had flattened into an unnatural angle. "Friend of yours?"

"He's the dim-witted fool who tattooed my head."

By now a crowd of men had begun to gather around them. Darius groaned inwardly, knowing that a quick, clean arrest was no longer an option.

Turning toward Zikir, he said, "Your servant, I believe."

Zikir gave a bitter smile. "You shall find it is not so."

A harassed-looking official pushed through the crowd. Darius recognized him as Pyrus's secretary. "What goes on here?"

272

"These men are being arrested for plotting against the king's life."

"Lord Darius! There must be some mistake. You are arresting Lord Pyrus's man for conspiracy against the king?"

Darius went still. "Lord Pyrus's man? Are you certain? Don't you mean Lord Zikir's servant?"

The secretary shook his head until his hat fell forward onto his forehead. He pushed it back into a dignified angle. "I am certain. This man came with Lord Pyrus from Persia. As I recall, he has served him since childhood."

Rubbing his eyes with his thumb and index finger, Darius tried to untangle the monstrous knot that this new revelation presented. He cast a look in Zikir's direction. "Did you bribe Pyrus's servant to work for you?"

Zikir said nothing.

"Time to visit the acting satrap," Darius announced. "If I have to put the whole lot of you in jail, I will. I will stuff all of Damascus into a prison cell and be done with this case. You have worn out my patience."

He changed direction toward Pyrus's chambers, walking with purposeful steps. Roxanna lingered close, followed by Meres and Arta who walked on either side of Zikir. Niq came next, frog-marching his prisoner, pronouncing loud admonishments like, "Serves you right for tattooing my head with seditious rubbish." His brother Nassir followed at a more sedate pace. Then came Pyrus's secretary and what seemed like half the Damascus court trailing behind him.

Darius's head was beginning to pound. He wished he could climb on top of Samson and ride like the wind in any direction as long as it was away from this place and the annoying crowd. He shot a glance in Zikir's direction. His face was devoid of any expression other than exhaustion.

Darius and his entourage burst into Pyrus's chamber without bothering to knock. The time for niceties was long over. The acting satrap put down the golden goblet of wine he was holding and came to his feet unsteadily.

"What is the meaning of this intrusion? What are all these people doing here?"

Darius did not bother with an answer. He turned to Pyrus's servant. "Listen. It's been a long five months chasing after you and your master. I'm in a foul mood, and I think planting my fist in your face might be exactly what I need to make me cheer up. Why don't you do yourself a favor and tell me who your real master is. It can make considerable difference in how you are treated."

The man's pale irises swam in the white of his eyes. He looked at Pyrus and then at Zikir. His mouth opened, but no sound came out.

Pyrus swayed as he sank down behind his desk again. Picking up his goblet, he took a long swallow. "Would you mind telling me why you are interrogating my servant?"

"I don't like his taste in tattoos."

"Then by all means, take off his head. I can't abide bad taste."

Darius studied Pyrus. The man was drunk as always. With sudden clarity he remembered Zikir's words from the morning. *That was not always the case.* Darius held his breath for a moment.

"Lord Pyrus, tell me, when did you start drinking so heavily?"

Chapter 21

Pyrus took another heavy mouthful of his wine. His round face had turned red. "That's none of your affair."

Darius persisted. "People grieve in odd ways. Loss affects everyone differently. Our friend Zikir here, for example, has worn mourning and struggled with melancholy since the death of his grandson. Another man might take to drink. Did you start drinking just before the Persian New Year?"

Pyrus's assistant who had managed to make his way into the room, thinking he was aiding his superior, said, "It is true, sir. Lord Pyrus drank in moderation until a few months ago. He received bad news. A friend's demise, I believe, though he would not say. He has been a good acting satrap. This is a passing problem."

Pyrus's florid skin lost its color. His hands shook around the stem of the goblet to which he clung. To Darius's surprise, he saw that Zikir had tears in his eyes. It came to him that some tragedy, which had given rise to the assassination attempt, affected both men. Whatever the nature of this mystery, it deserved some privacy.

"Everyone but my men, out. Now." Darius knew

how to project authority. His voice, his manner, his address had become regal, brooking no resistance. Although the residents of the palace assumed him to be a mere visitor from the king, ranked in their estimation below the acting satrap, they obeyed him without a murmur. Darius motioned for Arta to close the door.

Before he could speak again, Nassir came forward. "My lord. This is the man who commissioned me. I am certain of it." He pointed a finger at Pyrus.

Darius motioned toward Nassir. "Lord Pyrus, do you recognize this man? Do you now understand what I'm after?"

"Go to the demons."

"I'm afraid you are ahead of me in that line. Tell me why you did it. Why did you try to kill the king? How did you persuade Zikir's grandson to join you?"

"Are *you* the butcher who killed him?" Pyrus came to his feet, holding himself against the table with spread hands. "He was worth ten of you."

"He killed himself. Cut his own throat rather than face the possibility of betraying you. So you see, if anyone caused his death, it was you."

Pyrus hid his face in trembling fingers. "That's not true. I loved him." Lifting his head, he looked at Zikir. "I *loved* him."

Zikir rubbed a hand against his chest. "You ruined him. Xerxes was a good man until you came. You corrupted him, mind and body, and taught him to resent his betters."

"I taught him to have pride as befit his lineage!" Pyrus shouted. "Who is Artaxerxes? A nobody. A second son. He only came to the throne because the true prince regent was killed. And yet he sits on that throne as if he owns the world. As if he is superior to everyone.

"I'm from the same family as he, you know. But all my life, he has treated me like an insect. Because I'm not a soldier, because I'm not a remarkable marksman, I'm not good enough for him. Oh no. He barely tolerates me. This post is the first crumb he has thrown my way, and he only did it for the sake of my uncle. He didn't even tell me in person. Sent me a missive, penned by his scribe."

"This is the whining of a child. You stole my grandson from me for this? For this pathetic excuse of a grievance?"

"You'd turned Xerxes into a backwater peasant. He was the son of a king! Equal to Artaxerxes by blood and his superior by ability. He deserved to occupy a throne."

"I taught him to make the best of what life gave him. You got him killed. For the sake of your whimpering accusations, you taught him to hate. To murder. He's dead because of you."

Pyrus collapsed into his chair. His lips had turned white. "I loved him," he said again.

"I know," Zikir whispered. "I pity you for that

278

love, for I know, better than anyone, what you suffer."

Darius signaled Meres to arrest Pyrus, then came to stand before Zikir. "I accused you falsely. For that, I ask your forgiveness. Though in cases such as these, it is customary for the family of the perpetrator to suffer grave punishment as a warning to other miscreants, I will ask the king to spare you and your daughter. You had no part in this. I don't understand Pyrus's hold on your grandson. I don't know how he wielded so much influence over him. But it is obvious that Pyrus carries the greatest share of the blame. Xerxes has already paid the price of his indiscretion with his life. Pyrus's turn will come too."

Zikir collapsed on a stool. "It's small comfort to me, that man's death. I will never have my grandson again. And now his name will be dragged through the mud. I wished I could have spared him of that."

Darius thought for a moment. "Perhaps I can arrange to keep his role in this plot from becoming common knowledge. The important thing is that the king's life is safe. Tell me one thing, Zikir. When I gave you the opportunity to destroy Pyrus's reputation, why did you not take it? I understand that you wished to keep your grandson's memory unsullied. But you could have used many other ways to end Pyrus's reign here. I certainly gave you a lot of opportunity."

"Did you not notice how he suffers? What more could I do to him?"

Admiration for the old man filled Darius. He liked the dignity the grieving grandfather displayed. He also liked the pity that prevented him from destroying a ruined man like Pyrus. "I must leave Damascus soon," he said. "This place will need a steady rule in the wake of such a scandal. Will you agree to act as satrap until the king decides what to do?"

"I am tired. This position, the power that comes with it—none of it means anything now that Xerxes is dead."

Darius laid a hand on Zikir's shoulder. "It's never meaningless to serve your people and give them a better life. You are honest and wise. You can still make a difference for your nation. I know you are tired. Grief has devoured your heart. Still, I'm asking you to stay the course. Pay the price for the sake of the people you can help."

Zikir turned his face toward the wall. Darius could see rivulets of tears as they ran down his cheek. Slowly, the old man nodded.

Darius decided to spend the night in the modest inn where he had concealed Sarah. The thought of staying at the palace in Damascus turned his stomach. Too much bitterness lingered in the shadows of that place.

He had sent Pyrus and his servant, along with a

detachment of Persian soldiers stationed in Damascus, ahead to Susa. The king would deal with the details of the case. He had written a long letter, explaining everything that he had found out and asking for the king's clemency toward Zikir. Part of him wished to go ahead to Susa as well. He longed for the peace of home. But Sarah could not make such a long journey in her condition, and he had decided not to leave her alone again. She would have to remain Beyond the River until she delivered their child. So that was where he intended to stay.

Nassir and Niq had gone ahead to Susa with Pyrus's detachment to bring the strength of their personal testimonies to the case, and to plead with the king for the freedom of their brothers. Darius had included another plea on their behalf in his letter, asking for more clemency. Besides, he had plans for Niq.

His mouth twisted into a humorless smile as he remembered Niq teaching Roxanna a high kick— at her insistence, of course. She had landed him on the floor the first three times because he had refused to hurt a woman. By the fourth round, he had caught on that she wasn't just any woman, and Roxanna had gone flying up in the air and slammed so hard on the ground that her eyes had crossed. Darius tried not to enjoy that memory too much. That woman! She would be the bane of some poor man's existence one of these days. In the meantime, the service of the king was probably the best place for her.

She had insisted on inviting herself along to the inn. Darius had the uneasy feeling that he had not seen the last of her.

"Don't you have to go to Egypt? To deliver that grotesque robe the king sent for the satrap?" he asked her as they rode.

She had changed back into her women's garb halfway to their destination, saying she could not very well enter a public place such as a palace or an inn as a man and leave as a woman. It would lead to unpleasant talk. So she had found a tree to change behind. Now, hair demurely covered by a linen scarf, she looked the picture of sweet femininity.

"There's no hurry. Besides, you're going in my direction."

"That's a fearsome thought. All the way to Jerusalem, I suppose. It would be like Artaxerxes to get an added report out of one of his spies."

At the inn, they found Sarah, Lysander, and Pari gathered around a flimsy table, throwing dice. They were using pistachio shells to count the points. Pari had one left. Lysander had managed to hold on to six or seven. A mountain of them sat in front of his wife.

The unwanted warmth that at times filled him at the sight of her rushed over him. "Watch out. She cheats," he said, and walked in, trying to appear nonchalant.

"I do not!" Sarah bounced to her feet. He thought she would be unsteady, given the change in her body, and put his arm around her to keep her from wobbling. Once his hands found their way to her warm curves, though, they seemed unwilling to let go. Instead of stepping away as he intended, he pulled her into his embrace and held her there. She smelled of roses. He wondered how she had managed that in a dilapidated place like this, and drew her closer. He felt a torrent of emotions he could hardly recognize pass through him. It took him a few moments to discipline himself to step away.

He was breathing rapidly, the sound of his harsh inhalations strange in his own ears. He struggled with a confusion he found unfathomable. Uncertainty was not a familiar experience to him, and he found he did not like it. He had to admit that he had failed at growing indifferent toward her. Even her betrayal—her lies and manipulations—had failed to destroy his deepening attachment to her. She drew him in a way no one had managed to do since he was a child. He crossed his arms and leaned his shoulder against the wall, trying to give the impression of a man whose world wasn't turning on its head.

"Did you solve the mystery of the king's assassination attempt?" Lysander picked up his pistachio shells and stuffed them in his pocket. "Have you discovered the identity of the culprit?"

"And who might you be?" For once, Darius was glad for Roxanna's forward manner. He was in no mood for long explanations.

Lysander came to his feet, his movements deliberate. "I was about to ask you the same question."

There was a moment of silence as the two studied each other, neither willing to give in first. Sarah, the peacemaker, swept an arm toward Lysander. "Forgive me," she said. "I should have thought to introduce you. Lysander, this is Roxanna. She has been helping Darius in Damascus. Roxanna, meet Lysander of Sparta, a friend of Darius. He has accepted the commission to work with my husband on this case."

"Sparta?" Roxanna sounded shocked. Darius knew that since the battle of Thermopylae in the time of King Xerxes, the Persians had grown an unwilling respect for the courage of Spartans. They still considered them crude and uncultured, hardly worth mention, but the way those men fought to the death had left its mark on Persian memory.

"So you are a mercenary?" Roxanna said the words as if she was accusing Lysander of being a slimy earthworm. This was not going well, Darius thought.

"And what are you? By your accent you are Persian and highborn. What kind of aristocratic woman aids in the solving of royal crimes? I wouldn't be surprised to find you belonged to Artaxerxes' dirty-tricks department. Are you one of his famed spies?"

That's a bit too close for comfort, Darius thought. Trust Lysander to take one look at the girl and work her out. "Now, now, children. Shield your blades and try to get along. We have to be in each other's company for a while yet. Roxanna is coming as far as Jerusalem with us, before going on to Egypt."

He ordered dinner and, over bland food, filled in the details of the case for Lysander and Sarah.

"Poor Zikir," Sarah said.

"I agree. Though he would have saved us much trouble if he had shared his suspicions from the beginning." Darius stretched. "I hope this inn has sufficient rooms to accommodate all of us. After five months of chasing Pyrus, I am going to sleep well tonight."

Sarah was caught in the unrelenting grip of a nightmare. Since the miscarriage, they plagued her often, coming with the fierce darkness of a storm and lingering until she woke up, shaking. She never remembered the substance of them. The horror clung to her for long moments after waking, however.

She came to consciousness on a jarring gasp. The room was pitch black. She could feel arms around her. She fought them, filled with terror that some monster from her nightmare world had come to life.

"Stop fighting." Still groggy, Sarah did not recognize the voice. She continued to struggle, gasping, trying to get free.

"It's me, Sarah. Be calm now. Nothing is going to hurt you."

"Darius!" Sarah went still. How had he ended up here, she wondered. His room was next door. Had she made a great disturbance? She found the thought embarrassing. "I ask pardon. Did I wake you?"

"I wasn't asleep, and the walls are thin. I heard you cry out. You were having a nightmare."

She sat up and leaned against a pillow. "Just a bad dream. I have them sometimes. Since I lost the babe." She sensed rather than saw him search for the lamp. She didn't think she could face looking him in the eye right now. "Don't light that! Please."

She felt his hand against her cheek, trailing down over her shoulder. "You're shivering."

"It's nothing. It will pass."

In the dark, he rooted around the bed and found the blankets she had shoved to the bottom in her restless struggles. He pulled them up and tucked them around her.

"And you were looking forward to a good night's sleep. I'm a troublesome wife, I fear. More bother than I am worth." The dark was loosening her tongue. It was as if she could speak more freely, knowing that he could not see her.

"If you mean the nightmare, it's of no consequence. You cannot help what you dream." His body shifted, and she felt his hand find the rise in her abdomen. "I've missed this. All these months, wasted."

They said nothing for some time; just sat, linked by his hand and the indistinguishable heartbeat of their baby in her womb.

"Do you know, there is a lot you have to learn about being a wife," she said.

He leaned back, removing his hand. "Is that so?"

"Yes. I was always arrogant about the ease with which I learn. It's been a crushing blow to my pride that in the most important area of my life, I'm a dim-witted learner."

"I might regret asking this." She thought she heard the creeping edge of a smile in his voice. "What are we talking about?"

"About me, of course. What else is there to talk about?"

"You rarely speak about yourself." His fingers played with the blanket. "Do you want to discuss why you did not tell me about your pregnancy? You've done that already. It's of no use, Sarah. I cannot understand your reasoning."

She swallowed. "I don't mean to offer excuses, my lord. I sinned against you and against God.

But I do want you to understand where the root of that sin lies. What it is that makes me fight so hard to have my way sometimes."

"Say what you must." His tone warned that it would not make a difference.

She cleared her throat. "After my mother died when I was seven, I learned that I had to take care of myself. I don't mean physically. Between my father and aunt Leah, I never went cold or hungry. I never suffered abuse. But there are other things that a little girl needs in order to thrive. Love. Companionship. The knowledge that she is wanted and valued." She bunched the blanket in her fist. Its rough surface scratched her skin, and she forced herself to loosen her hold.

"I didn't have these things. If I wanted my father's company, I learned I had to devise a way to make that happen. I had to take charge of my life in order to receive a little of the care I longed for. Those years taught me to trust no one but myself. I was the one to take care of me. No one else could do that.

"And that's the kind of wife I've been to you. Unable to submit my life into your keeping. I took things into my own hands because I believed only I could provide for my well-being. You didn't deserve that, Darius. You are an excellent husband; you deserve my trust."

Darius shifted his weight away from her. "On that, at least, we can agree."

Sarah forced herself to go on. "I should have known that the most important thing was to surrender myself into your keeping. Even if it didn't feel like a safe option, I should have done it. I should have told you about the baby in spite of my fear that you would leave me behind, that I would have to go through this pregnancy and birth without you. Instead, I convinced myself that I knew what was best for me.

"You know the irony? All those things I was afraid might happen if I told you about my pregnancy happened anyway. I would have been much better off if I had done the right thing from the start."

Darius moved on the bed so that they were sitting side by side instead of facing each other, their legs stretched out, not touching. "So what are you saying? That because of your childhood, my marriage is forever going to be a bed of unrest and upheaval? Am I to helplessly await the next poisoned serpent that's going to raise its head and bite me when I least expect it?"

Sarah gave a choked moan. "I hope not. I don't know how many more times I can bear looking into the cracks in my character. The first time I betrayed you, it was at the wedding. We hadn't met yet. But I was so caught up in my own misery that I spared no thought for you and caused you awful distress because of it. What I learned then was the depth of my selfishness. I realized just how capable I was of considering my own needs above everyone else's.

"This time, I've learned that my life is not mine, anymore. It's yours."

"You want to be that kind of wife to me?" Darius's voice had grown husky.

"I do." She didn't tell him that she had another motive for wanting so badly to become a better wife. During these past weeks of separation, the Lord had shown her that she could not expect Darius not to make mistakes. Not to hurt her, even unintentionally. After all, he was only a man. But surrendering her life into his keeping meant that she trusted God to work out the details. She trusted the Lord of heaven and earth to cover her husband's insufficiencies, and provide for her needs in the midst of them. She trusted *God* to be her provider. Not Sarah. Not Darius. God.

She did not voice these thoughts, assuming that Darius would resent the mention of the Lord. She remained silent, praying that the Lord Himself would one day give her a marriage where she could share such considerations openly, without raising the ire of her husband.

In the darkness they both moved at the same time, and by accident their limbs touched. Sarah heard the sharp intake of Darius's breath. She was about to pull back and apologize for the unintended contact, when he drew her close to him. He held her clasped against the length of him for a moment and then kissed her, his touch searching at first, as if he was trying to know her again.

"Sarah." His breath was hot against the curve of her neck before he slanted his mouth over hers once more. Her heart was racing so fast, she thought they must be able to hear its beat next door. He hadn't touched her like this since Susa.

Sarah found herself getting lost in his touch. It had been so long! So—

With an abrupt move he pulled away. She could hear his breath coming fast and harsh, as if his lungs couldn't hold enough air. "I should leave," he said. He was off the bed and out of her chamber with such explosive speed that a flimsier door would have fallen off its hinges.

Part 3
The Restoration

Chapter 22

The return trip to Jerusalem took an eternity. Sarah knew that they had set the pace in order to accommodate her. They had also attempted to make the cart as comfortable as possible, placing thick mattresses on the floor and a removable canvas covering to ward off the elements. In spite of their care, she felt every bump in her lower back, like a sharp stab. She had to make frequent stops, be they convenient or not, and the jostling of the cart did not help. Her pregnancy affected her body more with every passing day.

She welcomed every hardship for the sake of her child. But she could not help wishing she were less awkward. To her surprise, Darius, who thrived on speed and normally would have chafed under the turtle pace of their convoy, displayed good cheer, even when she made him stop seven times in one day in order to answer the call of nature. She caught him laughing at her once, when she came back red-faced and grumpy from behind a thin bush. Although he didn't seek to touch her again the way he had at the inn, he had fostered a fragile truce between them since that night.

To Sarah's surprise, Roxanna and Lysander

remained at each other's throats every step of the way. The Persian girl had a knack for saying the wrong thing on purpose. Once, Lysander snarled, "I have whips softer than your tongue! Rein in your mouth, or I'll do it for you." Which was the closest Sarah had seen the Greek come to losing his temper.

Darius had had to step in. "Why are you so foul-tempered with her?"

"Why are you neglecting your wife?" was Lysander's retort.

Sarah's eyes grew round with shock. Darius's features became shuttered. "Shut up, both of you, or I will bind up your mouths with linen."

Roxanna began a new jibe. "Dirty linen!" Darius shouted, throwing both of them a hot glare that would have melted iron. Nobody spoke for a long time after that.

"Why do you think they hate each other so much?" Sarah asked Darius one night when the others were out of earshot.

"They don't hate each other. They like each other. That's their problem."

"They have a strange way of showing it. I've never seen two people so thorny around each other."

"I hope I can survive their constant bickering. They annoy the life out of my bones. I wish they would get together and be done."

"Get together? Might as well make Athens and

Persia best friends. It's hopeless, Darius. I can't imagine what makes you think they're attracted to each other."

The third day of their travel dawned sweltering even before the sun rose all the way in the sky. By noon, everyone was panting from the heat.

Lysander looked into the bright heavens and said, "I wish Apollo would not insist on showing off. It's hot enough to burn the feathers off a wet duck's back."

"Apollo!" Roxanna said, her voice dripping with sarcasm. "How can you believe in such a mercurial pantheon of gods? They are worse than you. Moody, vindictive, unreliable."

Lysander swatted at a group of flies that had gathered on his horse's neck. "It's not my fault you Persians are so stingy that you can only believe in two gods. One, Ahura Mazda, all good, and the other, Ahriman, all bad. How is a man to worship when his choices are so limited?

"As to you Jews," he nodded his head in Sarah's direction, "You are even worse. One God. What is a man to do if he gets on the wrong side of Him? You can't run into the embrace of a more sympathetic god. You can't receive help from a rival divinity. You're stuck."

Sarah laughed. "The Lord is merciful. He knows our weakness. I find that one God, if He is the right One, is more than sufficient for my soul."

Darius guided his horse near Lysander. "You

might as well give up. You'll never convince a Jew that your gods have anything of value to offer. She considers them idols. My mother was Jewish. She would have preferred to be beheaded than to give up on her Lord. They are acutely attached to their God."

Sarah stretched her feet in the cart. "You do realize, my lord, that since the time of the Jewish exile, our leaders have decreed that any man born of a Jewish mother is himself a Jew?"

"How convenient for your leaders. A little pronouncement and one's nationality is supposed to suddenly turn on its head."

They came upon Jerusalem one late afternoon, with the sun low behind an outcropping of brown hills to their west. Sarah sucked in an astounded breath when she had her first glimpse. "The walls!"

"They must be halfway up, my lady," Pari said, her voice high with awe.

Lysander's horse was prancing next to the cart. "That cousin of yours has achieved the impossible. I did not think anyone could pull off his grand scheme. And yet, here we are, fewer than thirty days since he started, and look at the state of that wall. It's a marvel."

"Do you call this a marvel in Sparta?" Roxanna asked. "They are just walls. And not very pretty ones at that."

Sarah rose on her knees to have a better view.

"You don't understand, Roxanna. When we first arrived—do you remember, Lysander? Jerusalem had been in the grip of such apathy that they couldn't even clean up the mess gathering around their ears. Now they have built a wall that spans the whole city. It may not be a work of art. Nonetheless, it will serve the purpose of bringing safety to Jerusalem. And they accomplished this without slaves, without an army, with only the people of Judah volunteering their time. In less than thirty days, these people who once had no unity have come together and rebuilt their city."

Nehemiah himself came to welcome them. Sarah noticed that his face was drawn and new lines had etched across his brow. She wondered when he had last enjoyed a good night's sleep.

"Cousin Nehemiah, how did you manage to raise the walls so high in such a short time?"

He gave her a warm smile. "The people work from first light until the stars come out. You look well, my dear. I take it the physician had good news for you?"

"Yes. All is well, thank the Lord."

"My heart rejoices to hear it. You have been in my prayers daily. Lord Darius, it's good to have you back. Did you conclude your business in Damascus to your satisfaction?"

"I did. We plan to stay here until after Sarah has delivered the babe."

Nehemiah nodded. "You are most welcome.

Now I am certain you are anxious to refresh yourselves after your journey. Sarah will show you to your lodgings. It's an old house and not comfortable, I fear. With the wall under construction, we don't have the time or the men to spare for another building project. The new residence for the governor must wait.

"We serve dinner in an hour. Please join us as my guests."

"I wished we could provide for our own meals," Sarah said when Nehemiah left. "I always feel guilty when I eat at Nehemiah's table."

Darius drew in his brows. "Why? As governor, he is entitled to a food allowance from the people of Judah."

"Entitled, he may be. But he refuses to accept it. He became aware when we first arrived that, due to recent famines and general poverty, the people had little to live on. In order to avoid being an added burden to them, he chose to waive the food allowance that was due to him and his officials. Previous governors had always insisted on receiving their share, laying heavy burdens on the people with their demands.

"Nehemiah has changed that practice. Instead, he uses his own savings and his regular salary in order to provide food for one hundred and fifty Jewish officials, as well as the visitors he often entertains from the surrounding nations."

"He is paying for this out of his own pocket?"

"Yes, and let me tell you, my lord, it is not a cheap undertaking. I used to keep his records before I came to Damascus. He pays for one ox, six sheep or goats, and a large number of poultry every day. And the wine! His guests seem to have a hole in their bellies, for they drink with the thirst of fish and he has to lay out large supplies of different wines every ten days."

Darius shook his head. "I've never heard of anyone giving up legal income."

"I asked him once why he did not charge the people the fee they owed him as governor.

"'Because I fear God!' he said. 'Do they not already carry a heavy burden? Have I not seen with my own eyes that they are poor and struggling to put bread on the table for their families as it is? Should I add to their hardship by virtue of the fact that I have the law on my side?'"

"He's an unusual man. Well, tonight we'll be his guests. But starting tomorrow, I will provide the rations for our company out of my own pocket." Sarah noticed that Darius became thoughtful after this exchange. He had never had the opportunity to come to know Nehemiah on intimate terms. Because he avoided her cousin when possible, he had had little discourse with him. Nehemiah remained a stranger, one he did not trust. Sarah hoped that seeing him at work in Jerusalem would help Darius come to understand the man, and grow to like and respect him.

Nehemiah was on a first-name basis with most of the workers and even knew their servants and wives. He carried dried nuts and dates for their children in his pockets and took their babies in his arms while he chatted with them as he inspected the wall. Not a day went by that Nehemiah did not visit some portion of the construction site.

Gone were his silk robes and golden jewels. Gone were his heeled shoes and curled hair. He was one of the people. The requirements of the Persian court already seemed far away and insignificant.

While making his regular circuit, Nehemiah breathed in the smell of dust, old stones, and fresh mortar. Construction smells. Against all reason, he had come to love them—he, who was accustomed to the scents of rose water, spring blossoms, and the spices of Arabia.

He came upon the Broad Wall where Uzziel the goldsmith and Hananiah, a manufacturer of perfumes, had charge of the repairs. This was by far the widest section of the wall around Jerusalem. The original had been built in the days of King Hezekiah. Its repair presented many difficulties due to its extra width.

Nehemiah shook his head. "You have done well. Even though your section is a good deal wider than the rest, you have managed to come up halfway, same as the others. You'd have to lay down five of me, head to toe, in order to match the width of this wall."

The goldsmith beat his sleeve with a dirty hand. A cloud of dust rose up in the air. His hair stood in tangled knots, and not a single piece of jewelry adorned him. He looked like he had not bathed in days. He had been too busy working, setting an example for his servants, Nehemiah knew. The delicate fingers that once purified silver and shaped gold were covered in calluses now.

"The people have been working with their whole hearts. And this enthusiasm is largely due to you, my lord Nehemiah. You have inspired us to persist and not give up. You show up in person every day. I've seen you pick up stones with your own hand, and I thought, if the governor of Judah can do this, then a goldsmith has no excuse. So here we are. Filthy but proud."

Nehemiah placed a hand on Uzziel's shoulder. "One day, people around the world will remember you for this accomplishment, my friend."

He was glad he had been able to enjoy that moment of celebration, for he had little peace from that moment. Sanballat, Tobiah, and their influential friends discovered how well the rebuilding of Jerusalem's walls was proceeding. This success infuriated them. Their enemies were more intent than ever to smash down their work and destroy them before they could taste further success.

In his office that night Nehemiah received the disturbing report that Sanballat, along with his friends the Ammonites and Ashdodites as well as a few other local tribes, intended to attack Jerusalem. It was the worst onslaught against them yet.

Nehemiah winced when he heard the news. He didn't feel fresh and strong. He didn't feel up to such a huge challenge. He was already stretched thin.

For Nehemiah, this journey had started months before. He had begun by fasting and praying and grieving for his people. For months he had carried on the delicate responsibilities of his regular work as the king's cupbearer while also carrying the burden of the wreck Judah had become. Immediately following those months, he had taken on the duties of organizing a large caravan and leading them through a long, incommodious and dangerous journey. He had borne the heavy pressure of protecting them. And then he had had to face the problems of Jerusalem.

Why now, when he was at his weakest, would God allow the worst to come against them?

Hanani, who was with him when the news came, said, "In a skirmish, we would be hopeless. If they plan to fight against us, there is little we can do to protect ourselves. Even with your Persian military escort we are shorthanded. Your escort was large enough to provide safe passage for a caravan, but it is too insignificant to make a real difference against so many enemies determined on our destruction."

Nehemiah did not answer. What could he say? He agreed with many of Hanani's concerns. Grey with weariness, he gathered those closest to him. Quoting Solomon, he reminded them, *"Unless the Lord builds a house, the work of the builders is wasted. Unless the Lord protects a city, guarding it with sentries will do no good.* We will pray and ask for God's guidance. He will show us the way, for human wisdom shall not prevail in these circumstances."

They prayed long and hard. In spite of his fatigue, Nehemiah persevered and would not give up. He knew God was their hope. Their strength. When they were finished, Nehemiah had a plan.

"We will guard the city day and night. We will protect ourselves as we build. And we will succeed." Strangely, with that resolution, he felt a new vigor. The discouragement that had over-whelmed him at the initial news of the impending attack lifted off him as if it had never been.

Before Nehemiah could put his plans into action, he received a visit from a group of men who represented the workers. "My lord," they said. "We are exhausted. For a month we have worked fourteen hours every day. The strength of the laborers is giving out. What's more, the conditions at the construction site are becoming untenable. There is more rubble than ever to contend with. The site has become downright dangerous in parts. The other day one of the children stumbled upon a piece of masonry and split his leg open from knee to ankle. We cannot rebuild the wall. Not under these conditions."

"I see."

The man reddened under Nehemiah's steady gaze. "We are tired. And now there are whispers that the enemy is going to attack us. The Judeans who live near those parts bring us repeated reports of Sanballat's imminent onslaught. If we aren't dead from weariness first, we'll die by their arrows."

Nehemiah placed a bracing hand on the speaker's arm. "In the midst of a significant building project, one has to face a point when it seems there is more chaos than there is progress. This is where you are. You've grown tired. You feel overcome. But do not set your mind on the disarray of the moment, for when God is in the building, chaos will eventually be replaced by His order. When things appear to be falling apart, God is in fact causing them to fall into place.

"Do not be swayed by Sanballat's threats. He has increased his attacks because he's afraid. The wall is so high that Sanballat and his friends are losing confidence. That's why they bear down so hard against us. Their new tactic is to terrorize us. To plant fear in our hearts so that we will give up.

But God is bigger than Sanballat. Although things seem to be falling apart, even now, in the midst of our worst disarray, the Lord is working to make them fall together for our future good." He took a deep breath and allowed his hand to fall away from the man's arm.

"I am making plans for the defense of Jerusalem. I will ensure that the workers have a short rest as I make preparations. Don't lose heart now. In your exhaustion, you feel overwhelmed. You want to give up. What you don't know is that you are close to victory."

Nehemiah invited Darius and Lysander for a private conference and explained the situation to them. Darius considered the news for a moment. "They mean to throw you into confusion. Thus far, your people have worked wholeheartedly. But this news is bound to shake their confidence. If they believe that coming to work on the wall means they'll be killed by an errant arrow, they are not going to feel as motivated as before to show up."

"So we must give them the feeling of security," Nehemiah said.

"The feeling and the reality. I don't think your enemies are making empty threats. They are intent on killing your workers. But only because they believe them to be easy prey. Once we give them the message that Jerusalem is not to be won so simply, they will give up their intention of attacking you."

After studying the map of the city, the three men decided upon a defense strategy. Nehemiah stationed some of his people behind the lowest points of the wall, where the city was most exposed. He posted families at strategic locations. Not only were they providing essential defense, but they were also located in positions where the enemy could spy them with ease. The glint of their weapons could be seen from leagues away. With a few well-placed guards, Nehemiah had managed to make Jerusalem appear like a fully defended garrison city.

Those who owned arms brought their own. A few even donned coats of mail. Nehemiah provided swords and spears and bows for the rest. He gave the workers a day of rest while he waited for the enemy to reconsider their plans.

Once he had inspected these defenses and determined their effectiveness, he called a gathering of the people and the nobles. As always, he opened the meeting with a simple prayer for the Lord's protection and guidance. And then he spoke to his countrymen. He had not prepared his speech beforehand. He relied on God to give him the words.

"People of Jerusalem, you have heard the rumors that Sanballat, Tobiah, and their friends intend to attack us. Do not fear! You have worked harder and better than they expected. You have accomplished an impossible task. You have completed half of the wall. That half is already providing an effective defense for us. Our men who stand behind it, guarding Jerusalem even as I speak, have enough covering to remain safe against an onslaught of arrows.

"Remember the Lord. He is great and glorious. Remember also your families, for you fight for your brothers, for your sons and your daughters. You fight for your wives and your homes."

There were tears in many eyes. Men wiped at their cheeks surreptitiously. Nehemiah took a deep breath and let silence settle over the crowd for a moment. He let his words sink in before beginning again.

"There is no other nation that can boast of your faithfulness. You have come from far and wide in Judah: from Tekoa, Gibeon, Mizpah, and Jerusalem's hinterland. You have worked long hours with no pay. You have sacrificed your comfort for the Lord.

"You come from every background conceivable. The high priest has been working alongside merchants and officials and women and rulers. You, Malkijah, although you are ruler of the district of Beth Hakkerem, you have been repairing the Dung Gate. Never once did I hear you whisper that it was beneath your dignity to work on that smelly stretch of land."

The crowd laughed. Malkijah bowed low until his forehead almost touched the ground. The crowd went wild.

"And you, Shallum, ruler of the half-district of Jerusalem, though you have no sons, you brought your daughters to help you repair the wall. I tell you, if I had a son half as strong as one of your daughters, I would count myself blessed."

"And they are all of marriageable age, lord governor!" Shallum shouted. "Just in case there is an interested bridegroom with a hefty bride price milling about."

A deafening cheer went up among the people. Nehemiah smiled.

The enemy still lurked at their door. The workers remained weary to the marrow of their bones. The work sites continued to be dangerous. Judea's economy was still in shambles. Nothing had changed in their circumstances. But Nehemiah knew that the spirit of the people had turned from fear and defeat to hope. And that was how victories were made. God was teaching him—and His people—that when it came to battle, what happened in the mind had far more power than what happened in the world.

Chapter 23

Sarah could not sleep. She did not know if it was the discomfort of her body or the constant worry about Jerusalem that kept her wakeful. If the rumors were to be believed, their enemy might charge against them at any moment. Giving up on rest, she abandoned her bed and, donning a linen robe loose enough to accommodate her increasing girth, she grabbed a light scarf and slipped out of her chamber. She decided to visit the courtyard, hoping the fresh air would help clear the cobwebs from her mind. A small lamp lit a narrow path as she navigated the uneven stairs. The hour had grown late, and she walked quietly to avoid disturbing the rest of the household. She was on the second to last step when a voice jolted her. "Sarah!"

She almost jumped out of her skin. Looking up, she saw Darius striding toward her. "I didn't mean to startle you," he said.

Behind him, the door of Nehemiah's office remained ajar, pouring soft light into the hall. "My lord! Have you been meeting with the governor so late?"

Close up, she noticed the hollows under his cheeks, the paleness of the usually robust skin.

Was anyone in Jerusalem not exhausted? Weariness had not robbed him of his startling beauty. Even after being with him for so many months, she sometimes found the sheer physical attraction of that face overwhelming. It made her as shy and tongue-tied as an adolescent girl. In the aftermath of the rupture in their relationship, these feelings had grown even more disruptive to her peace. She feared she could not hide them from his penetrating observation. His relentless intelligence came against her like an unleashed weapon, leaving no room for pride or self-preservation. It shattered something in her soul to acknowledge that he had no use for her responses anymore.

In spite of the uneasy truce they had entered since Damascus, he remained withdrawn from her. He had shut a part of himself up, locked it away, so that she could not reach it. When he sought her, it was no longer with the ease of dear friends. He felt awkward around her. And he spent his nights alone. It was the deepest sorrow of her heart. She surrendered it to the Lord day and night, but it always returned and weighed her down with the heaviness of a stone olive press.

Darius rubbed a hand against the back of his neck. "There are many details to oversee. Nehemiah is planning his defense strategy for the coming days." He put one foot on the bottom step and rested his elbow on his bent knee. "He is surprisingly astute, your cousin. I knew he was a talented administrator, but I didn't expect him to have any military sense. I underestimated him; it turns out he would do well as a general in time of war."

"Will there be a battle?"

He shrugged a wide shoulder. "No one knows for certain. We must prepare as if there will be."

Sarah sat on the stair and wrapped her arms around her legs.

"What are you doing out of bed?" Darius asked.

"I couldn't sleep. I thought fresh air might do me good."

"Come. I will accompany you. I could use some air myself."

The courtyard was dusty and smelled of horse dung. Not a single flower or herb plant adorned the place. Darius found a stone bench where they could sit side by side. He leaned against the wall behind them and gazed at the stars. The night blazed with them.

"I miss home," Sarah said. What had made her blurt that out? Would she never learn to have control over her mouth?

Darius turned to study her. "I thought this was home."

"In a way. Home to my spirit. But I think of your palace near Persepolis as my real home. If we were there, we could stroll in the gardens, with the sound of the pools trickling, and the scent of honeysuckle and lilies sweetening the air. Anousya would lick my toes and demand my attention. My friends and family would be gathered about me. And there wouldn't be an army at my door, seeking my blood."

"Are you sorry you came?"

"No. Just tired, I think. Tired of worrying."

"We've had a report that Sanballat and his allies have postponed their plans to come against us. Apparently, witnessing the evidence of Jerusalem's strong defense has put them off for now. Even if they choose to come against us, it will be in the form of a skirmish, directed at a portion of the wall. They would not come against the city itself. The king, while not concerned with minor disputes, might find an outright war against one of the regions under his rule offensive. Something these men would not risk. Rest easy, little Sarah. I won't let anything happen to you."

Sarah flashed a smile. "You are handy with an arrow, as I have good reason to know. Perhaps you should teach me."

"You'd probably take off my ear in your first attempt to use a bow. My thumb would be the victim of your second attempt. And the tip of my nose would be gone in the third. No. I confess I don't find it an appealing prospect."

"Are you disparaging my aim?"

"Absolutely. I've seen you throw a stick for Anousya."

"You are a wiser man than I gave you credit for. So, how will we go back to rebuilding the wall?"

"Without the help of your bow and arrow, you mean? I'm sure we'll manage."

Sarah laughed. "I mean Nehemiah had to stop the building project in order to station all those guards. If we start rebuilding again, won't we be vulnerable to attack? We only have enough men to either guard or build, it seems to me. We can't do both."

"Yes, we can. Nehemiah's plan is that half the men do the work while the other half, equipped with spears, shields, and armor, post themselves behind the workers. The Persian officers will help the guard. No doubt the sight of us will put off Sanballat. The work will go on, a little slower than before. But it will go on. I told you. Your cousin has a good head on his shoulders."

"You seem to have warmed up to him."

"I said he had talent. I didn't say he had become my dear friend." He stretched against the wall. "Roxanna and her servant leave for Egypt tomorrow. She can't delay her departure anymore."

"Are you sad to see her go?" she asked, trying to keep her voice casual. Would he miss the beautiful Roxanna?

"Sad? Relieved, more like. Never seen anyone like that girl for stirring trouble. I thought Lysander was in a foul mood while she was around. But he became worse since she announced her intention to leave. He's been acting like a wounded tiger all day. Heaven help us when she actually goes."

Nehemiah had arranged for the construction to begin again that morning. There weren't as many workers at the wall. But that could not be helped. Many of the stronger men had been posted as guards. He had spent the past hour walking the perimeter, trying to ascertain if certain sections needed more help. On one side of him walked a silent Darius, appraising their preparations with shrewd, experienced eyes.

On his other side, he was accompanied by a trumpeter who held his instrument at the ready. Before starting the work again, Nehemiah had told the laborers that he would use the trumpet as a signal. "The construction site is extensive and spread out and, now with fewer workers, our men are widely separated from each other. If we are attacked, I will use the trumpet as a signal."

At first the people had thought he wanted to give them a warning so that they could flee at the first sign of attack. Nehemiah had cleared up that misconception before it had a chance to take root.

"What I want you to do is follow the sound of the trumpet, for it will *lead* you to the fighting. We will aid our brothers who have come under enemy assault. Remember that we are not fighting in our own strength. Our God will fight for us!"

Now as he walked past the upper palace, near the court of the guard, a tired-looking man pulled on his sleeve. Nehemiah turned in polite inquiry.

"My lord, I live to the north of Judah, near Sanballat's territory. I am begging you to stop this work. Just yesterday we heard the news that he had made a promise to come and kill you all while you slept. Whatever you do, they will attack you. Your paltry defenses shall avail you nothing! You'll be murdered, and then what good will your wall be?"

If Nehemiah had heard this warning once, he had heard it ten times. It was becoming like an irritating toothache. It would not relent. At first, he had been annoyed. Now, he was beginning to grow concerned. Many of his leaders were already falling under its repetitive spell. If you hit the same patch of skin often enough, you would eventually form a tender bruise. Touch it again, and your victim would cry out from the pain. After so many warnings of impending disaster, the residents of Jerusalem were beginning to act like a bruised man.

Physical threat was the city's greatest fear. Though Babylon's invasion had occurred long before any of them had been born, the hearts of the people continued to bear the scars of that savage captivity. Over one hundred years of fear rose up at the threat of Sanballat's attack. It was a generational terror. To heal one man of the fear of invasion and violent death, God had to go three generations deep.

Repeated reports of imminent doom were taking their toll on the morale of the occupants of Jerusalem. The men who insisted on spreading their disheartening news had the best of intentions. They considered themselves faithful Judeans who were helping their countrymen. Instead, they were as effective as Sanballat in the proliferation of discouragement.

All around him, men were losing their heads. Nehemiah intended to keep his. It wasn't so much that he was immune to pressure. Far from it. He just knew that if he clung to God, he could push through this time of hardship. And if he persevered, he might be able to inspire others to do the same.

"Look," Nehemiah said to his uninvited companion, and pointed. Not far from them, Azariah and his servants were working on the wall beside Azariah's own house. "What do you see?"

"They are building the wall."

Nehemiah almost called the man a *genius,* before managing to clamp down on the sarcasm that wanted to boil over. That might bring him a moment's relief, but it would turn the heart of a man away. And he knew which had more value.

"Note those who are fetching and carrying. Do you see how with one hand they carry the instruments of their work—buckets, stones, spades—and in the other, they carry swords and daggers and spears?"

"Yes."

"Now the builders. Observe how each one has a sword buckled to his side."

"I see."

"Try to understand, my friend. We are ready for whatever may come. Stop being terrorized by a few menacing words. Put your hope in the Lord. Instead of bringing alarming news, make yourself useful and give Azariah a hand."

The man's jaw grew slack.

"Go on," Nehemiah said. "We're shorthanded. Your help would be welcome."

The man seemed dazed by the governor's response. Nehemiah imagined that he had expected weak-kneed dismay, not steely resolve. It seemed to have made an impression, for he obeyed Nehemiah's command and approached Azariah.

Darius gave a thin smile. "He looks like he can't figure out how he went from being the bearer of crucial news to helping in the very project he was disparaging moments ago."

Nehemiah ran an exasperated hand over his head. "With friends like this, Jerusalem doesn't need any enemies. They don't seem to understand that there are times in life when you must be both a builder and a warrior. One hand on a bucket and the other on a sword."

"Aren't you concerned about slowing down? With this strategy, you've lost a good part of your work force."

Nehemiah paused. "Sometimes you have to do less in order to achieve more. There are seasons in life when you have to slow down your productivity. I must use part of my strength to resist the foe, and part for the work of God. I can't bury my head in the sand and pretend that Judah has no enemies. My time and resources must reflect that fact, or I have already lost.

"God has asked me to build up Jerusalem. But He has also asked me to protect what He has already built. With one hand we will hold on to the instruments of building, with the other, we will grasp the weapons of protection."

Chapter 24

Roxanna left for Egypt the following morning. Sarah went to the courtyard to bid her fare well. She found Lysander already there, leaning against a wall, his arms crossed against his massive chest. His blond hair, newly washed, sparkled in the sunlight. His face bore such a thunderous expression that Sarah, intending to approach him with a hearty greeting, made a hasty retreat.

"I wished you didn't have to leave," Sarah said as Roxanna checked her horse's saddle. To her surprise, Sarah had grown to like the Persian girl. In spite of her barbed tongue, Roxanna's genuine interest in those around her made her a lively companion. Sarah suspected that if she had remained in Jerusalem, they would have formed the kind of deep friendship that her heart longed to have.

Roxanna played with the leather bridle of her horse, a massive creature that towered over her, though she did not seem to mind its menacing strength, or the danger it posed. "We Persians are slaves to our duty." She threw a quick look toward Lysander before returning her attention to Sarah. "I wish I didn't have to leave either." With disconcerting abandon, she threw her arms around Sarah and gave her an enveloping hug. "I'll miss you."

Sarah laughed. "I'll miss you too. Now, are you going to walk over there and say goodbye to him?"

Roxanna's fair skin suffused with color. "Why should I? He can come and take his leave of me as any polite man would do."

"Oh, if it was politeness you were expecting, then perhaps you shouldn't have been so rude to him for days on end."

Roxanna stiffened. "He deserved it." She signaled her servant, a lanky man with swarthy complexion, before jumping into the saddle. "Keep well, sweet scribe. And shield that husband of yours from trouble. He seems to have a liking for it."

She pressed her feet to the sides of her giant horse, and it sprung to life. It had barely taken three steps when Lysander threw himself in the path of the creature like a madman with no concern for his safety. Sarah gasped and clapped a hand over her mouth to keep a scream from escaping.

In the last moment, Roxanna managed to bring her horse under control before it crushed the Spartan under its prancing hooves. "Are you insane?" she shouted at the top of her lungs, her usually deep voice sounding squeaky.

Lysander pulled her off her horse with one fluid movement. "You didn't say goodbye."

Roxanna sputtered. "You've lost what little wit you had. I could have killed you!"

Lysander studied the tall woman through narrowed eyes, not bothering to explain his actions. Sarah didn't know whether to be outraged or delighted when, without warning, Lysander grabbed Roxanna and pulled her roughly into his arms and gave her a sound kiss that lasted far too long for decency. Sarah noted with interest that the Persian girl didn't exactly seem to fight the embrace. When he was done, Lysander walked away without a word. He couldn't speak; he was laughing too hard. Sarah found herself rooted to the spot. She had never heard him laugh out loud. It had a pleasant ring. One could grow accustomed to the sound of it. Observing Roxanna's expression, she worried for a moment that he might find a dagger buried in his back.

"Donkey," she screamed at him. "Spartan peasant!"

"See you back in Persia, shrew," he said, still laughing.

Sarah had a feeling that Lysander and Roxanna's story was far from over. The Greek's words held a firm promise. She felt certain that he would follow Roxanna, and that more adventures awaited them. A hint of pity for the Persian girl caused a wave of anxiety to shoot through Sarah. Being pursued by Lysander would be a little like being a besieged city.

• • •

Darius found himself alone with Nehemiah. He had sat through a protracted meeting while Nehemiah dealt with one complaint after another from his leaders. Darius knew he could have left at any point. These were not his problems. But he had found the governor's tactics fascinating and had lingered out of curiosity.

When everyone left, he asked, "Why do you think you have to spend so much of your time dealing with the difficulties that your own people are creating?"

Nehemiah stretched his legs and expelled a sigh that seemed to come from his depths. "Our men have grown accustomed to defeat. Remember that not long ago, they lost everything. Now, they measure every circumstance in life against that possibility. Even a small threat sends them scurrying for cover because they expect to lose. They expect the worst to come to pass. When we first started rebuilding the walls, they didn't believe they had the fortitude to be builders. Experience has taught them a different lesson. It is time they learn they can be warriors too.

"It's like in the days of Gideon. Did your mother ever tell you his story, my lord?"

"I don't recall."

"It was during the time of the judges. In those days, Israel did not have kings like other nations. The Lord was our King."

"I do remember my mother speaking of that time."

"It was an unusual period. Israel had enjoyed forty years of peace. In that season of prosperity, rather than drawing closer to God, we wandered. We worshiped the Lord. But we also worshiped the idols of Canaan. As a result, God allowed the Midianites to rule over our nation for seven cruel years. We became impoverished and were reduced to starvation by constant attacks.

"A young man from the tribe of Manasseh, named Gideon, grew up during those hard times. One day, the angel of the Lord came to visit him. Gideon was hiding at the bottom of a winepress, threshing wheat."

"Why would he thresh wheat in a winepress? Surely that must have been too confined a space?"

"Yes, but the Midianites intimidated him. They often swooped down on the people of Israel and plundered their food and cattle. Experience had taught Gideon to grow timid. To be afraid. So he hid at the bottom of a winepress. And God came to him there, at the height of his weakness, his indignity, his insecurity.

"And what do you think the angel of the Lord called Gideon, there, hiding in his winepress, clutching his bit of wheat?"

Darius shook his head. "Idiot? Coward?"

Nehemiah threw his head back and gave a deep

laugh. "You would think so. But no. He called Gideon a mighty warrior. A man of valor."

"What for? He sounds like a fainthearted weakling."

"That is how he had learned to live. His circumstances had caused him to see himself in those terms. He didn't accept the angel's words any more than you did, my lord. He said, *My clan is the weakest in Manasseh, and I am the least in my family.* In other words, he thought he was a nobody. A far cry from a man of valor.

"But God saw the real man. Not the person the circumstances had produced. Beneath all that, He perceived the man He had created. Someone strong and capable. A courageous champion. He saw a man who could be a judge over Israel during an arduous period. A man with strength enough to set Israel free from her enemies."

Darius raised his brows. "Did Gideon become a judge?"

"Yes. One of our greatest. And he went on to save Israel from the terror of Midian."

"Are you saying that the men of Judah have become like Gideon? They perceive themselves as less than they are?"

"Indeed, that is what I mean. We have grown timid and negative. Our enemies foster these lies. And so, like Gideon, we live our lives at the bottom of a winepress of our own making.

"But I don't think that is how God sees us,

because that is not how He created us. He is calling us forth, calling us to walk into our true nature. To be stouthearted. To become men and women of valor, like Gideon. He is calling us to crawl out of hiding and face our enemies, especially the ones that torment our mind. Enemies like fear and insecurity."

Darius bent to pick up a small clay tablet, which had rolled on the floor. He twirled it in the air before catching it with ease. "You've changed, cupbearer."

Nehemiah combed a hand through his beard. It had grown scruffy. "I dare say. Neither I nor my men have taken off our clothes in days. If I came before His Majesty in this state, he would place the heel of his leather-shod foot on the seat of my trousers and cast me out of his presence."

"I don't mean your appearance, though I own, I never thought to see you in such a state." Darius flipped the tablet higher this time, caught it again, and threw it back up. "You have become less of a courtier. More of a commander. You govern and lead your people as if you were born to it."

Nehemiah caught the tablet mid-twirl in the air. "I hope you are right, my lord. Most days, I feel I don't know what I'm doing. If it weren't for my faith in God and His guidance, I might have given up long ago."

As a military commander, Darius had seen his fair share of masterful leaders who pushed through difficult circumstances and accomplished the work, no matter how harrowing. He was accustomed to stubborn courage. As an aristocrat, he had spent years in the company of men and women whose autocratic confidence led the way out of many tangles—and sometimes into them. What had started to impress Darius about Nehemiah, however, was that alongside these qualities, he showed a profound understanding of the people under his care. He recognized their weakness, and yet instead of judging it, he sought ways to dissolve it.

What was more, Darius found Nehemiah's consideration for the suffering of the poor humbling. The first time he had visited the governor in his chamber he had been shocked by its diminutive modesty.

"These are your private quarters?" he had asked. He had been assigned a room twice as large.

Nehemiah had waved a hand. "I'm rarely here. No sense in taking the best room for myself."

"Sarah says you are paying the expenses of the household from your personal purse in order to spare the people."

"What else can I do? Bleed them dry? Someone has to take care of them."

The most shocking aspect of Nehemiah's character proved to be his openness. Darius had almost choked when he heard Judea's governor admit that he didn't know what he was doing. As the scion of one of the most important families in the Persian world, Darius had been raised never to confess his insecurity. Something in him had cringed with distaste when Nehemiah had said those words. Another part of him— something deeper and hidden—had leapt like a hungry lion toward that revelation. That level of transparency had appealed to a part of him he had not known existed.

He scratched his chin, which had begun to itch. Normally, in the summer months he adopted a clean-shaven look, like the Egyptians. It felt more comfortable in the heat. In Jerusalem, however, everything that required extra time had become untenable and he had stopped shaving.

The past few days had been tense, and everyone in Jerusalem lived as though under siege. In the urgency of constant danger, they kept their weapons strapped to their sides, even when they went for water.

Darius had volunteered to take guard duty at one of the sectors. No one could be spared any-more, neither the highest leader nor the lowest servant. Nehemiah had even asked the people who lived outside Jerusalem to move into the city at nights so that they and their men could help with the evening watch.

Darius made his way to the spot Nehemiah had assigned to him on the eastern wall, not far from the palace ruins. The location covered a residential area. Its proximity to the old part of Jerusalem, which the residents referred to as the City of David, made it a strategic portion. Darius had been stationed opposite a worker named Hanun, the sixth son of Zalaph.

"Good morning," he said as he took his position.

Hanun must have been close in age to Darius. His modest clothes and lack of servants marked him a poor man, but Hanun had a sparkle to his manner that seemed undimmed by poverty.

"Lord Darius! How blessed I am to have the flower of Persian aristocracy guard my back! The Lord has smiled upon me indeed. I doubt even the high priest himself has been honored with such grand protection." The wide mouth split into a guileless smile.

Darius returned the smile. "Perhaps the king has sent me to keep an eye on you. I hear you are a troublemaker."

"Ah, you must have me mixed up with this one over here." He pulled forward a little boy, no more than six or seven years old. "This is Benjamin, my son. He is the prince of troublemakers."

The boy had sturdy arms and legs and eyes the color of the night. He swatted Hanun on the thigh. "Father!" Turning to Darius, he said, "I am not a troublemaker. My father has taught me to be a good builder, because I'm strong. See?" He picked up a large piece of masonry. His face turned red with the effort.

"Impressive," Darius said. He meant it.

"Thank you! Just what I needed. Better give that to me in case I run out of stones, son." Hanun took the masonry from Benjamin before he could hurt himself and winked at Darius.

"I'm going to be a soldier, like you." Benjamin approached Darius, his manner confident. Before Darius could respond, a woman strolled over. She had the same dark eyes as Benjamin. Her pleasingly plump figure was encased in a simple woolen tunic cinched at the waist by a striped fabric sash he had noticed Judean women favored. Her scarf matched the wool of her dress. Neither one had been dyed. Dye cost money.

"Is my son making a pest of himself, my lord?"

"He's fine. He was sharing his plans for the future."

Hanun left the wall to join them. "Tirzah, my love." He kissed his wife with open tenderness. "Have you come to help?"

"I have. My chores at the house are done. I can lend you a hand the rest of the day."

Hanun addressed Darius. "This is my wife, Tirzah, my lord. Do you see my portion of the wall? These delicate, ivory hands have raised half of it."

Tirzah cuffed her husband on the shoulder and held out her hands. They were callused and work roughened. Where mud and dirt didn't cover the skin, it peeked through brown as wood from a walnut tree. "Neither delicate nor ivory, you foolish man. Now come and work, both of you, and leave the Persian lord to do his job."

Something squeezed Darius's heart as he saw the little family working side by side throughout the morning. They were openly affectionate with one another, often sharing laughter over inconsequential moments. Hanun helped his boy with a delicate wisdom that built his confidence without allowing him to do too much. The interplay between father and son moved Darius in ways he had not experienced before. He wondered if one day he would have the same tender relationship with the child that his wife carried. Would they laugh and play together with the same freedom? Would he know, with the ease and wisdom of Hanun, how to use everyday moments to plant lasting lessons in the heart of his child?

Hanun was no less loving with his Tirzah than he was with his son. Their open affection moved Darius with a power he found disconcerting. He felt a rush of longing that he could not squelch. Annoyed with himself, he tried to ignore the couple and the feelings they roused in him. Unbidden, he wondered if a day would come when he'd hold Sarah in the same high regard. Would they ever be able to draw that near to each other?

Up until then, he had blamed Sarah for the

distance that had come between them. For the first time, he had the uncomfortable feeling that the gap in their relationship was as much of his making as hers. He found it easy to blame her for her failures. But watching Hanun with his wife, he had to confess that he had never allowed Sarah that level of access to his heart. He had never been as open as Hanun.

He was relieved when Pari, accompanied by Meres, brought him lunch. The interruption helped to stop his intruding thoughts.

"My lady sends you this, with her compliments. She packed it herself," Pari said.

He had forbidden Sarah from coming near the construction site, worried that she might stumble and fall over the rubble. Somehow, she always managed to find his whereabouts and send someone with food and fresh water. He thanked Pari and opened the bundle she had brought. Sarah had sent enough food to satisfy five large men. There was no Shushan to prepare mouthwatering feasts for them. The fare was simple—vegetarian lentil stew, cheese, barley bread, and dates. But after a day in the hot sun, he could make do with anything.

He approached the little family who were busy at their task. Hanun had started work before sunrise and, except for a few short breaks, he and his family had worked straight through the day. It was now past the noonday hour.

"My wife has sent me enough food to feed the Egyptian army. I wondered if you would like to share my repast?"

Hanun sent him an uncomfortable glance and made a nervous sound in his throat. Darius said, "My wife is a Jew. She would not send food that does not meet with your regulations. Not in Jerusalem."

Hanun relaxed. "We would be honored to join you, my lord."

They could not take a long pause from their work. Meres took over the watch while Darius and the little family ate in haste.

"Tasty lentils!" Hanun said and dipped his bread into the bowl for another mouthful before he had swallowed the first.

"Slow down, husband, or Lord Darius is going to think we are an ill-mannered family who haven't seen the sight of food in a week." Tirzah put a small bite in her mouth and took her time chewing.

"Well, he would be right to think it. I don't know the last time I ate such a hearty meal. We're eating like kings, and I aim to enjoy it."

Darius felt a slow flush rising up. He thought of how he had criticized the fare for being too simple. To Hanun, the same food constituted a royal feast. Without making it obvious, he slowed down eating to leave more for the family who were his guests.

Hanun put a hand on Tirzah's cheek. "It may be delicious, but it's nothing to your cooking, love." Darius could not miss the melting adoration in the man's gaze as he looked at his wife.

She laughed. "If our ancestor Jacob had been half as talented as you are at flattery, both his wives would have been happy."

Darius chewed on a mouthful of barley bread, his mind in turmoil. When had he last praised Sarah? When had he told her he appreciated her company? When had he given her glances that were hot not merely with desire, but with plain affection? He swallowed, his throat dry.

Chapter 25

Sarah could not find a comfortable position. Her baby had grown at an amazing pace over the past month, and with it, her girth. At this rate, three months from now when her time came, she would be as big as Jerusalem itself. Perhaps she should tell cousin Nehemiah to expand the perimeter of the walls to ensure she could fit inside them. Sighing, she set aside the roll of parchment she had been working on, which kept track of Nehemiah's professional expenses. Running Judah was not cheap.

The door to her chamber opened and Darius walked in. He must have come straight from his watch. She rose and came to greet him. To her surprise, he wrapped his arm around her waist—or where her waist used to be—and drew her to him. He cradled her as if she were something fragile and precious. Sarah lifted up her face to try and read his expression; he raised his palm and cradled her cheek. Her breath caught. His hand, warm, and rough from years of archery, caressed her skin, making shivers run through her. Unable to resist, she turned her head and rested her lips against his palm.

He moved his hand from her cheek and trailed it down her shoulder. His kiss, when it came, was excruciating in its slow gentleness. He was kissing her as if his whole heart was in it. As if he wanted to swallow her up and take her inside himself. As if she were the best thing the whole world had to offer. She kissed him back with desperation, her arms wrapped about his neck.

Love for him welled up inside her. She thought she might burst if she did not put her feelings into words. The last time she had declared her love for him, he had told her he didn't care. Whatever he felt for her now, his anger had not disappeared. It lingered, under the surface of his passion and this new tenderness. Would he reject her again if she expressed her love in this fragile moment? What could he do to her? Rebuke her? Would that hurt worse than this separation?

"I love you, Darius," she whispered against his mouth. "You are the husband of my heart. The only man I'll ever love."

His whole body went still. He searched her face, the green of his eyes looking black and inscrutable in the lamplight. With slow deliberation, he bent his head to her again. Under the flat of her palm she could feel the hard beat of his heart. He leaned against the wall and pulled her with him. She was glad for his support; her legs felt like every single bone in them had melted. He never spoke. Never said what her words meant, or if they had pleased him. But Darius didn't leave that chamber until it was time to take up his watch again.

337

• • •

Nehemiah knew he had more trouble on his hands when some of the men and their wives lined up outside his office with the rising of the sun, making certain they caught him before he left for his rounds. *Now what?* he wondered, as he invited them inside. But the substance of their complaint turned out to be a complete surprise. Astonished, he listened to them as they told him about the state of their lives.

Jedaiah spoke first. He was a farmer who helped with the rebuilding. "My lord governor, we need your aid. God has blessed us with large families. But we don't have enough food for them. Working on the wall has prevented us from putting enough effort into our land. If things don't change, we'll have no harvest to sustain us through the coming months, and our children will starve."

Nehemiah, who had known of the poverty rampant in Judah, fisted his hands in agitation. He had not realized that some of the men working on the wall were making a choice between their families' survival and the survival of Jerusalem. He studied the faces of the people for confirmation. Men and women alike murmured their agreement.

Another man said, "We've had some lean years already, you see. We had to contend with famine and bad crops. Our storehouses grew empty. To survive, we mortgaged our fields and vineyards, even our homes. It was the only way to make it through those barren years." He stopped and drew a shaking breath, not lifting his gaze from the ground. Nehemiah could see shame eating at the man. It wasn't easy for him to admit that he had failed. He must be at the end of his tether to acknowledge his circumstances openly, Nehemiah thought.

"We are near to ruin," the man continued. "How are we to repay these mortgages? What future is there for us? You can build a wall around this city, but what will that mean to a man who can't provide for his family?" Some of the women wiped their wet cheeks with their scarves.

Before Nehemiah had a chance to respond, another man came forward. "It's even worse for some of us, my lord. Every year, the officials have been demanding taxes from us. Everyone who owns land, rich or poor, has to pay them. We've had to borrow money from our wealthier country-men in order to pay the king's tax on our fields and vineyards.

"But when the loans came due, we had no way of repaying them. To discharge our debt, we had to give parcels of our land to the moneylenders. We mortgaged the rest of our fields. When that wasn't enough, we had to allow our daughters to go to these Jewish noblemen as slaves. Soon, our sons will have to join them.

"Although we have the same heritage as these

wealthy men, and our children are as good as theirs, they have to go into slavery in order that we might have enough to eat!"

Nehemiah sank into his chair. His stomach turned into a hard knot of tension. Anger burned in him. What he had just found out did not merely jeopardize the building of the wall, though that was dire enough. It threatened the very fabric of God's society in Judah. Not only had the rich not cared for the poor, they were in fact exploiting them at the moment of their need, stripping them of their ancestral land, of their property, of their children, and of their dignity. Shocked, he said, "I will think about what you have said and decide what to do. Leave this matter to me."

In his outrage, Nehemiah's first impulse was to give the guilty parties a piece of his mind, pouring the full force of his fury on them. But venting his anger would merely cause a grievous rift. He needed resolution and healing, not the momentary relief of feelings, which would lead to further damage. The men involved in the situation came from some of the most powerful families in Judea. If they turned against him, he could forget about finishing the wall. He spent some hours thinking the matter through and praying about it.

It seemed the enemy wasn't always an outsider. Sometimes the people you knew best posed the hardest threat. They inflicted the deepest wounds. There was no sense in delaying what must be done, however. That same day, Nehemiah arranged to meet with the nobles and officials who had loaned money to the farmers.

"You are hurting your own countrymen by charging them interest when, in their desperation, they come to you for loans," Nehemiah said, his voice calm. "You're increasing your wealth by means of their misfortune. This isn't merely a matter of money. It's a matter of the soul. Do you not see that you are tarnishing your hearts? You can't separate the way you handle your finances from your standing before the Lord."

One of the officials came forward. "We have broken no laws, Lord Nehemiah."

"Not legally, that is true. But what about spiritual laws? Does not God demand that you love your neighbor as yourself? How is this callous exploitation of your brothers and sisters a demonstration of love? They are near to ruin! Do you not care? This is a sign of your lukewarm faith. Will you stay lukewarm forever? Will you love your comfort more than you love the poor?"

The official said nothing. Nehemiah turned his gaze upon the company, giving others the opportunity to come forward with comments. None did. He gave a heavy sigh. "You are turning your own brothers and sisters into slaves! I could not believe my ears when they told me of it."

His mouth had turned as dry as the wilderness.

He stopped for a moment to take a small sip of water. "Have they not suffered enough? Over the years, have not many of our Jewish relatives been sold to foreigners as slaves? Since my arrival, I have set aside a public budget for the recovery of such slaves. Now I find that some of you are selling Jewish people to our neighboring lands, while I am doing my best to free them. Others, you enslave for yourself, forcing them into unpaid labor. Have you no fear of God?"

No one said a word in his own defense. What could they say? Nehemiah had stripped every justification from them. What had seemed acceptable in the privacy of their minds now seemed unpardonable.

Nehemiah pressed his point home. "What you are doing is wrong. Will not the enemies of Judea mock you as you destroy your own people? Why should our enemies bother to rise up against us, when we do their job for them?"

Not one man could look him in the eye. Nehemiah bent his head. "My brothers and I have also been lending the people money and grain. But now let us stop exacting usury. You must restore these people's fields. Give back their vineyards and homes. Do not wait another day; do it immediately. And return the interest you have charged when you have loaned them money and food."

Heavy silence met his speech. Tension writhed in Nehemiah as the men refused to respond. To his inexpressible relief an influential leader stepped forward. "You have shamed me with your words, my lord. As for me and my house, we will restore everything we have taken." He looked around him and raised his voice. "I feel certain my colleagues will join me."

Several nodded. One said, "And we will not demand anything more from the people when we help them. We will do as you bid." At first, the agreements came halfheartedly. Mumbled words of resignation. As time passed and they discussed the outcome of such a decision—the increased prosperity of their homeland and the benefits of living in a more affluent nation—their agreements became earnest.

They took a short break to eat. Because to Nehemiah this was as much a spiritual matter as a practical one, he summoned the priests. He had two reasons for this. First, he wanted the officials to take an oath and to recognize that pledge as an act before God. Second, he had been annoyed with the priests for not stepping in sooner and correcting the officials' mistake. In this manner, both parties would learn to be accountable to one another.

After the officials made their oath before the priests, Nehemiah shook out the folds of his robe and said, "If you fail to keep your promise, may God shake you like this out of your homes and your property!"

The whole assembly agreed with him and cried out, "Amen!" There was no grumbling that day, though the men present stood to lose a great deal of property. Instead, they praised God as one man, and great joy filled them so that the sound of laughter filled the chamber. Nehemiah, feeling lighter than he had for a long time, observed with a wry smile that it was not often men lost so much wealth and rejoiced over it.

Benjamin chattered while Darius listened with half an ear. He kept his eye trained on the perimeter, fulfilling his guard duty while his mind insisted on reliving memories from the night before. Instead of diminishing his longing for Sarah, the hours he had held her in his arms had made him burn hotter. The thought half annoyed him and half invigorated him. He felt like he was on the edge of a monumental discovery. Which was a ridiculous thought. He was acting like a callow youth around his own wife.

He shifted his position behind the wall to have a better view of the territory beyond. A fan-tailed raven flew overhead. From the corner of his eye, he thought he saw a flash of color in the distance. His focus shifted, became sharp, and converged on a point behind a series of hills just beyond the wall. He sensed danger, though he could see nothing unusual. The hair stood on the back of his neck. Holding up his hand, he motioned Benjamin to be quiet as he walked a few steps farther. With unexpected speed, he saw a lone figure rise. Too late, Darius realized that he held a sling. It took less than a moment for the man to flick his wrist and release the stone. Darius saw the trajectory of the fast hurling object. It was coming straight at Benjamin.

He threw himself against the child, covering him with his own body. There was no time to pull them both out of harm's way. The whirling stone, smooth and rounded, found Darius's temple and collided with sharp pain. He was already squatting on one knee when the stone hit him; dizzy at the impact, he fell back. A trickle of blood ran into his cheek and eye, blurring his vision.

Hanun and Tirzah were running toward them. The frightened parents enveloped their son into their arms, ensuring that he remained unharmed. Darius breathed through his mouth, trying to control the onslaught of nausea. He forced himself to his feet, not liking how unsteady he felt. It was just a little stone, he thought with annoyance, wiping the blood from his face.

"My lord! You're hurt. Come and sit down." He had not noticed Hanun's approach. Glad of the man's support, he allowed himself to be led to a large piece of masonry and sat down.

"Fetch another guard," he said through stiff lips. "Tell him to investigate beyond those hills. I am certain this was the work of a lone man trying to foster panic. He was aiming at Benjamin. He knew if he hurt a child, the workers would be especially disheartened. I doubt we'll be able to catch up with him now. But we should try."

"Tirzah has already gone to fetch a guard. And find help for you."

"I don't need help," Darius said, exasperated by his own weakness. "He used a sling. A boy's toy."

Hanun's voice held the trace of a smile. "I would not underestimate the power of a sling, my lord. David brought Goliath down with one."

Darius knew the story. "How reassuring."

Tirzah knelt at his feet. "You saved my boy. I saw you. If not for your quick actions, Benjamin would . . ." She could not finish the sentence. "Your courage saved him. I don't know how to thank you." He heard the hint of tears in her voice.

He wiped his hands on his knees. "There's no need for that. Anyone would have done the same."

To his relief, he saw Meres running toward him. As soon as he reached Darius, he bent over and ran an experienced eye over the wound. "That's a nice one, my lord. You'll have a grand headache, no doubt about it. Being a hero doesn't come cheap."

Darius growled. No doubt Tirzah had cast him in the role of champion to anyone who would listen. Meres didn't bother to hide his annoying grin. "It's not funny," Darius said, clenching his teeth.

Meres's grin grew wider. "Not funny at all, my lord. Now let's take you to your chamber. I'll fetch Lysander to have a look at you."

Another wave of nausea convinced Darius that a few hours of rest in his chamber might not be a bad idea. "Get someone to replace me, in case that vermin decides to come back."

"Already done. Now put your arm around my shoulders."

"Don't make a fuss. I can walk."

"I have no doubt you can, my lord. If you prefer, I'll put my arm around *your* shoulders."

Darius did not feel well enough to rise to the bait. He tried to keep up with Meres's measured steps and stumbled.

Without comment, Meres placed a strong arm around his waist. "We'll have you home in no time at all."

Darius hoped he was right. He felt weaker with every step.

Chapter 26

Stubborn will kept Darius conscious during the long walk back to Nehemiah's residence. The combination of blood loss, heat, and the blow to his head packed a powerful punch. With relief, he spread out on his lumpy bed and closed his eyes. "Just let me sleep," he mumbled. "I don't need Lysander." Meres didn't acknowledge that he had heard him as he slipped out of the room.

Moments later he felt the bed dip next to him. "Leave me alone," he said, frustrated, thinking Lysander had come to apply his healing arts to his injury.

"Charming."

"Sarah." Darius forced himself to sit up. "Pardon. I thought you were Lysander." She looked pale and strained. She should not be in his chamber. He had not sent for her. Nor was he thrilled at the idea of her seeing him in this weakened state.

"I am all right, as you see." She did not take the hint. If anything, her hip shifted so that she was sitting closer.

"Why don't you go back to your quarters and rest? I'm going to sleep. I'll call for you when I awaken."

Even gripped by dizziness, he could see that he

had hurt her. She bit her lip and bent her head before rising. "As you wish, my lord," she said. She hadn't called him *my lord* last night. It had been *Darius* then. He frowned. A sudden wave of nausea made his stomach cramp. He whipped around looking for something to shove his head into, and regretted the abrupt motion.

Sarah must have sensed his need. Somewhere she found a bucket and held it before him. The contents of his stomach came up in violent waves. He kept on heaving even when there was nothing left to bring up. He noticed, through paroxysms of misery, that Sarah didn't flinch at the mess he was making. She remained efficient, her touch full of compassion. Exhausted, he leaned back against a pillow. His head pounded.

Sarah gave him water so that he could rinse his foul-tasting mouth, and ran a damp linen towel over his face, wiping the blood and the sweat. Even though he wished she wasn't there, he was glad for her ministrations. She brought him a cup of watered wine. He took one swallow and the cramps came rushing back.

"Why don't you close your eyes?" she said, her voice taut.

He did as she suggested. His ears were ringing, an annoying sound in his head that would not stop. Through the noise of it he heard the door creak. He slit his eyes open and saw Lysander. The Spartan took in the soiled bucket, the bloody towel, and the wound on Darius's temple with a comprehensive glance.

"I don't need you," Darius barked.

"Let's make certain. Between you and your wife, you sure know how to keep a physician busy."

"You're not a physician, and even if you were, I don't need one. Get out and take Sarah with you," Darius said, out of patience.

"Aren't we in a sweet temper." Lysander pulled a stool next to the bed and made himself comfortable on it. "Let's have a look at you." He examined Darius's temple, his vision, and his hearing before pulling herbs out of his box and making a poultice for his head.

Darius's ear kept ringing. He heard Sarah's voice as from a distance. "Will he be all right?" Clang. Clang. Clang.

"Oh, I imagine so. He has a hard head, if you hadn't noticed. I've seen him take a knock twice as hard as this and rejoin the fray by the following day. He has impressive powers of recovery. He should be his old self in a day or two." Mixing a few drops of a brown liquid into a goblet of watered wine, he held it to Darius's lips.

"I hope I throw it up over your shoes," Darius said as he drank. Lysander took a cautious step back, but to Darius's secret relief, he did not vomit again.

Sarah caressed his hair, her touch as soft as the wings of a butterfly. He decided that he liked the feel of her fingers in his hair. Through half-lowered eyes he saw her lips move and realized that she was praying for him. His heart softened. The annoyance of moments before evaporated. He felt a sense of peace in her presence, and was glad that she had stayed with him. Sleep came and, grateful for the reprieve from the pain and nausea, Darius surrendered to it. Sarah's white face, murmuring her prayers, was the last thing he saw.

He woke up once in the watches of the night. From his window he could see the moon, full and bright. His head still ached, but the noise in his ears had thankfully subsided, and his stomach had settled down. Sarah was perched at the foot of his bed, her head slumped against the wall. She looked fast asleep. He sat up, his movements careful. He saw that a trickle of thin drool hung against the corner of her open mouth, shining in the moonlight. A rush of warmth filled him at the sight of it. He could not credit how something as ridiculous as spittle had such an absurd effect on him. In her most helpless moments she seemed to wield the most power over him.

He stretched a finger and wiped the moisture from her skin. She jerked awake.

"Darius?"

"Go to bed, sweetheart." He frowned as that endearment slipped through his lips. It had been months since he had called her that, and he had not intended to use it now. He must be sicker than he realized. He cleared his throat. "You've been sitting with me for hours. Go to your own chamber."

She gave him a mutinous look and he saw that she intended to argue. "Think of our babe," he said, hardening his voice.

She ran the tip of her tongue over her lip. "Yes, my lord." Getting up took her some time. Annoyance filled him as he realized that her body had grown stiff in her uncomfortable vigil.

"Don't come back until I send for you," he said, sounding harsher than he had meant.

He was disconcerted when she narrowed her eyes. "I'll not abandon you when you are sick, Darius. I'll be here to take care of your needs."

He felt the tug of a smile and resisted. For such a soft creature, she had a backbone as hard as bronze. "Come back in the morning, then. First, rest a few hours. My child must be as creased as a pleated robe inside you, the way you have been wedged against the wall through the night."

She walked to the door. Before she pulled it open, she turned around to face him. "You called me sweetheart," she said, her eyes large and luminous.

"It doesn't mean anything." He felt heartless when he saw her face fall before she walked out.

Lysander examined Darius in the morning and declared that while he could not return to guard duty yet, he could leave his bed. He was already up when Sarah brought him a late breakfast. Of course, she had not waited for him to send for her. He studied her for signs of exhaustion and had to admit that she glowed with health.

She gave him an easy smile as she set the tray of food on a wooden table next to the bed. To his relief, she did not seem to hold his cruel words from the night before against him.

"You look much improved today, my lord," she said.

Back to *my lord* again, were they? He frowned. Even though he had been the one to build this distance between them, he found that he resented it.

"I feel better." His stomach rumbled with a loud protest. "I am famished. After I eat, I'd like a bath. I want you to help me."

Her eyes grew round and her skin took on a pink hue. He had never asked her to tend him in a bath. "You said you wanted to take care of my needs," he goaded.

She gulped. "Of course."

Darius could hardly hide his smile. Call me *my lord* now, wife. He found his mood improving with every bite, thoughts of Sarah tending to him in his bath accompanying each mouthful. Why had he never thought of arranging this before? He began to sing a snatch of song under his breath. If he looked in a mirror, he suspected he would find that he had the look of a prowling wolf that was sure of its prey: hungry and self-satisfied.

A couple of Nehemiah's servants hauled a wooden tub with buckets of warm water into his room, and with quick efficiency, filled the bath and left. The tub had high ends and dipped low in the middle; steam rose from the water invitingly. Sarah turned her back, busying herself with fetching scented oils, towels, and a washcloth.

Darius could no longer hide his smile. He focused on untying his fabric belt. He had not bothered to undress after the attack, preferring to sleep in his clothes than to go through the trouble of shedding them. During the night, the knot had grown tangled and now it refused to budge. His fingers struggled to loosen the tight folds to no avail. Frustrated, he let out a growling expletive under his breath.

He took a step forward, intending to ask Sarah for assistance, his eyes still focused on the knot as he tried to undo it. At the same moment, Sarah turned, her hands outstretched and full of bathing paraphernalia. The inevitable collision, when it came, was not hard, but it hit Darius at an odd angle, so that he lost his balance for a moment. He took a hasty step backward to regain equilibrium. The back of his leg hit the low edge of the tub. His eyes widened in disbelief as he pitched backward and landed fully dressed in the bath. He had managed to protect his head from hitting anything. Dignity, however, had gone overboard.

Sarah stood transfixed, both hands clapped over her mouth, towels and oil bottle scattered around her feet. Darius, stunned for a moment, could not resist the ridiculous humor of his predicament; he threw his head back and roared with laughter.

"Oh, Darius!" Sarah gasped and ran to his side. "Are you all right? I do beg your pardon. I don't know how it happened."

"No damage done. You weren't at fault. I wasn't paying attention." He laughed again. "You better help me out of these wet things. We might need a dagger for the belt; it's tangled beyond hope." He stood up, water dripping from his short tunic and trousers in wide rivulets.

"Let me try. I have smaller fingers." She plunged her hands into the knot at his waist and leaned against him as she tried to undo his belt. The scent of her filled his senses. Suddenly, he wasn't laughing anymore.

By the next day Darius had improved so much that Lysander pronounced him fit to take up his watch for half a day. He looked forward to being active again. At the same time, knowing that Hanun and Tirzah would insist on heaping him with thanks made him uncomfortable. He greeted them, his expression shuttered, hoping that the scowl on his face would keep them at bay.

They seemed to sense his mood, and apart from

a cheerful greeting and wide smiles, left him to his work. With relief, he took up his spot, noting that Benjamin was absent. He couldn't blame the parents for the precaution of keeping their son away from the construction site. Benjamin, no doubt, had pouted with disappointment. Poor boy! In his shoes, Darius would have wanted to be working alongside his father and mother too.

A pleasant breeze cooled the air. The buzzing of a bumblebee as it flew past Darius's nose made him smile. It was quieter than usual, and he could hear the conversation between Tirzah and Hanun with embarrassing clarity.

"I fear for you, beloved," Tirzah said. "When I'm not here by your side, I wonder what manner of trouble you might get into."

Hanun placed a soft kiss on his wife's cheek. "Have you no faith in my work? Do you think these stones will topple down on my head without you here to supervise my efforts?"

"I'm being serious, Hanun. What if the next time they use arrows? What if there is a skirmish and I lose you?"

"I don't dread losing my life. Death comes for all of us, and I can say with King David, *Surely goodness and mercy will follow me all the days of my life, and I will dwell in the house of the Lord forever.*

"But when I think of you and Benjamin alone, with no one to protect you—to provide for you—

it sends a chill down my back. I've left you with nothing. It grates on me, that failure to make certain you would be well cared for if something should happen to me."

Darius felt a frisson of shock at Hanun's admission. Not only did he concede to being afraid, he also acknowledged that he had failed his family. He spoke to his wife as if he held nothing back. As if he had no secrets from her. Darius had not unlocked his heart to anyone with such openness since childhood.

Part of him judged Hanun weak. No man should parade his darkest doubts into the light of day as if he could not handle the burden of them by himself. Wouldn't Tirzah think less of him? Wouldn't she, in a corner of her mind, reject him for his deficiency?

Another part of him had to acknowledge that, contrary to all reason, there was an undeniable closeness between husband and wife. They were devoted to each other in a way he had not personally experienced. Their intimacy drew him. It seemed as if the more they revealed their hearts to each other, the deeper their attachment grew.

Tirzah slapped her husband's arm. "What, and you think the Lord is unable to care for us? Does He not love the widow and the orphan?"

Sarah would have come to a similar conclusion, though she would never have spoken those words to him. For the first time, Darius began to wonder what it cost his wife not to be able to express her faith when they were together. That faith was such an integral part of who she was.

He remembered, with sudden and painful clarity, the final months of his mother's life. They had spent many hours in conversation about her faith. He had realized in those often awkward exchanges how lonely his mother had been in her marriage. She had loved Lord Vivan with a singular and faithful passion. Her love had never wavered. And yet, she had been solitary in the midst of it. She had been unable to share her deepest concerns with the man she loved above all else. Had he done that to Sarah?

He found himself squirming under that reflection. Until now, he had considered himself an exemplary husband. Had he not forgiven her for embarrassing him before the whole court? Had he not given her the unique position of being the only woman in his life? Had he not gone back to her after she had betrayed him by keeping her pregnancy a secret? He had been generous in his treatment of her. At every turn, he had sought the higher ground.

Yet the fact remained that not once had she spoken to him with the unselfconscious candidness of Tirzah. How could she? Whenever she had hinted at the Lord, Darius had shut her down. He had made it clear that he held no interest in her view of the world.

Neither had he revealed the inner workings of his mind to her as Hanun did to his beloved Tirzah. Would Sarah want that ridiculous level of transparency from him? His gut told him that she did. He felt certain that she would respond by loving him with an abandonment he could not begin to imagine. The thought of revealing every insecurity and fear turned his stomach sour, however. Weakness and timidity were not for him.

Darius ground his teeth. Being around Tirzah and Hanun had an unpleasant effect on him. They were poor and surrounded by danger. Starvation sat at their door from one season to the next. They belonged to a ravaged nation, one step away from utter destruction. And yet they made him examine his life and emerge discontented. He had begun to believe that for all their lack, they were richer than he could ever be. That conclusion grated on him. He should swap the location of his guard duty and rid himself of the thorn this family had become.

Chapter 27

Sarah crossed her ankles and then uncrossed them. Darius had returned home from his half day of work in a strange mood. He had not strung more than five words together as they ate lunch. Every once in a while she caught him staring at her, his eyes narrowed and thoughtful. She checked her green linen robe for an embarrassing stain and was relieved to find none. It had been weeks since she had worn the elaborate garments suited for the court. Now she garbed herself in simple linen robes, cool and loose enough to accommodate her condition. Did Darius find her appearance a disappointment? Did he think her fat and unattractive? She drew a nervous hand over her flowing skirts.

"How is Benjamin?" she asked, a fifth foray into conversation that seemed to go nowhere.

"He wasn't at the wall."

Sarah waited for him to elaborate. No further revelation was forthcoming, however. She sighed and leaned back, her appetite gone. "Is it me? Have I offended you in some way?"

"What?"

"You keep staring at me."

"Do I?"

Sarah let out a breath. "Shall I clear up our lunch? We seem to have both stopped eating."

Darius pushed away a full bowl of bean and garlic stew. "You prayed for me. When I was sick. I saw you, before I fell asleep."

Sarah's mouth turned dry. She tried to swallow, but could not. "I did . . . I ask your pardon. I did not think you were awake."

"I liked it. You may pray for me whenever you wish."

Eyes rounded, Sarah leaned forward. "Truly? You don't mind?"

"My mother used to do it. I had forgotten. When I was little, she would thank God for me every morning, and bless my day. In the months of her illness before she died, she would not allow a single day to go by without praying for me."

"She must have been an exceptional woman. I wish I had met her."

"I wish you had, too. She would have liked you. You could have talked to each other about the Lord to your heart's content."

"That would have been . . . a blessing."

"Sarah . . . I have not been fair to you. I've laid down an unspoken law, forbidding you to speak of the Lord. No doubt there have been many times when you've had to swallow what you wanted to say to me. I'm not promising that I will agree with your point of view, or even understand it. But I want you to be free to express what's in your heart.

"I remember when we were trying to solve the mystery of the intrigue against the king, and you tried to comfort me by pointing out that the Lord had helped us discover the plot in the first place, and that He would be faithful through the rest of our inquiries. You were so careful with your words, trying to avoid offending me. Still, I reacted harshly. I will try not to repeat that mistake."

Sarah sat stunned, her eyes glued to her husband, wondering where this change of heart came from. "I . . . don't know what to say."

"Finally rendered you speechless, have I?" His smile, slow and warm, settled on her like a cozy blanket. "I want you to be free. I want you to be yourself around me. I don't want you to have to pick and choose every word with care before you speak. You should be at your ease when we are together."

Sarah could not believe her ears. She felt like she was dreaming. Tears pricked her eyes and she lowered her lids to hide them.

"Don't," he whispered. Leaning forward, he lifted her chin. "You're doing it again. Hiding from me."

She stared into his beloved face, startled. The tears kept welling up. She could not stop them as they slid down her cheeks like fat rain drops. Darius wiped at them with his hand. Then he leaned over and kissed them away. "Don't cry, sweetheart."

That word again. She wouldn't chase after it like a hungry rabbit. She wouldn't. She gulped and said, "Pardon. I don't know what has come over me. I have no reason to cry."

"Yes, you do." He kissed her gently. "But not anymore. I promise you."

Sarah nodded, unable to trust her voice. Part of her wanted to jump up and dance and hug Darius until his ribs hurt. Another part of her began to tremble with dread. If she revealed herself, he might reject her. He had admitted that he might neither fathom nor agree with her understanding of the world. If she revealed to him her deepest feelings—if she began to tell him about things like her struggle to find her worth in her achievements instead of in God, perhaps he in time would find her so incomprehensible that any glimmer of affection he had for her would cool and die. Her faith in God might push him away and destroy their marriage.

Later that afternoon, Darius accepted Nehemiah's invitation to join him on his inspection round. "You seem to have recovered from your injuries," Nehemiah said as greeting.

Darius curled his lip. "A mere bump. Hardly worse than a mosquito bite."

Nehemiah gave a slight smile. "The mosquitoes in Persia must have grown more violent than I realized. I haven't seen such an impressive bruise in years. I didn't know that shade of purple existed. It brings out the green in your eyes."

Darius threw the governor a quelling look. The man refused to be intimidated. "In any case, you seem to have made an impression on Benjamin's parents. They have not stopped singing your praises since you protected their son from serious harm."

"They exaggerate. I did nothing that a little girl couldn't have managed."

Nehemiah tapped his bearded chin with a thumb. "I think you underestimate your actions. Benjamin is a special boy. Many would have grieved if harm had come to him."

"I enjoy his company. It would have been a sad day if he had been injured."

"Do you know, he reminds me of you when you were a boy. Not his looks, but his spirit. You had a similar charm."

"First you admire my eyes, and now you speak of my charm. Careful, my lord governor, or I might form the wrong conclusion," Darius said.

Nehemiah laughed. "I have been remembering you as a child. I was very fond of you, you know. It came to me when I was visiting with Hanun and his family that you were the same age as Benjamin when you left home. So young!"

Nonplussed by Nehemiah's odd comment, Darius frowned. "Pardon?"

"When your father sent you to the palace to start

your training, you were Benjamin's age. Just a little boy."

"I suppose I was. You were close to my parents at the time, I believe."

"We saw each other often. Your family had made Susa their primary residence, and so had I. As an official of the court, I understood your father's world. As a Jew, I understood your mother's. They had no one else in their lives that could relate to them both. We had much in common, which made our friendship a comfort and a joy."

"Strange. I don't remember meeting you as a child."

"I'm not surprised. You were very young at the time. Soon after you moved to the palace school, the king assigned your father to a permanent post in Babylon. He was gone for three years. Your parents traveled to visit you as often as they could, but the distance made frequent visits prohibitive."

"I had forgotten those years." Like a hazy dream, Darius remembered his life at the palace, deprived of mother and father for months at a time, living in an emotional desert. His chest tightened just thinking about it. He became aware that Nehemiah was guiding them toward one of the gates. None of the doors had been hung yet, and the opening in the partially raised wall looked like the gapped tooth in an old man's mouth.

"Where are we going?"

"I thought I would show you a new sight today," Nehemiah said.

Darius's brows knotted. "Outside the walls?"

"As far as possible, we planned the wall to follow the ancient foundations. But in places, we had to make the perimeter smaller. Beyond these gates is one such location. I thought you might find the old foundation interesting."

Darius was too polite to point out that he did not find the sight of old holes in the ground particularly thrilling and followed the governor's steps without comment. They did not have far to walk. Like a fat snake, the old foundation wound its way at the edge of the city's hills. Nehemiah stopped in front of a portion that must have been excavated at some point, stretching in the earth like a long gash.

Darius bent over and looked down. The original architects had made the foundation deep to accommodate the height and weight of the wall they had intended to build. "Is that soot and ash down there, covering the stones?"

"I should have known you would notice that. Yes. Ash from the fires of war."

"Babylon's conquest, you mean? But that was almost two hundred years ago! Wouldn't the wind and the rain of decades have cleaned this up?"

Nehemiah knelt a knee at the edge of the foundation and peered inside. "The passage of time alone cannot restore such vast damage.

Unless men went down there and physically cleaned up the mess, the deterioration of war leaves its mark." He turned his face away from the ravaged landscape to gaze at Darius. The intensity in the brown eyes made Darius shift in discomfort.

"I like to come here and sit by these ruins sometimes," Nehemiah said, unfolding his knees to stand once more. "They are a good reminder."

"Of your history?"

"Not just that. I have often thought how the heart of man is like that foundation. Under war. Attacked by forces that oppose and ruin it. And unable to repair itself. Time cannot heal wounds. Many of us walk around with gashes in our hearts, no different from this foundation, covered in the soot of life's fires."

Darius took a step away and grasped his wrist in a tight hold behind his back. "You're talking about me, aren't you?"

Nehemiah rose up, his movements deliberate. "Have you noticed how winsome Benjamin is? You were like that as a little boy, only more so. Full of affection and an open intelligence that charmed the adults around you. You loved passionately and were never afraid to demonstrate how you felt.

"Your father sent you to the palace school because it was expected of you. You would not have been able to fulfill your position as a Persian aristocrat without the appropriate training. He meant it for your best. He had no idea that tearing you from your home when you were only seven would have grave consequences. He himself had left home much later and did not understand the significance of your extreme youth."

"I've never blamed him for sending me."

"You paid a heavy due for that decision, whether you did it willingly or not. When you came back, you were different. Gone was the affectionate boy. You were self-contained and distant. There was a wall around your heart as high as the moon."

Darius kicked a pebble into the yawning hole of the foundation. It flew in the air before landing with a thud somewhere in the soot-covered depths. "Duty has a price. We all have to pay it with whatever currency is asked of us."

Nehemiah took a step that brought him closer. "Would you expect your own son to fulfill his duty in the same way? Your child will be born in three months. You might have a boy. Would you send him away from you in seven years? Would you want him to live a life similar to yours at that age? Would you desire for him to be separated from you, from Sarah, for months at a time? To grow up with cold teachers and distant sages who will never once hug him or express any love toward him?"

Darius paled. "I don't see how this is any of your concern."

"Forgive me, my lord." Nehemiah shoved a

hand through his hair, making the red filaments stand on end. In the pale rays of the sun, they seemed to catch fire, surrounding his head like a halo of flames. "Having once held you in my arms as a wriggling baby, I find it hard to remember that you are a man now, and more than able to make your own decisions. I should clarify something. When I spoke of your son, it wasn't because I doubted your ability to be a wonderful father. Like Lord Vivan, you already have the makings of the best of fathers.

"I only meant for you to remember your own experience—for your sake, not your child's. Often, we bury the wounds of our past. It's not until we consider someone we love going through the same hardship that we recognize how profound the damage to our soul really was. I wanted you to see . . ." He pointed a finger into the hole blanketed with ancient soot. "I wanted you to glimpse into your own heart and the ashes of an old war that came against you when you were very young. Perhaps it's time you dealt with it."

Without another word, Nehemiah began to walk away.

Darius felt rooted to the spot. His head had begun to pound and nausea roiled in his innards. Nehemiah had managed to summon the specter of a past he thought he had buried long ago.

Did he really have a wall around his heart that went as high as the moon? Nehemiah made him sound so cold and distant. Was he like that with Sarah?

He thought of the babe that would be born to him in a matter of months. *Would* he send him to the palace if he was a boy? Send him to be bullied and isolated, stripped of childish affection? Was the empire worth such a sacrifice?

The memories he had ignored for long years refused to be silenced anymore. They came upon him with such force that he stumbled, almost pitching into the gaping foundation. Like a man who had drunk too much wine, he took an unsteady step until his toe connected with a large piece of masonry. Shivering, he allowed his body to sink down until he half sat, half collapsed on the pale rock. He rested his head in his hands, taking deep breaths to steady his senses. The memories would not abate. They crashed over him with the fury of a gale, bringing with them the feelings he had forgotten.

Chapter 28

THE FIRST YEAR
OF KING ARTAXERXES' REIGN (426 BC)
PERSIA
(TWENTY YEARS EARLIER)

Long before his nurse came to fetch him, Darius sat up on his wide, gilt bed, heart thumping with excitement. It was his seventh birthday. He knew birthdays meant a full week of celebrations: presents; games; late nights with friends and family; an endless array of cakes and sweets. Even grown up Persians celebrated their birthdays with more festivities than the rest of the world could understand; but for him this was a magical time. A boy's seventh birthday marked an important rite of passage. After the birthday celebrations concluded, he would no longer have need of a nursemaid. Instead, leaving behind childhood, he would be introduced to the world of men. He would begin to learn a man's skills and acquire knowledge vital for an aristocrat.

Darius had already become an accomplished rider though he could not remember ever learning to ride. His father had told him that he had sat Darius astride a horse before he could walk. But now he would also be taught to use a bow and arrow as well as swords, daggers, spears, javelins, and would learn the enthralling secrets of the art of combat. He would study medicines and the mysteries of the forest and would train to survive in a desert. He would have to learn some boring things as well, like reading and writing, which his mother insisted upon, and the lengthy lessons of the magi about truth and justice. He thought he could put up with such annoyances so long as he could swap his dreaded nursemaid for sword-fighting and playing games all day long with other boys his age.

Too impatient to wait any longer, Darius slipped out of his warm bed and dressed himself quickly, donning his clothes from the day before. The garments were rumpled and carried the stains of a full day of fierce outdoor activity, which made them all the more comfortable in Darius's view. They sat askew on his solid form, thanks to the speed with which he put them on. His nurse would have been horrified by the results. Darius was more interested in starting the day than in her opinion.

He ran out of his spacious chamber, down a long corridor, and slipped into his mother's apartment. Her bedroom was still covered in darkness, an inconvenience he overcame by the simple expedience of pulling aside blue linen curtains.

Weak early sunlight found its sluggish way into the apartment, bringing to life the colorful mosaics that decorated the walls. Exotic birds seemed to take flight in a purple sky. Darius touched the royal blue and green image of a peacock and smiled. He loved this room. Turning, he saw that his mother slept on.

Tiptoeing with silent steps, he went toward his mother's sleeping form, intent on tickling her awake. He had barely reached her side when long graceful hands captured him and dragged him into bed. He squealed, startled.

"I've been awake all along, my darling monster." His mother's manicured fingers thwarted his plans by tickling him instead.

Darius laughed until his belly ached. "Stop!"

She obeyed his plea immediately.

"Do you know why today is special?" he asked, a serious note creeping into his voice.

"Today? No. Why? I know! It's father's birthday."

"No, it's not," Darius said, indignant. "It's mine!"

"You don't say? Come to think of it, you look more grown up. But how terrible! I forgot all about it. What shall I give you for your birthday present?" His mother gazed at him through thick curling lashes. "How about this robe?" She held out her morning wrap—a sheer confection made of pleated white silk with golden embroidery.

Darius made a horrified face.

"Oh well, I suppose not. What about my comb?

You must admit it's pretty." She offered him the long-toothed comb that sat on a table next to her lavish bed. Carved from ivory and encrusted in some kind of red jewel whose name Darius didn't know, it sparkled with feminine glitter.

He gave his mother an offended look and began to believe that she was not teasing him, after all. A terrible dread settled in the pit of his belly; had his mother truly forgotten his birthday?

She laughed. "What a face. I can see you don't like my comb, either. Perhaps you might find something more to your liking in my silver chest."

Darius's face lit up with renewed hope. He scrambled off the bed and ran to the chest. The lid, a carved affair inlaid with jewels and heavy obsidian, proved hefty. He pushed it up, using all his strength, his young muscles straining under the pressure, until it came to rest upright.

"Well done, little man. You are going to be very strong when you grow up." His mother had wrapped herself in her white morning robe and come to stand next to him. Her hair reached below her waist in a profusion of dark curls; Darius had heard more than one woman in his father's household sigh with envy over its beauty. At this moment, however, it presented a mere annoyance to him. He pushed the curls out of his way and focused on his task.

"I'm already strong," he said while making a visual search of the silver chest. Shoved to one corner, he found a long package wrapped in a length of yellow fabric.

Snatching it up with enthusiasm, he turned to his mother. "Is this mine?"

"It might be."

He grinned as he laid his bundle on top of the bed. Impatient fingers shoved the fabric wrapping aside. Darius gasped. A perfect bow with a leather quiver full of arrows appeared for his inspection. The limb of the bow was made of curved wood, its string fashioned out of sinew. He touched it with reverence and felt a thin layer of wax. Even as a boy he knew this was to protect the bow from moisture. He pulled out an arrow from the black-colored quiver and examined the bone tip with minute attention. It looked sharp and hard—not a child's toy, but an adult's hunting tool.

He tested the string with a tentative touch. It felt impossibly tight. For a moment his confidence wavered; perhaps he would not be strong enough to use it. With determined effort he pushed the doubt aside. No bow was going to defeat *him*. He resolved to beat all his friends with his perfect aim.

"Well," his mother's voice interrupted his musings. "Does the present meet with your approval, my lord?"

Instead of answering, Darius flung his arms around his mother's waist with fierce enthusiasm. It occurred to him, in a faint jumble of disorganized thought, that turning seven would somehow mean not living in the women's quarter of his father's house anymore. And that meant not having easy access to his mother anytime he wished.

The thought pierced him with the sharpness of one of his newly acquired arrows. Then he remembered the endless games he would play with his companions and forgot the fear of being apart from his mother.

"Rachel, shall we go and fetch—" said a deep voice from the door before breaking off into a deep, rumbling laugh. "I should have known the little rascal would be out of bed. Normally six trumpets and a rabid dog couldn't drag him awake this early in the day."

"Father!" Darius exclaimed with delight. "Look at what Mother gave me for my birthday." Fetching his bow and arrows, he brought them to Lord Vivan for his inspection.

His father examined first the bow, then the arrows with an experienced eye. "Straight shaft, sharp edge, tight string. An admirable weapon. I know my son shall prove worthy of it."

Darius felt his chest expand until he thought he would burst with joy. His father's approval always had that effect on him. "I will, Father."

Lord Vivan placed a hand on Darius's shoulder. "I suppose now *I* should present you with a gift."

Darius bit back a smile. "It is customary. I am seven today, you know."

"You amaze me. Truly? You are seven? Rachel, did you know this?"

"It comes as something of a surprise to me as well, my lord husband. Feels like only yesterday that he came into the world."

Lord Vivan approached his wife and took her into his arms. "How time flies with you, love."

Darius rolled his eyes. "It's *my* birthday, not hers."

"Did you want a cuddle too?" Vivan asked, and, without waiting for an answer, grabbed Darius into his wide embrace and threw him high in the sky. Before his son descended perilously close to the ground, he caught him up in his arms again and turned him upside down, holding him by the ankles. Darius, half blinded with the hair that streamed into his eyes, felt offended by a game that had always thrilled him before today.

"Put me down, please!" he demanded. "I'm not a baby anymore."

"I beg your pardon. Right you are." His father set him back on the floor, his blue eyes staring down at him with a serious expression.

Darius straightened his clothes and tried to recapture his injured dignity. "I used to like that. But now, I think I would prefer to play other games with you, Father. Perhaps you can take me hunting instead."

His father bit his lip. Darius scowled, trying to discern if Lord Vivan was laughing at him. But his father nodded, and reaching into his pocket, drew out an ornate box. "Perhaps this will help with our new game. Happy birthday, my son."

Darius forgot his injured pride and grasped the box. Made of light olive wood, the box had been carved into a long rectangle. Inside, he found a dagger, crafted from bronze, with a hilt slim enough to fit into a boy's hand. The dagger boasted no ornamentation. It was a young man's weapon, not a showpiece.

Darius beamed, delighted. He clasped the box with the dagger, and his bow and quiver of arrows to his chest. The new treasure trove barely fit in his arms. "I love my dagger. Thank you, Father. Let's go try everything out."

"I suggest we have breakfast first," Lord Vivan said. "Breaking in fresh weapons is hungry work."

Darius curbed his impatience as he ate with his parents. After all, eating breakfast with his father presented a rare opportunity. As customary with aristocratic Persian men, Lord Vivan had a large household. With two other wives besides Darius's mother, three concubines, two half-brothers, two half-sisters, and a baby on the way, Lord Vivan's domestic time remained limited. Darius's mother was his favorite by far, and the one woman he truly loved. Yet for the sake of family harmony he could not spend too much time with Lady Rachel and Darius. So rather than complain about the delay in learning how to handle his new weapons, Darius decided to enjoy this precious visit.

The breakfast spread boasted a variety of hot breads and soft cheeses. There were fig preserves and—his mother's favorite—bergamot jelly, as well as fresh eggs with yolks the color of the setting sun. Darius rolled a large piece of warm bread with thick sweet cream, topped it with grape jelly, and stuffed a huge bite into his mouth, noticing that his father was engaged in the same activity at exactly the same time.

His mother laughed. "Look at the two of you. No mistaking you are father and son. Except that you are fair-haired and blue-eyed, Vivan, and Darius has my dark coloring and green eyes, you are practically identical. Same straight nose, same long mouth, same grooves in your cheeks as you smile. And the same sweet tooth."

"You like sweets too, Mother. Even more than Father and me."

"No I don't," Rachel said before reaching a long arm and grabbing an almond cake from Darius's plate.

"That's mine! Give it back!"

His mother stuffed the round cake into her mouth until her cheeks puffed up like a squirrel. "Come and take it," she said through her full mouth.

Darius and his father dissolved into peals of laughter. With sudden clarity, Darius remembered his earlier concern. "Even though I'm almost grown up, I can still come and visit Mother whenever I wish, can't I, Father? It wouldn't be good for her to be alone too often."

He noticed the sheen of tears in his mother's large, dark eyes before she lowered her lashes. With a sticky hand he reached out to pat her arm.

Lord Vivan pushed away his golden plate and sat back. "You can't live in the women's quarters anymore, son. Now that you are seven, you need to start your education as befits a Persian lord. And that can only be done properly at the palace."

"Of course. I look forward to it. I can't wait to become a great warrior just like you, Father. But when I come home at night, after my studies are finished, may I still come to visit Mother?"

"You won't come home at night. You'll be living in Persepolis, in a dormitory with other boys your own age."

Darius went still. "I won't live with you and Mother anymore?"

"Once a month you will be allowed to visit us at home for two days. You will also come to us for a month during the New Year holidays. I have made arrangements for your mother and me to meet with you privately each week. You must not mention this to the other boys, however. I'm bending the rules, and they won't like it."

Darius gulped. He hadn't fully grasped what it would mean to see his parents only once a week—

to be away from home for such long stretches of time. But he did know that the thought of that separation filled him with an aching fear that made him want to cry like the baby he had claimed he no longer was. He swallowed his tears and vowed in the silence of his heart never to shame his parents by blubbering like a coward.

Forcing his head to move down in a nod of assent, he said, "As you wish, Father."

Chapter 29

Dawn remained a long way off when Darius jerked awake, thanks to the blaring clamor of a brass instrument. He groaned. He had slept less than six hours, having been awake late into the watches of the night, cleaning and oiling swords and daggers for the older boys. Ignoring the exhaustion that never seemed to leave him since he had arrived at Persepolis a month ago, he pushed himself out of his pallet and washed with cold water.

He had scant minutes to be dressed and ready for their daily morning run, led by two of the older boys. They would run for over an hour, covering almost two *parsangs** before returning for a grueling round of lessons.

The first week, Darius had vomited more than once before they returned to their dormitory. He was not the only boy; most of his company of fifty new apprentices were similarly afflicted. Their commanders merely allowed them to fetch water from a freezing stream afterward in order to clean up before returning.

Life in the palace turned out to be nothing like

* Each *parsang* measured approximately four miles.

Darius's imaginings. His world did not resemble an endless round of fun games. The physical training proved arduous, pushing him beyond his strength. He was being taught endurance, and the only way to learn that particular lesson was to *endure* no matter what kind of hardship he faced.

His treasured birthday gifts from his parents had been put away unused; his teachers considered him too young for swordplay and archery. Instead, they gave him repetitive exercises that left his muscles sore and aching. Some days, he had to hold up a stone for long silent minutes at a time, until his arm began to burn.

Another common exercise required him to crouch until his thighs gave out. Several times a day he found himself carrying heavy equipment for the older boys who were more capable of carrying their own gear than a seven-year-old. Yet this too was deemed an important means of building up his strength in preparation for the time when his combat training would begin in earnest.

"You have no muscles, boy," one of his masters had told him more than once when his arms began to tremble during weight training. "How can you be so puny?" Unaccustomed to indiscriminate criticism, Darius had locked his jaw, determined to hold up the heavy weights for as long as necessary. He never wanted to be considered *puny* again.

To his disappointment, the masters frowned on

attempts at friendship. He had noticed that the boys who had been at the palace for several years seemed to have fostered deep connections. But new arrivals like him were expected to grow used to a solitary existence.

Their combat and sports instructors were hard and distant. The magi—Persian scientists, astronomers, and religious leaders—had begun to teach his company of fresh recruits about the virtues of honesty, loyalty, and gratitude. They demonstrated indiscriminate kindness to the boys. But they tempered that kindness by an impersonal manner that discouraged any form of attachment or warmth. Darius had no one to talk to.

Life in the palace had turned out to be a disappointment. It was lonely, exhausting, and tedious. Darius had seen other boys cry tears of solitude. Tears of pain. He resolved not to give in to such an outward show of weakness—to swallow the storm of his emotions and show nothing of his feelings. He simply had to push through.

He determined to make his father proud. But he missed home so much that sometimes his body trembled with the strain of it. It wasn't the physical hardship, the tasteless food, the endless chores that felt unbearable to him. He could endure all that. It was the isolation that gnawed at him. His life before now had been filled with love and companionship. The sudden and intentional loss of every form of meaningful relationship felt heavier than any of the weights he had to carry for training.

At night when he crawled into his lumpy pallet, bruised and spent, he would pull the scratchy blanket over his head and think of home. He would smell the delectable hot food served to him at his whim. He would feel the softness of his linen sheets. He would relive the warmth of a cozy fire.

He didn't dare think of his mother's voice or embrace often, afraid that he would lose control and demand to be sent home. But sometimes, when he lingered somewhere between sleep and wakefulness, he sensed her presence with him—the loving presence that seemed to make every hurt disappear. And he clung to that sensation even though he knew it wasn't real.

Darius was pulling on his trousers when another boy from his company named Cambyses walked past him. Without a word, he aimed a vicious kick against Darius's shins. Darius lost his balance and fell hard. He didn't cry out. Instead, he pushed himself up, and finished dressing with the economical movements of a soldier, which he had already learned.

"I saw that," a boy named Arya said. A couple of other boys added their assent. "He's a block-head," Arya added.

Darius nodded. Cambyses had been born the son of a satrap—the governor of one of the largest territories in the empire—an accident of birth that had pumped him full of self-importance. He had taken a dislike to Darius when Darius beat him in their first race. Now Cambyses tormented him every chance he found. Because the boys were encouraged never to tell tales, Darius chose not to complain. But Cambyses' increasing bully tactics were becoming a real nuisance. Darius added that to the list of things he had to do something about.

At least he would be going home this afternoon for a two-day visit. His first in a month. A few more hours and he would be home. *Home.*

His father came personally to fetch him. When he entered the enclosed carriage, he saw his mother waiting for him with open arms. Darius hesitated for a fraction of a moment before catapulting himself, body and soul, into her welcoming embrace. His mother wept. That carriage ride was the first time in a month that Darius felt something like peace.

That peace helped him make an important decision. He had formed a plan over the past few weeks. An escape route. A way of pleasing his father by fulfilling his responsibilities as a Persian nobleman, while at the same time surviving the experience. He had not been sure that he would approach his parents with his proposal. He did not wish to worry them by saying too much about the misery of his life. But he decided during the carriage ride, with his father's arm around his shoulder and his mother's smile enveloping him like a warm blanket, to speak to them.

A private dinner was served in his mother's apartments. His parents were full of questions. Although they had visited him each week, their time together had been stifled by the need for secrecy and haste. Now they showered him with every manner of inquiry, especially his mother to whom his new world was a complete mystery. Darius tried to keep his responses light. He noticed a softening in his father's gaze as he painted an insouciant picture of his life. His father, he realized, must know from his own experience that the training of young Persian boys entailed more than fun races and hilarious lessons in the recognition of edible wild plants.

Finally his mother said, "Enough. The poor boy has hardly had a chance to eat. Let us cease pestering him so that he can taste his food. I had the cooks prepare your favorite dishes, darling. Try the stuffed grape leaves."

Darius closed his eyes as he took a mouthful. The stuffing, enriched with the scent of exotic herbs and the flavor of spiced ground lamb, slid down his throat in an explosion of incredible flavors. The grape leaf was tender and surprisingly fresh considering the season. Darius groaned with the pleasure of it.

Lord Vivan laughed. "What do they feed you? Bread and cardamom and broiled meat?"

"Barley cakes too, for treats. Morning noon and night, it's the same fare."

"The ingredients haven't changed since my boyhood, then. I remember those years well."

"Did you also live in Persepolis, Father?"

"Not until I turned sixteen. Back then, only the older boys moved into the dormitories. They didn't have enough room for the younger ones."

Darius had found out this bit of information by happenstance from one of the senior boys. This presented the precise opening he needed to present his plan.

He drank down a gulp of grape juice to fortify himself, and then launched into speech. "I was thinking, Father, why don't I do the same? I could attend my lessons at the palace, and then come home to spend the night here, as you did when you were my age. In the evenings, boys my age have no lessons. Instead, we perform chores. Often, we are given the gear of the older boys to clean or oil. Sometimes, we have to write out or memorize an assignment the magi have given us. I could bring my chores home and finish them here, and then ride back to Persepolis very early, in time for our morning exercises."

His father went very quiet. "Why?" he asked, after several moments of tense silence.

"I want to be home, with you and Mother. I will learn everything well, I promise. I will excel at my training. I just want to be home."

"No," his father said, his tone implacable. He offered no explanation.

Darius was astounded. "But—"

"No buts. *No.* That is final."

Darius turned to his mother, sure that she would speak up for him. Instead, she turned her face away, staring at the wall. For a moment, he thought he saw a glint of unshed tears in her eyes, saw her fingers tremble before she clutched them into fists. But he must have been wrong, for she said nothing. Not a single plea on his behalf. Not one word to show she understood his need to come home.

Darius tried one last time. He swallowed the bitter taste of pride, something he had been taught to guard since he could remember. *Surely they do not understand. If they knew, they would never force me to go back.* He said, his voice small and trembling with a childlikeness he hated, "I miss home. I miss *you.*"

"That is enough, son. I said no. I meant it. You shall train as other boys your age and station. You shall fulfill your duty to your family and empire. And you shall never try to shirk that duty again."

Darius rose from his seat, turning pale. Without a word, he ran out of his mother's apartment and wound his way back to his own chamber. He climbed into bed fully clothed, hardly noticing the thick luxury of lying in abundant comfort after weeks of a lumpy pallet. His father's words burned into his mind like a brand. He felt utterly ashamed. Had he really tried to shirk his duty by wanting to remain at home?

He could not understand his parents' reasoning. Their response shocked him. He had expected that they would grant his request; their refusal was beyond his comprehension. He never doubted that they loved him. His whole life had been shaped by that knowledge. But he began to realize that being loved did not mean that you would be wanted. Love, it seemed, was powerless to give you what you desperately wanted. It could not fix problems. As far as it concerned his parents, duty overshadowed love.

He thought of his duty at the palace, the endless round of lessons that challenged his mind and body, stretching him to excruciating limits. And yet, if he didn't cherish his parents so much, he could tolerate his new life. There would be no longing for them every day. He wouldn't miss them. He would adjust to his new life without them, the way they had adjusted to their lives without him. He felt crushed at the realization that his parents could let him go with such ease.

Why don't Father and Mother want me? There's no one for me anymore. If I can't rely on Father and Mother, is there anyone in this whole world on whom I can depend?

He spent half the night awake, his thoughts

tortured. He knew one thing. His parents' rejection hurt worse than bullies and fistfights and swords.

A miserable welcome awaited Darius at the palace. The first person he ran into turned out to be Cambyses. They were alone in a dark hallway. Cambyses was a year older than Darius—having started his training late due to his father's travels—and half a head taller. Without a word of explanation, he jammed his elbow into Darius's stomach.

The pain wrapped about Darius with an intensity that robbed his breath. He bent over double, wondering if he was going to die, because hard as he tried, he could not pull any air into his body. When he could finally catch his breath, he straightened, feeling shaky.

Cambyses smirked. "Look at those fat tears swimming in your eyes. How pretty! Are you going to cry? You're nothing but a baby."

Darius swallowed the tears. He swallowed the hurt and the rejection. He made a fist, and putting all his weight behind it, he rammed it into Cambyses' middle. The boy yelled and retched with pain.

Darius felt nothing. Not relief or pride or regret. He liked this separation from his feelings. He flicked his finger against Cambyses' ear, and with the dispassion of an aloof observer, watched it turn red. As he walked away, he knew he had found a way to make his time at the palace bearable. He would just stop feeling. Every day, he would practice walking away from his feelings until he learned to master them. Until he learned not to be a baby anymore.

Darius raised his head and stared blindly into the horizon. With astonishment, he realized that his cheeks were wet with tears. Over twenty years had passed since those wretched months. And still they had the power to haunt him. To rule him. His life continued to be affected by those devastating separations. Even his marriage was damaged by them. Nehemiah was right. A hole as deep and soot-covered as the foundation of Jerusalem's wall ran through his heart. And he had no way of repairing it.

Sarah gazed out of the narrow window in the passageway adjoining her chamber, her eyes straining to see into the dark, hoping for a glimpse of Darius. He was so late! Worry gnawed at her. He had left with Nehemiah hours before and had yet to return. No one knew where he was. Unable to remain inside, she grabbed one of the torches in the corridor and walked out to the courtyard. She didn't dare stray too far from the house unescorted, knowing that Darius would be displeased by the risk she took. Instead, she lingered at the side of the dirt road close to their residence. Something dark and large flew past her face and she gasped, beating at it with a flailing hand. A bat! Her flesh crawled.

Darius, where are you?

Her arm began to ache, and she passed the torch from one hand to another. She wished she could find a comfortable seat, but the roadside was bare. In the distance, she glimpsed a lone figure moving toward her. Sarah took a few slow steps, trying to distinguish the man's features. Her hesitant steps turned into a lumbering jog, the best she could manage with her protruding stomach, as she recognized Darius's form. There was something forlorn about the heavy steps, the stooped shoulders, the lowered head.

"Darius!" she cried.

"Sarah?" He sounded dazed. "What are you doing out here?"

"Looking for you. You've been gone so long. I grew anxious." She drew abreast of him and came to a stop. In the torchlight his eyes had a faraway look. His breathing was labored and harsh. Something about his expression made her gasp. "What's wrong?"

He opened his mouth, but no sound came out. His throat convulsed and he pressed his lips into a hard line and shook his head.

"Are you sick?"

"No." His voice was low.

"Did something bad happen? Was someone injured?"

His laughter had a cold edge, like the sound of iron clanging against iron. It sent a chill down her spine. "You don't wish to confide in me?" she asked, feeling the old hurt lashing at her.

Slowly, he raised a hand. His fingers tangled in her robe and pulled her close. He bent his face and buried it in the side of her neck. Fearful that she might scorch him, she threw the torch on the ground and wrapped her arms around him. She felt something melt in him, and the rigid hold he had on his body began to give. "Just some bad memories I thought I had forgotten." His voice was muffled against the heat of her flesh.

Sarah stroked his back soothingly. She didn't know what to say. Darius had never revealed such vulnerability to her. She held him tight as if he were a little boy and tried to comfort him with her presence.

He placed a possessive hand over her abdomen. "He might be a boy." His voice trembled.

"You would be disappointed if he were?"

"Of course not. But . . . if he were a boy, he would have to go to the palace school when he turned seven. Like me."

Sarah sucked in a shocked breath. "I'd forgotten about that."

"It's a hard place for a little boy."

"Perhaps we don't have to send him."

He stepped away from her. "If we don't, he won't receive the training he needs in order to succeed. He will have a title and riches, but no respect from his peers. We'll spare him of hardship in his youth. But will he thank us for that, do you think, when he grows into manhood and is treated with disgrace?"

"Why does he need to go to the palace to learn what he needs? You and I can train him. Or hire tutors."

"You don't understand, Sarah. The separation is part of the training. He needs to learn endurance. Toughness. Those of us who were sent to the palace that early developed incredible fortitude and strength. I can survive things you couldn't begin to imagine. But there is a price to pay. It was as if my heart . . . shrank in those years. I grow sick to think of my son paying such a price."

Sarah grasped his hand. "We still have some years to think of a solution. Don't torment yourself with these questions now."

He hung his head. "I can find no peace. My memories plague me." He raised his head, and stared straight into her eyes. In the light of the dying torch, the torment in his gaze pierced her soul. "Sarah, will you pray for me? To your God? My mother's God? Perhaps He can help me."

Chapter 30

As Nehemiah began his customary circuit around the perimeter of the city, he was amazed to find that not a single gap remained in the wall. He had not ordered the doors to be hung in the gates yet. The builders were preparing special scaffolding that made it possible for the heavy doors to be set in place. The debris still needed to be removed as well, but they had accomplished the impossible. They had built the wall itself. He barely had a chance to complete that thought when a messenger brought him a missive from Sanballat and Geshem.

When would these men give up? Nehemiah was tired. Tired! He had no patience for their continuous mischief. With an abrupt movement he broke the seal and began to read.

Come, Nehemiah. Let us meet together in one of the villages on the plain of Ono.

The invitation sounded innocuous, but Nehemiah suspected this was no peace offering. In spite of the fact that the letter sounded like a step toward reaching a new accord, he detected another scheme brewing. Until now, they had tried to harm the wall. The people. Jerusalem. Finally, they had realized that if they could get him out of the way, tearing down the new walls would be a much easier prospect.

Nehemiah ambled to his office in order to write a response. On his way, he noticed how empty Jerusalem remained, its inhabitants refusing to return to the city while it was not fully fortified. Hope thrilled through his veins at the thought of the proliferation of the city. One day soon, the population would explode; merchants and musicians and farmers and fishermen and their children and families would return. All manner of people would enliven the city because it would be safe. The battle for that safety was not over yet. Nehemiah sighed as he pushed the door into his sparse office.

Sarah was leaning against his desk, taking careful note of his accounts.

"I am glad you are here!" he said, feeling cheered by her presence. "Will you act as my scribe and fashion a letter to Sanballat and Geshem?"

Sarah set aside the wet clay tablet she had been working on. "Haven't they given up yet? What do they want now?"

Nehemiah told her about their message. "Write them the following message," he said.

I am carrying on an important work and I cannot come down. Why should I cause the work to stop while I go down to meet with you?

He gave a satisfied nod when Sarah read it

back to him. "These men are not as important as they think they are," he said. "I refuse to be sidetracked by their constant interruptions."

"Do you not worry that the leaders of Judah might take offense at your rudeness in response to what seems like an invitation to restore peace?" Sarah blew on the parchment to speed the drying process. "Many here remain attached to these men."

Nehemiah shrugged. "I will deal with their objections if they come. I cannot make decisions based on other people's opinion of me."

Sanballat would not give up. Like a stubborn horsefly, he kept coming back no matter how hard Nehemiah swatted him away. Four times his enemies sent him the same message, and each time, Nehemiah wrote back the same answer.

Out of patience, the fifth time Sanballat sent his own aide rather than a simple messenger. The man came armed with an unsealed letter. Nehemiah wondered how many times it had been read along the way, spreading its bitter lies amongst friend and foe alike. No doubt, that was the reason the senders had chosen not to seal it. He read it under the cold eye of the Samaritan aide.

It is reported among the surrounding nations— and Geshem who has many friends and relatives among your people confirms it—that you and the Jews are plotting to revolt against Persia. They say this is your motive for building your wall. According to these reports, you are about to set yourself up as the king of Judah. You have even appointed prophets to make the proclamation that there is now a king in Judah! You can be certain that this report will get back to King Artaxerxes. So come, let us confer together before he sends his army to destroy you.

Nehemiah curled his lip. "Is that the best your commander can come up with? Now you go and tell him that I said there is no truth in any part of his story. He has made up a child's tale."

Darius, drawn by the appearance of Sanballat's aide, had come to linger nearby in case Nehemiah should need help. It was typical of Darius, who had avoided him since the awkward conversation about his childhood, to set aside his personal anger in order to lend his support in national matters. Nehemiah gave him a warm smile as they watched Sanballat's servant, red-faced, make his way toward the Sheep Gate.

"You must hand it to the man. He is persistent," Darius said.

"They are trying to intimidate me."

"But you're not intimidated?"

Nehemiah rubbed his chest. "Of course I am. But this is not about my feelings. It concerns the will of God. They can destroy my name, but what can they do to the Lord? They imagine they can discourage me by spreading rumors and trashing my reputation. They want me to stop the work at any cost. And that, I will never do."

"Because God wants you to complete the wall?"

"Exactly!" He slapped a hand on Darius's shoulder. "You begin to understand the Jewish way."

"I doubt it," Darius said, his voice a drawl.

"These interminable attacks make me even more determined to push through. As soon as the scaffolding and the doors are ready, I will have them installed."

When he returned to the quiet of his chamber, Nehemiah prostrated himself on the floor and prayed. *Lord, strengthen my hands. Give me the fortitude to ignore these rumors. You are my vindicator. Enable me to shut my ears to these unjust accusations. Help me not waste my time and vigor by giving in to the desire to defend myself. Don't let me stop before Your time. Help me push through. When I am at my weakest, lend me Your strength so that I can go on.*

Shemaiah, a self-professed prophet, sent an invitation for Nehemiah to visit him later that evening. In spite of a busy schedule, Nehemiah accepted the invitation, wondering why Shemaiah desired to see him. He did not have long to wait in order to find out. He had hardly had a chance to greet Shemaiah when the man pounced on him, his bent fingers digging into Nehemiah's arm.

"I've asked you here in order to save your life. Here is a prophecy that you would do well to heed. Your enemies are coming to kill you tonight. Let us hide inside the Temple and bolt the doors shut. They won't dare come against you there."

"Hide in the Temple? Have you lost your senses, Shemaiah? A layman like me has no business in there. Furthermore, what will the people think if their governor barricades himself in the house of the Lord? Do you wish me to be discredited? I will do no such thing."

Shemaiah's face turned stony. "If you prefer to die by the hand of your enemies, go your way. You're such a stubborn mule, there is no talking reason to you."

For a moment fear grasped Nehemiah's heart so that he could not breathe. Were there men out to murder him at this very moment? Facing fear was not a new challenge to Nehemiah. Many were the times he had had to act in spite of being afraid. In the silence of his heart, he asked God for inspiration, and focused on controlling his overwhelming desire to give in to Shemaiah's warnings.

The more he resisted the urging of fear, the more it faded. With sudden clarity he said, "I don't believe God sent you to me at all. This is not a prophecy from the Lord, is it Shemaiah? Tobiah and Sanballat have hired you to intimidate me. They were hoping that I would be terrorized by your lies and violate the Lord's house, and thereby become discredited by my own actions." He shook his head. "May God remember how you tried to tempt me into betraying Him tonight."

Walls that had lain in ruin for over a century were restored in under two months. In spite of incessant enemy attacks and internal disharmony, the ambitious rebuilding project was concluded in a mere fifty-two days. Nehemiah's gaze took in the enormous gates, which had finally been hung that day. A number of them even sported guardrooms that provided shelter for the men who would stand as sentinels over the city's entrances.

The pale limestone of the walls, washed clean and unblemished by moss, twinkled in the sun. Nehemiah noticed that from certain angles the stones looked golden. Beyond the walls, several farms were visible. It was the early days of autumn, and the last of the crops had come in. The tawny heads of wheat and barley waved in the breeze like a gold band about the walls. A harvest of gold—the walls and the grain—one bringing safety, the other nourishment. God had achieved the impossible. He had provided for Jerusalem. In spite of all their fears, in spite of their faithlessness, in spite of their doubts and self-pity.

God. Had. Provided.

Looking at that sight made Nehemiah want to fall on his face and worship. Never before had he been so utterly aware of the Lord's provision. His might could overcome every enemy. How often Nehemiah had been told that he chased after an impossible dream.

But God had achieved the impossible. Not Nehemiah. God.

By remaining faithful to Him, by refusing to give up, by persisting, Israel had reaped a harvest that changed its future. A harvest of gold.

His brother Hanani was with him. Awe had kept them both silent, sunk in their private reveries. "Nehemiah, is it real?" Hanani said, his voice a whisper.

Nehemiah laughed. "I hope so." His voice shook with emotion.

"This should silence our enemies."

"You would think so. But when it comes to the work of God, I am learning that the battle never stops. Tobiah, who has many ties to Israel, continues to send me letters, trying to intimidate me. I don't know what he expects me to do. Run out with a hammer and personally bring the wall down because I'm so afraid of him?"

Hanani grinned. "If your friends are as faithful as your enemies, you are a blessed man."

"I *am* a blessed man. In the meantime, we must return to work."

Hanani looked dismayed. "What work? Everything is finished."

"This is just the beginning. We cannot stop with the wall. We need to rebuild houses and roads. If we wish for Jerusalem to grow its population again, we have to provide a well-ordered city with sufficient habitation to attract more citizens. And Hanani, this has never been about a mere building project. God wants to restore the people back to Himself. He seeks to draw our hearts to Him.

"With so much to accomplish, Jerusalem needs someone who is in charge of it. I was thinking of you, little brother."

"Me!"

"You. Along with Hananiah, the commander of the citadel. He is a man of integrity who loves God above all else. I trust you both."

"How could you trust me with a position this significant?" Hanani dropped his head, avoiding his brother's gaze. "Over the past two months, I have doubted you many times. You must have found me trying on more than one occasion."

Nehemiah shook his head. "The worst character defect that can plague a leader is arrogance. Do you know the cure for arrogance?"

"What is it?"

"Failure. The Lord loves to place those who have failed in positions of power. They know their limitations and rely on Him more. You have grown through the trials of the past weeks. You have seen how God can surpass our weakness. It has humbled you, Hanani. You won't ever make the mistake of being arrogant."

"I am honored you believe I make a good leader for Jerusalem, even if you think my only qualification lies in the fact that I am a failure."

Nehemiah gave a hearty laugh. "Perhaps you have other valuable qualifications as well. Here are your first orders, then. The gates of Jerusalem are not to be opened until later in the morning when the sun has grown hot. Set the gatekeepers from the Temple on guard duty, for they are not needed as often in the house of the Lord. Make sure that they shut the doors and bar them in the evening. Furthermore, appoint residents of Jerusalem as additional guards, some at their posts, and others near their houses. Men are bound to be more vigilant when their homes are at stake.

"I also intend to register the people of Judah by families. We need a record of those who have returned from captivity. There must be over forty thousand people living in the area surrounding Jerusalem."

Hanani gave a weak nod.

From the corner of his eye Nehemiah saw a glint of color. Turning, he found Darius waiting. He was surprised at the young man's humble patience. As the king's cousin and a high lord in his own right, Darius would have been within his right to walk right up, unconcerned with interrupting a conversation.

Nehemiah left Hanani and approached Darius. He hadn't had a chance to open his mouth in greeting when Darius spoke.

"You were right about me."

Chapter 31

His arm about Darius's shoulder, Nehemiah drew the young man to the privacy of a hill and settled them under a myrtle tree with a twisted trunk. The silence stretched. After seeking him out and spitting out his initial confession, Darius seemed to have lost the power of speech. Nehemiah waited with patient compassion. It wouldn't be easy to break the discipline of a lifetime and begin to express deeply private thoughts.

"Lord Nehemiah . . . You said that my childhood was like the foundation of Jerusalem's walls, bearing a damage that time had not erased. You were right. I have . . . no idea how to . . . to be the man I want to be. I don't . . . love my wife the way she deserves or wants."

He exhaled a tortured breath. "In order to survive the pain of losing my parents and living in the harsh isolation of the palace school, I learned to shut down my heart. Every time I come close to giving Sarah my whole heart, I find an excuse to . . . to run. I have blamed her for the trouble in our marriage. But I'm as much to blame. And I don't know how to change. I am . . . I am afraid."

Nehemiah could imagine what such an admission had cost the young man. "Of what?"

"Of never being able to change. Never becoming the kind of man who is worthy of true respect."

Nehemiah sighed. "My young friend, you won't like my solution."

Darius's laugh lacked humor. "I like the knot that refuses to leave my insides even less. Go ahead. Tell me what you wish. That's why I have come."

"I only know of one source of healing. The One who made you can renew your soul. He can undo the hurt of your past and make you into the husband and father you desire to become."

Darius nodded. "I thought you might say something like that. I've been thinking about it since the day we spoke." He drew up his knee and rested a fist against it. "My father's heart will break if I turn to your God. But my heart will stay broken if I don't."

Nehemiah let out a deep breath. He knew Lord Vivan would feel betrayed by what he was about to do. Their friendship might not survive the weight of this decision. Then again, he knew what the Lord expected of him. And while losing Vivan's good opinion and warm regard would hurt, disobeying God would prove far more painful.

"Darius, the Lord sometimes calls us to build something. Something that is important in His sight. He called me to this broken down city in order to rebuild these ruins. He has called you to build a marriage with Sarah. In order to do that, you have to rebuild the ruins of your early life."

Darius lifted his head. "I never thought of it that way."

"Just as my efforts to restore Jerusalem were opposed, your marriage will also face opposition. Your soul has enemies that are as persistent and devious as Sanballat."

"What enemies?"

"Sin. The wiles of the world. The dark forces of evil that come against us. Nagging doubts. Lies. Forces that have already come against you in your childhood."

"What can I do against an enemy I can't even see? An enemy that seems to be inside me?"

"You need God's weapons of war to survive. You are a warrior. You know what it's like when you come under attack. You know how to build up defensive walls, how to retreat, how to charge. You have to be a warrior for your marriage, Darius."

Darius lowered his brows. "I do know how to be a warrior. What are these weapons that you speak of?"

"This world offers powerful weapons. Bitterness. Detachment. Unforgiveness. You can win an argument with these weapons. You can make yourself feel justified. Feel right. In the end, however, they will rob you of any chance at happiness. Like swords, they can sever the best of unions. These are the only weapons you have known how to wield thus far.

"But the Lord can equip you with godly weapons instead. Weapons that have power to protect you from your enemy's attacks. Learn to pray. Fight for your family. Study the Law of Moses and live according to its principles."

Darius was silent for long moments. "My first step is to commit my life to my mother's God, isn't it?"

"Well, unless He becomes *your* God, you won't have access to His power. He cannot transform you if you don't belong to Him."

Darius covered his fist with an open palm. His teeth were clenched so tight, Nehemiah worried that he might crack them. With a jerk, the young man gave a nod of affirmation. "I will do as you say, Lord Nehemiah."

For the first time Nehemiah noticed that Darius had been calling him *lord,* a rank that was not strictly true. Darius's perceptions of worth were already changing as he drew near to the Lord. He was elevating Nehemiah because he could sense that by God's standards Nehemiah was a man of authority.

"I think I always avoided you because I sensed that you could draw me near to God," Darius said suddenly. "That was the real reason I didn't like you."

Nehemiah laughed. "You are going to like me even less by the time we are finished. For one thing, you will have to be circumcised."

Darius went still. He bit out a long and fluid expletive.

"And you'll have to give up doing that."

Sarah tried to reach a small casket containing some of her writing paraphernalia, which Pari had stored on a high shelf. Too short to reach the box directly, she tried to rise on tiptoe. The awkward bulk of her figure got in the way, and she gave a vexed groan as she failed to lift it. A high-pitched squeak escaped her throat as a long arm reached over her head unexpectedly and grasped the casket with one hand.

"You should ask for help, Sarah. It's no hardship for me to give you a hand." Darius placed the carved wooden box on the table.

"I didn't hear you come in!"

"I thought I could persuade you to rest for a while."

"It's the middle of the afternoon."

"You haven't been sleeping well at night. A short nap would revive you."

Sarah hid her surprise. She had tried to conceal her nightly struggles with sleeplessness and the ensuing exhaustion that trailed her steps into the daylight hours. She should have known that little escaped his notice.

"Come. I will bide with you." Before Sarah could respond, Darius swept her into his arms and carried her to bed.

Sarah made a squeaking sound in protest. "Put me down! I weigh as much as a house."

Darius made a face. "I own armor heavier than you."

He sat on the bed behind her, her back against his chest, his knees raised on either side of her body like a bronze fence. To her delight, he began to rub her shoulders, his fingers tender. She gave a sigh of pleasure.

"Do you know, there is a lot you have to learn about being a husband," he said.

"Hmm?" She opened her eyes and tried to emerge from her pleasure-induced haze. Vaguely, she remembered saying those words to him late in the night while they were in Damascus. She wondered what he had up his sleeve now. In recent weeks, he had managed to shock her out of her skin more than once. Not that she was complaining. He seemed to have read her list of secret longings and decided to make them come true. Leaning against him, she said, "Is that so?"

"Yes. I was always arrogant about the ease with which I learn. It's been a crushing blow to my pride that in the most important area of my life, I'm a dim-witted learner."

Sarah began to giggle. "Are you mocking me?"

"Not at all. I thought you captured the sentiment

rather well, and now that it's my turn, I decided to use your own words. I hoped it would win your favor."

Sarah went still. "You cannot win what you already own."

She felt Darius heave a deep sigh against her back. Coming up on her knees, she turned around to face him. A rush of tears blurred her vision. Her throat was thick with them as she whispered, "Darius, please, will you forgive me for not telling you I was carrying our child?"

He turned pale and Sarah squeezed her eyes shut, not wanting to see the bitterness that he wouldn't be able to hide. Fingers grasped her chin. "Look at me," he demanded.

Sarah forced her eyes to open, trying to veil her disappointment.

"I forgive you, Sarah. I forgive you."

She gasped. Words failed her as she tried to take in his declaration. His mouth pressed against hers in a hungry kiss. Against her lips he murmured, "I forgive you with all my heart."

Sarah wept, relief and hope washing through her in overpowering waves. Darius clung to her, his arms caressing her back, cradling her against him. There was something different in the way he held her. In his embrace she had always detected an impenetrable reserve, as though he held some part of himself back—some part of his soul that he allowed no one to come near. In an inexplicable way, she sensed now that he had removed that barrier.

It was as if a wall had crumpled between them, drawing them nearer than they had ever been. She had never felt so close to anyone. She felt that she belonged entirely to him, and he to her. She knew he did not love her. For the first time, she did not care. He was giving her everything he had to give. Everything but his heart.

"You forgive me?" she asked, to make certain that she hadn't dreamt this moment up.

"I do forgive you. Hush, now, sweetheart. Don't cry so hard. I meant for you to rest."

Sarah blew her nose in the handkerchief he held out for her. "You've freed me from an unbearable burden. Thank you."

His chest expanded under her cheek. "Then I should ask *your* pardon—for withholding my forgiveness such a long time."

"I give it, freely. I hurt you with my actions, Darius. I cannot tell you how much I regret it."

He waved a hand. "Sarah, I know I have not been the best husband to you. I haven't given you reason to trust me. I've been a blind fool, thinking so proudly of myself. I've only seen the good I've done, and ignored my failures toward you. I've been a harsh judge to you."

Sarah caressed his cheek. His beard had grown in thick, and it tickled her hand. She smiled at the sensation, and at the pure joy of knowing that she could touch him in freedom, without worry that he might spurn her. "You make me happy just by being with me, Darius. Just by wanting me."

He drew his thumb down the inside of her arm, making her shiver. "And you make *me* happy. I do have some good news for you."

"More good news?"

"Nehemiah is arranging for my circumcision."

For a short moment Sarah's mind went blank. Then the meaning of his words sank in, and she squeaked an inarticulate cry before drowning him in kisses. "It can't be true! . . . The Lord be praised! . . . Is it real? . . . I am so overjoyed!" she exclaimed breathlessly between kisses. "And so proud of you, husband."

Darius laughed soundlessly before prying her loose. "You Jewish women are a blood-thirsty lot. I tell you your husband is about to have a very precious part of him dissected, and you whoop with jubilation."

Sarah laughed and hugged him to her with all her strength. She became aware that his hands had curled into hard fists, and his mouth had become a hard line.

"Sarah, there are still many things left unsaid between us." His face had turned the color of ash.

"You don't have to tell me anything you don't want to."

"That's not true. It's too easy for me to avoid personal topics. I prefer to contain my feelings, I admit. But I have discovered that only gets in the way of our marriage."

Sarah caressed his fisted hands, trying to imbue him with comfort. She felt overwhelmed by his admission. It was a surprise to her that he was even aware of his tendency to keep his emotions hidden, let alone realize that by doing so, he hurt her. Hurt their marriage.

He gulped. It was an endearing sound coming from a man who seemed unfailingly elegant in his manners. "I've never told you about my life at the palace," he said.

Chapter 32

The day the wall was completed, Nehemiah sent the workers back to their homes for a few days of rest, with instructions that they were to return to Jerusalem on the first day of the seventh month. It wasn't in Darius's nature to postpone an unpleasant task. He asked Nehemiah to arrange for his circumcision at the earliest possible hour. He knew the governor had grand plans for the feast of the seventh month, and he intended to be present and recovered by the time of those ceremonies.

On the appointed day, the whole community gathered together to praise God for His great favor toward Israel. Nehemiah had ordered a high wooden platform to be built just inside the Water Gate. The land was still shrouded in predawn darkness when every man, woman, and child old enough to understand congregated there, waiting for Ezra the priest.

Darius asked Nehemiah why he refused to read the law himself. "You are the governor, the chosen of the king. You did all the hard work. Why should you not enjoy the glory now?"

"A good leader knows when to step into the shadows," Nehemiah said with a smile. "Ezra is a scholar and a priest. He has the learning and the consecration needed for this task. He will glorify God better than I ever could. He will help the people understand what the Lord desires from them.

"Do not worry. I am not abandoning Israel. At the right time, I will join forces with Ezra, and together we will strengthen God's people. Faith and diplomacy shall make a powerful union." The corners of his mouth turned down. "Which means I must convince Artaxerxes to do without me for a while yet. I shall definitely need both diplomacy and faith to accomplish that feat!"

As the sun splashed the sky with its light, Ezra arrived, followed by thirteen handpicked assistants, some of whom helped carry a large scroll with great care. The old priest stepped onto the platform, with a man on each side of him to help unroll the scroll of the Book of the Law. When the waiting crowds saw Ezra open the book, they rose to their feet as one man.

Darius took his place near Sarah. From a corner of his eye he caught a glimpse of his friend Lysander amongst a small group of foreigners who had gathered at a respectful distance. Lysander stood, feet slightly apart, his massive arms crossed, his face an impenetrable mask. He had made no secret of his disdain for Darius's decision to be circumcised.

"They have hijacked your brains, these people," he had said, his mouth curling. "Why do you want to go and do a stupid thing like that?"

To his own amazement, Darius had felt no irritation with Lysander's contempt. Because of his mother, Darius had always harbored a certain respect for the Jewish faith, even when he had run from it. But he could understand his friend's scorn. Lysander would not have minded if Darius had offered a sacrifice or two to the God of the Jews. He could not, however, accept with equanimity a commitment so encompassing that it even marked his friend's flesh. Darius had spent enough of his life avoiding the Lord to be able to feel a bittersweet compassion for his friend's derision.

Next to Lysander he spied Pari, her head bent, her hands folded before her. Pari's demeanor, in stark contrast to the Spartan, displayed deference. She had spent many hours in Sarah's company, asking questions about the Lord. Sarah had told him that she even prayed with her.

Darius turned his attention back to Ezra. The old priest began the day by praising the Lord. Everyone lifted up their hands and shouted, "Amen!"

Then Ezra began to read from the ancient book before him. The law was written in Hebrew, and unlike his wife, Darius understood little of what was being read. He was not the only one afflicted with incomprehension. Knowing how many of the Israelites themselves had lost the ability to understand Hebrew since the years of their captivity in Babylon, Nehemiah had arranged for Ezra to read a section of the law and then stop. A number of Levites had been stationed among the people, assigned to translate Ezra's words into Aramaic. They made certain that the people understood the significance of each passage and gained a deeper insight into God's intentions.

Darius felt his whole body tingle with an unusual excitement. The words flowed through him with power, and he realized that he was measuring his life by them.

> The Lord is God and there is no other . . .
> The Lord is our God, the Lord alone. You must love the Lord your God with all your heart, all your soul, and all your strength. You must not worship any of the gods of neighboring nations, for the Lord your God, who lives among you, is a jealous God.

It dawned on Darius that God demanded more than duty or loyalty, though He wanted those things. He wanted Darius's heart. He wanted an all-consuming love.

Darius became aware of a strange silence. The whole world seemed to have faded around him.

Sarah, Ezra, the Levites, the crowds. They disappeared from his consciousness. It felt as though he alone stood before the Lord, his soul bare. He could not tolerate such a scrutiny. He felt his own failures, unhidden, overpowering him, and fell to his knees.

I don't know how to love You! I don't know how to love. Not the way You demand.

With a disconcerting jolt, he became mindful of those around him once again. The voice of the Levite near him penetrated his mind.

> The Lord did not set His heart on you and choose you because you were more numerous than other nations, for you were the smallest of all nations! Rather, it was simply that the Lord loves you . . . He is the faithful God who keeps His covenant for a thousand generations and lavishes His unfailing love on those who love Him and obey His commands . . .

Darius sensed that God wanted him to understand the significance of those verses not only for Israel, but also for him. As a man. His fingers dug in the dirt where he knelt, spasmodically clenching and unclenching. The Lord cared for him as an individual. That knowledge began to permeate his mind, and then deeper. Past his emotions, past his thoughts, it sank into his inmost being. He had not chosen God; God had chosen *him!*

He had not been chosen because he was the strongest or the best. God had not chosen Darius because of his mother or his relatives. God had chosen him simply because the Lord of the universe *loved* him. He loved Darius with an *unfailing* love.

Darius's strength deserted him. His muscles, always strong and in control, became like a mass of wet silk, unable to support him. Darius fell forward, his face on the ground.

Lord, I have failed You! I have failed You all my life. And I can't even promise that I will stop. But Your love has never failed me and never shall. Your faithfulness is beyond my comprehension.

He felt as though that love covered him like a blanket. The weight of it was so overwhelming that Darius could not move. Awe pumped through his veins so that he could barely breathe. He knew that the Lord's hand had deigned to touch him. In spite of his rebellious years running from God, running from His rule and His mercy, God was choosing to impart His forgiveness and acceptance to him.

Darius wept like a small boy and felt no shame for it. His face was drenched in tears, and he did not care. It sank into his benumbed mind that the Lord had been with him through every single moment of the ravages of his childhood. When he had thought himself alone, the Lord had been with him, loving him, guiding him. The Lord had known every sorrow, every childish fear, and had never—*never*—abandoned him.

Slowly, Darius felt something crack in his heart, like an old crust as hard and cold as marble. The love of God permeated the ancient shell that had been his protection from childhood. Now God Himself would be his protection.

> The Lord your God will change your heart and the hearts of all your descendants, so that you will love Him with all your heart and soul and so you may live!

The Lord was changing Darius's heart, restoring it, teaching it to love again. He felt the heavy weight ease and was able to move his head. The first thing he saw was Sarah kneeling next to him, her eyes closed, her face glowing in spite of the tears that ran down the length of it.

He was struck by such a wave of love for her that his breath caught. Like an inexperienced youth he stared at her, his mouth half-open, overwhelmed with affection so deep he lost the power of speech. It had been here all along, this love, from the early days of their union. Only he had been unable to give it rein.

With sharp clarity, he remembered the first time he had seen Sarah on the hill outside the palace in

Persepolis. He had been chasing a lion that had escaped the hunting grounds and had stumbled upon her in his search. She had faced him, her cheeks pink from a recent nap, her shapeless robe askew, her large eyes filled with humor and fearless intelligence. Six unbroken generations of Persian aristocracy running through his veins snapped into rapt attention when she confronted him with the fire of challenge instead of a simpering giggle. She had been far from beautiful that morning, with her rumpled scribal garb and her disheveled hair, but she had charmed him within moments of his meeting her like few women ever had.

He had had to aim his arrow just past her, at the lion that was crouching behind her, and she had stood still as an old soldier, forbearing the danger that faced her from two directions. He had not fallen in love with her there, but he had been captivated enough to feel threatened. Which was doubtless why he had chosen to believe that she was just another sycophant, seeking to promote herself by flattering him. He had pushed her away as fast as he could by coming up with a likely fault to attach to her, so it was the fault he had seen, and not the sweetness of the woman who attracted him with unreasonable power.

He had not allowed himself to feel his true emotions. His austere childhood had left its mark, making him incapable of displaying that depth of vulnerability. Love had let him down once. He had learned not to give it that opportunity again. Even after they had been married long enough for him to know Sarah, to know that she was caring and loyal and generous, he could not surrender his heart. He feasted on her love like a starving babe, but he could not offer his own.

Now that the Lord had shattered the cold walls with which he had surrounded himself since boyhood, he could no longer detach himself from her. Nor did he want to.

He loved Sarah. The realization filled him with joy.

Darius staggered up, his movements awkward. From a corner of his eye he saw Lysander. The Spartan was on his knees, his face covered in perspiration. The blue eyes were wide and shocked. Darius had a suspicion that the Lord had made His presence known to his friend in a way he was not likely to forget soon. Pari was lying on the ground, her face in the dirt, much like his own moments before.

Darius widened the scope of his gaze and became aware that most of the people were weeping, some silently like Sarah, others wailing like inconsolable children. The Lord's presence hung over the crowd like an invisible mist.

Darius had walked through the wealthiest

palaces in the world. He had experienced the lushest riches that human imagination could offer. Nothing had compared in majesty to the grandeur of God's presence in this small, barren city. He realized that the scope of the Lord's presence on that day was so wide and encompassing that every man, woman, and child there was bound to experience an unforgettable shift in their souls. No one would be the same after this day. The Lord had revived the zeal of His people. They hungered and thirsted for a righteousness they knew they did not possess.

Nehemiah joined Ezra on the platform. A new gentleness colored his voice as he said, "This day is sacred. Don't mourn. The Lord is holy, but His mercy rises even higher than our shame. Stop grieving now."

The Levites joined Nehemiah, calming the people with their reassurances. The governor charged the gathered crowd to rest. "Go and celebrate the Lord's goodness with rich foods and sweet drinks. Share your bounty with those who have nothing prepared so that they won't go hungry.

"Wipe your tears. The joy of the Lord is your strength! Let His love fill you with joy, and you will overcome."

On his way to his chambers, Darius ran into Nehemiah. Without a word the older man pulled him into a fatherly embrace. Darius could feel his eyes welling up again. "Lord Nehemiah, I never knew it could be like this."

"Nor I, my son. Nor I."

Darius felt like he had a colony of ants taking residence inside him. He longed to be alone with his wife and dreaded it at the same time. He had faced fierce enemies on numberless battlefields. Yet never had he been reduced to such a puddle of fear. And all because he wished to express to his own wife how dear she was to him. He could have kicked himself for his folly. But he could not outrun the weakness that caused a veneer of perspiration to cover his forehead.

In his room, Pari served a small feast. Darius dismissed her with a stiff wave before she had finished laying out their food. His throat was parched and he took a large swallow of sweet wine.

Sarah's voice was hushed as she said, "I'll never be the same after this day. I feel like Job: *my ears had heard of You, but now my eyes have seen You.*"

"I feel the same. I imagine most of Israel has had a similar experience today."

Sarah was busy unwrapping warm bread from a napkin. He took the bread from her and set it distractedly atop a bowl. It sank into the contents. Sarah made a small sound of protest and tried to rescue the bread.

"Leave it!"

She turned to him with a frown. He forced out a long breath and moistened his dry lips. Her hands were arrested midway to the bowl. He captured them in his own. His fingers were trembling and he could not steady them.

"Sarah. Sarah . . . I love you."

"What did you say?"

"I love you, sweetheart."

A heavy silence met his hard-won declaration. For a moment his heart sank. Would she reject him? Would she walk away now that he had bared his soul?

Her voice sounded brittle when at last she spoke. "Say it again."

With sudden insight he recognized that it was not coldness that drove her, but doubt. After hammering her month after month with his dispassionate assurance that he would never love her, she could not take in his declaration. He was not a poetic man. But for her sake, he tried.

"I want to grow old with you. I want your face to be the first thing I see in the morning and the last thing I see at night. I want to feel my children growing inside you. Sarah, my love. I want to worship the Lord with you, and hear your laughter until the day I die."

"What changed?" she asked, her voice unsteady. "You said yourself that you could not feel that way toward me. Are you driven by duty to say these things now? You called me sweetheart before, but didn't mean it. Is your new faith the source of this pretty speech?"

"Of course not! Could I lie to please the Lord? You should ignore everything I said before. I was an idiot. I meant it when I called you sweetheart. I meant that and more."

Her smile was sad. "I know I'm not pretty enough for you. You would have chosen someone like Roxanna as your wife if you had been free to make your own decision. Someone athletic and stunning. Someone highborn, like you."

Darius wrapped his hand around her forearm and pulled her toward him. His face contorted with frustration. "I could have married Roxanna years ago if I had wanted. Which I didn't."

"But you didn't want me either."

"I wanted you almost from the start. I think I fell in love with you before we arrived at Ecbatana. I was just too dense to admit it to myself. Sarah, my darling, I have not desired another woman but you since then."

He saw doubt in her eyes, and beyond it, the lack of confidence that drove it. He had caused some of that insecurity. He ached when he thought that his own behavior had diminished her ability to receive his love. To trust it.

He pulled her against his chest, his movements laced with tenderness. He kissed her forehead, her chin, her neck, her cheeks. Desire washed over him in powerful waves. He had always wanted her with an intensity that seemed to grow regardless of their circumstances. But now, he tried to instill into her the reality of his feelings. It wasn't just her body that he wanted. It was all of her.

"God gave me the desire of my heart when I married you, Sarah, and I did not know it. He gave me a marriage of love. The Lord made my most cherished dream come to pass, and I was too ornery to notice. I don't deserve such loving-kindness from the Lord. You are my gift from Him. And I aim to keep you, my darling. And to cherish you until you believe me."

He moved away from her and examined her expression. She was smiling, her face illuminated with an inner light that made his heart pound. "You really love me, don't you?" she whispered.

"With all my soul." He kissed her until he felt dizzy with wanting.

"I love you, Darius."

As he drew her hard against him, their child poked him with such a firm thrust of a little limb that he felt it through his clothing. Sarah made a short sound of protest.

"Are you all right? That must have hurt."

"He was just making his approval known." She laid her head against his chest. And then she called him *sweetheart,* which she had never done before. Darius decided that he would not grow tired of hearing that particular endearment until the day he died.

Chapter 33

How could one small woman bear so much pain? Darius wondered. If he saw her swallow one more scream, he would become unhinged. He had suffered numerous injuries in battle—knife stabs, dislocated shoulders, head wounds, broken ribs. Weathering them had been easy. But he found Sarah's suffering unbearable. She had been in labor over one whole day and night. And still she pushed and heaved. And still the child would not come.

In between the ravages of pain, sometimes she lost consciousness, a mercy for which he was grateful. At other times, she vomited with a violence that made him wince.

Lysander had found an experienced midwife who came with glowing recommendations from the lords of Judah, and they both attended Sarah. Neither seemed particularly worried. To judge by their expressions, watching a woman being torn asunder by contractions was the most prosaic thing the world had to offer. Darius had learned to keep his mouth shut in the early stages of the birthing process. Lysander had threatened to expel him from the room if he did not stop making annoying comments. As it was, he had had to argue his way into being allowed to stay for the labor.

His fingers had long since lost feeling as Sarah pressed them when the pains came upon her, which were closer and closer together.

"Good one, Sarah," the midwife cried. "One more like that and his head will be out."

Darius snapped into focus. He no longer cared about the birth of the child. He only wanted Sarah to be free of this infernal anguish. Sarah screamed. It wasn't a human sound. Darius felt his whole body go rigid. Perspiration drenched every orifice. He realized that he was praying with the desperation of a petrified man. Darius Pasargadae, scion of the great king Cyrus, was shaking with fear.

"His head is out!" Lysander shouted. "The hardest part is over. One more push now, Sarah."

Sarah groaned, her voice hoarse. She had been kneeling on the mattress, Pari behind her to support her back. Her body bent over, and she pushed. The midwife had her hands on her belly, helping the body's natural contractions. Darius's eyes grew large as he saw a bluish grey creature emerge from his wife's body. Half his mind was captured by the image of the child, which lay as still as a wooden statue in Lysander's large hands, and the other half grappled horrified with the large gush of fresh blood which suddenly soaked the sheets beneath Sarah. She collapsed backward into Pari's arms. With exquisite care, the handmaiden laid her mistress on the pillows behind her.

Sarah's lips had turned a purplish hue. She was as still as the child she had birthed. "Sarah!" Darius cried, and laid a desperate hand against the side of her neck to ensure she lived. He felt the thud of her pulse. It was weaker than it should have been.

He could tell that it took all her strength to open her eyes. "My baby," she whispered. "Why isn't he crying?"

Darius looked over to where Lysander held the child by the ankles, upside down. He slapped its back once. Then again. Nothing. Darius's heart sank. The child was dead. Lord have mercy! After all this, the child was dead.

And then suddenly, without warning, the baby took a breath—its first upon the earth.

"It's all right, Sarah. He breathes. He lives! We have a boy. A son!"

As soon as he had taken that initial breath, their son began to wail, making his displeasure known to everyone in the room. Darius didn't begrudge his vociferous objections. He would not have enjoyed the indignity of being held upside down, and the additional insult of a none-too-gentle slap, either.

Darius spent a short moment thanking God for that miracle before returning his gaze to the midwife who had been tending Sarah. Once the entire afterbirth had been pushed out, the midwife did what she could to stop the unnatural flow of blood. She caught his distraught gaze and gave him a reassuring smile.

"She's fine now. The bleeding has slowed. We'll have to watch over her for the next few days. She's bound to be frail at first. But the immediate danger has passed, and with proper care, your wife should recover and give you many more children."

Darius leaned against the wall, too weak to stand without help.

"You want to hold your son? He's a noisy little Persian," Lysander said.

Darius saw the longing look in Sarah's eyes. "Give him to his mother, first."

Lysander had washed the babe with warm water and salt and rubbed olive oil into his skin after cutting and knotting the umbilical cord. He placed the wriggling bundle, cleaned now and pink, covered in soft cotton swaddling, onto Sarah's chest. Her arms went around him weakly. Tears streamed down her face as she beheld him. "He's your very image, Darius," she murmured.

Darius studied the wrinkled face surrounded by the thick shock of dark hair and kept his remark to himself. The babe stopped his wailing as soon as his mother's arms wrapped around him. His son had good taste.

Pari, who was quietly cleaning away the bloody sheets, whispered, "The Lord be praised!" She had come to believe in the Lord as the true living God the day Ezra had read the Law. Darius smiled at her and nodded agreement.

He drew a gentle finger down the side of his son's face. The tiny mouth gathered and made a suckling motion. He felt a powerful tug on his heart. His soul rose up with the desire to protect this helpless creature against every danger.

"Your boy is hungry," the midwife said. She arranged him against Sarah's breast. Darius looked at the unfamiliar scene, fascinated. His wife held on to the baby with an emotional strength that overcame her physical weakness. Pride washed through Darius. Pride that this woman and this child belonged to him. And then he was humbled by the thought that God had chosen to gift him with both.

He bent over and kissed Sarah on the crown of her head. "I love you," he whispered. "I love you more than I can say." For the first time since he was a child, a sense of completeness filled him. He felt utterly at peace. In spite of not knowing how to meet the challenges the future would offer him and his family, he felt bathed in the assurance of the Lord.

He thought of the walls of Jerusalem, and how they had been rebuilt in spite of incessant danger and threat. How the ravages of the past had been overcome by the persistent faithfulness of one man. It occurred to him at that moment, when exhaustion still had ahold of him, that God had restored his own life no less than He had Jerusalem. Nehemiah had once called the walls around Jerusalem a harvest of gold.

Darius looked at his little son, eating his fill at his wife's breast, and acknowledged that God had given him a harvest, as well.

AUTHOR'S NOTES

According to some archaeologists, during the time of Nehemiah the population of Jerusalem might have been as low as several hundred inhabitants. Other scholars estimate as many as three or four thousand. Certainly, the city had shrunk substantially since the days of Solomon, and I try to capture that tragic loss in the plot.

We are unable to fully reconstruct the location of the walls in Nehemiah's day or even to know what the walls would have looked like. Many of the landmarks mentioned in Nehemiah's letter were destroyed during Herod the Great's renovations four hundred years later. My description of the walls is based on a combination of archaeological discoveries from that period, biblical narrative, and of course, literary license.

According to the lunar calendar, in the year 445 BC the month of Nisan occurred between April and May, which was unusually late. This means that Nehemiah must have accomplished the arrangements for travel from Susa in an astonishingly rapid manner and arrived in Jerusalem earlier than the average caravan would have.

As always, where possible, I have tried to

remain faithful to history. The plot on Artaxerxes' life is inspired by two unrelated stories from the Achaemenid period as reported by Greek historians. In one case, Histiaeus, planning insurrection against the Persians, sends a secret message to his nephew, tattooing the words on his slave's shaved head to prevent discovery. In another, the plot to kill the king involves a knife that is poisoned only on one side. I combined the two stories in order to create the fictional plot against Artaxerxes. Pyrus is also a figment of my imagination.

The description of Megabyzus's rebellion against Artaxerxes, and the king's benevolent response, is historical and based loosely on Ctesias's account. It seems likely that Megabyzus really was the satrap of the Trans-Euphrates at the time of this novel.

The education of aristocratic Persian boys, as well as the role of magi in their instruction, has been captured by a number of ancient writers. According to one Greek historian, boys did not live in palace dormitories until the age of sixteen or seventeen. Others don't distinguish the age the boys were sent to live in the palace, only the fact that their education started between the ages of five and seven, and that they lived in the palace while being educated. The plot makes use of both these details. I found it fascinating that the magi were not only the astrologers, philosophers, teachers, and scientists of their age, but also the seekers of highest truth. To several such men, the Truth they sought with such passion would one day be revealed in a simple manger.

A number of early rabbinic scholars claim that Nehemiah was a eunuch. Most historians find no evidence of this assertion. I have portrayed him as a single man, because the Bible mentions no wife. That he was an extraordinary man—at once courtier, project manager, politician, and military leader—one cannot doubt. Few in history equal his perseverance and faith. I chose to loosely base one of his proclamations on a speech given by Winston Churchill in the early days of WWII, because I think the two men would have understood the concept of working against great odds while holding on to the hope of victory.

Harvest of Gold is a love story. But at its core, it is also a novel about overcoming in the midst of battle. Jerusalem is under attack. The king's life is threatened. Darius and Sarah's marriage is slowly unraveling. How do you respond to the interior and exterior forces that threaten to destroy you? *Harvest of Gold* tries to answer that question based on the timeless principles we find in the book of Nehemiah.

As always, the best way to study the Bible is not through a novel, but simply to read the original. This story can in no way replace the trans-formative power that the reader will encounter in the Scriptures. For the biblical account of the rebuilding of Jerusalem, please refer to the books of Ezra and Nehemiah.

I hope you have enjoyed Sarah and Darius's adventures, which began with *Harvest of Rubies*. After so many years of working with them, they feel like old friends to me.

DISCUSSION QUESTIONS

Harvest of Gold

1. In the first two chapters of the novel, we glimpse certain strengths in Sarah and Darius's relationship. But we also become aware that this marriage is already in trouble. Identify some of the strengths and weaknesses you see in Sarah and Darius's relationship.

2. Most of the characters in *Harvest of Gold* seem to be engaged in a battle. The king is battling to save his life. The Babylonian brothers are trying to preserve their freedom. Nehemiah is striving to save Jerusalem. Sarah and Darius are desperate to keep their marriage intact. Where are the places you see a battle in your life?

3. What do you see in your life that is worth fighting for? What have you given up on?

4. What are some of the lessons we can learn from Nehemiah to help us overcome in the midst of the battles of life?

5. In Chapter 12 Sarah has a miscarriage and Nehemiah prays for her. How can *you* help and comfort others as they grieve? How do you personally cope with loss?

6. In Chapter 24, Nehemiah talks about Gideon. Are there places in your life where you are hiding in a metaphorical winepress? What are you afraid of? (For example, failure, disappointment, suffering, ending up alone . . .)

7. Gideon's perception of himself differed from the way God saw him. Do you think you are like Gideon in that respect? How do you think God sees you? In contrast, how do you see yourself?

8. Describe Darius. How do you think Darius's emotional distance affects his marriage? Can you relate?

9. What prevents Darius from placing his trust in the Lord? In the end, what causes him to change?

10. We sometimes build walls around our hearts that need to come down: walls of fear, defensiveness, pride, emotional distance. But there are also godly defensive walls that we should establish around our lives: walls that

protect our relationship with God and with others, walls that safeguard our destiny and our soul. But like Jerusalem, many of us have allowed these walls to fall into ruin. Talk about areas of your life where the wrong walls have to come down, and areas where new protective structures have to be raised up.

11. Nehemiah has a special role in Sarah and Darius's lives. In your own words, describe their relationship. Do you have a Nehemiah in your life? Are you a Nehemiah in someone else's life?

12. What caused Nehemiah to overcome all the odds against him?

13. Who is your favorite character in this book? Why?

14. Which character can you identify with the most? Why?

15. What are some of the scenes in this story that touched your heart? Why?

ACKNOWLEDGMENTS

The gracious expertise and help of many people made this novel possible. I would like to thank my agent, Wendy Lawton, whose efforts on my behalf continue to pave the way for me as a writer. I was blessed the day we met. To Deb Keiser at River North, whose support of this project has remained unstinting from its conception, and Pam Pugh my editor: simply, thank you.

Thanks to my dearest friend, Rebecca Rhee who, in spite of being very pregnant with her first baby, applied her inveterate knowledge of the Hebrew Bible and love of literature to *Harvest of Gold* and made it a far better book with her insights. I don't know how many hours I have spent boring her with my fears and plotline problems in this book. But she has always been there to hold my hand. I am profoundly grateful for my friends Beth and Rob Bull who never cease to encourage and support me along this path. Thanks for believing in me, guys! It's the best gift you could give me. As always, my sister Emi Trowbridge's undeserved faith in me sustains me every day.

Special acknowledgment is due to Tegan Willard for her astute suggestions and incredible editing. My faithful and encouraging critique partners, Cindy McDowell and Lauren Yarger, occupy a special place in the completion of this book. Cindy's suggestion to use a poor couple as Darius's inspiration for change added a new dimension to the story. Deryk and Christy Richenburg provided unstinting support and incredibly helpful hints on male psychology. I deeply appreciate their constant grace. Others worthy of mention include author Karl A. Bacon for his editorial suggestions.

Professor Glenn Sunshine, a genius in matters of history and most things theological, turned out to be a wealth of information on Chinese martial arts. The brilliant Rabbi Paul Saul spent a whole afternoon trying to explain the book of Nehemiah from a Jewish perspective. I am grateful for the Reverend Halvor Ronning's suggestions regarding Nehemiah's wall. Any deviations or mistakes in the manuscript are due to my error and not the fault of these eminent scholars.

A book's life is complicated and there are many who are essential in the process. My profound thanks to Michele Forrider, Jeane Wynne, and Janis Backing for helping to release my novels into many hands. A special note of appreciation is due to the sales force, who manage to land these books in the most astonishing locations. You folks are amazing.

And to my fans, who write Facebook messages, emails, and best of all read my books, you are a true joy to me—my beloved companions on this adventure.

Center Point Large Print
600 Brooks Road / PO Box 1
Thorndike ME 04986-0001 USA

(207) 568-3717

US & Canada:
1 800 929-9108
www.centerpointlargeprint.com